W9-BUP-272

HAPPINESS™

Will Ferguson is the author of several books including the critically acclaimed travel memoir *Hokkaido Highway Blues* (Canongate 2000), *The Hitchhiker's Guide to Japan* and the controversial cultural critique, *Why I Hate Canadians*. His first three books were plucked from the slush pile. *Happiness™* is his first novel. He lives in Calgary in the foothills of the Canadian Rockies.

HAPPINESS™

WILL FERGUSON

CANONGATE

Originally published under the title *Generica* by
Penguin Books Canada in 2001

First published in Great Britain
in 2002 by Canongate Books Ltd,
14 High Street, Edinburgh EH1 1TE

This edition published in 2003

10 9 8 7 6 5 4 3 2 1

Copyright © 2002 by Will Ferguson
The moral right of the author has been asserted

British Library Cataloguing-in-Publication Data
A catalogue record for this book is available on
request from the British Library

ISBN 1 84195 351 2

Printed and bound in Great Britain by
Clays Ltd, St Ives plc

www.canongate.net

America is a vast conspiracy to make you happy

John Updike

Acknowledgments

I would like to thank my agent, Carolyn Swayze, for her support and enthusiasm, and I would also like to thank publicist Terrilee Bulger whose passing comment first provided the idea for this book.

Thanks also to Mark Olson who gave me a room to hide away in while I was writing the first draft. And a big thank you to my production editor, Shannon Proulx, for service above and beyond the call of duty. And last, but not least, I would like to thank my editor, Michael Schellenberg—who was not, I hasten to add, in any way the basis for the character of Edwin.

Acknowledgments

Caveat Emptor
(A Disclaimer of Sorts)

This is a book about the end of the world, and as such, it involves diet cookbooks, self-help gurus, sewer-crawling convicts, overworked editors, the economic collapse of the United States of America and the widespread tilling of alfalfa fields. And I think one of the characters loses a finger at some point, too. This is the story of apocalypse: Apocalypse Nice. It tells of a devastating plague of human happiness, an epidemic of warm fuzzy hugs, and a mysterious trailer on the edge of a desert . . .

It could be worse. The original draft of this manuscript ended with a full-scale military invasion of the U.S. by an army of French Canadians. Honest. But my cold-hearted editor made me cut that entire subplot, which brings us to the real question: editors—necessary evil or evil necessity? (*redundancy, no?—ed.*)

Happiness™ began two and a half years ago. It started with an off-hand comment by a book publicist in response to an observation I had made—namely, that the authors of self-help books are always the most screwed-up people you ever meet on any book tour. The publicist in question replied, just in passing, "I'll tell you one thing. If anyone ever wrote a self-help book that actually worked, we'd all be in trouble." She was speaking about publishing in general, but as her comment rattled about in my already cluttered brain, I realized that the ramifications were far worse than she had ever imagined. If someone ever wrote a self-help book that actually worked, one that cured our woes and banished our bad habits, the results would be catastrophic.

It took me two more years to wrestle the idea into its present form. Even as I juggled other assignments and worked on reference books and hockey guides, I kept returning to this single central idea, reworking it, rewriting it, reshaping it. At some point, the characters in the book staged a *coup d'état* and took over entirely. They began dictating to me how the tale would be played out—which is to say, I take no responsibility for anything that Edwin or May or any of the others get up to.

This book is a work of fiction. It is completely made up. As far as I know, there are no such things as Shilo trees or MK-47s or magnesium-tipped bullets. The Latin terms that Edwin banters about are real, as are the various self-help theories discussed. The "untranslatables" that appear are real as well. Some of them came from my own notes, made during my time in Asia, but most are from Howard Rheingold's wonderful lexicon, *They Have a Word for It*. And that's about it. Everything else in this book is a lie.

Just keep in mind that *Happiness™* is set in the future—the near future. Oh, let's say, ten minutes from now.

Part I

Life on Grand Avenue

Chapter

Life on Grand Avenue

Chapter
One

Grand Avenue cuts through the very heart of the city, from 71st Street all the way to the harbourfront, and although it is eight lanes wide, with a treed boulevard running down the middle, the Avenue feels claustrophobic and narrow.

Rising up in straight verticals, and flanking either side, are Grand Avenue's imposing Edwardian buildings, their facades creating two continuous walls. Many of these edifices were built during the Great Potash Boom of the late 1920s, with all that that entails: sombre Calvinistic capitalist features and a grim, heavy-handed feel. Buildings without laughter. From up on high, where the angels sit, Grand Avenue looks very handsome indeed, a veritable showcase of architectural dignity. But down below, on the level of the street, it is a far different scenario, one of littered, gritty, noisy lanes choked with exhaust and angry taxis, of mad rambling panhandlers and scurrying office workers. A world of constant din, where the echoing noise of traffic ricochets off the buildings in a crashing, cacophonous roar. The noise is an eternal presence here. With nowhere to go and no way to escape, it is caught in a perpetual standing wave, a never-ending feedback of cityscape clatter. Static of the Gods.

But if the dominant sense from on high is visual, and on the street level aural, down below, in the depths of the Loop, it is the sense of smell that is most saturated and most abused. Here, in a miasma of fumes, trains rattle-bang on an endless Möbius strip of work, sweat, salt and grubby lucre. A merry-go-round where the horses have emphysema, the paint is peeling and the smell of halitosis and body odour swirls in oily whirls through the air, in the air—*is* the air. Bodies inhaling dioxide, recycling waste, pressed into wedges already sticky in this: the morning rush-hour crush. In the city, the bottom layer, the lowest level, is one of smell.

Edwin Vincent de Valu (a.k.a. Ed, a.k.a. Eddie, a.k.a. Edwynne in his poetry-reading college dorm days) emerges from the underground at Faust and Broadview like a gopher into a towering canyon. On Grand Avenue, the rain is dirty before it hits the ground. Edwin had once caught a solo drop on the back of his hand, had stopped and marvelled at that single bead of water, already streaked with soot.

Edwin is a thin, officious young man with a tall, scarecrow walk and dry straw hair that refuses to hold a part. Even when dressed in a designer overcoat and polished turtle-cut Dicanni shoes, Edwin de Valu has a singular lack of presence. A lack of substance. He is a lightweight, in every sense of the word, and the morning's commute almost sweeps him under. In the urban Darwinism of rush hour, Edwin has to fight just to keep afloat, has to strain just to keep his head above the deluge. No one—least of all Edwin himself—could ever have suspected that the entire fate of the Western World would soon rest upon his narrow shoulders.

On Grand Avenue, the eastside underscore of sour milk and stale urine, so ever-present you start to taste it on your tongue, greeted Edwin like a familiar slap to the face. Like a worn-out motif. A metaphor for something else. Something worse.

As Edwin crossed Grand Avenue, en masse with a crush of rumpled jackets, damp shirts, and groaning attaché cases, and as the traffic echoed into white noise around him and the queasy smells of the city trailed in his wake . . . he looked up, up to where the morning sun was catching the high edge of the buildings, a mocking gold glow out of reach and almost out of sight. And he thought to himself, as he did every day at precisely this spot and precisely this moment: *I hate this fuckin' city*.

For all its architectural facades and historic pretensions, Grand Avenue is little more than a crowded assemblage of filing cabinets, lined up, squeezed in, one after the other, relentless and almost endless. Inside these filing cabinets you will find ad agencies, business consultants, secret sweatshops and modern software developers, pyramid schemes and investment firms, small dreams and big dreams, executives and peons, plastic cafeterias and anonymous love affairs, accountants, attorneys, contortionists and chiropractors, moneymen and mountebanks, systems analysts, cosmetics salesmen and stock-market financiers: gymnasiums of the absurd and self-cancelling circuses of unrequited desire.

You will find all this and more filed away on Grand Avenue. But most importantly, you will find publishers, an entire dizzying procession of publishers: some little more than a name on a door, some cogs in vast multimedia empires; some responsible for launching great literary careers, others responsible for Sidney Sheldon—and every one of them clinging to the cachet of a Grand Avenue address.

Publishers infiltrate Grand Avenue like larval termites. Hidden in the maze of cubicles and corridors that lie in wait behind the sombre Edwardian facades, you will find dozens upon dozens of these publishers, swilling their swamp of words, churning the muck, breeding in captivity. Here, manuscripts are stacked high, and great mounds of festering papers accumulate. Here, women without makeup and men without fashion sense sit huddled, sharpened blue pencils in hand, scratching, scratching, endlessly scratching at the voluminous outpourings of that most egotistical of creatures: the writer.

This is the belly of the beast, the ulcerous stomach of the nation's book publishing-world, and Edwin de Valu, crossing Grand Avenue en route to his cubicle at Panderic Books Incorporated, is smack dab in the swampy middle of the quagmire.

Panderic Inc. stands near the top of the food chain. Not one of the Cabal Clan, not Bantam or Doubleday perhaps, but certainly head and shoulders above the other mid-size publishing houses. Which is to say, Panderic has no John Grisham or Stephen King on its roster, but it does have a Robert James Waller or two. Each season, Panderic publishes a full slate, not of books, but of "titles" (in the jargon of the industry, books are reduced to their very vapour essence)—titles that range from celebrity diet fads to forty-pound vampyre gothics. Panderic puts out more than 250 titles a year. It barely recoups its investment from half of them, loses money on more than a third, and reaps a small profit on the remaining handful. Those magic titles, those rare few money-makers, somehow manage to fuel the entire sprawling enterprise. In the world of American publishing, Panderic is considered financially sound.

Although Panderic's specialty is non-fiction and genre novels, on occasion—and mainly by accident—a genuine masterpiece slips through, a book so humourless and slowly paced, so plodding and laden with arcana, that you just knew it had to be Great Literature. It was Panderic, after all, that had first published *The Shame of the Tulip*, an "intellectual mystery" set in a medieval nunnery in Bastilla, whose hero was a middle-aged mathematician turned semiotician. The author, a middle-aged mathematician turned semiotician, had swept into Panderic's office, thrown down his hefty manuscript like an invitation to a duel and had pronounced his work to be the height of "postmodern hyper-authenticity." He then flung himself from the room and into a full-time career as an aphorist and keynote speaker ($500 an aphorism, $6,000 a note). All this in spite of, or perhaps because of, the fact that he had never had a single lucid thought in his entire life. Publishing is an odd industry indeed. And as Ray Charles once said, "Ain't no son of a bitch nowhere knows what's going to hit."

It was into this world, this postmodern, hyper-authentic reality, that Edwin de Valu now came.

Edwin has been working at Panderic for more than four years, ever since he abandoned his original career plans of becoming a professional bon vivant. (Turns out there were very few openings in the bon vivant category.) Edwin works on the fourteenth floor of 813 Grand Avenue, in Panderic's Non-Fiction Department. Today, as he does every day, Edwin stops outside to buy two cups of coffee to go from Louie (of Louie's Hot Dog and Pickle Stand). Most of the editors at Panderic favour the more genteel, la-di-da-type coffee shops, but not our Edwin. He has a rugged sense of the common man about him. Oh, yes, Edwin is the type of guy who prefers Louie's down-home java over Café Croissant's hand-roasted house blend, a guy who likes his coffee raw and real. Edwin slaps his money on the counter, says, "Keep the change."

"You want cinnamon sprinkles on your caffe-latte mochaccino, or would you prefer white-almond chocolate?" asks Louie, wet cigar in mouth, two days of stubble on his chin(s).

Every working day for the past four years, Edwin has stopped here at Louie's stand, every damn day, and never, not once, has Louie remembered him. "Nutmeg and cinnamon," Ed says wearily. "With a dash of sun-dried saffron. Extra froth."

"Comin' up," says Louie. "Comin' up."

Inside the lobby of 813 Grand Avenue, the sound is suddenly muted: echoing footsteps, the distant ping of elevators, the murmur of a hundred impending heart attacks. Only this. Gone is the constant white noise of traffic outside. Gone is the cymbal-crash symphony of the city.

On Grand Avenue, this is about as close as you can get to deliverance.

It took Edwin several years to realize he actually worked on the thirteenth floor. Technically, the address of Panderic Inc. was suite 1407, but this wasn't exactly true, as Edwin discovered one day when he happened to notice, absent-mindedly, that although the double row of buttons inside the elevator *began* odd-even (1-2, 3-4, 5-6 . . .), the order had been reversed at the top of the panel and was now even-odd (. . . 16-17, 18-19, 20-21). It was only when Edwin retraced the numbers that he realized what had happened: number 13 was missing. This omission skewered everything, and threw the entire sequence off. Panderic wasn't located on the fourteenth floor; it was located on the thirteenth. When Edwin mentioned this oddity to the other editors, they just shrugged it off—everyone except the occult editor, who blanched a bit.

With his two cups of coffee held before him (and well we might wonder for whom the second cup was meant), Edwin pushed open the glass doors of the office with his shoulder and entered sideways into a world of words. A world of words and frantic shuffling papers, a world where all those people in college English courses who had such promise, such potential, ended up: editing grammar, marking up manuscripts, scratching away and dreaming of the day they would open a window and stretch their hands outwards to touch the gold-rimmed edge at the top of the city, up to the higher reaches, where the sunlight reached . . . Until then, they had books to edit, cover copy to produce, long green fluorescent hallways to traverse, photocopies to make, deadlines to meet, pruning shears to wield, prose to emasculate.

Ten past nine and already the place was humming. People rushed past, hurrying nowhere with great purpose. The plants at Panderic were plastic, and even then they looked as though they were dying from a lack of sun.

As Edwin passed his own sorry little cardboard-and-Scotch-tape cubicle, his heart sank. There, stacked high on his desk, was a tower of paper. Thick slabs of manuscript. Slush. Unsolicited, unagented, unloved. This was where dreams came to die. Book proposals, cover letters, entire manuscripts—they gathered like so much detritus on the desks of publishers everywhere. Edwin's cubicle was thick with the stuff. "What the hell?" By the time he reached May's office at the end of the hall, Edwin was well into a slow boil. May's door, as always, was not entirely open, but not entirely shut either. ("Ajar," his editor's parsimonious mind immediately chimed in, wanting to pare down that previous sentence to the starkest elements possible, editors being notoriously unsympathetic to rambling author asides.)

"What the hell," he said as he entered May's office, "is that pile of slush doing on my desk? I thought we hired an intern."

May looked up from her desk. "And a good morning to you, too." In the context of publishing, May Weatherhill was considered successful—a young modern career woman with a suitably overblown, underpaid title: Associate Editor-in-Chief, Non-Fiction, Excluding Biographies but Including Angels and Alien Abductions (which, many claimed, really should have been handled by the fiction department anyway). May was a slightly plump, slightly shy, slightly attractive woman. Well, plump isn't exactly correct. She was heavy-set. "I don't have breasts," she joked. "I have a bosom. I'm a neo-Victorian in that respect." Where Edwin was thin and taut, May was filled with folds and half-hidden hollows.

Oddly enough, and unbeknownst to her, May's most notable attribute was not her bosom, ample though it was, but her lips, her red waxy lips. They were of a shade found almost nowhere outside of Crayola. It was as though they had been painted on, as though they really were made of wax, stuck on as a party prank and then never removed. People didn't look May in the eye when they talked to her. Instead, they stared, fascinated, at her lips. Like most editors, May was pale to the point of anemic—but with May, it went far beyond that. May Weatherhill was made of porcelain. Soft porcelain. Warm porcelain. But porcelain nonetheless. Beautiful and breakable. Even when she laughed and even when she smiled, it always looked as though her thoughts were somewhere else. "Existential eyes": that was the alliterative description Edwin had once given her. "Hazel," she had replied. "You're confusing hazel eyes with French philosophy." "Perhaps," said Edwin. "And perhaps not." May was constantly veering from one diet plan to the next, something that had long baffled Edwin. When you had existential eyes, who needed to diet?

Still, if nothing else, May did have that indefinable substance called power. Power surrounded her, power permeated her; it was her own brand of perfume. This was partly because of her position at Panderic, but more importantly, it was because she had the Ear of the Publisher Himself. ("And his balls," one of the more catty male editors had suggested.) May Weatherhill, middle manager, confidante of the CEO, head of the department, had hired Edwin de Valu, and she could have fired him as well. Could have fired him at any time, could have fired him right then and there, could have fired him almost on whim—and God knows it wasn't like Edwin didn't give ample cause for termination. But she never did. She never used threats, veiled or otherwise, against Edwin because . . . well, there was the Incident at the Sheraton Timberland Lodge. And that had changed everything.

It was during a book conference upstate when, heady on champagne and silliness, Edwin and May had tumbled into bed, half-laughing, the way friends sometimes do. And then, next thing you know, they were breathing hard and pulling at each other's clothes and licking sweat from each other's necks—and *not* in the way friends sometimes do. The next day, while attending a mind-numbing presentation by "an acclaimed author" (or perhaps it was an acclaimed agent), May had felt a slow single trickle—the "essence of Ed," so to speak—creep down her thigh, and she knew then that nothing would ever be the same between them.

They never talked about it. They circled around it at times, dancing dangerously close to the cliff, but they never mentioned the words, now anathema, "Sheraton Timberland Lodge." It had become their Alamo, their Waterloo, the synecdoche watershed of their friendship.

May had recently edited a quirky lexicon of obscure words for Panderic. It was titled *The Untranslatables*, and was a light-hearted look at certain terms that were lacking in the English language. Entire feelings, entire concepts, went unexpressed, simply because no word had ever been coined to capture them. Words like *mono-no-aware*, "the sadness of things," a Japanese term that defined the ever-present pathos that lurks just below the surface of life. Words like *mokita*, from the Kiriwina language of New Guinea, meaning "the truth which no one speaks." It refers to the tacit agreement among people to avoid openly referring to certain shared secrets, like Aunt Louise's drinking problem or Uncle Fred's covert homosexuality. Or the Incident at the Sheraton Timberland Lodge. Or the fact that Edwin is married. These, too, were *mokita*. This is what drew Edwin and May together, and this was what kept them apart: a thin, impenetrable wall of *mokita* lay between them.

"He's a married man, he's a married man." May would repeat this to herself whenever her self-control began to lapse. Whenever she was tempted to touch him, softly, on the nape of the neck. "He's a married man." And yet the more she repeated this phrase, the more sexy it started to sound. "We did have an intern," said May, smiling her thanks as Edwin placed the cup of coffee before her. Not a deep smile, you understand, and certainly not a flirtatious one, but rather a small smile that said, "I know why you bring me coffee every day. And I know that you know that I know. And yet I find it strangely endearing nonetheless." (May could say a lot with a single smile.)

"So why isn't the intern handling the slush pile?" said Edwin. "I mean, how hard is it to stuff rejection letters into an envelope?"

"The intern quit. Mr. Mead had her washing his car and running laundry errands. Turns out, it wasn't what she had in mind when she said she was looking for an 'entry-level position in publishing.' Apparently, she was expecting something more fulfilling. I believe she is now shovelling out the pens down at the docks. Said it wasn't a big difference."

Edwin sipped his coffee. "Bloody interns. Whatever happened to the good ol' American work ethic?" The cream in his mocha latte had uncongealed—if that is the word for it—creating an unpleasant oil slick of unsaturated fat. Louie's cappuccinos were the best—if indeed that was how you pluralized "cappuccino."

"Until we get someone new," said May, "we're all going to have to chip in. I gathered up last week's submissions—I think there were around 140 manuscripts, and maybe as many proposals—and I divided them among editors, more or less at random. I think you got a dozen of them, and yes, I already printed off a stack of 'after careful considerations' for you to reply with."

"Why do we even bother? Why not just hire a trained chimp to go through them?"

"Remember the General? Remember his unagented, over-the-transom offer for—and I quote—'an insider's look at the war in Kosovo'? Remember how fast we turned that around?"

"Ah, yes, the General. Mad Dog Mulligan himself. How could I forget? The last of the NATO bombs hadn't even hit the ground and *Operation Balkan Eagle* was already on the stands. We scooped Doubleday and Bantam by a week. It was . . ."

"Magnificent?"

"No, that's not the word I'm searching for. It was awful. Absolutely awful. As far as I'm concerned, *Balkan Eagle* was both the apex and the nadir of disposable publishing."

"Apex? Nadir? I love it when you talk dirty to me," and as soon as she said it, she regretted it, wished she could backspace delete the comment. "Edwin, just do it, okay? Clear the slush as fast as you can, because more is on its way."

"The slush never stops coming, does it." It was less a question than it was a statement of fact.

"Never," said May. "It's a hallmark of civilization: unwanted, unagented dreams. The slush pile is one of the few irreducible elements of life. Just think of yourself as—oh, I don't know—Sisyphus with a shovel, I suppose. And don't forget, there's a meeting at ten."

"Oh, God. Is Fuck-Face back already?"

"Edwin! You have got to stop referring to him like that. You were an

English major, for God's sake, you would think you'd have a better repertoire."

"I'm sorry. *Mea culpa. Mea maxima culpa.* What I meant to say was, 'Is Shit-for-Brains back already?'"

She sighed. It was the sigh of someone who has given up on ever reforming a lost cause. "Yes, Mr. Mead has indeed returned. He flew in early this morning and he wants everyone in Conference Room 2 at ten o'clock—*sharp.*"

"Got it. Room 10 at two o'clock."

"Goodbye, Edwin."

He turned to leave and then stopped. "Why don't you have any slush?"

"Pardon?"

"When you divvied up the manuscripts, why didn't you take some, you know, to share the misery?"

"I did. I took thirty manuscripts and maybe a dozen proposals home with me Friday. I did them that night."

"Ah, I see." Edwin paused just a beat too long. Long enough to let the comment hang in the air. Long enough to underline the fact that May had spent Friday night alone, with her cat, reading book proposals and unsolicited manuscripts. "I should, ah, get back to my cubicle," said Edwin. "Meeting starts in half an hour. I figure I'll be able to get through most of the slush by then."

May watched him leave. Drank her coffee. Thought about all the many *mokitas* that clutter our lives and give it its texture and meaning.

Chapter
Two

Edwin de Valu pulled the first manuscript out from the top of the pile. A stack of rejection letters was on hand, ready to go.

The first submission was from a writer in Vermont, and the cover letter began: "Hello, Mr. Jones!" (Jones was the fake name they gave out when writers phoned asking for the acquisitions editor. Having something arrive marked URGENT FOR MR. JONES! was a tipoff to reroute it to the slush pile.)

"Hello, Mr. Jones! I have written a fictional novel about—" and that was as far as Edwin got.

> *On behalf of Panderic Inc. I would like to thank you for your very interesting proposal. Unfortunately, after careful consideration . . .*

Edwin took the next manuscript from the pile. "Dear Mr. Jones: Enclosed is my novel, *The Moons of Thoxth-Aqogxnir*. This is the first of a three-part trilogy that will—"

. . . and much editorial debate, we have regrettably concluded that your book does not meet our current editorial needs.

"Mr. Jones! My blockbuster book, *Lawyer on the Lam*, is a guaranteed bestseller, and is certainly much better than the kind of stuff Mr. Big Shot John Grisham writes and everyone thinks is so hot. P.S. I single-spaced the manuscript to save on paper. Hope you don't mind. :-)"

. . . We wish you the best of luck placing your work with another publisher, and we are deeply sorry we weren't able to offer you a contract at this time.

"Dear Sirs: How little we know about refrigerator repair mainte-nance, and yet what a long and fascinating history this field has."

. . . Have you considered submitting your manuscript instead to HarperCollins or perhaps Random House? (Panderic had been feuding with HarperCollins and Random House for years, and they kept redirecting their slush to each other on a regular basis.)

"Dear Mr. Jones: 'Watch out! Watch out! Watch out! Get down! Duck!' The red-hot bullets sprayed around Agent McDermit's head, trained to kill with his bear hands . . . That is the beginning of my action-packed adventure novel, *To Kill a Killer!* If you want to find out more, you'll have to ask me for the full manuscript and see for yourself." But Edwin inserted another standard "after careful consideration" letter, and that was the last he ever head of Agent McDermit.

Mind you, Edwin did make note of the "bear hands" line to add to the bulletin board in the staff room, the one filled with odd clips and outrageously bad writing. The collection was known as The Wall of Bad Writing. Also known as, Gems from the Unsolicited and Unagented. Also known as, It Came from the Slush Pile! Examples of the scintillat-ing prose contained therein included the following:

"She stood on the hillside, her jet blonde hair blowing in the breeze."

And: "What a big bunch of baloney," he hissed.

As well as the now-classic: "She said nothing. She just bit her lower lip and licked her upper lip . . ." (which triggered a wave of editors twisting their mouths around while they tried to perform the feat described).

Agent McDermit's "bear hands" might make The Wall of Bad Writing, but that was about it. Edwin sighed.

Every submission, whether it was a full manuscript or just a proposal, contained a self-addressed stamped envelope (or SASE, as it is known), which made Edwin's chore somewhat easier: open, skim, reject and stuff. It was a fairly mechanical exercise in literary evaluation. Edwin rarely got through the first paragraph of any cover letter; he didn't even bother starting those printed on bright pink paper or in dot matrix, or those entirely in caps or italics (there was even one in all caps *and* italics, surely a record of sorts) or anything in fancy non-standard fonts. He just fished out the SASE the writer had included, inserted the requisite "after careful consideration" and then tossed it into the OUT box.

It was a miserable lot, even by slush-pile standards. Edwin took a swallow of cold coffee, opened the last manuscript—a great thick stack of paper in an oversized envelope—and was about to reject it on the basis of sheer mass alone when Nigel stuck his big inflated head into Ed's cubicle entrance.

"Edwin! Confab in five. G.T.L.O."

"G.T.L.O.?"

"Get the lead out. Boss is waiting."

Nigel should have had slicked-back hair and an oily smile; he should have had a gold tooth and a snakeskin belt. It would have suited him. But he was in fact impeccably dressed, at once carefully casual and artfully tousled. Among editors, Nigel Simms was a suave and sexy young man. Mind you, when you considered his competition (other male editors) and the people who were doing the actual appraisal (female editors), it wasn't an especially ringing endorsement. In a normal human environment, Nigel would have been average-looking at best, but in the rabbit-hutch, just-one-notch-above-librarians-in-the-hilarity-and-sex-appeal category of book editing, Nigel shone like a freshly groomed stallion. Edwin hated Nigel. Hated him for all the obvious, trivial reasons. Hated him for being a reverse funhouse mirror, one that reflected back the cleaner, smoother, better version of himself. Hated him for being so competent. Hated him for *not* smoking. Hated him for everything.

Not that Edwin de Valu was any slouch when it came to fashion. No sir. Edwin always made a point of looking sharp, or at least not overly blunted. Clothes hung well on Edwin, in the same way an Armani jacket will hang well on a coat hanger. The problem came when Edwin had to remove that jacket, or wear shorts and sandals, or—worst-case scenario—get undressed within near proximity of witnesses and/or a mirror. Edwin's lanky frame, all arms and legs and elbows, was the bane of his existence. Indeed, Edwin had once gone through an intense, almost neurotic, six-month bout of bodybuilding and power protein shakes in an effort to "bulk up" and become "a manly man." It was as though a fever had gripped his brain. He oiled his skin, pumped his iron, and hoisted heavy cartoon weights above his head until his legs began twitching, his back began to spasm and his face began making comical Hulk Hogan grimaces (but with less artistic flare), even as some Cro-Magnon steroid-knotted trainer yelled motivational abuse at him. Edwin had risked a brain hemorrhage on several occasions, had dragged his weary carcass home night after night, and for what? A physique that was no longer skinny, true, but rather one that was now wiry *and* skinny. Edwin's muscles hadn't grown, they had simply become more taut. "Like a skinned lemur," is how Edwin described it when he caught a glimpse of himself, naked, in a mirror.

Nigel Simms looked like one of the background models in a men's fashion magazine, the ones who are not handsome enough to hold their own on the cover but still worthy of a photo shoot. Edwin, on the other hand, looked like the "before" picture in a vintage Charles Atlas comic-book ad. The guy who keeps getting sand kicked into his face down through eternity.

"One more manuscript," said Edwin, looking at the last of his pile. "One more to go. I'll make this quick." He pulled the flop from its wrapping. It was huge, at least two reams' worth, more than a thousand pages. Jesus. Trees had died for this. The cover letter (and indeed, the entire manuscript, when Edwin flipped through to check) had been hand-pecked on an old manual typewriter, a sight so unusual that it stopped Edwin in mid–rejection letter. He turned to the title page. It was called *What I Learned on the Mountain*, by someone named Rajee Tupak Soiree. Sprinkled across the page—and here Edwin all but guffawed—were little stickers of daisies (daisies, mind you), and along the bottom was a handwritten note that read *"Live! Love! Learn!"*

Edwin chortled in spite of himself. *Live! Love! Learn!* His mind was already churning up rejoinders: *Go! Fuck! Yourself!* Edwin pulled out the accompanying cover letter and began to read:

> To whomever is in charge of the slush pile, and I presume this means you, the very person who is now looking at this letter I have written, perhaps silently mocking my sunny three-word life-affirming motto, even as you sit in your office, in your weary grey office, or perhaps not even an office, not even weary grey—perhaps you are lost in a cubicle, a small box among larger boxes, as anonymous and unfulfilled as your own hopes and failed dreams, the ones you keep locked in the cabinet, the ones you whisper to yourself late at night when no one can hear. No one except God. If He exists. And what if He doesn't? What then? The emptiness that lies at the heart of one's life does not go unanswered, it is simply pushed down, kept at bay . . . Ah, but you knew that already, didn't you?

Edwin felt his chest tighten ever so slightly. His smile faded and a crawly feeling came over him, made his skin shiver. It was the feeling you get when you know someone is watching you, and it was all Edwin could do not to close the hallway blinds and hunker down under his desk awhile. Fortunately, Edwin's cubicle did not have a window, so he didn't have to worry about peeping Toms, random sniper fire, or even worse, being distracted by a view.

My prescription for humanity—calling it "a book" does-n't do it justice—is the product of an intense seven-month hermitage I took on a mountain high in Tibet, where I sat in deep meditation, without food or water, for days on end. Slowly, the interconnected problems and solutions of mankind unfolded before me. I offer them to you now. I permit you the right of publishing this impor-tant work. What will this "book" of mine do? It will pro-vide happiness to anyone who reads it. It will help people lose weight and stop smoking. It will cure gambling addiction, alcoholism and drug dependency. It will help people achieve inner balance. It will show them how to release their left-brain intuitive creative energy, find empowerment, seek solace, make money, enjoy life and improve their sexual lives (through my breakthrough Li Bok Lovemaking Technique). Readers will become more confident, more self-reliant, more considerate, more con-nected, more at peace. It will also help them improve their posture and spelling, and will give their lives mean-ing and purpose. It is everything they have ever wanted, everything they have been yearning for. It will bring the world happiness. [And here the word "happiness" was underlined several times with a ballpoint pen. Another flurry of daisy stickers lined the bottom margin of the let-ter.] To the person in the small, drab cubicle, I offer you light. True light. Sincerely, Tupak Soiree.

Dear Mr. Soiree: Well, this is certainly a first. I don't know where you got the idea that insulting the acquisitions editor of a fine and distinguished publishing house such as Panderic Inc. was the way to go, but trust me it didn't work. (And by the way, I work in a spacious room lined with polished oak and overlooking the ocean, and not, as you so presumptuously assumed, some dismal grey cubicle.) I was going to send your hand-pecked collection of silly little feel-good prescriptions back to you, but seeing as how you are clearly some crackpot

> *whacked-out loony-tune nutcase, I am instead going to use*
> *your manuscript to wipe my—*

But of course, that isn't what Edwin wrote. No. He pulled out yet another standard rejection letter that "regretfully informed" Mr. Soiree of his decision and suggested he try submitting his manuscript—and indeed as many more manuscripts as he might have—to Harper-Collins or perhaps Random House. "Tell 'em Panderic sent you," Edwin scribbled at the bottom.

Still, there was something about the tone of that cover letter. Something both hypnotic and ominous, akin to the fear you feel when a street person suddenly calls out your name just as you're passing by. Great books have been pulled from the slush pile, Edwin reminded himself. So have evil ones. *Anne of Green Gables* was pulled from the slush pile. So, legend has it, was *Mein Kampf.* And that name, that name: Tupak Soiree. Where had he heard that name before?

"Edwin, will you hurry up?" It was May, and she looked frantic. "Mr. Mead is waiting! I slipped out on the diversionary pretext of getting a file. The meeting's already started, so get in there!"

Edwin rotated in his chair and smiled up at her. "Wow. You used 'diversionary pretext' in a sentence."

"Just move it!" she said. "I have to get back." And she was gone.

"All right, all right." Edwin fumbled with the manuscript, looking for the required SASE. But there was none. He checked the envelope, looked all over his desk, and even on the floor in case it had fallen out. Nothing. "So you didn't think to include an SASE? Well, screw you, Mr. Soiree." Company policy stated that any unsolicited manuscript not accompanied by an SASE would *not* be returned, but that was a bluff. Non-SASEs were returned all the time. But not today. It was Monday, Edwin's ulcer was acting up, his boneheaded boss was waiting for him in the meeting room, and Tupak Soiree's submission had already annoyed him enough. Edwin stuffed the thick, bloated manuscript and cover letter back into its original envelope, folded the top, and slam-dunked it into the wastepaper basket.

"So much for you," he muttered as he grabbed his notepad and hurried out of the cubicle. And that was the end of Tupak Soiree. Or so Edwin thought.

Chapter
Three

The meeting was well under way by the time Edwin arrived. Which is to say, all the good muffins had been taken. As Edwin picked through the dismal offerings that remained—the blueberry and banana were the first to go and there was always that one piece of zucchini-pumpkin-bran crap that no one wanted—the almighty Mr. Mead turned from his overhead projector and said, smiling down on Edwin in patronizing schoolmarmish waves, "Edwin. So good of you to join us."

Mr. Mead was a Baby Boomer in the worst sense of the word. He was in his early fifties, but he kept trying to pass himself off as, well, hip. Or something. He wore jeans to work but didn't allow anyone else to. (This was to show that while he was not "uptight," he was still "the Man," or some damn thing.) Mr. Mead was going bald, and his thinning grey hair—dyed grey, it was rumoured because his actual grey didn't look quite natural enough—was pulled back in a tight, tiny ponytail "like a chihuahua's penis," in Edwin's memorable description. As with every male Baby Boomer who ever went bald, Mr. Mead had grown a beard in compensation (or distraction, it was hard to say which). Mr. Mead wore glasses, some weird octagonal shape meant to suggest that here was a man on the cutting edge of eyewear and—by extension—politics, business and life. Edwin hated Mr. Mead. Edwin hated a lot of people, but he especially hated Mr. Corduroy-Tie-Wearing-Did-I-Ever-Tell-You-Kids-about-the-True-Spirit-of-Woodstock Mead. He especially hated it when Mr. Mead pointed out how bad Edwin's work habits were, how unpunctual he was, how young and fallow. *Of course* Edwin's work habits were bad. Of course he was unpunctual. Of course he was disorganized. But Mr. Mead didn't have to point these things out with such relentless glee.

Mr. Mead's full name was Léon Mead, but everyone knew it was just plain Leon, the accent being strictly an affectation. His last name, however, always struck Edwin as the perfect Baby Boomer emblem, combining as it did "me" and "need," the summation of an entire generation.

It was while adrift in this mindless-meeting frame of mind, as he picked his way through the pumpkin bran and tried not to keel over dead from sheer boredom, that Edwin suddenly got an unnerving feeling that people were staring at him, that they were waiting for him to say something. It was similar to what he had experienced just a short time ago while reading the cover letter for that book about the mountain (the title was already fading from the Etch-a-Sketch surface of Edwin's consciousness). But this time it was no mere hunch.

When Edwin looked up, everyone around the conference table—Mr. Mead with a patronizing smile, May with a look of abject consternation and Nigel with an evil grin—every last one of them was staring intently at Edwin.

"Well?" said Mr. Mead. A single syllable, but oh how thick and wet it lay on Edwin's mind. He frantically began flipping through his short-term memory, trying in vain to connect what they had been talking about back to himself. Edwin's notepad was no help; it was filled with squiggly doodles and inspirational slogans like "chihuahua" and "blah blah blah blah." He looked over at May. Her face was so strained with expectant anxiety that he thought she might go into labour at any moment. This was beyond pregnant. This was a full-scale multiple-birth, where-are-the-painkillers, someone-call-an-ambulance pause.

"Yes?" said Edwin.

Mr. Mead had been going over the unexpected hole in their fall cata-logue. Every October for the past six or seven years, Panderic had pub-lished a book by a doctor down in Georgia who went by the name of Mr. Ethics: *The Everyperson's Guide to Ethics* one year, *An Introduction to Ethics for the Modern Manager* the next, *How to Live an Ethical Life in This Crazy Mixed-Up World of Ours* the following year and so on. (The more successful Mr. Ethics had become, the longer his book titles had grown and the thinner the content. It was said his last book was dictated to his secretary while he shaved in the mornings.) Mr. Ethics' most recent work, *The Seven Habits of Highly Ethical People—and the Life Lessons They Can Teach You!*, was already in the copy-edit stage. Unfortunately, Mr. Ethics had been picked up by the IRS on tax-evasion charges a couple of weeks earlier, and he was now facing eight-to-ten even with a plea bargain. The entire Mr. Ethics line of self-help books was on hold. What any of this had to do with Edwin was unclear.

"We're all waiting," said Mr. Mead, his smile still in place.

"Waiting, sir?"

"For your proposal."

"My proposal?"

"That's right, your proposal. Remember the little chat we had just before I left last week? I asked you how your aunt was doing. You said she's doing fine. We talked about holding off on the next Mr. Ethics book. I said, 'Gosh, how are we going to fill the hole in our catalogue?' And you said, 'Don't worry. I have a brilliant idea for a fall self-help book.' And I said, 'Terrific, let's hear about it when I get back.' And you said, 'Sure!' Don't you remember *any* of that?"

"But I don't have an aunt."

"For God's sake, man, this has nothing to do with your aunt! Now what do you have to show us?" Mr. Mead's demeanour was growing sterner. His patience was clearly wearing thin.

Edwin swallowed hard, felt a flutter of blood in his temples and said, with a quavering voice, "Well, sir. I am presently working on something."

"Which is?"

"It's, um, a book. A very exciting book. That's what I'm working on. A book."

"Go on," said Mr. Mead.

22

Nigel was smiling sadistically. "Yes, please go on. We're very interested in what you have to say."

Edwin cleared his throat, attempted to stay calm, and said: "It's a book about how to lose weight."

"Plenty of those already," said Mr. Mead. "What's the angle?"

"Well, it also tells readers how to quit smoking."

"Checkout-counter pulp. We need a front-list, self-help, trade paperback. Something with real meat to it. Dieting? Smoking? I was gone for almost two weeks, and that's the best you came up with?"

"Well, no. This book also tells readers how to improve their sex lives. Something called the, um, Li Pok Technique—or perhaps Li Bok. It's revolutionary. Very sexy."

Mr. Mead frowned, but in an approving manner. "Sex," he said. "I like that." And the next thing Edwin knew, the momentum of the moment ran away with him. He was caught in a positive-feedback loop: the more he piled it on, the more enthusiastic Mr. Mead became, the more thoughtful the frowning and the more vigorous the nodding.

"This book will also tell people how to make money."

"Excellent."

"And how to release their creativity. And achieve inner balance."

"Good, good. Go on."

"And how to become empowered and self-confident and more compassionate, and there's also, um, some recipes and tips on the stock market. It's everything you could possibly want. Money. Sex. Weight loss. Meaning of Life."

"Hey, I like this," said Mr. Mead. "It's kind of the ultimate self-help book."

Across the table, Nigel's smile had gone beyond evil; it was now Lucifer's mien itself. Mr. Mead, however, was beaming with delight. May looked distraught. Edwin felt like he was going to faint.

"Terrific," said Mr. Mead. "Have it on my desk when I get back next Monday." (Mr. Mead was always en route to somewhere else, whether it was the Publishing Subsidy Symposium or the Frankfurt Book Fair.) "Oh, and what did you say the title was?"

"The title?"

"Yes, man, the title. What is it?"

"That would be the title of the book?"

"Don't be so damn thick. Of course the title of the book. What are you going to call it?"

"It's called, um, *What I Learned on the Mountain*."

"The mountain? I don't get it. What mountain?"

"It's a mountain, sir. A very big mountain. In Nepal. Or maybe Tibet. The author learned many things on this mountain. Hence the, ah, title."

"*What I Learned on the Mountain*." Mr. Mead rubbed his jaw. "No. Don't like it. Don't like it one bit. Not snappy enough."

"We could expand on the theme in the subtitle. Maybe something along the lines of *Great Sex, Lose Weight, Make Money*. Throw in some gratuitous exclamation marks for emphasis, maybe even—"

"No, no, too wordy. Long titles don't sell in today's market. You want to keep it short, precise. Maybe just a single, stark word. Or an allusion to a popular movie. Something that signals to the reader the type of 'magical journey' upon which they are about to embark. *The Wizard of Oz* perhaps."

"Or *Invasion of the Pod People*," said Edwin, under his breath.

"As for the specific length of the title," said Mr. Mead, "there's a survey of non-fiction titles in last month's *Publishers Weekly*. It turns out, the average length of a book title is—what did it say, Nigel?"

"It said 4.6 words."

"That's right, 4.6. That's the optimum word count for a successful non-fiction title. So let's work within those parameters, shall we?"

"And what exactly," said Edwin, "would 0.6 of a word be, you stupid, brain-dead, grey-haired, washed-up, over-the-hill twit?"

But that wasn't exactly how Edwin phrased his question. What he actually said was, "Point six, sir?"

"That's right. That would be something like—" Mr. Mead thought about it for a moment. "Well, like a contraction. Or perhaps a preposition: *a, an, the*. Or wait! A hyphenated word. That would be 1.6 of a word, don't you think?"

This was followed by a long meandering discussion on whether "an" or "the" counted as a full word or just point six of a word.

"Perhaps," said Mr. Mead, "we should do our own in-house survey. Take the average number of words in our titles from the past ten catalogues, divide that by 0.6 and take it from there?"

"I'll get right on it, Mr. Mead," said Nigel as he furiously scribbled gibberish in his notepad. (By the end of the day, Mr. Mead would have completely forgotten about the request.)

"Good, good. And don't forget prefixes, Nigel. I don't think we can rule out prefixes. Those might very well count as 0.6 of a word as well."

"I'll make a special note of it," said Nigel.

"And let's keep the total length of the book to 309 pages exactly. That's the average for current bestsellers. So make sure it comes in at exactly—what did I say? Three hundred and nine pages. Okay, Edwin?"

But by that point, Edwin had already threaded a rope over the rafters and was even now swinging lifelessly from the end of it.

Mr. Mead turned to May. "What is your take on this? What do you think? Be honest."

"I don't think it's something we need to spend a lot of time on," said May.

"Exactly. You're right. We're just wasting our energy bickering over details." And then, with a contemptuous wave in Edwin's direction, "I don't know why he even brought it up. Focus, Eddie. That's what your generation lacks. Focus. It reminds me of an analect by Confucius, one that was very much in currency when I was younger. It was when I was at Woodstock, or maybe that was Selma. But the resonance has stayed with me ever since. Of course, it reads better in the original Mandarin, but the gist of it, if you will, was that in any hierarchy—oh, wait, maybe that's the Peter Principle I'm thinking of, not Confucius."

"Sir?" It was May, trying once again to nudge the discussion back towards reality. "We were going over changes to the fall catalogue?"

"Oh, yes, the fall catalogue. That's right. Good point, May. Glad you brought it up. Now then, as you all know, with our Mr. Ethics line on indefinite hold, we'll have to roll up our sleeves and pull up our boot-straps and blah, blah, blah, blah, blah, chihuahua's penis."

Edwin had already tuned the blather out as effectively as a single twist of a radio dial can drown out a fundamentalist preacher with static. Although he sat through the remainder of the meeting behind a veneer of calm, his heart was gripped with panic. He was trapped. He had talked his way into a corner, had sealed all exits, locked the door and swallowed the key. Only one man could save him now: Tupak Soiree.

"—and that's when I decided to devote my life to something more meaningful, something on a higher moral plane." Mr. Mead was wrapping up some tangential anecdote or other. "And ever since then, I have never looked back. Never."

It was all Edwin could do not to leap to his feet, applaud madly and shout, "Bravo! Bravo!"

The Sixties never died, they just got really, really boring.

As the staff filed out of the conference room, Nigel fell in step beside Edwin. "Great presentation, Ed. What was that? 'Makes money, tastes great, cures cancer'?"

"Go piss up a rope, Nigel."

"That would be the same rope you just used to hang yourself with, correct?"

Edwin picked up the pace, pulling away from Nigel, who stopped and called out, cheerfully, "She's fine, by the way!"

Edwin turned. "Who is?"

"My aunt Priscilla. She's fine. Turns out it was just a mild flu. But good luck with your book. It sounds much more exciting than the project I was working on."

You son of a bitch.

"Tah!" said Nigel as he disappeared into his office. With a view.

Edwin stomped back to his cubicle, grumbling muttered vows and King Lear invective under his breath. "I'll show them. I'll show them all."

May was waiting for him when he arrived. "You know," she said, looking around the walls of his cubicle, "there's no law against posting pictures or adding personal touches. Mr. Mead encourages it. Says it 'nurtures worker spontaneity.' I swear, this cubicle of yours has got to be the most barren, most—"

"It's a protest," he said. "I'm protesting flowers and balloons and pictures of babies and cute cartoons clipped from the funny pages."

"It certainly is Zen-like."

May sat on Edwin's desk and leaned an elbow on the pile of

manuscripts that was now stacked in the OUT tray. "So tell me," she said. "*What I Learned on the Mountain*? Which hat did you pull that one out of? I've never heard of it, and I'm the one dishing out assignments. Tell me you didn't just make it up on the spot. Please tell me you didn't."

"May, you don't understand. I was trapped."

"Edwin, we need to go back to Mr. Mead, right now, right this instant, and explain to him that in a moment of weakness, in the grips of Monday morning fatigue, you—"

"May, listen to me. I can pull this off. Do you remember when you hired me? Do you remember my very first assignment? Editing Panderic's most successful line of self-help books ever: *Chicken Broth for Your Aching, Needy Heart*. And do you remember what you said to me? You said, 'Don't worry, the books practically write themselves. People send in their uplifting anecdotes, and the so-called authors of these books simply gather up the various sob stories and attach a clever variation on the title. The only thing the editor has to do is check the punctuation and spelling.' Piece of cake, remember? And then what happened? My second week on the Chicken Broth beat—my *second* week—and in come the authors, all tan and sorrowful, with gold glinting from every appendage. And what did they tell me? 'We've hit a snag.' It was for Chicken Broth #217: *Chicken Broth for Your Fallen Arches*. And what did they say? They said, 'We can't do it. We've run out of heart-warming stories about young children dying of bone cancer. There are no more uplifting anecdotes left. We have exhausted the supply.' And what did I do? What did I do, May?"

"You know, I really hate it when a writer tries to disguise exposition as dialogue," said May.

"Did I run crying to you? Did I give in? Did I admit defeat? No. I sucked it up, and I said, 'All right, gentlemen. There's only one thing to do in a situation like this: fake it.' We went back through the archives and culled the two least memorable anecdotes from each of the previous 216 Chicken Broth books, repackaged it as *A Big Ol' Heapin' Helpin' of Warmed-Up Leftovers for Your Needy Soul*. And you remember what happened?"

"Yes," said May. "I remember."

"Seventeen weeks on the *Times* bestseller list. Seventeen fuckin' weeks. That was two weeks better than *Balkan Eagle*. Seventeen weeks and no one, not a single reader, not a single reviewer, not a single goddam bookseller, ever caught on. Not one person ever realized we had simply rehashed previous material. So don't tell me I can't pull this one off. A book that promises health, happiness and great sex? Not a problem. Chicken feed. I can do this, May. I can pull this off."

"But, Edwin. You only have one week. Mr. Mead will expect a manuscript waiting for him when he gets back from his trip, and you have nothing to show him. Nothing."

"Ah, but that's where you're wrong. For I know something that you do not. I have just such a manuscript!" Edwin stepped from behind his desk and, with a flourish, plunged his hand triumphantly into his wastebasket to retrieve the discarded manuscript.

The basket was empty.

Chapter
Four

"Shit." This was the only word Edwin could conjure up, the only word that formed in his mind, the only word to trip off his tongue, to roll across his palate. Two million years of human evolution, 500,000 years of language, 450 years of modern English. The rich heritage of Shakespeare and Wordsworth at his beck and call, and all that Edwin could come up with was "shit."

His wastepaper basket was empty. The fat manuscript reeking of self-help and false promises was gone, and so was any hope of Edwin finessing his way out of the hyperbolic sales pitch he had just made to Mr. Mead.

"Shit," he said.

Shit was, as you may have guessed, one of Edwin's all-time favourite words. When Mr. Mead had given out coupons for discount therapy sessions (in lieu of a Christmas bonus), Edwin had answered the question "Life is a field of _____" in a predictable manner. Apparently the correct answer was something along the line of "flowers." But as Edwin quickly pointed out, "flowers grow in shit, and thus, *ipso facto*, the word 'shit' is both logically and temporally prior to 'flowers.'" At which point, the therapist had complained of a headache and ended the session early. Now, faced with this empty wastepaper basket, faced with the horrible ramifications that it suggested, Edwin had resorted to type.

"Shit."

"What's wrong?" said May.

"The wastepaper basket. It's empty. I put my hand in and it was empty, and now—it's still empty."

"Yes," said May as she got up to leave. "Well, that was certainly the lamest magic trick I have ever seen."

"No, you don't understand. The manuscript was here. It was right here."

And then Edwin heard it, a single elusive sound, faint under the hum of fluorescence and the muffled mummy voices huddling behind cubicle walls: a squeak. A thin, plaintive squeak, one faint note. Ed knew the sound, understood full well its significance. It was the squeak of the garbage bin, the one with the wobbly tire that always drove him to distraction and set his fillings on edge whenever—what was his name? *Rory!*—whenever Rory the janitor wheeled it through, twice a day, emptying bins of paper and listlessly sweeping the floor.

Rory was indeed a listless man, and it was this very listlessness that might yet prove to be Edwin's salvation. If Edwin could somehow catch up to Rory before he got away, if he could manage to retrieve the thick envelope with the—

Ah, but at this point, Edwin was already in full mad dash.

"Where are you going?" shouted May.

"On a quest," he yelled back, even as he ran through the maze of cubicles, weaving his way among the bystanders. "On a quest!"

Edwin cut through the chug-a-chug of the copier room, out the side hall and past the staff room, sprinting through snippets of gossip and wafts of perfume and lingering editorial ennui. Edwin was a flash, a burst of energy, a bolt of desperate speed, lightning unleashed. "Slow down," yelled the extras in the scene as they stepped aside. "Slow down!"

Edwin heard the squeak grow louder and louder as he closed the gap between himself and Rory, and then, as he bolted around the corridor, he saw—a heel. It was the Heel of Rory, just as it disappeared into a freight elevator. And at this point, an odd occurrence of competing velocity and narrowing distance created a strange optical illusion: as the doors of the elevator slowly closed, Edwin hit maximum warp drive. He was flying, his feet barely touching the floor. He had only to reach the elevator and thrust a hand dramatically between the doors, watch them bounce back and say, in an equally dramatic voice, fists on hips, "Give me the manuscript." But no. In a perfect Zeno paradox of time and distance, the slow, slow elevator doors closed even as Edwin all but ran headlong into them (the skid marks from his shoes can still be seen on the floor tiles).

"Shit," said Edwin.

No matter. Although basically a man of letters and a true literary soul, Edwin still went to the movies (a lot), and he knew full well what to do next.

Down the stairs and around the corner, down the stairs and around the corner, down the stairs and around the corner, down the stairs and around the corner, down the stairs and around the corner, down the stairs and around the corner . . . By the time he reached the eighth floor, Edwin's head was spinning, his knees had gone wobbly and he realized with a certain dismay that real life was not like the movies. No editorial ellipse would save him, no bursting into the stairwell, followed moments later by a shot of Ed bursting back out on the ground floor, just in time to meet the freight elevator. No. Edwin would have to run every damn step of every damn flight of every damn stair. This came as a mild surprise. He knew full well that books lied, especially self-help books, but he had always sort of assumed that movies were real. (Back in his English lit. campus days, he would often slip out to watch Schwarzenegger movies where there were no hidden themes to be discussed, no depths of human motivation to be plumbed. His favourite was *Conan the Barbarian*, even if Arnie did quote Nietzsche in it, which sort of ruined the mood.) Had Edwin's literary friends known that instead of musing on T. S. Eliot and Ezra Pound, he had in fact been sitting through repeated matinees of *Conan*, he would have been ostracized from the group. Or at least given the intellectual equivalent of a headlock noogie. Throughout his university days, Edwin had lived this shameful double life, well-read and aristocratic on the surface, but crass and populist in his heart. And now, in heroic pursuit of Rory the Janitor down a seemingly endless series of stairs, Edwin de Valu had come face-to-face with a disturbing truth: Conan the Barbarian movies may not entirely reflect reality.

So Edwin did what any true protagonist would do in such circumstances: he gave up. Staggering out at the seventh floor—"Lucky seven," he gasped—Edwin surprised a receptionist sitting on guard at her desk.

"Where did you come from?" she wanted to know, her voice full of huff, as Edwin limped over to the elevators and pushed a button.

"From the thirteenth floor," he said weakly.

"There is no thirteenth floor."

"Exactly," said Edwin. "Exactly."

As the elevator made its slow descent, Edwin could hear the medieval creak and moan of chain and pulley. Down, down he went, into the darkest sub-basements of the building. If he could just find Rory, everything would be fine, of this Edwin was certain. Rory liked Edwin, Edwin could tell. Even though he was a highly respected editor with a powerful publishing company, Edwin was careful not to let it go to his head. He always made that extra effort to "stay in touch" with the working man. Whenever Rory wheeled his squeaking cart through Panderic Inc., Edwin made a point of engaging in a bit of uplifting chit-chat. "Hey there, Jimbo!" he would say. "How is life treating you?" (On second thought, maybe his name was Jimbo, not Rory. No. Definitely Rory. There must be another janitor somewhere named Jimbo.) Sometimes Edwin would pretend to punch Rory on the shoulder and say, "Hey there, ho there," or ask him about ice hockey. Rory really liked ice hockey. Edwin knew this because one time Rory had said, "I really like ice hockey." So Ed would say, "How about them Raiders?" and Rory would say—something. Edwin couldn't remember what. Probably something along the lines of "the Raiders are lookin' good, my man." You know, sports talk. That kind of thing. Rory liked Edwin, Edwin could tell.

So, by the time the elevator had descended to the very end of its tether, Edwin was in high spirits. Everything would work out. Edwin would pretend to punch Rory on the shoulder, ask him about "them Raiders" and then mention, just in passing, how he had accidentally discarded a very important package. He would let Rory go and fetch it for him, and by way of thanks, Edwin would say, "Let's get together for a beer sometime," and they never would. Everything would be just fine.

But first he had to find Rory. Or possibly Jimbo.

Edwin ended up wandering from one dark level to another like a character in a minimalist play. Storage rooms led to abandoned underground parkades, and the parkades in turn led back to littered corridors and empty hallways. The entire place was dank, dark and dripping, and filled with the echoed plonk of waterdrops falling. The scent of sulphur and carbon monoxide seemed to have seeped into the very walls. At some point, Edwin began to whistle.

In much the same way that a rat will solve a maze by random attempts at passage, Edwin eventually discovered Janitorial Storage and Waste Management #3. He had already tried numbers 1 and 2 to no avail, and there didn't seem to be a 4, so . . .

"Hey there, ho there, hi there. Rory, my man! How the heck is life treating you?"

Rory, a dishevelled, soft-featured fellow in his middle years, turned and said, "Edwin? From up in Panderic?"

"That's me!" Big grin.

"And you got my name right. Usually you call me Jimbo."

"Oh, that." Edwin pshawed it away. "It's just that you remind me of a chap—a guy we used to call Jim. So I gave you that nickname. I was just being wacky. You know, kiddin' around and whatnot."

"I suppose." Rory was emptying a dustpan into a large cloth bag. "What brings you down to my depths?"

"Oh, well. You see, I accidentally threw out a very important envelope, about yey thick, from someone named Soiree. Anyway, you emptied my trash, and I need to retrieve that package, so . . ."

"Jeez. I must have already dumped it into the compressor. Hang on." Rory stepped over to a battered control panel, hit a large red button and a noise Edwin hadn't even noticed suddenly ceased. "We pack it, then we take it up to the loading dock for transport. Why don't you climb in and have a look, and I'll go through a couple of the bins that haven't been emptied yet."

"In?"

Edwin rummaged around for more than twenty minutes. It was hopeless. When he finally crawled out—having hardly trusted Rory not to start up the compressor while he was still inside—Edwin was covered in a wet wash of coffee grinds and eggshells.

"That'll be from the cafeteria," said Rory. "Second floor. Maybe you ought to try the bigger refuse container out back."

So again Edwin took a deep breath, and again he plunged inside. But this time, instead of wet garbage and coffee grinds, it was Death by a Thousand Paper Cuts. This was definitely Panderic trash: reams of pages and stacks of discarded canisters of ink that stained Edwin's fingers blue. Photocopy fluid had soaked into everything (a not unpleasant smell, but probably one with a cumulative toxic effect, Edwin decided).

"For cryin' out loud, don't you sort the trash around here? You know, recycle?"

"Supposed to," said Rory.

After going through Panderic's morning trash, envelope by envelope, manuscript by manuscript, knee deep in words and ink, Edwin admitted defeat.

"I checked every goddamn package in there," he said. "Nothing. Nada. Not a goddamn thing."

"And this particular package, it's important, is it?"

"Yes."

"Very important?"

"Yes, yes," said Edwin impatiently. "It's very, very important. I thought we had established that already. I have to find it, Rory. My entire career depends upon it."

"I'm not sure if I can help you. I get off in about an hour—I'm working the early shift. Maybe Dave or Marty can help you. They're in at noon."

"No, dammit! I can't wait until noon."

And then, suddenly, softly, Rory said, "Wait a sec. This package of yours, fairly thick, was it? With stickers of daisies on the front page?"

"Yes!" Edwin's eyes lit up. "Daisies! Where is it?"

"It's gone. It was in the first bin, and there was some extra space in the morning run, so I bagged it with the earlier batch."

"Meaning?"

"It's probably on the scow right now."

Edwin could feel his life spiralling away from him. "The scow? *The scow?* What scow?" It sounded positively Stygian. And it was.

"The garbage scow. Departs every day, right about"—Rory peered at his wristwatch—"now."

Which is how Edwin Vincent de Valu found himself on Belfry Island amid mountains of refuse, scrambling over loose shuffles of garbage bags, stumbling down avalanches of plastic, searching in vain for one specific bag of wastepaper in an entire vast landscape of wastepaper. Bulldozers pushed steaming piles of garbage into gullies, flattening and rearranging the ever-shifting expanse. Seagulls picked and squawked and reeled in the sky as the sun lifted wavering sheets of heat and humidity. The stench was almost transcendental.

Edwin, morose beyond belief, was covered with flicks of eggshells, coffee grinds, printer's ink and now this: seagull shit. Drippings of white yogurt-like feces. "Just when I think my life can't get any worse. Just when I think I can't possibly sink any lower . . ."

He called May from a dockside pay phone, amid the blare of tugboats and the constant screech and cry of seagulls.

"I'm at the dump," he said.

"*In* the dumps?"

"*At*—both. Whatever."

"For Chrissake, get back here. Mr. Mead has been looking for you all afternoon. Said he wants to discuss that 'nifty' concept you had for a fall title."

"Tell him I called in sick. Bubonic plague. Seagull excrement. Broken spirit. Anything. It doesn't matter any more."

"Edwin, I can't keep covering for you like this."

"I know, I know." He suddenly felt weary, weary beyond words. This morning he had been happy. Cranky, bitter and weighed down with life, but otherwise generally happy. He had been in a groove, or at least a very comfortable rut. His life, such as it was, fit together. But ever since this morning, ever since that manuscript landed on his desk, it was as though everything had begun to unravel. The end of the wharf and the deep waters beckoned . . .

"Edwin? Are you still there?"

"Hmm?"

"Are you okay?"

"I think I'm going to go home now." His voice was faint and distant. "Tell Mr. Mead that she's all right."

"Who is?"

"My aunt. She's fine. Turns out it was just a mild flu."

Chapter
Five

Edwin lived on Upper South Central Boulevard, in a row of brownstone townhouses built along a scrub of grass and a scraggly line of tumorous trees filled with chain-smoking squirrels and wet-hacking birds of indistinguishable breed. And even then, even here, Edwin was living beyond his means. With two incomes combined, Edwin and his wife could barely manage the mortgage payments, could just afford to cling to this address on Upper South Central Boulevard—an address that was at once elegant and elegiac.

The Great Potash Boom that had helped line Grand Avenue with handsome Edwardian buildings had also helped create Ed's own neighbourhood: a procession of grand manors, now subdivided into townhouses. It was like living in a castle long after the lord had died.

Edwin had taken a cab from the ferry dock to the nearest subway station, had taken the Grey Line north to 47th and then changed first onto the LRT and then to the CTR and the ABC and the XYZ. His life was a daily soup of commuter routes, an alphabet of repetition. Sometimes he thought about stepping off, of floating up and out, beyond words, beyond the city, into the never-never of dreamland. Somewhere beyond consciousness and the burden it inevitably brings.

Edwin's brownstone was distinguished from the rest on his block by only two things: its number (668, "the neighbour of the beast" as he liked to call it) and the sunshiny yellow shutters in the front window.

Jenni—Edwin's younger, smarter, better-looking wife—worked as an online consultant for an out-of-state brokerage firm, and most of her time was spent in the spare bedroom (now a high-powered virtual office), moving packets of electronic information back and forth. Both Edwin and his wife spent their time submerged in words, but the difference was both profound and subtle. Edwin dealt with paper, stark black on white, the letters like holes punched through the surface, revealing the darkness on the other side. Those were the words Edwin waded through every day. Jenni's words were luminescent green. They shone in an eerie glow like renderings on a radar screen; they emitted light; they shimmered and scrolled up the surface of the monitor, they slid along phone lines, seeped into mainframes, lived inside fibre-optic cables. "You know, you can change the settings on that," Edwin had pointed out. "You don't have to make the letters luminescent green; you can make them black on white if you want." But Jenni had just smiled and said, "I like my words to glow."

Jenni worked at home, which is to say she had an awful lot of free time on her hands. Hence the always-fresh, always-scooped kitty litter box for Mr. Muggins. Hence the regularly changed air fresheners in the hall toilet (the one they never used, reserved as it was for the guest poop of visitors). Hence the knick-knacks, hence the hobbies, hence the endless fad diets and the meta-vitamin therapy sessions. Half the quack doctors on the lower southside were being funded through generous donations from Edwin's wife.

Jenni *believed*. What she believed didn't matter, just that she believed. She saw cosmic purpose in random chance; she saw portents of a greater cause enveloped in everyday coincidence. When they went out for Chinese food, she would hover her hand above the fortune cookies, picking up vibes, feeling the flow of the universe directing her choice. "They're just cookies!" Edwin wanted to yell. "They mass-produce them in a factory in Newark. They come wrapped in plastic, for God's sake." But he never did. Edwin, in his heart of hearts, was afraid of Jenni. She had fooled everyone else, but she had never quite fooled him. He knew that a blade of thin steel ran straight through her core. She was a candied apple, the kind you hear about in urban legends and Halloween scare stories—the kind with a razor blade hidden inside. And Edwin knew it was only a matter of time before he bit into it.

And now, here he was, home again. Up the four steps, key in door, shoulders slouched, Edwin was like a younger, less noble version of Willy Loman. (Loman didn't normally enter stage left adorned with bird shit and eggshells. At least, not in the version of the play Edwin and Jenni had seen. "That's me," Edwin had said afterwards. "That's me in twenty years." "Don't be silly," his wife had replied. "That actor was much shorter than you are.")

Edwin took off his overcoat. Took off his necktie. Stared at himself in the hallway mirror, his face haggard, his eyes like two holes burnt in cheap linoleum. "I really should have been a writer," he thought. "I have a knack for simile."

So focused was Edwin on this reverse-narcissistic fascination with his own downtrodden features that he almost missed the yellow square of paper stuck to the lower corner of the mirror. It was a Post-it Note, and it said: "Cheer up! You're better than you think you are."

What the . . .

"Hello, honey! You're home early!" His wife bounded across the hall-way from the kitchen back into the living room, a sudden purple-and-pink flash of spandex. Faint in the background, a Mesmer's chant could be heard. "Ah-one and ah-two and ah-three. Make it burn, make it burn."

Their cat—Jenni's cat—rubbed up against Edwin's shins, intrigued by the smells of rotting fish and produce that still clung to his hems, purring, tail twitching. "You never learn, do you?" said Edwin as he kicked the cat down the hall. It yelped once and disappeared, threading its way through the furniture in a single liquid ripple.

As Edwin walked down the hallway, he saw more and more yellow squares of paper, a tickertape parade of motivational messages. "Remember: you are just as good as you say you are! Even better!" "Knowing how to live is the first step in knowing how to love." "Yes, you can! Yes, you will!"

What the . . .

He grabbed one square of paper as he passed. On it, in cheery hand-writing, was written: "Did *you* remember to hug yourself today?"

"Hun!" he called out as he entered the living room. (She had always assumed his little nickname for her was an abbreviated form of "honey." It wasn't.) "Hun," he said. "Why are there—"

"Do I look fat?" She was in the middle of a series of deep knee bends and had paused to look up at him. Her hair, shimmering auburn and pulled up with a band, continued bouncing long after she herself had stopped. Of course she wasn't fat. Jenni was trim. Fit. She had to make an effort to squeeze together enough cellulite to worry about. This didn't make her especially popular with her friends.

"I'm so fat." Some people fished for compliments. Jenni sent out bottom-trawling Liberian fleets to scour the ocean floor.

Aren't you going to ask why I reek of garbage and have seagull droppings on my head? Aren't you curious as to why I'm home so early? Or how I have managed to single-handedly sink my career at Panderic?

"You're not fat," he said for the 327,304th time since they were married. "You're not fat."

"How about in plaid? Do you think I look fat in plaid?"

"Plaid?"

"That's right, plaid. Be honest. How do you really feel about plaid?"

"How do I feel? *How do I feel?* I don't give a shit is how I feel. You ruined my life. I never should have married you, you horrible, horrible person." But of course, that's not really what he said. Edwin was afraid of Jenni, and he said instead, "You look fine in plaid."

"Honest? You're not just saying that, right? Because I do feel fat today. I don't know why, I just do. Are you sure I haven't put on some weight?"

Edwin sighed. "A writer named Betty Jane Wylie once said, 'Most people feel that their life would be complete if they could just lose ten pounds.'"

"Well," said Jenni. "That's certainly true."

"Which is true?" Edwin asked, more testily than he had intended. "Your syntax is imprecise. Do you mean that most people do think that way, or that it is factually true? That their lives *would* be complete if they just lost ten pounds."

"I don't know. Both, I guess. Hey, look, Post-it Notes!" She picked up a booklet and held it aloft.

"Yes, I was meaning to ask what—"

"Swirl," she said, as though that explained everything. Sure enough, this month's issue of *Swirl* magazine had arrived and was sitting in proud view on the coffee table. And sure enough, one of the cover articles was "Better Living Thru Post-it Notes!"

"You write self-motivating principles to yourself and then put them up around the house as reminders."

"Reminders?"

"To be happy! Here, you want to try?"

She handed him the pad and a pen, but all he could think of were things like "Try to get through the day without killing somebody," which was not, he suspected, quite what Jenni had in mind.

Edwin wandered through the halls of their home like a stranger in someone else's life. Often, while sitting quietly, alone in the living room, he would look around him and try to find something—anything—that could be identified with *him*. The entire decor reeked of Jenni, from the sunny colours to the wildflower motifs to the polished untouched upright piano in the far corner. There was nothing of Edwin invested anywhere in the room. He was merely a tenant.

Yellow Post-it Notes were everywhere: in the kitchen, in the dining room, even, no doubt, in the washroom. There were Post-it Notes on the lampshade ("Energy consumption! Think about the big blue planet!"), above the dishwasher ("Clean dishes! Clean mind!"), and on the front of the fridge ("Better health and a more beautiful body"—and wasn't it revealing, Jenni's choice of words? Not "a beautiful body" but "a *more* beautiful body"). Edwin swung the fridge door open and reached inside for a can of beer. On the can—on every beer in the case—was a little reminder from Jenni: "Are you sure you need that beer? Are you really sure? Seems someone has been drinkin' an awful lot lately."

With a deep sense of relief, Edwin finally knew the answer to one of Jenni's Post-it Note questions. *Was he really sure he needed a beer?* "Abso-fuckin'-lutely." Edwin popped a tab and drained the beer more or less directly down his gullet. "I got the workin' man's blues," he said, wistfully, to himself.

Edwin had once been a Swedish liqueur and mahogany cognac sort of fellow, someone who lingered and sipped and massaged his tongue with nuance. But when he entered the bumper-car world of the publishing business, when he decided to get "a job," he knew he had to steel his reserve, had to become more grounded in daily reality. So he made the conscious and, to him, courageous decision to drink only domestic beer. Straight out of the can. The way real Americans drank. (Though, truth is, he liked beer. Preferred it to cognac or peppermint schnapps. And anyway, this wasn't just beer. No sir. It was "genuine cold-filtered, beechwood-aged draft." Not that Edwin knew what that meant. Not that anyone knew what that meant.)

Jenni bounded into the kitchen as Edwin finished the last of his beer. "Your day," she said. "How was it?"

"My day? Let's see . . ." he popped the top of another can. "I made rash promises that I couldn't keep, I rummaged through human refuse, I was shat upon by flying feathered rats and—oh, yes—I destroyed my career at Panderic."

"What, again?" This was the third time this month that Edwin had destroyed his career at Panderic.

"But this time it's for real. We'll have to sell off our mortgage, live in a cardboard box, scrounge for cold cheese on discarded pizza boxes, push our belongings around in shopping carts. That kind of thing." He swallowed hard and grimaced. "And how was your day?"

"Wonderful! I got Post-it Notes."

Edwin chugged the second can of beer so quickly it almost frothed up from his nose. "Ah, yes. Post-it Notes." He held the cold can against his temple, thought about escape.

"Honey," she said. "You've been drinking a lot of beer lately, and I'm starting to get concerned. Now, I know a friend of a friend who knows a hypnotist, down in the Village, who—"

"Hun, listen. I'm fine. My career is in ruins. I am about to be fired. I have probably contracted fifteen different types of infectious disease. But other than that, everything is just peachy-keen. My life is one big parade of limericks and happy skipping summer songs. Everything is fine. The beer is fine. I'm fine. We're all fine," he swallowed hard. "Anyway, Hun. You can't become a full-blown degenerate on beer alone.

Trust me, you have to switch to harder stuff. If you see me kicking back the Lonesome Charlie or Southern Comfort straight from a paper bag, that's when you have to worry. But not till then."

"Okay. If you insist, but . . ." and she slapped a Post-it Note on his chest with more force than was really necessary. It read: "Somebody needs a hug."

"Come here," he said as he pulled her into his embrace.

"Yuck. Why so smelly?"

"It's a long story," he said. "A long, long story."

Chapter
Six

That night, Edwin dreamed of daisies. An endless field of daisies, stretching to the horizon. But they weren't real daisies; they were scratch-and-sniff Post-it Note daisies left in wild abandon by a loud, laughing voice. When Edwin stooped to smell them, he woke up gagging.

"The daisies," he said. There was something about the daisies. Something important. Something he had missed.

He lay awake, listening to Jenni's soft angelic snores (even her snores were endearing—closer to a purr than a seagull's squawk), and then, unable to recapture oblivion, he got up and plodded naked into the kitchen, kicking the cat out of the way as he went. (Truth be told, the cat wasn't really in the way. Edwin had to make a short detour to get to Mr. Muggins.)

Earlier, after Edwin had showered and shaved, Jenni had invited him to (a) make love; (b) have sex; or (c) engage in marital intercourse. As always, it had been predictable, uninspired, and mildly disappointing. Which is to say, the correct answer had been (c). At one point in the proceedings, at the height of their stale passion (married couples can pretty much make love without even paying attention), as he nuzzled his face between her legs, he found, attached to her inner thigh, a Post-it Note that read: *"Remember, small circles and not too much direct pressure!"*

What the hell is this? Lessons in cunnilingus?

So there he was, turning small circles with his tongue, carefully avoiding direct pressure, thinking about somewhere else . . . someone else.

And now, his naked buttocks sticking to the kitchen chair with the residue of love sheen and sweat, Edwin thumbed through Jenni's stack of *Swirls*. He wasn't really paying attention; he was just sort of marvelling at the never-ending supply of "advice" and "tips" when, with a sudden head-thwack of energy, Edwin said, "Hey! Wait a minute. I can do this. This is tripe." He thumbed through more magazines, quickly and with a growing sense of excitement. Quizzes were mandatory, apparently ("How Sexy Are You?" "Are You Married to the Right Man?" "The Wrong Man?" "Do You Take Magazine Quizzes Way Too Seriously? Take the *Swirl* Quiz and Find Out!"). There were several handy articles on "driving men crazy," another one on "how to make yourself irresistible to men," and another on how "you don't need a man to be happy." (The magazines were obsessed with men and why women didn't need them.)

Edwin was overjoyed at the weak level of writing, the thin ideas, the chatty grade-school style of composition. "Ha! This stuff is easy. It practically writes itself. To hell with Tupak Soiree, I'll write my own damn self-help book."

Edwin gathered up a stack of magazines and grabbed a notebook and an assortment of pencils. He sat down with fresh determination. It was two in the morning, the streets were sleeping and Edwin felt good. He stretched his arms, cracked his knuckles, and set himself to the task.

"Okay. Here we go. Let's be logical about this, Edwin. Novels are regularly 90,000 words or more. But with self-help, 60,000 will do. We can even fluff out 50,000 in a pinch: widen the margins, increase the spacing between lines, use a bigger typeface." Mr. Ethics books, for example, had become thinner and thinner each year, forcing Panderic to expand the margins of the last one to such an extent that there was almost more white space than text ("Stark and bold," was how the salespeople described the layout to booksellers). And it worked. The general public is never turned off by having to read less. *The Bridges of Madison County* and *The Notebook* were enduring evidence of this. The same principle applied to self-help: promise the max while demanding the least from your readers. It was almost axiomatic in the trade.

"Now then," said Edwin. "What was it I promised? Stop smoking, lose weight, better sex, happiness, meaning, purpose . . ." He wrote out a list of the many areas mentioned at the meeting. There were twenty-four. Perfect. That worked out to one chapter per insight (though "happiness" could probably be covered in the introduction). "Okay, let's move happiness to the intro and divvy up the rest. That makes twenty-three chapters, at 60,000 words, which works out to be—let's see—roughly 2,600 words per chapter. No problem." (If Edwin couldn't come up with 2,600 words on "how to achieve inner balance" or "how to discover your purpose in life," he wasn't worthy of being dubbed a hack editor.)

"Let's start with the simplest: kicking the tobacco habit." How hard could that be? Edwin had quit smoking at least a dozen times. He wrote the chapter heading across the top of the page and underlined it forcibly: "How to Stop Smoking: *Step One.*" He sat back. Mulled it over. Scratched his scrotum thoughtfully for a moment. Sniffed his fingertips. Drummed the pencil on the tabletop. Thought some more, chewed on the end of the eraser, and then crossed out "How to Stop Smoking" and wrote above it "How to Lose Weight the Easy Way: A Modern Miracle Breakthrough!" Weight loss was a better start. He'd cover smoking later. Diets were easier; after all, during his marriage to Jenni he had had a front-row spectator's seat to at least a dozen fly-by-night diet regimes. If only he had paid more attention . . .

After a few more fruitless moments of frowning, scratching and sniffing, Edwin decided to sort of "help" the writing process along.

"It is very hard to distinguish plagiarism from paraphrasing," he reminded himself. "And no one can copyright an idea." These were the first two commandments of the Derivative School of Book Publishing, and Edwin began opening Jenni's magazines at random, looking for pointers to steal. Or rather, "repackage." After a dozen or so forays, all he was was confused. Cholesterol seemed to be a big factor in most of the articles, but Edwin didn't exactly know what cholesterol was. Figuring out your proper height-to-weight ratio was also apparently a factor, but Edwin was never much of a whiz when it came to math. (That was why he became an English major in the first place. There were no facts involved in English lit., only interpretations.) No. The hard-edged, number-saturated information would have to wait. Edwin would start with something more abstract instead. Something more ephemeral, more obtuse, where his true talents could best be put to use.

Aha! A cover story in one of the back issues of *Swirl* was entitled "Motivation: The Key to Losing Weight." Perfect. Motivation was both vague and abstract enough that Edwin could ruminate without fear of being asked to provide empirical evidence. It was just like being back in English lit. again.

"Okay, here we go, Edwin. Let's get down to business. 'Losing Weight: Step One.'" And with a flourish, he wrote, "The key is motivation. If you are motivated to lose weight, this will prove to be a key. Indeed, some might say, as far as keys to losing weight go, that motivation is one of the most important, if not the most important, key involved. But how do we motivate ourselves?" Edwin stopped a moment, looked at the ceiling. Frowned some more. "This is a very good question," he wrote. "Indeed, many people feel that this question is the most important key there is (regarding motivation)." Then, in a sudden spurt of inspiration, so blindingly bright he almost cackled out loud when it came to him, Edwin wrote, "Post-it Notes! Post-it Notes are a very good way to create the motivation needed to lose weight. For example, you could leave motivational messages on your fridge door. Messages like: '*Don't eat so much, you big fat pig.*'"

Edwin stopped. He re-read the last sentence and, realizing that the sentiments expressed therein might be misconstrued as insensitive, crossed out the word "big."

At this point, Edwin got up, stretched, and briefly considered making a pot of coffee. But all they had was a pressurized steam-milk latte machine that would have woken up Hun and half the neighbourhood. Instead, he did a quick word count of what he had written so far. It came in at around 405 words. So he put "big" back in: 406 words. He jotted down the calculations: 60,000 words minus 406. That left 59,594 to go. Mr. Mead came back in seven days. So Edwin had to come up with roughly 8,500 words a day before then. Edwin did these calculations three times, got a different total each time and then took the average. No matter how he juggled it, the outlook was grim. So far, it had taken Edwin—he checked the kitchen clock—just over two hours to come up with 406 words. Which meant he was writing at a rate of 203 words an hour, so (he worked it out on a pad) Edwin would have to spend the next week writing 42 hours a day, every day, which was, thanks to Einstein's theory of relativity, scientifically impossible.

Edwin pushed the pad away and gently laid down his pen.

"I'm doomed," he said.

Chapter
Seven

"The copy editor's gone crazy," said May.

They were sitting in O'Malley's on Donovan Street, amid polished wood and brass, drinking black pitch beer and manufactured Irish moods. Edwin hadn't gone to the office, had called in to say he was "working at home today," but that was a lie. To have worked at home would have meant spending the day with Jenni, something that ranked just below spending a day in the chair of a hiccupping dentist in Edwin's continually amended, always-growing list of Things I Try to Avoid. Instead, he had gone on an extended pub crawl, beginning at O'Callaghan's and then moving on to O'Toole's and then O'Reilly's and eventually O'Feldman's before ending up here, at—where were they again?—O'Malley's. On Donovan Street. Edwin had called May, half-sloshed, and had pleaded with her to join him. "Come have a drink with a corpse," he said, slurring his words into the phone. "Come keep a dead boy company."

"Gosh," said May dryly. "How could a girl resist an invitation like that?" But she came anyway.

Edwin hailed her like a returning general. "May! May! Over here!" He was rumpled but shaven, and May took this as a good omen. He hadn't sunk that far yet, hadn't reached full-metal caricature. Not yet. But he was, she noted, smoking again. And not just smoking, but smoking furiously. Edwin was wreathed in a pall of blue haze and the ashtray in front of him was stuffed with the smouldering butts of slow suicide.

So they sat and they drank, and Edwin smoked and May shared small anecdotes, and Edwin waved his hand for more beer and he laughed just a little too long and a little too hard at May's jokes.

"I realize that copy editors are paid to be anal-retentive," she said. "But this guy has gone over the edge. He really has. He flagged the phrase 'hand-written manuscript,' said it was a redundancy. The Latin root being *manus*, or 'hand.'"

"Ha!" said Edwin. "Latin! *E pluribus unum*. *Carpe diem*. *Dum spiro, spero!* Copy editors, ha! R'all crazy. Crazy, I tell you."

It was true. The only thing worse than a copy editor with a tin ear and a ramrod up his ass (speaking of redundancies) were the lawyers Panderic hired to go over their books, page by page, line by line, and suck the life out of them one by one. A particularly anal lawyer—this is true—once flagged the phrase "today's politicians are brimming with bromides," noting that this "implies drug use." Apparently, the word "bromide," beyond meaning a trite expression, also suggests "a sedative."

"Brimming with bromides!" roared Edwin. "Remember that May? Remember what's-his-face? The writer. What was his name?"

"Berenson."

"That's right, Berenson. Flipped out when he saw they had flagged 'brimming with bromides.' D'you 'member him storming into our office, throwing chairs upside down, threatening to kill the lawyer and any-one—what was it he said?"

"Anyone who 'tampered with the sanctity of his prose.'"

"That's right. Sanctity. Ha!"

May leaned in, closer. "Listen, Edwin. This isn't good what you're doing. I know you're under a lot of strain, but—"

"I promised a book and then I threw it away. Or maybe it was the other way around. Doesn't matter. An' not just any book, but the great-est damn self-help book in the history of the universe. A book that fell from Heaven itself."

"So we tell Mr. Mead that the deal collapsed. We tell him the author asked for an unreasonable advance, or got snippy, or we had a falling out and he pulled the manuscript, took it to Random House—you know how paranoid Mr. Mead is about Random House, how he always thinks they're out to get us. Even if Random House denies stealing our author, it'll just confirm his deepest suspicions. It will get you off the hook, Edwin. And remember," she said, "it's just a book."

"No, no. It's not just the book. It's everything. Another screw-up, another . . . I don't know." His head was down. He was mumbling something into his chest, but now he swung his face up, focused his gaze on May and said, suddenly and with a softness so sincere it almost broke her heart, "God, you're beautiful."

"Stop it."

"It's true."

"Stop it *right now*."

"You are. You are so very, very beautiful."

"And you," she said pointedly, "are so very, very drunk. Come on. I'm going to take you home."

"My wife," he said, lurching over to one side and breathing into May's neck, "my wife is a cow."

At this, May went rigid. "Edwin, let me give you some advice. If you're a married man trying to hit on a single girl, don't slag off your wife, okay? It doesn't impress anyone."

"But it's true," he said. "She's a cow. She's horrible." He began to make loud, sad mooing noises, even as he leaned in farther, even as his hand rested on May's knee.

May shifted her body away from him, stood up. "Come on. I'm taking you home."

"Don't wanna go home. Wife is insane. It's like the *Stepford Wives*, 'member that? My wife is so insane she *appears* to be sane. But she isn't. I'm afraid of her, May. I'm afraid of her sanity."

"Well, then," and her voice now had a hard, serrated edge. "Why don't you just leave her?"

"I can't," he said sorrowfully.

"And why not?"

"Because I love her so much."

"Get your jacket," said May. "We're leaving."

Jenni was bouncin' to the oldies (Van Halen and Bon Jovi) when the cab pulled up out front. She went to the door, still wiping her face with a small towel as she turned the deadlock.

"So there you are!" she said.

Edwin was propped up against the jamb, with May keeping him on his feet.

"He's had too much to drink," said May, superfluously.

"Did you, honey? Is that true?"

But Edwin said nothing. He only made low mooing noises as Jenni led him into the entranceway. "Thanks so much, May. You're the best."

Unlike Edwin, May didn't hate very many people. But she did hate Jenni. Hated her not with a passion, but with a cold, clinical detachment. "If the world ever ends, if society collapses and martial law rules the streets," thought May, "the first thing I am going to do is track down Jenni and kill her."

Edwin continued to moo soulfully, eyes shut, as he kicked uselessly at his shoes.

"We were at a bar," said May. "Together. Just the two of us. He had a lot to drink—with me—so I called a cab." It was dark out and May was returning a rumpled husband to his wife.

Jenni looked up from untying Edwin's shoes. "Owe you one, May," she said cheerfully. "Now let's get you into bed, shall we, honey?"

"Moo," said Edwin. "Mooooo."

"I don't know what bothers me more," said May as she stood on the doorstep outside. "That I once had sex with her husband, or that she doesn't even see me as a threat. Not even on the periphery."

The cab driver was waiting with a meter-running grin. "So," he said, "where to next?"

The entire night was spread out before her like the city itself, in a wash of lights and possibilities. "Home," she said.

"What, so soon? A lovely young lady like yourself? Come on, the night is young and so are you."

"No," she said. "No, I'm not."

Chapter
Eight

Over the next few days, a strange sort of calm settled upon Edwin. It was the calm of a man who has accepted his fate, whether it be death by firing squad, death by lethal injection or having to face a domineering boss with nothing but empty apologies and weak excuses. It was a deep, existential calm. One that allowed Edwin to glide over the surface of storm-tossed waves with the greatest of aplomb. Grace, even. Aplomb and grace, those were the qualities that Edwin now sought to cultivate.

When Nigel chided him about the missing self-help book—"the one that would have changed humanity itself," as Nigel derisively described it—and asked Edwin if the author was also preparing to walk on water, maybe cure the blind and heal the lame, Edwin would turn and say with the utmost dignity, "Fuck off and die, Nigel." Just like that, with aplomb and grace: "Fuck off and die."

"Hey, Edwin, you know what they say. Sticks and stones . . ." Nigel was standing over Edwin's desk, his face scrunched up into something that was meant to resemble a smile.

"Oh, words *will* hurt you, Nigel. Ever had an unabridged dictionary smack you on top of the head? Want to find out how it feels?"

"Come on, Edwin. If I can't take joy in your impending self-destruction, what can I take joy in?"

"*Schadenfreude*," said Edwin. It was one of May's untranslatables: "The pleasure one feels from witnessing another's misfortunes." A German word (natch).

Edwin turned to Nigel and said, sweetly, "Why don't you take your *schadenfreude* sympathy and shove it up your—"

"Know what your problem is, Edwin?"

Edwin thrust a self-righteous finger at Nigel's chest. "Yeah. I don't play the game."

"Oh, no. You play the game. You just play it really badly. I mean, why on earth would you promise something so outlandish? What were you thinking? It's like that book you championed last season. What was it called?"

Edwin turned away. "Leave me alone," he said.

"*Die, Baby Boomers, Die!* That was it. That was the title, right? 'A generation on the brink of death faces old age, greying pubic hair, sexual impotence and prostate cancer. The generation that thought it would stay young forever now sinks into pathos and decrepitude. They are going bald, getting flatulent, becoming fat and flabby.' That was it, right? That was your pitch. What the hell were you thinking? And you presented it as a humour book, for God's sake."

"Well, *I* found it funny."

"Listen . . ." Nigel was leaning over Edwin so closely that his tie was dangling on the desktop. "What did I try to tell you when you first concocted that proposal? I said, 'Baby Boomers can dish it out, but they can't take it. And they hate to be mocked.' I told you this, and did you listen? No. You told me to F-off. Those were your words, to put it euphemistically. F-off. You're always so crude, Edwin."

"That Baby Boomer book would have sold. It would have sold by the shitload."

"Edwin, North American Baby Boomers feel superior to everyone. Superior to their parents, superior to us. And when it comes to their own place in history, they are absolutely humourless. You know that, I know that, everybody knows that."

"Yeah, well. I thought we could buck the trend. I thought we might show some backbone for a change."

But what Nigel didn't know, what even May didn't know, was that the author of *Die, Baby Boomers, Die!*, Douglas C. Upland, was in fact a pseudonym for "Edwin Vincent de Valu." It was his own book he had pitched at the meeting, it was his own manuscript that Mr. Mead had denounced as "puerile, jejune and any other adjective that means 'young.'" And even now, as Nigel chastised him, Edwin's manuscript sat secretly in his drawer, breathing, throbbing with life, refusing to die. (And who knew how many other editors had similar secret manuscripts hidden in drawers, breathing softly, waiting for the right moment to appear . . . Perhaps even Mr. Mead had one or two stashed away in the darker recesses of his office.)

"Nigel," said Edwin, "I don't know if you've figured this part out yet, but I despise you. You make my skin crawl."

Nigel leaned in, tie hanging, voice even more condescending than usual. "You don't hate me, Edwin. You hate what I represent. You hate the success I have garnered, even with the deck stacked against us." (By "us," he meant, of course, Generation X. Nigel spoke of it as though it were some noble fraternity, rather than a demographic lump of directionless young adults.) "It's not me you hate, Edwin."

"Oh, yes it is," said Edwin, smiling, even as he fed Nigel's tie into the pencil sharpener. "It is definitely you."

"Listen, if you want me to help out with Mr. Mead when he gets back, I'll—*hey!* What the—" he was starting to choke. "Damn it, Edwin!" Gasping at the tightened knot, Nigel pulled his tie, now twisted and half-shredded, free from the sharpener, the handle reversing itself in fits and starts. "Damn it! Damn it all to hell!"

"Ah, ah, ah," said Edwin, wagging a finger. "Language."

Nigel was red in the face and sputtering by the time he had extracted the remains of his tie from Edwin's pencil sharpener. "That was pure silk!"

"Well, now it's pure shit."

"You'll be getting a bill from me," said Nigel, in full snit, as he stormed out of Edwin's cubicle. "You can count on it."

"Come again!" said Edwin. "Door is always open!"

Edwin leaned back, arms behind his head, and marvelled again at the deep calm he felt. His ulcer was behaving; his head felt clear; he was enjoying himself. Enjoying himself in the same way a skydiver whose chute doesn't open enjoys the breeze. I'm in free fall, he thought. And I have just shredded Nigel's necktie.

He couldn't stop giggling.

And so passed the week. Edwin felt calmer and more filled with aplomb than he ever had before, so calm that he almost reached a state of *satori*. Or stasis. It was hard to tell at times. He knew that he was about to crash and burn, knew full well that May's plan ("the deal fell through") would never work. Anyone else at Panderic might have managed to pull it off, but not Edwin. There would be questions. Follow-up calls to Random House. Threats, accusations, blistering replies, and then—slowly—the noose would tighten and it would all come back on Edwin. Mr. Mead had never fully trusted him, and for good reason. Edwin, after all, had once killed off a particularly bothersome writer. Killed him dead, as it were. Not literally, of course. He had simply cut off the relationship, and then, confronted unexpectedly by the marketing department, had said, "He, um, died." No. Edwin would never dream of *actually* killing one of his authors. He hoped one day to cross paths with the mysterious Mr. Soiree so that he could properly thank him. Thank him for sending in that huge hand-typed manuscript. Thank him for triggering the crisis that forced Edwin out of publishing, that forced him into poverty, that forced him into a cardboard box and a diet of cold cheese scraped from discarded pizza trays. Forced him out of his rut.

As the hours and days counted down to Mr. Mead's return, Edwin spent his time putting his life in boxes. He cleaned out his desk, pilfered some computer disks and said goodbye to those of his fellow workers he could stand—and vice versa. (The list was very short. It consisted solely of May.) Nigel presented him with a bill for $136 for the necktie he had ruined, and Edwin dutifully stuffed the bill down his shorts and spent the rest of the day sitting on it. It was a wonderful, joyous time. Edwin even managed to make a belated and awkward apology to May. "I'm sorry," he said. "You know, for pawing at you in the cab that day I called in sick. I am truly sorry, and I just want you to know: I never would have done that if I hadn't been so drunk. Really, I would never have made a pass at you otherwise."

Strangely, this didn't seem to make her feel better. "I know you wouldn't have," she said. *I know*.

Edwin invited her out for a drink after work on Friday, but May didn't say much. She just sat, toying with her mineral water, answering in nods and shrugs, her heavy red lipstick leaving muted pastel wounds on the edge of her glass.

Chapter
Nine

Early morning, Monday.

Edwin sat bolt upright in bed like a jump-cut in a bad horror movie. Of course! The daisies! In a surge, Edwin understood everything, understood the meaning of the daisies, knew why they were so crucial, knew why he had been dreaming about them night after night—had been dreaming about them ever since he first lost the manuscript.

It was 5:47 a.m. The liquid neon of the bedside clock glowed soft green. His wife lay beside him, purring and snoring, snoring and purring, and the bedroom curtains were moving on a faint wisp of wind, breathing in and out, in and out: slow inhalations, long exhalations. It was 5:47 in the morning, and Edwin wanted to leap in the air and yell "Eureka!" at the top of his voice. He gathered up his clothes and hopped into his pants even as he stumbled down the hall. The daisies. Of course! Exultant, he ran out the front door. Stopped. Came back in, kicked the cat, and then ran back outside. A wet mist was falling, soft as dew, but Edwin didn't care. He charged down the middle of the dawn-washed streets all the way to the nearest subway station.

By the time Edwin reached Faust and Broadview, his heart was singing. He bounded up the underground stairs, emerged into the Edwardian canyon of Grand Avenue and sprinted down the sidewalk, overcoat flapping behind him like a cape.

"Give me your money, muthafucker!" It was one of Grand Avenue's resident muggers, showing a certain early morning initiative, trying to catch the first wave of commuters.

"Sorry," shouted Edwin as he sprinted by. "Not today. Catch you next time."

And on he ran, down Grand Avenue and then up to the front doors of 813, which he pounded, palms open, until the security guard inside was sufficiently roused to come over and investigate. Edwin flashed the guard his ID and then loped down the high-ceiling entrance, where he caught a freight elevator and made his descent.

Janitorial Storage and Waste Management #3: Rory was down there, his back turned, as he leafed loose papers into the incinerator. Steam and the smell of sulphur already lay heavy in the stale recycled air of the basement.

"Jimbo!" yelled Edwin as he ran towards him. "The daisies! How did you know there were daisies on the title page? I put the manuscript back in the envelope before I—"

But it wasn't Rory. It was someone else in Rory's uniform, a slacker with red hair and a pointed beard who turned, sleepy-eyed, and said, "Rory. He gone."

Edwin skidded to a halt. "He *gone*?" he said, more in reference to the man's abysmal grammar than to the significance of what had been said. "He gone?"

"That right."

"That right? He gone? What kind dismal illiterate dialect are you speaking? Where go Rory?"

"He go home."

"Home? What, he doesn't work today?"

"Not today. Not tomorrow. Not anytime. He quit."

"He quit? What kind of dismal—" Edwin started and then stopped when he realized that "he quit" is in fact proper English.

"He quit?"

"That right. Call in, said, 'I got to realign the possibilities of who I am.'"

"Just like that?"

The slacker nodded. "Just like that."

Edwin turned to leave, not sure what to try next. "Well, that doesn't do me much good."

"You Mr. Edwin, down from the book place, right?"

"That's right. Why?"

The man laughed. "Oh, you everything Rory said you be."

Edwin managed to bribe the demonic janitor with promises of free copies of Panderic's next instalment in its Womyn's Erotica Empowerment series (or "stroke books," as they were known in the biz), and the man scrawled Rory's home address on a scrap of brown paper. It was a tenement not far from Grand Avenue. "You run it, maybe take ten minutes."

So Edward ran it. Ran like the wind (though by this point, his pace was starting to get ragged and he had to stop several times with a stitch in his side). Rory's building was a paint-peeling affair in front of a vacant lot ringed with rusting chain-link fences. The Great Potash Boom had passed this neighbourhood by entirely. It was a neighbourhood that had tried, and failed, to become a sort of lower-rate bohemian hangout, where artists and playwrights and other such societal flotsam could gather to play out the scenes in their own private Jack Kerouac fantasies. Instead, the neighborhood had sunk into working-class poverty, with the tenants trading low rents for high crime and getting through life day by day, paycheque to paycheque. Angry graffiti and gang tags were splashed across walls, marking turf like a dog's scent. Who knew what invisible boundaries of authority Edwin was crossing right now. Who knew which arcane inner-city protocol he was breaching at this very moment.

The darkened windows looked down. The front door opened on a dry hinge, not with a creak, but a moan. In the hallways, the lights hung broken in the sockets, shards of glass impossible to twist out, impossible to replace. Darkness and the smell of mildew—that was all. When he reached Rory's apartment, Edwin knocked, tentatively at first and then with growing urgency. Nothing. As his eyes slowly adjusted to the dark, and the details emerged, Edwin noticed a small cardboard sign hanging from the doorhandle. It read, simply: "Gone fishin'."

Then, from behind, a figure stepped out of the shadows. "Mr. Edwin?" it said.

"Yes?" He turned slowly, expecting the worse.

The face was still cloaked in darkness. The voice was low and resonant. "I suspect you'll be looking for Rory."

Edwin's voice, when it came out, was high-pitched, almost helium-filled in its squeakiness. "Yes. That would be correct."

"He said you might be coming around."

"Will he be back soon? Should I return some other time?"

There was a low rich chuckle. "Ah, Mr. Edwin. He's gone."

"Gone? You mean gone fishing?"

"No. He's gone. Moved out last week."

Edwin cleared his throat, nervously, and forced the quaver out of his voice. "And how would one go about finding him?"

"Oh, no," another deep chuckle. "You don't find him, Mr. Edwin. He'll find you." The voice rolled back into darkness and the figure melted away.

Shaken, but still riding a wash of adrenalin, Edwin escaped the tenement at a barely controlled stride. (Indeed, so brisk was his stride it would probably be more accurate to describe it as "fleeing.")

And as he left, blood pounding, Edwin went right by a large billboard sign, freshly painted with big bold letters. It announced an upcoming project of some kind, but Edwin hurried past without stopping. Which is a shame, because had he stopped to read it, he would certainly have found it of interest:

> COMING SOON! THE RORY P. WILHACKER FOUNDATION
> PRESENTS "A RESTORATION OF PRIDE IN THE INNER
> CITY." THE TENANTS OF THIS BUILDING ARE LAUNCHING
> AN INNOVATIVE NEW APPROACH TO PROFITABLE CO-OP
> TIME SHARES WITH A 500 PER CENT RETURN ON INVEST-
> MENTS. NO ONE DISPLACED. NO ONE EVICTED. "A NEW
> DAWN IS BREAKING!"

By the time Edwin returned to Grand Avenue, the morning rush was well under way. The white-noise echo of traffic was already ricocheting between buildings, and waves of commuters were ebbing and flowing on traffic-light authority. As Edwin crossed the Avenue at 41st, he thought to himself, as he did every day at precisely this spot and precisely this moment: *I hate this fuckin' city*.

Today was D-day. Final act. Mr. Mead was back from whichever regulatory junket he had sponsored himself for, and Edwin was scheduled to meet with him first thing in the morning to present his "exciting new self-help book." If nothing else, Edwin was going to go out guns blazing. He had been inventing and rehearsing various exit scenes, ranging from the sublime ("Mr. Mead, you have greatly disappointed me. You run this company like a second-rate campus paper, and I do believe it is time for me to move on") to the overt ("Puke face! Puke face! I don't care, I quit! Do you hear me? I quit!"). He even considered a succinct non-verbal message—a single strong yank on Mr. Mead's ridiculous little ponytail—but even then, in his heart of hearts, Edwin knew that was not the way the denouement would play out. There would be self-recrimination, sad appeals to mercy, the gleeful gloating of Nigel. Having to say goodbye to May. Maybe forever.

Edwin stopped for his final cup of joe at Louie's Hot Dog and Pickle Stand. "Two coffees," he said with a sigh as he pulled out his wallet. "One regular and one—" But before he could finish, Louie spoke, wet cigar still clamped between his teeth.

"The usual?"

"Yes," said Edwin, almost tearing up with joy. "Yes, the usual. I will have the usual. That's what I will have. I come here every morning, and that is what I am going to have. The usual."

Louie got it right, too. "Let's see: extra froth, nutmeg, cinnamon and just a dash of saffron. Sun-dried, of course."

"Thank you, Louie," said Edwin, heartfelt and drenchingly sincere. "Thank you so very much."

"My name's not Louie, kid. It's Thad. Louie's just the corporate trademark. We're owned by Coca-Cola."

"Well, thank you anyway, Thad. I'm going to miss you. I truly am."

"Whatever you say, kid."

And Edwin felt wonderful. Wonderful that he worked in such a rough-and-tumble city, that a guy named Louie (or Thad) had called him "kid," that he had someone like May to annoy. Someone like Nigel to loathe. He hated to see it all come to an end.

Edwin paid for the coffee and turned to leave. And that's when the limousine pulled up.

It was sleek, long, and obsidian black. It appeared out of nowhere like a shark, sliding in silently, keeping pace with Edwin as he walked along the sidewalk. Slowly, Edwin realized he was being stalked. He turned, and the limo rolled to a stop. A tinted window was lowered and a hand appeared, a hand heavy with gold. It beckoned to Edwin.

"Rory?"

"Hello, Mr. de Valu."

Edwin peered inside. Rory was there, dressed in what looked to be hand-cut Italian silk, and beside him was a radiant woman, smiling beatifically at Edwin.

"Edwin, you remember my wife, Sarah?"

Sarah leaned over, beaming. "Hiya, Eddie."

"Sarah, is it? I'm sorry, have we met?"

"Staff party," said Rory. "You thought she was the cleaning lady. Asked her to empty the ashtrays."

"Oh, really? I'm sorry, I don't remember."

"Of course you don't," said Rory, his voice warm and soothing. He had a smile, a smile of such profound serenity that Edwin was reminded of Buddhist statuary. It was a smile of utter contentment, a smile of utter satisfaction.

"You have the manuscript," said Edwin. "You've had it all along."

"Ah, Edwin. I wondered how long it would take before you figured it out. I wondered how long before you would check the work orders from that morning and discover there was no early garbage run."

"It was the daisies that tipped me off. You mentioned them, but they were inside the envelope. You couldn't have known unless you had opened the package and looked inside. It was while I was rummaging around in the trash compactor, right?"

"Oh, no. It was before that. When I saw you running for the elevator—I was holding the 'close' button the entire time, by the way—I knew you must have thrown away something of great value." Rory laughed, a gentle, unnerving laugh, a laugh (if such a thing were possible) that was absolutely devoid of malice. It was a laugh in tune with the flow and folly of the universe. "Oh, I certainly sent you on a wild chase, didn't I? The image of you, rooting around in a huge pile of garbage, it warmed my heart." And the laughter resurfaced, calm as ever.

"But why?"

"Why? Because I don't like you, Edwin. I've never liked you. Not now, not ever. And neither does my wife. Isn't that right, dear?"

"Oh, yes," she said, still smiling away. "We can't stand you, Edwin." They spoke as though reciting a simple and obvious statement of fact, in much the same tone as one might say "the sky is blue" or "rain falls down, balloons rise up."

"You hate me?" said Edwin, dumbfounded.

"We despise you." A secret compartment in the limo cabinet slid open, and Rory reached inside with both hands. "I imagine you'll be needing this," he said, handing the thick manuscript through the open window.

Edwin discarded the coffee he had just purchased and accepted the manuscript with a mix of disbelief and amazement. It had been removed from the envelope and was now bound with rubber bands, but it was just as hefty as ever. The stickers of daisies still adorned the front page, and the cover letter was folded over and tucked in. *Ah, Mr. Soiree, we meet again . . .*

"And trust me," said Rory, "Li Bok really works. Doesn't it, honey?"

His wife tittered and leaned over to give him a swat on the arm. "Oh, stop it," she said.

Edwin turned his attention back to the former janitor and his wife. "The limo, the clothes. How?"

"Oh, that," tut-tutted Rory. "Just money, really. Once you recognize that money is not a mathematical creation but rather an organic entity, it all starts to make sense."

"But—"

"I invested in short-term T-bills at 4.85 per cent on a convertible blue-chip bond and then rolled it over before the twenty-four-hour disclosure requirements took effect. I then cascaded the return into several mutual funds, reinvested the principle and cashed out on mid-cycle. After that, it was just a matter of reinvesting the excess and repeating the process. With the three-hour, four-zone time difference between the East Coast and the

West Coast, I was able to turn my money over several times a day. I then took a compound return on the difference and, well, here I am."

"You did all that in one week?"

"Oh, no. It only took a couple of days. Time zones, Edwin. Time zones are the key. Imagine your investments as a giant snowball rolling down one steep snowy incline and up another. The distance grows shorter and shorter even as the speed increases and the snowball grows and grows. When it reaches maximum mass, it comes to a rest. Money makes money, Edwin. Momentum feeds mass. Ah, but listen to me. I'm just quoting from the book." And the way he said "the book" it sounded positively spiritual.

"That's . . . that's incredible," said Edwin.

"Oh, no. It's just elementary organic economics," said Rory. "Of course, that will change once word gets out. The entire system is self-cancelling, much like the snowball that grows into a boulder so big it can't move. But by then, the entire basis of our economy will have shifted to micro-cooperative economic circles. The next step, the real challenge, is to 'make the money sing.'"

"Sing?" said Edwin.

"Yes. To make it do your bidding, rather than the other way around. To use money as a catalyst to fulfilment, rather than simply as an end in itself. Ah, but listen to me. Again, I'm just repeating what a much wiser man has written. The book," said Rory, "you must publish the book."

"Absolutely. I'll start editing it right away."

"As is," said Rory. "Publish it just as it is. Don't change a single word. Not one single word. It all fits together, Edwin. Remove a part of the whole and you lose everything."

"Well, I can't promise we won't edit it. I mean, come on. It's huge. Must be a thousand pages here."

"Not one word," said Rory. "Not one word. Oh, yes. One other thing, before I forget. It's the *Rangers*, not the Raiders, you stupid prick." He said this with the same calm serenity, the same detachment with which he had said everything. "Goodbye, Edwin. I never want to see you again as long as I live."

And with that, the window slid up silently and the long, sleek limo pulled back into the flow of traffic along Grand Avenue.

"Well, I'll be damned," said Edwin (literally, as it turned out).

Chapter
Ten

Edwin de Valu bounded up the front steps of 813 Grand Avenue and spun himself through the revolving door so quickly he sent several stragglers flying. He ran past the security desk and down the hallway to the elevators. He was holding the heavy manuscript to his chest the way one might embrace a baby or an idea.

He had done it! He had managed to slip free. The blindfold had been in place, the last cigarette smoked, the order to aim had been given . . . but Edwin the Magnificent, the Houdini of the Cubicles, had somehow escaped. "No prison can hold me!" he wanted to shout. "I laugh in the face of fate."

By the time he reached the fourteenth/thirteenth floor, he was grinning so widely it looked as though he might pop a facial muscle. When the elevator doors opened, he leapt out in full sprint.

"Mr. Mead is in his office!" yelled May. "You're late."

"I love you, May!" he shouted as he passed by. Nigel stepped out from behind his office door and tapped his wristwatch as Edwin ran past. "You're in G.B.O."

"Spare me the abbreviations, dickbreath. I have the manuscript!" And he held it aloft, proudly, with two hands, heavy over his head like a defused bomb, like an enemy's head held high in victory. Through the polished doors he ran, through the polished doors and into the large office with the expansive view.

"You're late," said Mr. Mead without bothering to look up. He was working at his desk, a wide swath of mahogany separating his Royal Self from Edwin. "I was just about to leave," he said. "I'm on my way to the Wacoma Writer's Workshop. I'm the keynote speaker, and I can't afford to miss my flight. Well?" He looked up from behind his octagonal glasses.

Edwin flopped the manuscript down on the desk.

"Here it is, sir. The self-help book, just like I promised. It's everything I said it would be."

"Jesus, man. It's a foot thick. How many pages?"

"Um," Edwin frantically checked the upper corner of the last page. "It came in at 1,165 pages, sir."

"Good God! That's not a manuscript, that's a mini-series."

"Well, of course I'll be editing it down. Saving the good bits."

"All right, Edwin." Mr. Mead rolled his chair back, put his hands behind his head. "Sell it to me."

"Sorry?"

"The manuscript. Give me your best pitch. How does it start? How does it grab the reader? What is the main angle? The target market? The table of contents? The style? Lay it on me."

At which point, Edwin walked slowly across the room, opened the window and leapt to his death.

"Well, sir," he said, "I'm still working on the specifics of that. I've been talking with the people down in marketing, trying to figure out the best way to position it via other books, *ipso facto*, in the genre. So to speak." (When in doubt, use Latin.)

"I see," said Mr. Mead. "You've been talking with the people down in marketing."

"That's right, I have."

"No. You haven't. Our people in marketing have never heard of this book. I wasn't just sitting on my keister doing nothing while I was waiting for you to grace me with your presence. I called marketing, talked with Sasha. She didn't know anything about it. Neither did anyone in distribution. Or advertising. Or the art department. Other than May, no one on the entire editorial board would vouch for whether such a manuscript even existed. Until you brought it in just now, I was beginning to have my doubts as well. Thought maybe you were trying to pull a fast one on old Uncle Léon. In fact, Nigel tells me you were barely here last week."

Yes, well, that's because Nigel is a scum-sucking poisonous toad with bile in his veins.

"Yes, well, that's because Nigel isn't aware that I have been working very hard at home, devoting all my time and resources to this very, very exciting project."

"Time and resources, huh? So tell me, what are the main themes of the book?"

"Themes?"

"How about the structure? Is it mainly anecdotal? Or statistical? Does it appeal to a specific age range, or is it one of those awful 'something for everyone' books?"

"Well, sir. It's hard to explain, in so many words."

"You haven't read it, have you?"

"No, sir. Not exactly. Not *per se*."

Mr. Mead sighed, pushed back his chair and stood up. While putting on his jacket, he leaned over and pressed his intercom. "Steve, have the car meet me around back. I've got a twelve o'clock flight I need to make."

Edwin straightened his shoulders, decided to go with the "puke face! puke face!" approach and, stepping forward, said, "Sir, if I may say something before you depart—"

"Offer $5,000 up front and 7 per cent on the first 10,000 copies, with standard escalating rates thereafter. You can go as high as $15,000 for the advance, but don't give away British rights or first serial. Buckingham Press has been whining about past commitments for overseas distribution, and we need to throw them a bone."

"Sir?"

"Don't feel bad, son," said Mr. Mead as he gathered up some loose files and put them in his briefcase. "I didn't read half the books I purchased for Panderic back when I was in acquistions. Just make sure you have it ready to go to print by mid-August. You can take over the Mr. Ethics slot on the printing schedule. And don't forget to let the art department know. Tell them I need a preliminary cover in two or three weeks. We'll have to reissue our catalogue, or maybe we'll just send out an insert. With Mr. Ethics gone, we're going to have to scramble." Mr. Mead closed his briefcase, pulled a scarf across his shoulders. "You heard he was denied bail?"

"Yes, sir. And we're all very sad. I know I speak for everyone in the editorial department when I say that Mr. Ethics was a vital part of our—"

"Ah, to hell with him. The man was an idiot. Everyone knows you don't leave a paper trail when you're moving funds to the Cayman Islands. That's the first place people look. Anyway, our entire Mr. Ethics line has nose-dived. We've been swamped with returns on his last six books. Barnes and Noble, Borders, even Amazon.com—they're all bailing on us. The press has been making snide cracks. Leno is having a field day. 'Mr. Ethics? In jail? Golly, gee.' It's beyond saving. We're going to have to write off the entire line. So whatever it is you have, Edwin, it had better be good."

Edwin swallowed hard. "I'll do my best."

"*Your* best? Your best isn't good enough. Do Nigel's best. Or May's." He punched Edwin once, lightly, on the shoulder. "Just kidding, Eddie. Don't look so tense. Oh, and speaking of Nigel—I told accounting to deduct the money you owe him for the necktie from your next pay-cheque. I like hijinks and fun-and-games as much as the next person, but Edwin, come on. You don't touch a man's necktie."

And with a tally-ho and a fare-thee-well, he was gone, leaving Edwin alone in the office with the expansive view and the mahogany desk. Edwin picked up the manuscript, flipped through the pages. Mr. Mead hadn't bothered to take a close look or even remove the rubber bands. "I could have bluffed him," said Edwin. "I could have just stormed in with a cover page and stack of blank paper tied up with a bow." He turned out the light as he left.

"Well," he said, "live and learn."

Chapter
Eleven

"Mr. Soiree? Is that you? Hello, my name is Edwin de Valu. I'm calling you today regarding—"

"Soiree ain't in. He's out in the desert or some damn thing."

There was heavy static on the line, as though Edwin were calling another century. Another time. Another place. The far side of the moon, perhaps. Or even more remote, the town of Paradise Flats, down in Dacob County. The town itself had originally been named Salt Flats, in honour of the sun-baked salt mines that had first attracted investors to the area. But the town founders quickly changed it to Paradise—the better to lure in rail lines and gullible settlers. ("Paradise Flats! What a swell name. That's the place for me.") Which is to say, Paradise Flats was a town settled largely by suckers. An outpost, lost in the middle of nowhere, Paradise Flats basted in its heat and anonymity. In Paradise Flats, the desert was the one almighty fact of life, and it was into the desert that Tupak Soiree had now vanished. Edwin couldn't believe what he was hearing.

"The desert?" he said.

"That's right. Dry, arid place. Maybe you've heard of it? Mr. Soiree spends his time out there, meditating and doing mystical stuff. Says he's in tune with the interconnectedness of the universe. The guy's a friggin' crackpot, if you ask me."

"And to whom am I speaking?"

"Whom? *Whom?* Listen to you, with your prep-school grammar and your pretentious vocab. Who am I? I'm Jack McGreary. I'm his landlord, that's *whom.* Mr. Soiree owes me two months of back rent, so if you're a loan collector, get in line, pal."

"No, no. I'm calling from Panderic Incorporated. Mr. Soiree sent us a manuscript, and we're interested in publishing it—this fall, as a matter of fact."

A long, static-ridden pause. For a moment, Edwin thought they had been disconnected, but no, the voice on the other end reappeared. "You got a contract offer or somethin'?"

"That's correct. Listen, why don't I fax a copy of our standard agreement—our boilerplate, as we call it—and Mr. Soiree can look it over and get back to us. Does he have a fax number?"

"Sure. Send it care of the Paradise Flats Municipal Library. If he ain't in the desert, the odds are he's hangin' out in the library. I never knew a guy who read so many damn books. He's a friggin' fruit loop, if you ask me. Anyway, I've got the library's fax number here somewhere. Hang on a sec."

So Edwin faxed the twelve pages of intricate legalese and hidden land mines to Mr. Soiree, along with an initial offer of $3,000 and 5 per cent royalties on the cover price. Much to Edwin's surprise, a reply came back just a few hours later. It was a single page saying, simply, "I accept the terms as they are." Edwin stopped short. *As they are?* This was unheard of. No changes in a boilerplate? Boilerplates were designed to be changed. That was the whole idea. Several outrageous clauses were inserted specifically to be removed, so that agents and writers would have something to demand, so that publishers would have something "to cede." Things like Panderic's infamous option clause, which required authors to give them their next two books, complete and finished, and then allow Panderic six months to decide whether to bid. Or the termination clause, which made it nearly impossible for an author to regain rights to the work even after it was out of print and had been remaindered. Or the clause that allowed Panderic to withhold "a reasonable amount" of royalties against possible future returns of the book. (In the world of publishing, booksellers return the product for a full refund if it doesn't sell. Virtually no industry on earth operates this way.) "A reasonable amount against returns" was never defined, of course, and in some cases, Panderic managed to hold back 50 per cent of an author's income on the mere possibility of said returns. Or how about the clause requiring the author to repay all advance monies within six (6) months if the work was deemed "editorially unsuitable upon submission"? Cash advances to authors were, in principle, non-returnable, but that didn't stop Panderic from trying. And what about that innocuous clause dealing with "electronic rights and any technologies which currently exist or which may exist anytime in the future"?

Edwin was taken aback. Mr. Soiree was willing to sign over everything to Panderic—*everything*—and for what? A meagre advance and poor royalty rates. Edwin was still shaking his head in disbelief when he noticed, below the initial message, a short note that read: "Any changes to the contract must come from you, Mr. Edwin. You know full well the hidden pitfalls contained therein. A cash advance returnable on demand? Come now, Mr. Edwin. Surely you don't take me for a stupid man? Make the changes—and you know which changes they are—and I will happily sign. Live, love, and learn. Tupak Soiree."

There it was again. That feeling. That feeling that someone was watching you over your shoulder, that someone was two moves ahead of you all the way. Edwin took a moment to collect his thoughts and then, with a deep breath, he began . . .

For the first time in the history of publishing—for the first time ever—an editor sat down to change a contract *in the writer's favour* without being forced to. Edwin crossed out the second half of the termination clause, put the copyright back in the author's name, removed the rider regarding the advance—did everything an agent would have done. He even increased the royalty rates and pencilled in a 1 in front of the $3,000. For all the talk about "partnerships" and "working together," when it comes to negotiating a contract, writers and publishers are mortal adversaries and the process is always heavily slanted in favour of the publisher. And yet, here was Edwin de Valu, junior editor, doing the unthinkable: he was putting the author first. It was a strange and somehow unnerving experience. It felt as though everything had shifted slightly, as though the bedrock of the entire publishing industry and the ingrained unspoken hierarchy it contained (namely, that the author is always at the absolute bottom of the woodpile) had suddenly become malleable.

It took Edwin more than an hour to go through the contract and remove the various hidden booby traps and insert the proper protections. By the time Edwin was done, Tupak Soiree had one of the most equitable contracts Panderic had ever offered. "What can I say," said Edwin with a certain grudging respect. "The man drives a hard bargain."

Outside, dark clouds were gathering.

Chapter
Twelve

"Everyone talks about the banality of evil," said May over mineral water and spinach salad. "But no one ever writes about the banality of talent."

Edwin and May had worked late and were now sharing supper and conversation at O'Tanner's Irish Pub and Old Towne Restaurant™. Edwin was quaffing great quantities of beer and eating onion rings and deep-fried cheez sticks. May, however, was in the grips of yet another weight-loss plan, one she read about in *O*: an all-you-can-stomach-mineral-water-and-spinach-salad diet.

"The banality of talent?" said Edwin.

"You know, like when you really admire an author's work, and then you meet him. Remember *Why I Hate Ukrainians*?"

"Ah, yes. 'A searing indictment of the pysanka mindset.'"

"Exactly. And then you meet the author, and he's just some kid with a scraggly goatee and a penchant for self-referential, self-indulgent humour. It's always such a letdown. For example, just this morning I got a call from marketing. Our publicists were swamped, absolutely swamped. Everyone was overbooked, so I ended up driving Nilös Javonich around."

"No kidding? Javonich, the Great Poet of Slovakia?"

"None other. I believe 'Great' is actually his first name. I think he had it legally changed to 'the Great Javonich.' I've certainly never heard him referred to in any other manner. So anyway, I took the Great Javonich to interviews, photo sessions and even a book-signing over on the Strand. Truth is, I wanted to. I loved his books. I loved *Insignificance* and *Humility* and *I Am But a Speck*, and when I heard our publicists were in trouble, I readily volunteered. It got me out of the office, and hey, it was a chance to hobnob with the Great Nilös Javonich. But then I meet the man, and he's awful. Loud. Lewd. Petulant. Self-important. Arrogant. Banal. That's what I'm talking about: the banality of talent. Someone should write a book about it." (That was, of course, one of the most common sentences in any publishing house: "Someone should write a book about that.")

"What is the deal with publicists, anyway?" Edwin wanted to know. "Why do they all have names ending in -y or -i? I'm serious. We have a Kelly and a Lucy. MacMillan has a Jamie and a Marnie. And there's Cathy and Holly over at Doubleday. The senior publicist at M&R is Lindsey, and Hornblower has a Terri."

"Terri*lee*," said May.

"Double whammy. So what is it? Is it some sort of self-fulfilling prophecy? Their parents gave them such perky names that they had no choice but to pursue an equally perky career? Let's face it, you need an inordinate amount of perkiness to succeed in the field of publicity."

"I know," said May. "Look at Jerri."

"Or Larry. Remember him?"

They both laughed. Larry was the smilingest, sing-songiest, most upbeat publicist in the entire history of publicists. Then one day he snapped and began driving authors off the Maynard Gate Bridge. They had to fish Larry and a couple of very soggy authors out of the drink on more than one occasion. He ended up attacking one young writer in mid-interview, live, on-air. (The author had turned to Larry and snapped his fingers for more water, as though beckoning a waiter.)

"Good ol' Larry," said Edwin. "When does he get out?"

May was still laughing. "I think it's two years with good behaviour. Perhaps they'll put him in a jail cell with Mr. Ethics. Now *that* would be fun."

"Hey," said Edwin. "Maybe they'll write a prison exposé together. Prison books always sell fairly well, in a certain voyeuristic, God-I'm-glad-that's-not-me sort of way. Or maybe Ethics and Larry will stage the Great Escape. Tunnel their way to freedom."

"I doubt they'll be in the same facility," said May. "Didn't you hear? Mr. Ethics is going to be doing some very hard time. He's looking at three consecutive life sentences."

"What? For tax evasion?"

"No, it turns out they found the bodies of the last three auditors the IRS sent over buried in his backyard."

"And he's going to get life for that?"

May was just as baffled. "I know. You wouldn't think killing a tax auditor would be a felony. A misdemeanour, maybe, but not a felony. Anyway, our Mr. Ethics is going to spend the rest of his life behind bars."

"Ah, serves him right," said Edwin. "The man was an idiot. Everyone knows you don't bury the bodies in your own backyard. That's the first place people look."

May was now on her third spinach salad, extra dressing, extra Parmesan cheese, extra bacon bits. Edwin didn't want to draw attention to this, but he was fairly sure that the Oprah diet plan was based on just one salad per sitting. No matter. Life was good. Edwin felt at ease with the world. True, Grand Avenue was still a canyon of despair, Mr. Mead was still getting in everyone's way, Nigel was still a sewer-dwelling weasel inhabiting the skin of a human being and Jenni was still . . . well, Jenni. But no matter. Edwin had managed to produce a manuscript, almost from thin air, had once again, and with no small amount of amazement, managed to keep his job.

"So how is it?" asked May. "Your book, *What I Learned on the Mountain*. Does it really deliver everything you promised?"

"Oh, yes. And then some," said Edwin. "I faxed Mr. Soiree a contract, he signed and I started a preliminary read-through this afternoon. It's a very strange manuscript. It's long, convoluted, and as far as I can tell, it has no discernible shape or structure. I had assumed it would be laid out in the usual way, divided into separate chapters—you know, one on smoking, one on financial planning, another on achieving inner happiness, etc., etc.—but instead it reads like one long, rambling monologue with the separate elements interwoven into a single whole. And yet, it's the weirdest thing. There isn't any structure—not in the classic sense—but there is a definite flow. Everything is related to everything else. Soiree twists each argument into the next, so you never really know where one section ends and the next begins. It's a mishmash. A dollop of Norman Vincent Peale, a dash of Chopra, a pinch of Dale Carnegie. He bases an entire passage on the Hindu concept of *moksha*—if I'm pronouncing that right—which represents liberation from wrong desire."

"'Liberation from wrong desire': it sounds like one of my untranslatables," said May.

"It does, doesn't it? *Moksha*. It's based on the idea that life is a journey from one stage to another. First, we desire sensual pleasure, which is the hedonistic phase of our lives. Then we seek material success, which is the wealth-and-trinkets phase. Then we seek fame or, failing that, something of lasting importance, a legacy of some kind. Something to leave our children, or even our grandchildren. This might sound noble on the surface, but—according to Tupak Soiree anyway—it's simply a sublimated fear of death. And—" Edwin broke off.

"What?"

"It's just that I had a feeling, when I read that passage, that it was the one moment when Soiree let his guard down. Fear of death and the desire to live on, somehow, if only through our children. Or our grandchildren. A Quixotic quest for immortality. It's sad and heroic and doomed—all at the same time. Mind you, Soiree doesn't stop there. The final phase, and one very few people attain, is that of absolute inner calm. Enlightenment. Most of us get entangled in one or more of the 'false desires' along the way. Tupak Soiree's goal is to help everyone move towards that fourth and final level. Pretty heady stuff, don't you think? It's very deep and spiritual and then—pow!—he gives us a Fun! Five-Point! *Cosmo*-style Quiz to see where we are on the Great Hindu Journey of Life. It's like riding a roller coaster. It's like"—and here Edwin hesitated, because he didn't like the ramifications of what he was suggesting—"it's like reading the mad ravings of a lunatic. Someone locked away in a padded cell, someone who has read far too many books. Or maybe the mad ravings of"—and again Edwin hesitated, because he wasn't sure he liked the ramifications of this either—"a genius."

"Madman. Genius. Those aren't mutually exclusive terms," said May.

"Or maybe it was a committee. Maybe more than one person wrote this book. The voice and style change abruptly at times. It's like a collage. A kind of pasted-together, slapdash pastiche. At one point, Soiree mixes Buddhist moral philosophy with libertarian-style capitalism. And the strange thing is, it works."

"Hmmm. Sounds more like philosophy than self-help," said May, frowning. (There is nothing worse than a book that refuses to be pigeonholed.)

"It is, it is," said Edwin. "It is philosophy. And psychology. And physics. And tips on dieting. I've never seen such a hodgepodge of ideas—highbrow and lowbrow, silly and sublime—stuck together like a magpie's nest. He borrows from a wide range of sources, but then he puts his own weird spin on it. For example, there's a Hindu proverb that says: *The finger that points to the moon is not the moon*. What they mean by this is that we shouldn't confuse the symbols of faith with the underlying reality they represent. Statues. Icons. Fingers. They shouldn't be mistaken for the numinous object itself, which is beyond words, beyond representation. But Tupak Soiree takes it even further. He writes: *The same finger that points to the moon picks our nose*."

May laughed. "It's earthy, I suppose."

"Oh, it's earthy. And pretentious. And banal. It's all of the above and then some. At one point, he tells us that it's okay to take a break from our past, to hang up a sign and say to the world, 'Gone fishin'.'"

"Gone fishin'?"

"That's right: *Gone fishin'*. Can you imagine anything so trite? But then, in the very next paragraph, he goes off on a tangent about the physics behind karma and the eternal balance of energy forces within the universe. He quotes Spinoza on one page, deconstructs Keynesian economic theory on the next, and then he talks about the importance of giving 'kissable kisses' and 'huggable hugs.' Everything is thrown together: ideas, advice, philosophical concepts. And yet, at times it can be electrifying. It leaves your head buzzing. I've never read anything quite like it."

"Meaning?"

"We have a problem. A very big problem. If we publish this book as is, it's going to bomb. We'll be lucky if we recoup our initial costs. It's simply too strange. Who would buy it? It has no niche market, unless you count 'people who feel something is missing in their lives' as a viable market. And what is that? Half the population?"

"Oh, more than that," said May. "Everyone has something they wish they could change, something they wish they could capture. Or recapture. Youth. A memory. A moment. Some missing piece of the puzzle. But you're right, it sounds as though this book's appeal is far too broad for specialized sales—"

"And far too eclectic for general sales. Still, I think I can save it. If I can just get through it, keep the standard self-help bits and remove the mysticism and the metaphysics, divide it into chapters, cut the length in half, and come up with a clever title and a catchy cover, it just might work. *What doesn't kill us makes us stronger.* We might yet have a winner. The real problem is time. I've got only a week or so to do an edit and get it off to the author for his approval. But you know something, May? I think I can do it. I think I can pull this off." He smiled at his own determination.

May returned the smile, raised a glass. "Salutations!"

"To me!" said Edwin as they clinked. And then, as an afterthought, but one that would have a deeper significance as the events of the next few months unfolded, Edwin said, "It's odd, but several parts of the manuscript seemed very familiar, you know? I said it reads like one extended pastiche, and it does. It's as though every self-help book in existence was put into a blender and then strained through cheesecloth, somehow capturing the very essence of the genre. He even had a section called 'The Essential Laws Governing Money' that sounded just a little *too* familiar, you know? And then it hit me. There was this book I read back in college; I studied it for a course I took. It was called *The Seven Laws of Money*, and I started to think, What if Soiree is out-and-out stealing material from other books?"

"Plagiarism, paraphrasing—it's very difficult to prove one over the other," said May, quoting the Second Commandment.

"Oh, I know. And you can't copyright an idea. But still, there was something about what Tupak wrote that made me uneasy. I mean, it was almost exactly how I remembered *The Seven Laws of Money*. So on my lunch break I went down to that big second-hand book emporium on 5th Street. You know the one."

"Bryant's Books?"

"No, the other one, farther down. Across from the grocer's. Anyway, *The Seven Laws of Money* is no longer in print, but I did manage to track down a copy. It's by someone named Phillips. And the thing is, Tupak Soiree *did* base that section of his book directly on what Phillips wrote. It's obvious."

May sat up at this. "Plagiarism?"

"No. Not plagiarism," said Edwin. "But here's the thing: he didn't really paraphrase it either. He got some of it wrong, he muddled other parts together and altered the rest. Do you know what it was, May? It was as though he were writing it from memory. Tupak Soiree's version was actually closer to how I remembered *The Seven Laws of Money*. Our memory always changes things: some details fade, some become stronger, others become subtly transformed. That's what happened here. It was as though Soiree intentionally summarized not the original book itself, but our memory of it. It's unsettling. And the people who buy self-help don't want to be unsettled. They want to have their self-worth reaffirmed. They want to be stroked and suckled and placated with platitudes—"

"'Placated with platitudes'? I like that." (May was a sucker for alliteration. It was one of her weaknesses as an editor. Give her a glass of wine and a couple of clever alliterative quips, and she was all yours. She had hired Edwin in the first place partly because she liked the idea of an *ed.* named Ed.)

"I'm worried," said Edwin. "Panderic hasn't had a strong hit in years—not since *Balkan Eagle*. True, the Chicken Broth franchise is still doing well, but we haven't had a genuine blockbuster for a long time. We need a money-maker."

"That last self-help book you edited. What was it?"

"*Be Who You're Not*," said Edwin.

"That one did fine."

Even Edwin had to admit that *Be Who You're Not* had sold fairly well. "But still . . ."

"Not to worry," said May. "I'll let you in on a little secret. Our biography department is just about to cut a deal with a cleaning lady who says she had sex with both the Vice President *and* the Speaker of the House"—May paused for full dramatic effect—"at the same time."

"Oh, my God," said Edwin. "The VP is a Democrat and the Speaker is a Republican."

"I know. Is that shocking, or what? The scandal alone will cover the cost of our entire fall line. So don't worry too much about your self-help book. As long as we earn out our costs and turn a small profit, you'll be fine. With our upcoming *Sex in the Capitol* exposé, Panderic stands to make millions."

"Wow. A Republican *and* a Democrat."

"At the same time," said May.

"Unbelievable." Edwin struck a match, lit just the second cigarette of the evening (he was trying to cut back) and inhaled deeply. "Well," he said, quoting the First Commandment, "sex certainly does sell. People can't get enough of it. It's like some kind of hunger." And the concept—or rather, the image—of sex hung between them like a heavy, wet promise. It was a long time dissipating.

"*Mokita*," said May, under her breath but loud enough for Edwin to hear. *Mokita*.

Chapter
Thirteen

He arrived back at his house to find the Post-it Notes gone, as though they had migrated south like butterflies. Jenni was knee-deep in *feng shui* now, and had spent the day rearranging furniture to better suit the spirit world. The blue objects in the house were now clustered in the east corner. Yellow had been banished to the west and pink to the north. Both the television and the refrigerator had been turned at odd, unnatural angles—"to facilitate energy flow"—and the shower-curtain rings had been painted a weird Day-Glo orange. This was supposed to make Edwin and Jenni wealthy and successful. (The gods are apparently crazy about glowing orange shower-curtain rings.)

As Edwin wandered through this latest self-improvement binge by Jenni, he thought of something May had once said to him. Something she called the Bruce Springsteen High School Compatibility Test.

"I was reading a magazine article about Springsteen back when he married his first wife," May had said. "She was a jet-setting model named Julianne something-or-other. The editors at the magazine had dug up some old high school yearbook photographs of the bride and groom, and they published them, side by side, with the article. And you know what? In high school, Julianne would never have given Bruce the time of day. She was a wealthy suburban prom queen. A cheerleader, a student councillor. She was Miss Popularity. She was one of the *in* crowd. Bruce's yearbook photo, on the other hand, is one of an awkward, shy social outcast. Julianne was from Lake Oswego, an upper-class bedroom community on the West Coast. It was a far cry from the factory lines and seedy barrooms of New Jersey. Bruce and Julianne came from different worlds. If they had gone to the same high school, Julianne would have looked down her nose at him. And now, here they are getting married? I said, right then and there, based solely on their yearbook photographs, that their marriage was doomed. And I was right. He eventually left her for his backup singer, Patti Scialfa, a good ol' Jersey girl. In high school, Patti and Bruce would have gotten along fine."

May called it a compatibility test: people who never would have associated in high school should never get married later on. "We never really rise above our high-school days," she said. "We just suppress them. Who we are never truthfully changes. A homecoming queen in high school will always be a homecoming queen. And a misfit will always be a misfit."

May had been talking in generalities, but her observations had a certain barbed sting to them. Edwin pretended he hadn't been paying close attention—"Interesting theory. Are you ready to order? The special looks good"—inside, however, it ate away at him. He had seen Jenni's yearbook, knew that she had been the most popular girl in a very status-conscious uptown high school. He knew that if he had met Jenni back then, with his acne and his thick glasses and his *Norton Anthology* tucked under his arm, a lanky figure known primarily for quoting Latin and making dry sarcastic asides, she would have never deigned speak to him. And it would have crushed Edwin. (Although contemptuous of his peers, he craved their approval nonetheless.) Edwin de Valu had spent much of his school years trying to ingratiate himself with people much dumber than he. And though this had given him a healthy ego and a certain arrogant streak, it had also underlined his own position as a permanent outsider. When Jenni had first—miraculously—agreed to go out with him, just shortly after he started at

Panderic, it was as though he had somehow, finally, been validated as a person. When she first laughed at his easy wit (a wit practised in front of a mirror the night before), when she readily agreed to go out with him again, Edwin knew that he would marry her. Knew it before they ever went on their second date. He would marry her to appease his former self. He would marry her so he could erase his own yearbook photo, so he could say to himself: "See, you did it!"

Now this. The brass ring was turning green. The house was aligned according to some arbitrary colour scheme, his televison was angled along imaginary energy lines, and he felt as though he were sharing his life with a stand-in. Jenni hardly seemed real. Seemed more like a yearbook photograph herself. A cut-out, full-size rendition. A permanent prom queen.

Maybe May was right. Maybe her theory contained a hard kernel of truth. Maybe none of us ever does move beyond high school. If nothing else, it had given Edwin a certain affinity and grudging sympathy for Bruce Springsteen.

Chapter
Fourteen

That night, something strange happened.

Edwin was at home, with the manuscript spread out before him, struggling to wrestle Tupak Soiree's behemoth into some kind of manageable form. He had already identified and isolated several basic thematic threads, cut most of the minor ones, ditched the more abstract musings, condensed the long meandering passage on love down to a neat seven-point summary, and was wading through a densely written section on "the cognitive dissonance of self," when he stumbled upon Tupak Soiree's directions on how to stop smoking, even—and here's an uncanny coincidence—as he reached for his next cigarette.

"Listen to me!" Tupak had written. "Listen. Right now, right at this very moment, gather every cigarette you have and fill a glass a quarter full with warm water. Now remove one—and only one—cigarette. This is the last cigarette you will ever smoke. This moment, right now. You are about to stop smoking forever. Go to the toilet and empty the rest of the cigarettes into it, but do not flush. Look at the cigarettes floating there. Now look at yourself in the mirror. Light that one last cigarette.

The last cigarette you will ever smoke. But do not savour it. Oh, no. Do not smoke it slowly. Do not caress it. Do not enjoy it. You should not linger over your last cigarette. If you do, it most certainly will *not* be your last cigarette. Instead, I want you to smoke it as quickly as possible, as fast as you can, choke back the smoke, do not stop for a fresh breath. Smoke! Smoke! Quick! Do it now!"

Edwin coughed and hacked, gulping back as quickly as he could, sucking in the smoke as the paper crackled from the draw, the orange-red coal growing to a spike.

"Now quickly drop it in the glass. Drop it in the glass and let it sit. Look at it floating in there, sodden, turning the water slowly black. There it is. The last cigarette you will ever smoke. The very last. Now raise the glass to your lips . . ."

So there stood Edwin, his mouth filled with foul water, the butt floating in his mouth as he stared intently at the mirror. He fought the urge to gag and swallow, to spit and vomit. He stood and stared, and began what Tupak Soiree called "the separation of traits from identity."

"It goes beyond smoking or not smoking. It goes beyond gambling or eating too much or eating too little. Those are merely the symptoms of an unbalanced soul. Those are but traits misaligned. Focus your mind on realigning these traits. Allow them to float into position, one by one."

And something shifted. Something just below the surface, like a vein under skin. It was as though the various layers of Edwin's personality—the various flaws and quirks, the tics and traits that combined to make him who he was—were slowly starting to separate. He could almost see it in the mirror, right before his eyes. If he just released his mind, the process would . . .

Edwin hacked and spit up the water, spit the butt into the toilet, flushed hard again and again. His head was reeling. It felt as though he had brushed up against something dark and warm and powerful. He rinsed his mouth out, threw cold water on his face, looked into the mirror.

"I am Edwin de Valu," he said. "I am Edwin Vincent de Valu, and I smoke too much. This is who I am."

He felt the panic in his chest slowly subside. He had almost lost grip on his identity; had almost let it disintegrate and drift into its composite parts; had almost lost the whole.

"Hun! I'm going out to get some cigarettes!" Edwin tugged on his overcoat.

Jenni came down the hall, bathrobed and barefoot, hair swept up in a towel. "Do you honestly need a cigarette? At this time of night?"

"No," said Edwin. "I don't. I honestly don't. That's why I'm going."

He trudged out in a rainy gloom-lit night, searching for a corner store still open, searching for nicotine, searching for bad habits.

Meanwhile, back in 668, Jenni sat down at the kitchen table. She looked at the manuscript, piled this way and that, and then, without really thinking, she picked up a page or two and began to read.

Chapter
Fifteen

What I Learned on the Mountain continued to frustrate Edwin's editorial need for coherence. Parts of the manuscript came from sources as ancient as the *Tibetan Book of the Dead*. Other sections had apparently been lifted directly out of today's newspapers.

Right in the middle of his Tantric reinterpretation of the Kama Sutra, amid flowery, moist New Age erotica, Soiree suddenly began quoting a recent scientific study which had produced evidence that regular sex boosts one's immunity levels. "A report in the *Natural Health* magazine cited research showing that people who have sex once or twice a week have 29 per cent more immunoglobulin (IgA), a chemical that helps fight disease." This dry, scientific passage was plonked down in the midst of a discussion on "the trembling of the jade stalk in the warm pool of the lily." It was mind-boggling. It was like trying to read a palimpsest, a parchment that had been written on and erased, again and again, leaving only shadow images. That's what this is, thought Edwin, it's a *palimpsest*. (And as events would later prove, Edwin was right. It was indeed a palimpsest, though not perhaps of the type he had assumed.) Reading *What I Learned on the Mountain* was like reading a dozen different books superimposed, one on top of the other. It was like trying to edit an entire library in one go. It was . . . it was damn well annoying, is what it was. To the editorial mind, *What I Learned on the Mountain* was an affront to the basic codes of composition and clarity. It didn't just break the rules—it rewrote them.

There weren't even any chapter breaks. Indeed, Soiree barely paused to catch his breath before plunging headlong into his next topic. There was no reprieve. The prose spilled out, unchecked, across the page. Each idea was interlaced with the next, in one extended daisy chain of tangled concepts. An overgrown rose garden, more thorns than flowers, *What I Learned on the Mountain* required a well-aimed axe.

Edwin began circling certain catchphrases for use as possible chapter headings, but the list soon bogged down:

1. Yesterday's Weather
2. Gone Fishin'
3. The Illusion of Diets (and the Diet of Illusion)
4. The Finger That Points to the Moon
5. Capturing Your Bliss
6. The Art of Kissing
7. The Kiss of Art
8. Making the Money Sing
9. An Introduction to Organic Economics
10. My Mother's Favourite Recipe for Turnip Stew

And that was just the first 100 pages.

The fifth item on the list ("capturing your bliss") was particularly vexing. Soiree used the word "bliss" the way some writers use punctuation, and the message was both muddled and forceful, like reading a poem in a language you only half understand. "Capture your bliss. Your bliss is all you have. Follow it where it will lead you, and lead it where you will. Follow it even as it leads you, and you lead it." To which Edwin's only editorial comment had been "?". (What else could he possibly say? It made no damn sense.) And as Edwin pushed on, into the thicket of prose, deeper, ever deeper, as the sentences piled up and the syntax became more and more convoluted and the arguments more and more circular, he felt almost as though he were being hypnotized. Numbed to death by words. Perhaps our mysterious Tupak Soiree was actually a master hypnotist, a mentalist who spun a fine, perplexing web of interwoven . . . Edwin shook his mind clear, took a deep breath and told himself, "It's only a book, Edwin. It's only a book."

The next morning, he began to slash and burn.

Time was running out. No more Mr. Nice Guy. (Often, at this stage in editing, Edwin would knot a banzai headband around his forehead and hang a sign reading "No Mercy!" above his desk.) Edwin went in swinging his machete. He hacked out entire sections of the manuscript, almost at random. He saved only the most cliché-ridden (i.e., sellable) parts and discarded the rest. He reduced the passage on smoking to a single boxed insert: "Here's a handy, helpful tip! When it comes time to quit, don't savour your last cigarette. Smoke it quickly and be done with it. You don't want any positive memories of 'your last smoke.'" Gone were the sections on "disassembling your personality" and gone were the semi-hypnotic exercises in "realigning your character traits."

A sunny, happy book—fair brimming with bromides—slowly began to emerge from Edwin's editorial assault, and Edwin felt a surge of excitement somewhat akin to that which an artist feels as his work first begins to take shape. Except that, as an editor, Edwin's would always be a negative craft—one of removal, not creation. No matter. Edwin felt good. Who knows, Tupak Soiree's book might well prove to be Panderic's next *Chicken Broth*. "Always prepare for success," Mr. Mead had said. Which is why they would need a new, improved title. One that could easily be turned into a running series, should sales warrant it. True, they could call the follow-up book *What I Learned in the Sky*, and then *What I Learned on the Sea*, and *What I Learned in the Forest* and so on, but Edwin was looking for something catchier. Besides, they would quickly run out of inspirational natural locales, and then where would they be? (*What I Learned on the Isthmus, What I Learned on the Tundra, What I Learned in the Semi-Boreal Woodlands*.)

"How about something with flowers?" said May.

Although Edwin was working at home, he and May had agreed to meet halfway between the office and his house.

"Eat, eat," said Edwin. "O'Connor's serves a fairly decent Reuben. Comes with kosher pickles."

"Can't. I'm on a strict cottage-cheese-and-tonic-water regimen." May had been reading the latest issue of *O*, and Edwin had to stop himself from saying, "You don't need to lose weight, May. You're beautiful." But he couldn't say it. He couldn't say it because it would have caused an awkward silence, would have brought the Sheraton Timberland Lodge crashing back into their world. Instead, he said, "Flowers?"

"For the title. Something like *A Bouquet of Roses to Help You Grow*. There's an almost endless list of flowers, Edwin. *A Vase Filled with Tulips, A Gathering of Daisies, A Handful of Bluebells*. You could spin that out indefinitely."

"Not bad," said Edwin. "Not bad at all. I was thinking more of something with 'potpourri' in the title. To emphasize the mixed nature of the book. It does touch on a wide variety of topics. Soup to nuts, so to speak."

"I've got it!" said May. "Chocolates. *An Assortment of Chocolates to Nibble On*. We'll use flowing cursive text on the cover, maybe even a silk ribbon spelling out the title, and put a picture of a heart-shaped box on the front with each chocolate labelled with a different heading: love, happiness, work, money."

"Chocolates," said Edwin. "I like that. I like that a lot." He reached for his pack of cigarettes, forced himself to light one, inhaled bitter smoke, tried not to gag. It felt horrible, but he forced himself to smoke anyway, to make at least a token effort. Halfway through, he finally admitted defeat and put it out. He had a sickening, oily feel in his veins.

"Chocolates," he said as he filled his mouth with Guinness, trying to get both the taste of tobacco and the cluster of associations it now held for him out of his mouth. "That's brilliant, May. Absolutely brilliant. I'm getting goosebumps just thinking about it."

And then, for no reason whatsoever, the Sheraton Timberland Lodge came crashing down around them. They smiled at each other, just a little too long and a little too warmly.

"Chocolates," said May after a drawn-out silence. "Chocolates for the soul. That's what they need, and that's what we'll give them."

Chapter
Sixteen

After his latest marathon round of editorial carnage, as he cut and slashed and scribbled increasingly incoherent editorial asides, Edwin's eyesight began to go. His eyes started to throb, and his vision became blurred and unfocused. If writers suffered from repeat-strike syndrome, editors suffered just as surely from "exhausted-eye syndrome." He held an ice pack against his closed lids, splashed water repeatedly onto his face, even tried some impromptu eyeball aerobics, but to no avail. Time to call it a night.

He yawned, stretched, and said aloud, "The glamorous life of an editor. Can't be beat."

This session hadn't been entirely uneventful. Just after midnight, as Edwin was raging across the manuscript with his mighty blue pencil, killing words with reckless abandon, he happened to turn one page over and caught, from the corner of his eye, something written on the back. It was a message, handwritten in what could only be described as a drunken scrawl. *"Oliver Reed is dead, and I don't feel so good myself."*

This caught Edwin by surprise.

Oliver Reed? Who the hell was Oliver Reed? The name sounded familiar in a nagging sort of way. A singer? A musician? Maybe an actor? But what did Oliver Reed have to do with anything? What did he have to do with Tupak Soiree and the pursuit of human happiness?

Edwin's entire head was now throbbing; both his cerebellum and his eye sockets were aching from the exertion (mental and otherwise). He clicked off the table lamp and staggered to bed. Oliver Reed? Who the hell was Oliver Reed?

Something was waiting for Edwin when he crawled in wearily between the covers, something wild and untamed. A tigress. A seductress. His wife. She slunk over onto him, under, around, across, like a long, wet lick.

"Hun? No, really. I . . ."

"Grrrrr," she said.

"No, really. I'm not in the mood. I'm exhausted. Honest, I am."

She ran her fingers up his rib cage, almost as though she were counting it out. She stopped at a specific spot, and then, with her other hand, she slid her thumb up his inner thigh and pressed. A shock of electricity, a zap, and suddenly she was on top of him. She slithered across his body, and before he could comprehend what was happening, he was inside her, caught in her rhythm, trembling the way a fly trembles in a web. Jenni was doing *something* deep inside, a kind of counter-thrust with the angle pressed against him that sent sparks of lightning from his pores and fireworks tumbling through his synapses. It was as though she had poured brandy over his body and set it alight. He could hear her breathing softly as their rhythm reached its crescendo, sighs interlaid with sobs, sobs interlaid with moans. He knew she was about to come, could feel it building, and then, at the same moment—at that exact same cosmic moment—Edwin came as well, explosion following explosion, one after the other, an almost musical finale.

In the aftermath, Jenni slid off, curled up on one side and was instantly asleep, purring and snoring, snoring and purring. Edwin lay there, his body hot and wet between the sheets, agog at what had just happened. He could feel his thigh shaking in small spasms, and there was nothing he could do to stop it. Edwin de Valu, you see, had never had a multiple orgasm before. His head was reeling, his emotions were spinning like a loose top. It was, in its way, terrifying.

And as he lay there, listening to his heart pound and feeling his leg twitch, he noticed, with an odd sense of foreboding, that the bed was still perfectly made. The sheets and blankets hadn't become the least bit tangled during any of what had transpired. They weren't even rumpled.

Edwin was a long time falling asleep.

The next night, Jenni slithered over to Edwin's side of the bed and performed the same erotic assault as before. And the next night. And the next. Each attack was as passionate and as electrifying as the previous one. And each attack was absolutely the same. Edwin would never have thought it possible: sexual ecstasy by rote.

It wasn't until much later that he reached the part of the manuscript that described the Li Bok Technique, with its bizarre mix of blunt gynecological information on "angle of penetration" and "counter-pressure" and "soft-tissue ridges" and its romantic, flowery passages about the Song of Solomon and the mystical union of opposites. It was enough to make your brain hurt. Edwin had said that reading the manuscript caused his head to buzz, and he was right. (He always had a knack for simile.) Like bees in an empty pickle jar, Tupak Soiree's ideas drove you crazy. They harassed you to distraction, until all you could do was either give in and accept it as the truth, or flee.

As an editor, Edwin could do neither. So his eyes continued to blur and ache, his head continued to buzz and his nights continued to be filled with staccato bursts of intense sexual pleasure.

"You should study the Li Bok section," Jenni would coo. "It's supposed to work better in tandem. Woman. Man. In conjunction."

"I know, I know," said Edwin. "Men are from Mars. Women are from Venus."

"Exactly," said Jenni, eyes shining. "But together they live on Jupiter. Don't you see?"

But of course Edwin didn't. It never jelled; it never made sense. None of it. He found the entire *What I Learned on the Mountain* experience to be a quagmire of contradictions.

"It's like one of those Magic Eye 3-D images," Rory the Janitor had said. "The ones where you see only a wash of dots at first, but then suddenly—*click!*—a figure emerges. It's like magic. One moment you perceive nothing but chaos, and the next moment a shape, with real mass and dimension, appears. That is what it's like with Tupak Soiree and his writing. When it comes together, it happens suddenly. In a flash."

Unfortunately, some people can stare at a Magic Eye 3-D image for hours, can stare until their eyes hurt, and never see anything emerge. And that was how Edwin felt while sifting through Soiree's sea of verbiage, trying to shape it into something simpler. Something safer.

Chapter
Seventeen

Edwin de Valu worked harder over the next four days than he had during the previous six months. He cut and chopped and flailed away. The manuscript, like some mythical beast, had to be beaten down, or at least subdued, and Edwin could not afford to flinch. Not now. So it was, that after wading through and leaving his path littered with the scoured remnants of blood-spattered prose, he finally—against all odds—managed to pare down *What I Learned on the Mountain* to just over three hundred pages. What had once been a swamp of words was now a quick, light read. He broke the text into "handy pointers" and "helpful tricks" and "li'l reminders." He added notes for graphics and suggestions for possible clip-art embellishments: a rose here, a little cartoon of a chocolate heart there. The pages were covered in editorial squiggles and quick-scrawl asides, but Edwin had won the battle. The first batch of *Chocolates* was almost ready. He packed up the edited manuscript, sent it overnight via FedEx to Tupak Soiree, care of the Paradise Flats Trailer Park, and then let out a tired but triumphant sigh. He didn't have the energy to cheer, or even lift his arms above his head, but he did want to celebrate. He hadn't had a full night's sleep in almost a week, and his body felt drained (in every sense of the word), but what the hell. He gave May a call.

A quick drink became a light lunch and a light lunch became a long late-night talk. Edwin felt as though a great burden had been lifted. He felt as though he might float away at any moment, as though his chest was filled with helium. And May was smiling at him, a warm expanse of mauve from across her wine glass. (She had switched her shade of lipstick, going for a softer approach, but it was still of the Crayola line of cosmetics.) Edwin the Human Coat Hanger and May of the Mauve Lips—they made an unlikely pair, sitting in the half dark, ordering wine and beer, laughing at nothing. Well, that wasn't really true. They were laughing at Mr. Mead, which amounted to more or less the same thing.

"Come on, Edwin, you have to give the man credit. I mean, he *earned* his scars. Mr. Mead has paid his dues; he worked his way up the ladder the hard way. Christ, the man spent six years as a fact-checker for Tom Clancy. Six years! That's a record that may never be broken. The only one who came close was that other guy, the one who spent four and a half years fact-checking Clancy. And he ended up in an asylum, spouting techno-babble and speaking in foot-long words. Mr. Mead got out alive."

Edwin knew the story, had heard it many times. It was whispered as Mr. Mead went by, whispered in tones of awe and deference. "That's the man who spent six years fact-checking Tom Clancy." Within the publishing industry, Mr. Mead commanded the type of respect usually reserved for battle-hardened Vietnam vets. "Six years, mind you. Six years."

"Hey," said Edwin, "you ever heard of something called the Li Bok Technique?"

"Mmm?" May's mouth was filled with chocolate cheesecake. This was a "day off" from her diet, she had decided (a diet of celery and uncarbonated soda), and May was making the most of it.

"Li Bok," said Edwin. "It's a lovemaking technique. The woman initiates it, but because the angle matches the, um, rhythm, both the man and the woman usually end up, you know, reaching a climax at the same time. It's in Soiree's book. It's amazing. It'll replace the G-spot, I swear."

"No," said May in mock horror. "Not the G-spot."

"It's true. This Li Bok thing, it works. It really does."

"Well," said May dryly, "that assumes one has a partner to work with."

"No, no," said Edwin a little too quickly. "I mean, you don't *need* a partner. Single people can do it, too. There's a whole section about self-love. You know"—his voice dropped—"masturbation."

"And why," said May with a distinct chill in her voice, "would that be of particular interest to me?"

"It's just that, well—"

"Edwin, for all you know, I have a dozen moonstruck lovers writing me poetry. For all you know, I have men driving by my window late at night, pining away. For all you know, I have *women* driving by my window late at night. For all you know, I come home to an orgy every day of the week."

"Okay, okay," said Edwin. "I believe you. No need to get graphic. And anyway, I realize that you, as a high-powered female executive, never, *ever* masturbate."

"*Au contraire*," said May blithely. "I did just the other night. And I was thinking about you the whole time."

He laughed. "Touché." But what Edwin didn't realize, what he couldn't have realized, was that May was telling the truth.

"And anyway," said May. "What about same-sex marriages? It looks like your Mr. Soiree didn't think of everything."

"Actually, he did. There's a variation of Li Bok for gay couples. Granted, it's a bit sketchy."

May smiled more mauve at him. "Well, then," she said. "You'll have to test it out, won't you? Make sure it works for gays, too."

"No problem," said Edwin. "I'll ask Nigel to help. Why not? He's been screwing me for years anyway."

May laughed and Edwin ordered another drink.

"Oliver Reed," said Edwin. "The actor. What do you know about him?"

"Superman?"

"No, not Reeve. *Reed*. Oliver. A British actor, born in Wimbledon. February 13, 1938. I ran his name through Panderic's listing of celebrity bios. You remember that big gladiator movie? Oliver Reed was in that. It was his last film; he died while he was on location. In

Italy or something. Apparently, he hadn't filmed all his scenes yet, so they added his face on someone else's body, digitally."

"That's a bit creepy," said May.

"Oliver Reed started out acting in shlock horror films. If anything, he was kind of the anti-Superman. The films he made sound absolutely awful, hardly noble or heroic. I've got the list here somewhere . . . Here it is. His first starring role was in *The Curse of the Werewolf*. He was also in *The Two Faces of Dr. Jekyll*. What else? *Night Creatures, Blood in the Streets, The Pit and the Pendulum*. He also did swashbucklers: *The Pirates of Blood River, Sword of Sherwood Forest, The Three Musketeers, The Four Musketeers*, and so on. He played a villain in the musical *Oliver!* and a ballet dancer in *The League of Gentlemen*. But generally, he was a sort of second-rate he-man for hire. Blue eyes. Smouldering good looks. A string of scandalous affairs with leading ladies, several barroom brawls—that sort of thing. Reed was a prize boxer at one point, and a notorious drunk as well. The man made more than sixty films, but I'll be damned if I remember seeing any of them. It's very odd. As far as I know, Oliver Reed never read a single self-help book. He said his only regret in life was that he didn't drink every pub dry and sleep with every woman on the planet."

"Charming," said May.

Edwin nodded. "He wasn't exactly a touchy-feely sort of person."

"And?" said May.

Edwin shrugged. "And nothing. It's just—well, it's just that Tupak Soiree scribbled a note about Oliver Reed on the back of one of the manuscript pages, by accident apparently, and I can't figure it out for the life of me. What does Oliver Reed have to do with anything? What does he have to do with seeking spiritual enlightenment or attaining inner calm?"

"Maybe Soiree was talking on the phone," said May. "You know how you'll jot something down on whatever piece of paper is handy. He was probably chatting with a friend of his, one who happened to be a film buff, and his friend mentioned Oliver Reed—and Soiree just sort of wrote it down, absent-mindedly. I don't think you need to look for any hidden significance in something an author scribbles on the back of a manuscript."

"You're right," said Edwin. "That's probably what happened. He just jotted it down, I mean, what could a werewolf and Dr. Jekyll have in common with Tupak Soiree, right? Right? But still . . ." His thoughts trailed inward. Intuitively, Edwin knew there was more to it than that, knew, perhaps, that the death of Oliver Reed was the key to understanding the true intent of Tupak Soiree. But what was the connection? And why the addendum: ". . . *and I don't feel so good myself?*" What was Tupak Soiree trying to say? And why would a saintly guru who ostensibly eschews alcohol appear to have written such a note while under the influence?

"Hello?" said May. "Ground control to Major Tom."

"Sorry," said Edwin, snapping out of it. "My mind was elsewhere."

"I can see that," said May. "I realize I'm not the most scintillating conversationalist around, but I would like to think that you and I can spend an evening together without you lapsing into silence every five minutes."

"Hmm?" said Edwin. He had already started to drift away again.

May laughed. "I was just saying how well we communicate, you and I. The Japanese call it *ah-un*, the unspoken communication of old friends and—" she stopped herself. The phrase referred to lovers as well.

Edwin was about to reply when something caught his attention. Something outside. Through the window, he could see a night crew, lights blinking, backup sirens bleeping, as they raised a billboard. It was enormous, and as it swung into place on the front of an abandoned building, Edwin read "Another upcoming project by the Rory P. Wilhacker Foundation!" And he forgot all about Oliver Reed.

"I wonder," said Edwin, more to himself than to May. "Do you think there are any banks open this time of night?"

"Wilhacker?" said May. "Didn't we used to have a—"

"Yes, a janitor. He used to be a janitor. Do you think," he turned to May, "that First National over on Sullivan Street is still open?"

She checked her watch. "I think so. I think they're open till eleven. But deposits and transfer banking only."

"Perfect!" said Edwin, swigging back the rest of his beer. "Gotta run. See you. Bye." And he was gone, without even bothering to pull on his overcoat as he ran out the door, hand already raised, signalling for a taxi.

May watched him leave in stunned, befuddled silence. The night had ended on an off-note, and May didn't quite know what to make of it.

She felt insulted. And even worse, she could already feel the guilty gloom of too much cheesecake descend upon her.

"Well," she said, "so much for using my feminine wiles to ensnare a married man. Of course"—and now she was being just plain nasty—"I use 'man' in the loosest sense of the word."

And once again, May wondered what exactly she saw in such a jumpy, skittish, skinny, sarcastic, compulsive man as our Edwin. And once again, she had no answer. (No one ever does. Not really.)

"More cheesecake!" she said, beckoning the waiter like a wounded soldier calling for a medic. "More cheesecake!"

Chapter
Eighteen

By the time Edwin jumped out of the cab in front of First National, he knew exactly what he had to do. On the ride over, he had rummaged through his briefcase and retrieved the manuscript pages that dealt with organic economics.

Edwin moved what little savings he had—it was less than $2,000—into a new account, which he then dumped into short-term T-bills (now at 3.94 per cent) on a convertible blue-chip bond.

"This won't go through until tomorrow," said the clerk, ensconced behind her bulletproof glass.

"That's fine," said Edwin. "I have twenty-four hours to roll it over."

Edwin set up a cascade account first thing in the morning. He then reinvested the principal and cashed out in mid-cycle. By carefully playing off the time difference between the East Coast and the West Coast, Edwin managed to move his money back and forth across the country five times before the week was out. By the following Monday, his initial investment was worth $18,000. By Tuesday, it was worth $167,000. By Wednesday, $680,000. And on Thursday, the feds showed up.

They were waiting for Edwin when he sauntered in to work that day. There were two of them in standard-issue sunglasses and dark severe suits and suitably grim expressions. They were members of the FBI, where the motto is "We don't think that's very funny."

"Mr. de Valu," said the first man. "I'm Agent Blah, and this is Agent So-and-so." (There's no reason to remember their names.)

Edwin slung his jacket onto the desk. Then, with a smile, said, "You guys go to the same tailor, right?" Sadly, this attempt at humour did not win them over. (See: above motto.)

"This is a small and rather humble work environment," said one of the agents as he looked around Edwin's little cubicle, "for a millionaire. Don't you think?"

Hot damn! "Really?" said Edwin. "A million? It was just under when I went to bed last night, and I wasn't sure if it would hit a million today or not. I mean, math has never been my strong suit, but I figured that with—"

"Two point five million, to be exact," said Agent Blah.

"*Ha, ha!* Excellent! Now, gentlemen, if you'll excuse me for just a moment, there's a ponytail I have to yank and a co-worker I need to beat senseless. I'll be back in a jiff to clean out my desk, and we can continue this conversation somewhere else—like on a private jet to the South Pacific, perhaps."

"I wouldn't do that if I were you."

"Have a seat, Mr. de Valu." The agent was sitting in the only chair in the cubicle.

"I think I'll stand," said Edwin.

"As you wish, but be advised that if you decide to flee, we will be forced to fire upon you."

There was a pause. "You're kidding, right?"

"We never kid, Mr. de Valu."

"You'd fire on me?"

"We'd fire on you."

"Innocent bystanders be damned?" said Edwin.

"Innocent bystanders be damned."

"Wow," said Edwin. "I mean, they *are* just editors. They're expendable, but still . . ." And for the first time since he'd found the two FBI men in his cubicle, Edwin de Valu realized he might very well be in trouble. Serious trouble. This entire scenario might not end with him lounging on a beach in Bali, eating chilled strawberries while a lackey slowly fanned him with a large frond and Nigel dangled upside down over an open septic tank. It might very well end in a different manner entirely.

"Your account has been frozen, Mr. de Valu. Future transactions have been blocked, and a full audit is now under way."

"Is what I did a crime?" asked Edwin.

"We're not sure."

So Edwin signed a waiver and was taken in for questioning. They didn't shine a bright light in his eyes or beat him with a rubber hose or anything, but they did make him wait an unreasonably long time alone in an interrogation room while the Muzak version of *Cats* was piped in. Edwin didn't think that was part of the actual interrogation, but you could never be sure. Who knows? Perhaps a panel of headphone-wearing men in shirt sleeves was watching from behind the one-way mirror at that very moment, waiting for Edwin to crack. "Still no sign? Crank up the volume, increase the bathos setting. Hell, we'll go to full lyrics if we have to."

Edwin's sudden wealth was now held in limbo. The investigation could take years; he might never see his money again. Apparently, an entire wave of millionaires had recently emerged, almost overnight, all within a ten-mile radius of the city and all with the same *modus operandi*. They had slipped through the gates, turned fortunes over in a week, and had sucked millions—if not billions—out through innocuous loopholes in the banking laws. And some of those loopholes were exceedingly thin; it was like sucking a water buffalo through a drinking straw. As investigators closed in, the concentric circles of investors closed in around one man: Rory Patrice Wilhacker. Everyone involved in the scam (if it could be called that) was either a friend of Wilhacker's or a relative or a former neighbour or a friend of a neighbour or a neighbour of a friend. It was an entire network of sudden stealth wealth. Unfortunately, by the time the government had moved in, most of the money had melted away, disappearing into offshore accounts and recently chartered charities. More than two hundred different non-profit foundations had sprung up in the past week alone. They all claimed to be doing good work for good causes—"making the money sing," as they said—but the FBI and the IRS clearly didn't believe them.

"It was like an inverted pyramid scheme," one of the agents explained. "Instead of shrinking, it got bigger and bigger. The base wealth kept expanding against every known law of exponential mathematics. It was as though they had turned economic theory upside down. And they bilked the system for a fortune."

"Really? Did people lose money because of what they were doing?" asked Edwin.

This proved to be an embarrassing question.

"No, not exactly. As I said, it goes against expectation. They weren't injecting resources into the system. They weren't contributing anything, they weren't producing anything. And no, they weren't skimming cash from other accounts. The money wasn't filched from somewhere else; it just sort of *grew*. The math doesn't make any sense, it doesn't add up, but apparently—"

And Edwin thought of something Rory had said: "Money is not a mathematical creation. It's organic. It lives. It breathes. It grows." He started to laugh.

"You think this is funny? Do you, smart boy?"

"No, sir."

"Because we don't think it's funny."

"I know," said Edwin apologetically. "I saw the motto on the way in. I'm sorry. Really. But I still don't understand what crime has been committed. Which laws have been broken exactly?"

"We haven't decided yet. But I would advise you not to cross state lines until further notice."

No one was ever arrested or formally charged in the Rory P. Wilhacker Affair, and with the sole exception of Edwin de Valu, no one lost a penny to the government. Only poor Edwin, in too late and bad of luck, was caught. Only Edwin had his funds trapped in a net of ad hoc regulations. Edwin had always known it was too good to be true. The rise and fall of the Edwin de Valu fortune had occurred within the space of one week. It was too much, too fast. And though it had been a heady wild ride, somewhat akin to a sudden run of good luck at a roulette wheel, Edwin had always suspected it would come crashing to an end. And it did.

Not long after, the government began issuing complex rules regarding the use of cascade accounts and regulations aimed at preventing further "time-zone surfing" (as it was now known), but by that point more than a thousand new millionaires and multi-millionaires had been created. And all through word of mouth.

For Edwin, it was as though he had woken up from a particularly cozy dream, one of easy wealth and unlimited possibilities, and had fallen back to earth, back to the daily grind of life on Grand Avenue. No matter. For one moment, for one brief, shining moment, Edwin de Valu had had it all. For one moment, he had been obscenely wealthy. For one brief moment, he had been something more than an editor.

Chapter
Nineteen

Life continued. Work went on. The gears and wheels continued to turn. Tupak Soiree sent a fax to Edwin informing him that the edited manuscript had indeed arrived. "I will look it over and return it as soon as I am able. Live, love, and learn, Tupak Soiree."

The people in marketing were already scheming out the niches and working out the angles. The art department was drafting a preliminary cover ("Chocolates and satin," Edwin had stressed), and May had hired a new intern, which meant that there were no more unwieldy stacks of unsolicited manuscripts to wade through; they were sloughed off on Irwin. (Irwin the Intern. Edwin suspected May had hired him solely on the appeal of the alliteration.) Irwin hadn't exactly got off on the right foot. His first major gaffe came when, on being introduced, he had noted the similarities between his name and Edwin's.

"Ed-*win*, Ir-*win*. Quite the coincidence, don't you think? Especially when you consider how similar our jobs are."

"Our jobs aren't similar," Edwin had snapped. "They aren't similar at all. *You* spend your time shovelling out steaming piles of unwanted manuscripts. *I* spend my time finely honing and improving upon literary works of art. Shovelling vs. honing. They're not even in the same league, Irwin. Now go fetch me a sandwich."

Irwin tried his best, he really did, but he just wasn't fully in sync with what was required of him. He wasn't jaded enough (yet). His spirit hadn't been properly crushed (yet). "Give him another week," said May. "He'll be fine." Still, a day hardly passed without Irwin running up with some "great find" or another that he had discovered in the slush pile. He even tracked down Myers in sci-fi and said, breathlessly, "I just went over this proposal for a novel set in the future, and I think it's amazing. It has this big surprise ending, right? The world has been destroyed, right? Complete nuclear annihilation. But not everyone dies. One man and one woman manage to survive. And, on the very last page, the man turns to the woman and he says—"

"'Hello, my name is Adam,'" said Myers, his voice flat, as though reciting it from memory.

"Um, yeah," said Irwin. "How did you know?"

"And then she turns and says, 'My name is Eve.' They join hands and watch the sun rise."

"Right. Have you read it already?"

"Oh, yes," said Myers. "Many times. Many, many times."

Still, Irwin the Intern was a good kid. Even if he was a trifle earnest and a bit too, you know, *nice*.

Everything was going well. The office was humming. Things were starting to click, the pieces were falling into place. And then the boss showed up and ruined everything. Mr. Mead had just returned after spending four days at a publishers' seminar in Antigua. ("Four days of non-stop, intensive brain-storming," is how Mr. Mead described it.) When Edwin came in to work, there was a note from Mr. Mead taped to his chair. It said: "Check your e-mail, Edwin." So he checked his e-mail, and sure enough, there was a message from Mr. Mead waiting for him. It said: "Go to the front desk, Edwin. There's a memo there for you." So Edwin trudged down to the front desk and picked up the memo. It said: "Edwin, come to my office right away. Signed: Mr. Mead."

"Thank God we live in the Information Age," said Edwin. (As nonsensical as that chain of events appeared, it did have its own odd internal logic.

Mr. Mead had sent the memo to the front desk first, and then, wondering if Edwin would think to pick it up, had sent Edwin an e-mail reminder. And then, thinking, "Well, what if Edwin doesn't check his e-mail right away when he gets in?" Mr. Mead had gone down to Edwin's cubicle and written a quick note telling him not to forget to check his e-mail. Hence the chain of events. Such was the type of tight ship that Mr. Mead ran.)

Edwin passed May in the hall. "On your way to Mead's office?" she asked.

Edwin nodded. "I'm taking the scenic route, via my e-mail and the front desk."

"If you are going to see Mr. Mead, be warned: he's been reading *The Financial Times*."

"Oh, no," said Edwin, his pace slowing considerably. "Not again." *Not again*.

"Think of it as a Theatre of the Absurd," said May, smiling.

Edwin entered Mr. Mead's office with his shoulders already stooped in pre-emptive defeat.

"You wanted to see me, sir?"

Sometimes creativity needs a little boost. Sometimes genius needs a helping hand. On days like that, Léon Mead liked to whip up an inspirational cocktail of illicit chemicals—uppers, downers, sidewinders—and then wash it down with a mix of crystalline AZD followed by a trimethyl concentrate chaser, with maybe a quick snort of snow as the capper. And then, as the lotus flower of enhanced awareness blossomed around him, he would . . . well, he would usually topple over onto the floor, but not before he had managed to harvest an "insight" or two. Today was one of his better days. Mr. Mead had managed to adjust the inspiration in his bloodstream to optimum levels, but without stumbling headlong into unconsciousness. Spontaneity crackled through his veins, it leapt in arc-light bursts across his brain, it hummed with an intense heat that—

"Edwin! Come in, come in. Quick, close the door behind you. We have important things to discuss."

"How was Antigua, sir?"

Mr. Mead's thinning hair and tiny ponytail were now sun-bleached blond and his face was so tan his lips looked white. "It was very tough. We worked day and night, night and day, I can assure you. People say that publishing companies will run themselves if they're left alone. Well, that just isn't true. Look at me, Edwin. I don't believe in hands-off publishing."

"No, sir, you certainly don't." Alas.

"Oh, yes, I like to get right in there and really muck about, get my hands dirty."

"I know you do, sir. We often call you Dirty Hands Mead."

"Do you? That's terrific. Come in, have a seat. Can I get you something? A drink? Cigar?"

"A raise would be nice."

"Ha, ha," said Mr. Mead. (He didn't laugh; he actually said "ha, ha" in a painfully insincere approximation of laughter.) "You've got a good sense of humour, Edwin. I like that in a"—he almost said peon—"person. Now then, first of all, a great big thumbs up on the work you've done with *Chocolates for the Soul*. Mind you, I am a little worried that the booksellers may misfile it; you know how annoying they can be. They might end up shelving it under 'Desserts' or some such nonsense. Remember what happened with *Chicken Broth*? They put those in the cookbook section for years."

"I know, sir. But I think with the right marketing campaign, the right advertising and promotion, we can position *Chocolates* in such a way that—"

"Promo? Marketing? No, no. There won't be any of that."

"Sir?"

"Oh, no. Our entire self-help line is a write-off this season. I included your project so that we could fill the hole in the catalogue and keep our distributors happy. Forget about *Chocolates for the Soul*."

"Forget it? Sir?"

"I've got something much bigger. Something I want you to work on personally as our lead title for the spring."

Edwin could feel his ulcer starting to flare. Could feel his impotent anger starting to rise. "Forget *Chocolates for the Soul*?"

"That's right, Edwin. I was reading *The Financial Times* on the flight back from Antigua—"

Oh, Christ. Here we go.

"—and I came across an article, and I think you'll be as excited about this as I am: pork-belly futures *are up*."

"Pork bellies, sir?"

"Oh, yes. Pork bellies are selling like hotcakes. And in that same paper, in that very same paper, I read another article—under 'Trends,' I believe—that says women today are more concerned than ever about eating right and losing weight. Especially women in their middle years. Well, you put those two trends together and what do you have?"

"I wouldn't begin to guess, sir."

Mr. Mead sighed. "That's the problem with people your age, isn't it? That's the problem with your whole generation. You don't see the full pattern; you don't see the big picture. Lateral thinking, Edwin, that's what you need to work on. Lateral thinking. Women, pork: it's obvious. I want you to put together a self-help book for overweight women telling them how they can eat pork and lose weight. It'll be a new theory. We can call it 'the pork paradox.'"

There was a pause. A long, long pause. So long it was more of an epoch than a pause. Continents drifted. Glaciers crept down mountainsides.

"Well?" said Mr. Mead. "What do you think?"

"Let me get this straight," said Edwin. "Let's see if I understand what you're saying. You want me—a university graduate with an M.A. in comparative literature, whose thesis, 'Understanding Proust from a Postmodern Perspective,' was described by the review committee as, and I quote, 'well-researched'—you want *me* to put together a book for fat housewives telling them they should eat more pork. Is that what you're asking? Is it, you stupid, born-at-the-right-time, wouldn't-know-your-ass-from-a-hole-in-the-ground, self-important Baby Boomer son-of-a-bitch? Is that what you're asking?"

But of course, Edwin didn't really say that. What he said was, "I'll get right on it, sir."

"Great. Oh, yes, before you go: that same report on pork bellies stated—and I'm relying on *The Times* for accuracy until I can confirm it independently—that there was also a huge bumper crop of canola in southern Saskatchewan last year."

"Canola, sir?"

"You may know it by its Latin name, *Brassica campestris*. It's a cash crop, Edwin, a member of the *Cruciferae* family. Thought to have originated in the Mediterranean region some four thousand years ago, though some sources cite the foothills of the Himalayan Mountains. Mixed with the right ingredients, it can be used to create a lethal explosive. But generally speaking, canola is used to make oil. Edible oil. Take note of that, Edwin: edible oil products. In particular, edible *cooking* oil." He gave Edwin a knowing look. "Well, I think you can see the significance of this."

"Which is?"

"Better make it a *fried*-pork diet book."

At which point Edwin leapt from his chair, grabbed the letter opener from the desk and began plunging it repeatedly into Mr. Mead's chest, searching, in vain, for a heart.

"I'll see what I can do, sir."

"Thanks. I knew I could count on you. Tell me, did Nigel ever reimburse you for that necktie of yours he ruined? It seems to me he owed you some money or something."

"No, sir. I'm afraid Nigel still hasn't paid me for that. Perhaps you could remind him."

"Oh, I will, don't you worry. He's not got going to get away with it."

"Thank you, sir."

May was waiting for Edwin when he came out of Mr. Mead's office, and she had a look of absolute glee on her face. It was the look of someone who has long been collecting anecdotes about her boss and can't wait to add a new one.

"You don't want to know," said Edwin as he stomped past.

"Come on, you have to tell me. I'm dying to know. What's his latest brainstorm?" She fell in beside Edwin as he walked down the corridor.

"He wants me to put together a book telling overweight housewives they should eat more pork."

May stopped in her tracks. "No," she laughed. "I don't believe it."

Edwin turned to face her. "Oh, believe it, sister. And not just pork, but *fried* pork. He wants a full report on his desk by next Wednesday."

"But what about *Chocolates for the Soul*?"

Edwin stepped in closer, his voice so low it was almost a growl. "Mr. Mead has already written it off. He was just keeping the distributors happy. He never had any intention of promoting it or trying to turn it into a series. Which means that I sifted through seagull shit and went four days without any sleep for nothing. Meanwhile, Galloping Head has already charged madly off in a new direction." Edwin turned and looked out over the sea of cubicles. "This isn't an office," he said. "This is Hell with fluorescent lighting."

"I'll meet you down at your desk," said May. "It's not as bad as you think."

"Oh, yes, it is," he said. "You're forgetting: I used to be a millionaire." And he trudged through the maze, past clusters of workers and co-workers, interchangeable in their shared anonymity, as disposable as he was. "I hate my job," he muttered. "I hate my boss. I hate this place." He passed Nigel. "And I really hate *you*."

"Hey, Edwin!" yelled Nigel. "How's your self-help book coming? The chocolate one? How long before it melts and makes a big mess?"

Edwin spun around and said, without thinking, "Tupak Soiree's book is going to sell 100,000 copies and make us all a lot of money."

"If you say so. Isn't that the same prediction you made about that Baby Boomer book of yours? Remember that? *Die, Baby Boomers, Die!*"

"Nice necktie, Nigel. Why don't you come a little closer?"

"Watch it, mister." Nigel raised an angry finger—but he didn't step any nearer. "You still owe me for that."

"A kick in the ass is what I owe you."

"Gentlemen! *Please!*" It was May. She was carrying a stack of files and paperwork. "Edwin, I brought some material over to help you with your new project. Nigel, you go back to your side of the pound. Okay?"

"What is it about this guy?" asked Nigel, at once disgusted and genuinely puzzled. "Why do you always bail him out, May? He's bringing the entire department down. Why do you always make allowances for him?"

"Nigel, we're all in this together, okay?" She was referring to Panderic, but Nigel mistook it for a reference to their generation, that Gen-X camaraderie thing.

"I know, I know. We have to show solidarity. It's just that Edwin here puts us all in a bad light." And he sulked off to seethe a while.

"Edwin," said May once Nigel had left, "why *do* I always make allowances for you?"

"I don't know. Because you're smitten with me? Because you admire the way I carry myself with such quiet dignity?"

"Sure," said May. "Your quiet dignity. That must be it."

113

Chapter
Twenty

Edwin had protested the assignment—saying that he had never done a cookbook before, that he was self-help, not cookbook—but Mr. Mead had brushed these objections aside.

"You'll do fine, Edwin. Don't be so rigid in your thought processes. Self-help. Cookbooks. Who's to say where one ends and another begins? Borders blur, Edwin. Concepts overlap. And anyway, this book *will* be more self-help than anything. I even have a title worked out: *Eat Pork, Be Happy!*"

"Shouldn't that be *fried* pork, sir?"

"Yes, I know. But you have to be careful when you're using declarative sentences in a title. You don't want to overdo it. Today's readers are always on the go. They don't have the time to make it all the way through a long title. Best to keep it short. A single word would be ideal."

May, meanwhile, had piled Edwin's desk high with files, contact lists, nutritional charts, author resumes and sales listings for Panderic's previous line of cookbooks, *The Healthy Eater*. (They had had to discontinue the line when it was discovered that one of the recipes caused people's palms to become a bright carotene yellow. And another recipe had apparently caused heart flutters. Still, Panderic had done very well with *The Healthy Eater*, and it was now considered something of a template for future works. Except for the part about the yellowing skin and the heart palpitations.)

"Whatever happened to the good old days?" said Edwin wistfully.

"Like when we were still young and free?" said May.

"No. Like last Friday, before I got this stupid assignment."

"Look, here's a list of doctors who have written diet and self-help books. Start at the top and work your way down."

Edwin nodded, took the list.

The trouble started immediately.

"Hello, Dr. Aaron? Edwin de Valu here, at Panderic Books. I just wanted to thank you again for that macrobiotic cookbook you wrote for us last year. I'm wondering if you'd be interested in a new project we're working on. It's very exciting . . . You're interested? Good . . . It's a diet book about pork . . . No, not how to avoid it . . . No, no. Not how to find substitutes for it. It is one that would, um, encourage overweight people to eat more pork, especially fried pork—*hello?* Hello?"

"Dr. Betcherman? Edwin de Valu here, at Panderic Books . . ."

Edwin went through the entire list, top to bottom. He had so many phones slammed in his ear that his cranium began to ring like a tuning fork. One doctor asked if he was on *Candid Camera*. "No?" *Slam!*

May had pulled a chair into Edwin's cubicle and was going through folders on private research labs, trying to find one that would agree to fudge some results. (For *Eat Pork, Be Happy!* to succeed, they would have to support their claims with some sort of medical report, if only to establish credibility.)

"This isn't going to work," said Edwin after the last dietician on the list, Dr. Zeimer, hung up in a particularly dramatic fashion. "We're going to have to ghost it. Dr. Yaz sounded like he might do it—he kind of hesitated before he slammed down the phone—but there's no way he'd ever put his name on it. Do we have a list of people with phony doctorates? You know, experts?"

"Sure. There's a whole file. It's just behind you."

Edwin began searching through the profiles. He was looking for someone with an impressive string of post-graduate initials after his or her name, which could then be displayed prominently on a front cover. "Wow," he said. "Look at all the letters behind this guy's name: M.Sc., B.A., QED, NbR. Hey, he has a doctorate as well. A Ph.D. from the Wisconsin Correspondence School and Institute of Plumbing."

May looked up from her files. "What was his doctorate in?"

"Cryptozoology. What's that?"

"Hmmm. I think that's the study of monsters. You know, sasquatches, Ogopogo, Nessie. That kind of thing."

Sure enough, there was a photo of the good doctor holding up a huge plaster cast of a sasquatch footprint. "Excellent photo," said Edwin. "The man looks very authoritative. I mean, we'll have to crop out the giant plaster monkey's foot, of course. But I think this might be the guy. He has a great name as well: Dr. Richard Geoffrey III. If someone with a name like that tells you to eat more pork, you believe him."

"Aha!" said May. "I think I have it. This laboratory sounds like it might be the one to test our fried-pork recipes and give them a seal of approval: the Carlos Brothers Discount Food and Drug Testing Centre, where the motto is '*Hey! What's a few decimal points between friends?*'"

It was in the middle of this, while Edwin was submerged in paper and May was in the photocopy room running off lists of contact numbers, that the front desk buzzed.

"Mr. de Valu? There's a message from your wife. She said to tell you she's 'in the mood for some Li Bok tonight.' I'm not sure what that means, but she asked me to pass it on. And she said to make sure you take your vitamins before you come home."

Edwin shivered in dread. He couldn't face another night of great sex. He couldn't. It had become oppressive.

"Oh, yes. And there's a courier down in the front lobby. He's got a package for you. Said his instructions are 'to place it personally in the radiant hands of Mr. de Valu himself.'"

Those instructions could have come from only one person: Tupak Soiree. It was the edited manuscript, just in the nick of time. Edwin would quickly go over the author's comments, send it out to be copyedited, notify the typesetter, confirm the print order.

"Sure," said Edwin. "Send him up. My radiant hands are waiting."

Edwin was on the phone with the Carlos brothers when the courier arrived. "Yes, yes. It's a health book. We're an established publisher, but for credibility, we need an outside firm to test our recipes and confirm— hang on a sec. *Over here!*"

The courier, a bicycle fiend with sleek pants and predatory sunglasses, turned, slouched over and handed the package to Edwin. "You'll have to sign for it."

Edwin scrawled a signature and then cradled the phone in his shoulder as he unwrapped the manuscript. "We'll need the usual tests: nutritional breakdowns, charts, laboratory results. It's a diet based solely upon— *Holy shit!* No, sorry. Not you. No, the study isn't about— *Jesus!* Look, can I call you back later?"

Edwin hung up the phone quietly and looked in stunned silence at what he had unwrapped. It was the manuscript, all right. A fresh photocopy of the original. He flipped through the pages: nothing. The heroic editorial work Edwin had achieved, the massive reconstructive surgery he had performed—gone. Tupak Soiree had simply tossed away the edited manuscript and returned a clean copy of the original. All those changes, all that blue pencil, all those structural alterations. Gone. All gone. Edwin was right back to square one.

A letter was attached:

> Ah, Mr. de Valu. Your presumptuous conclusion that my manuscript needed to be edited was, indeed, an unfortunate decision on your part. Listen to me, Edwin, and do pay attention: You may not change one word of my manuscript, not one single word. *What I Learned on the Mountain* is a complete holistic whole. It cannot be tampered with. It cannot be altered. And it certainly cannot be improved upon. Not the title, nor the content, nor the style. Publish it exactly as is. Do not change even the errors or eccentricities of grammar and spelling. Even those are an essential part of my book—my gift, if you will, to mankind. Live, Love, Learn. Tupak Soiree.
>
> P.S.: If you do make any changes, I'll sue your ass so fast your head will spin.

Edwin felt dizzy. His face became flush. He turned, hesitated, and then ran. *May*, he had to talk to May. May would know what to do. He ran first to the copy room, but she had just left, so he hurried to her office, found her at her desk, burst in, said, "Quick! Can we edit a book against an author's wishes?" He was almost hyperventilating. "I have to know, May. Can we override an author's directives?"

May hesitated. "It is proper protocol to get the author's approval. But especially in non-fiction, small editorial changes don't necessarily require—"

"No. I don't mean small changes. I mean an entire overhaul. A complete restructuring. If we have to, can we do that without an author's approval?"

"Sure. Clause 12(a) of our boilerplate. It gives us the right to override any objections that we find 'unreasonable.'"

Edwin felt a knot form in his stomach. "And what if someone crossed out that clause in the contract?"

"Oh. Well, then we'd have a problem. But remember, under clause 6(b), if an author refuses to entertain editorial changes, he or she is required to repay the full advance—plus a penalty."

Edwin's voice was becoming almost sickly at this point. "And what if someone crossed out clause 6(b) as well? What if *both* clauses had been crossed out? Could the author sue us if we still went ahead with the changes?"

"Clause 6(b) as well? He'd have to drive a hard bargain to get us to remove both of those. Usually we give up one or the other, depending on the clout of the author. But if *both* of those clauses were removed and we *still* went ahead with a massive edit? Sure, the author could sue us. And he'd probably win."

Edwin walked back to his cubicle on wobbly, anemic legs. There, on his desk, sat the newly unpacked, crisp, clean copy of *What I Learned on the Mountain*. Around it, strewn in all directions, stacked in piles and overflowing from cardboard boxes, were the many countless disparate aspects of the pork book that Edwin was even now desperately trying to coordinate. In the middle of this, Tupak Soiree's package had landed like a jest of God.

I don't have time for this, goddammit!

Edwin took a deep breath, steeled himself and straightened his shoulders. His priorities were clear: Mr. Mead had said as much himself. *Eat Pork, Be Happy!* was to be Panderic's lead title for the spring catalogue. The Soiree book was a simply a space filler. Edwin couldn't afford to spend any more time on it.

And so, Edwin Vincent de Valu made a momentous and far-reaching decision, and one he would rue for years to come . . .

Cue: ominous music.

Chapter
Twenty-one

"Irwin, get in here. Right now." Edwin was pacing back and forth—at least as much as that is possible in a tiny cubicle crammed with loose papers and stacked files. It was more of a one-step stop-and-turn rhythm, the kind you see among stir-crazy polar bears at the zoo.

"Mr. de Valu?" It was Irwin. "You called?"

"Get in here. We have work to do."

"Actually, I was on my way to lunch, and I'm hypoglycemic, so I really should—"

"Not now, Irwin. We all have to make the occasional sacrifice. Do you have a pen and notepad? Good. You'll need to take notes, because I'm going to go fast. The manuscript for *What I Learned on the Mountain*, here on my desk, goes to the inputter as is. Tell them to scan it in with character recognition software and then send it directly to the typesetter. We'll reduce the margins to the minimum settings, use the smallest size font we have, squeeze the text in and try to keep it under 800 pages. Cancel the hardcover order. We'll go straight to paperback, on pulp and at the lowest price offered. Cut the print run from 7,500 copies to a token 1,000—no, wait, I think the minimum run is 3,000. Anyway, we'll go with whatever the minimum is. And even then, tell the warehouse to stand by, ready to remainder and dump as soon as the six-month deadline is up. This book is going to go down in flames, Irwin, and we have to cut our losses any way we can. Call up Gunter Braun at that German firm, Edelweiss Inc., or whatever it is. They repackage and reprint. Once this book goes to remainders, maybe we can foist it off on them and recoup some of our initial costs. Call the advance people on the West Coast and tell them—"

Just then, Christopher Smith from the art department showed up. "Hey there, Edwin! I have with me the cover for that book on chocolates. The one you put a rush order on." As always, Christopher was dressed completely in off-maroon. (He thought he was dressing in black, but he was colour-blind and no one ever had the heart to tell him.) Christopher wore a lush goatee and dark-tinted glasses. He insisted on signing his name *X-opher* and was always offering to show people his pierced nipple. "It didn't hurt," he'd say. "Not as much as you'd think."

Christopher stood in front of Edwin and, with a certain art-school flare, held up a display card with a picture of chocolates on it. They were arranged on a silk background with the title spelled out in ribbon, just as May had suggested. "Here is what you originally asked for," said Christopher.

"It looks fine," said Edwin. "However, I'm afraid—"

"But then I started thinking: silk, satin, stockings. What do these suggest?"

"Chris, I'm sorry but there's been a change of plans."

"Sex. Right? That's what they suggest. The feel of silk on your body. The taste of chocolate. These are just sensory stand-ins for sex. And where does sex lead us? That's right: death. So I was thinking, instead of going with the original concept, why not do something a little more creative, a little more risqué, a little more—how shall I say—*intriguing*?" ("Intriguing" was Christopher's favourite word. He picked it up from his second-year design instructor at York University. It had since become something of a Christopher trademark.) And then, with an even greater flourish, he unveiled his follow-up design. It was a mound of rotting skulls piled on top of a silk pillow, with a snake sliding out of one of the eye sockets. There wasn't a chocolate in sight.

"Chris, listen—"

"X-opher, *please*. X for short."

"Okay. Listen to me, X. Everything's changed. We aren't using that title or that cover design. All I need are block letters on a solid background: *What I Learned on the Mountain* by Tupak Soiree. That's it. No skulls. No snakes. No silk sheets. Just block letters and a two-tone cover, okay? I don't want you to spend a lot of energy on this. What is the shortest increment of time you charge us for?"

"Temporally or spiritually?"

"Time. Real time. Like what people live their lives in."

"I charge by blocks of fifteen minutes."

"Great. Fine. I don't want you to bill us for anything over fifteen minutes. That's the maximum amount of time I want you to allot for this cover. Got it?"

"I suppose so."

"Good, because there is a much more important project coming down the line, a specialty cookbook about fried pork, and I'll need your complete creative energy for that one."

Christopher nodded, stroked his goatee the way you might stroke the vulva of the one you love and said, "Pork, eh? Well, you know what *that* suggests."

"Mr. de Valu?" It was Irwin. His face was pale and his voice was starting to quaver. "I'm sorry. I don't mean to bother you, but I am starting to feel a little lightheaded. Would you happen to have a muffin or a sandwich or something?"

And with that, his eyes rolled back, his knees gave out and he keeled over onto the floor.

What I Learned on the Mountain went to bed the following Monday, without fanfare and without advance publicity. In an irony-laden "celebration party/book launch," Edwin and May stopped for a drink after work. They were in high spirits, what the Germans call *Feierabend*, an untranslatable that signifies "the uniquely festive mood that overtakes people at the end of a working day." A sort of warm, relaxed euphoria. Those Germans, they have a word for everything.

"Here's to Tupak Soiree," said Edwin as they raised their glasses in toast. "Goodbye and good riddance."

"Hear! Hear!" said May.

"You know what?" said Edwin. "If the IRS ever does release my lost millions, the first thing I'm going to do is take you on a holiday. Somewhere far away, where no one reads books, and where the wind is always warm."

"Why, thank you, Edwin, for that wonderful gesture that doesn't cost you anything."

He laughed. "Not a problem. When it comes to imaginary gifts, I'm a generous man. You can have any non-existent thing you want, May."

"Story of my life."

"But I'll tell you one thing. If I ever do get back my millions, I'm not going to bother pulling Mr. Mead's ponytail."

"No?"

"Naw. I think I'll dip it in rubbing alcohol and set it on fire instead. Maintain that quiet dignity of mine you find so attractive."

"Edwin," she said. "Let's go for a walk."

"A walk? Where?"

"Anywhere."

And so, even as *What I Learned on the Mountain* rumbled off the press and was stacked and wrapped in boxes, even as Tupak Soiree's words were punched out again and again and again, Edwin and May went for a long twilight walk in the park.

They had no idea—none whatsoever—that they had just unleashed the Plague.

Part II

The End of the World
(As We Know It)

Chapter
Twenty-two

The end of the world began with a small notice on the third page of *The Times-Herald*.

The story had come in over the wires late in the day, and many papers hadn't even bothered running it. *The Times-Herald* treated it as a minor item, tucked in among advertisements and editorials. It was easy to miss. The heading read: "Tobacco Companies Report Unexpected Drop In Sales."

This was a few months after *What I Learned on the Mountain* was first published, and although there was no direct correlation between the two events—between the tobacco company losses and the publication of Tupak Soiree's book, that is—the article stopped Edwin de Valu cold nonetheless. He was reading it while standing cheek to jowl with the usual evening rush hour, crushed into the endless loop that was his life. He had his paper folded in on itself and was reading another mindless editorial on—what? The environment? The economy? The growing number of desertions in the U.S. Armed Forces? Edwin's mind had already begun leaking information, sieve-like, when his eyes wandered down to the article in the lower left corner.

> Spokespersons for the Tobacco Institute today confirmed rumours that a sudden, unexpected drop in cigarette sales occurred last week. "It is just a short-term, self-correcting anomaly," said Ms. Grey of the institute in a statement released Tuesday afternoon. "A spike, nothing more." Ms. Grey was referring to reports that cigarette sales suddenly bottomed out, dropping 42 points on the Marshall Index in just a single week. Liquor manufacturers have reported a similar drop, fuelling speculation that the two industries are experiencing a major upheaval in consumer buying patterns. "That simply isn't true," said Ms. Grey. "There is no paradigm shift. There is no reason to panic. This is merely a one-time, unexpected adjustment, and we are confident that within a week, sales will be back up at projected levels, if not higher. A blip on the screen, nothing more. Certainly nothing to be alarmed about."

That in itself was a fairly ho-hum, turn-the-page, what's-Cathy-up-to-today sort of news story. But then Edwin got to the end of the article and his head snapped back as though he had been given a sudden, severe jolt.

> The president of Philip Morris Tobacco was unavailable for comment amid rumours that he had resigned unexpectedly. Sources inside the company report that the only notification given was a hand-drawn sign taped to his office door that read: *"Gone fishin'."* The president of Philip Morris was not known to be an avid angler, and speculation over his whereabouts continues.

"Oh, my God," said Edwin. "It's started."

Edwin had been waiting for omens and portents of impending doom. He had been waiting for weeks, had been waiting for them ever since May first mentioned, in passing and just shortly after *What I Learned on the Mountain* was first shipped, that "Barnes and Noble called. It was about the Soiree book."

"*Uggmgk!*" Edwin had said, his mouth full of sourdough bagel at the time. "Forget it!" he shouted once he had managed to choke it down (both the bagel and the news). "No way are we going to accept returns that quickly. We shipped the book only a week or so ago. The agreement was for—"

"Not returns," said May. "Orders. They want to re-order."

"So soon?" Edwin was suitably impressed. "But they took 800 copies already."

"They asked for 35,000 more. We've only got a couple hundred copies still in stock, so we're scrambling to get a second print run going."

"That's got to be a typo," said Edwin. "Did they fax the order? They must have meant 3,500."

May leaned in closer, and her voice became very calm and very, very serious. "I phoned back and asked three times to be sure. They want 35,000. Said they have a waiting list of customers almost 12,000 strong. Told us to stand by for further orders. Edwin, something is going on."

The shipment went out, and two weeks later another fax came through. "Priority: 50,000 copies to be shipped immediately: *What I Learned on the Mountain*. Soiree, Tupak. ISBN: 176661313. Rush Order. Hurry!"

By the end of the week, the book had surged to the top of the local bestseller lists, and by the week after that, it had gone national. Suddenly, all of Panderic was talking about it. The cries of "We have a winner!" and "Random House can kiss our ass!" echoed down the hallways. Edwin was heralded as a marketing genius, Mr. Mead was openly considering promoting him, and even Nigel had to give him half-hearted credit.

"None of us saw *that* coming," he said.

"Hey, Nigel. What did I tell you? One hundred thousand copies. It's going to make us all rich."

In fact, it topped 100,000 copies that same month and still showed no signs of slowing down. It hit the top of *The Times* bestseller list and stayed there, parked at number one, week after week after week. And that's when Edwin started to become uneasy.

"This isn't right," he said to May, voice hushed, as they sat in a darkened corner of O'Connor's. "This just isn't right."

"What are you talking about? Lighten up, Edwin. Your unheralded self-help book is this year's *Madison County*. Enjoy it while it lasts, kiddo, because it's got to end sometime, and then it's back to the grindstone for you. As it is, you're Mr. Mead's prize prodigy right now. He's already taking credit for teaching you everything you know. Might even move you up to your own office in the fall. Think about that: no more cubicle, no more 'head pop-ins.' And imagine how you'll be able to gloat over Nigel. *What I Learned on the Mountain* is the biggest seller we've had in years, and trust me, we've got nothing else on the near horizon."

"But what about your sex-scandal book?"

"Oh, you mean the woman who had sex with the Vice President and the Speaker of the House? Turns out she also had sex with Elvis. Onboard a UFO."

"Oh. So are we cutting her book from the catalogue?"

"Nope. We'll just move it from biography to New Age. But it won't sell as well, political scandals are much hotter than UFOs right now. The main thing is, Edwin, your book is doing wonderfully well and you are about to reap all kinds of benefits, fringe and otherwise. *What I Learned on the Mountain* has made you a star at Panderic. Revel in this while it lasts, because it will end sometime. It'll have to."

"But what if it doesn't?" said Edwin, an irrational panic creeping into his voice. "What if it just keeps on going, forever and ever and ever? Like some kind of Energizer Bunny from Hell."

May leaned back in the booth, looked carefully at Edwin, pursed her lips and said, slowly: "We are talking about a book, right? A self-help book. One that purports to help people improve their lives. That is what we're talking about, right? Just a book."

"Is it?" he hissed. "Are you sure that's all it is?"

"When your eyes get all buggy and crazed like that, I find it a bit disconcerting. I think you've been working too hard, Edwin. How's the fried-pork diet book going? Have you tried any of the recipes? I saw one of them, fried rinds soaked in Slim-Fast. Seems a bit like cheating, don't you think?"

"What if it isn't just a book, May? What if it is *the* book? The one everyone has been waiting for. The one that will cure all our problems, fix our frailties, resolve our inner conflicts. What if this is the one? What if Tupak Soiree managed to come up with the master formula? There's always a germ of truth in different books, but no one ever gets it completely right. Or even comes close. I mean, the entire reason we have so many damn self-help books is because they don't work! If anyone ever wrote a self-help book that actually worked, I'd be out of a job, goddammit!!"

"*Edwin!* Your voice. Calm down. You're starting to yell. Look, why don't you go home. Get some rest, maybe—"

"I can't," he said, eyes flashing. "Can't go home. My wife is trying to kill me."

"Your wife is trying to kill you?"

"That's right. She's trying to kill me with sex. It's horrible. Every night, the same thing. The same perfect technique, the same incredible orgasms. It's killing me, May! Sure, laugh if you want. But it's true. She's trying to kill me. If it weren't for her menstrual cycle, I'd never get the chance to recuperate. And she's always yammering away, saying, 'Read the book, Edwin. You must read the book. After all, you edited it. Read the section on Li Bok. It's supposed to work better if both partners use the same counter-pressure points.' It's like some kind of cult. It's like she's joined Amway or something. And every night, every goddamn night. It's like I'm trapped. Like I'm trapped in a—in a, I don't know, something. Something terrible. I can't even think straight. Haven't you noticed how gaunt I've become?"

"You *are* gaunt, Edwin. You've always been gaunt."

"Oh, yeah? Well, how about this?" He leaned in, close, his voice a faint whisper. "I have an erection all the time now. I have an erection right now."

May whispered back. "And what exactly would you like me to do about that?"

In spite of himself, Edwin laughed. "Well," he said, keeping the whisper going, "whatever you do, don't touch it."

"Okay, Edwin. I won't. I promise." And then, in a normal volume voice, she said, "You see? What is that? A smile? There, that's the old

Edwin de Valu I know and hate. Let's order, I'm hungry. This celery-
and-uncarbonated-soda diet I'm on just isn't cutting it."

"But what if this *is* the book, May? What if this is the one?"

"Oh, Jesus, Edwin. Look, you have got to stop getting so—"

"What if Tupak Soiree managed to hit the jackpot? What if all the
numbers, all the parts, all the words, what if it came together, in the
right order, at the right time? Like a thousand monkeys typing for a
thousand years. You know, what if Tupak Soiree somehow hit all the
right keys in all the right order?"

"Edwin, first off, it's not a thousand monkeys typing for a thousand
years. It's a thousand monkeys typing for an eternity. The theory is,
given enough time, they would eventually turn out *Hamlet* or *Gone with
the Wind*."

"Or *What I Learned on the Mountain*."

"Are you suggesting monkeys wrote that book?"

"No, no, of course not. What I'm saying is that, theoretically, if someone ever wrote a book that had everything arranged in just the right
way—"

"Edwin, those monkeys would have to type forever. We're talking
infinity."

"Ah, yes! But infinity *includes* all numbers. Any event that will happen—quote—'sometime during infinity' has the same chance of
occurring two seconds from now as it does a million years from now.
The odds are exactly the same. Mathematically speaking, those monkeys have the same chance of typing *Hamlet* on their very first try as
they would on their thousandth. Why? Because there is no outside
limit to infinity, so there is also no difference in the odds. Tupak Soiree
could just as easily have hit the jackpot now as at any time in the next
million billion years."

"How do you know all that? I thought you were terrible at math."

"I am. I was watching *Stargate* last night. But the physics involved is
still sound. And what about his name? *Tupak* spelled backwards, what
does that tell you? It makes you think, May. It really makes you think."

"No, Edwin. It doesn't make me think. It doesn't make me think at
all. Too much work, not enough sleep, and bad science-fiction. That's
what I see at work here."

"Okay, well, what about chaos theory? You know, how a butterfly flapping its wings in China can cause gale-force winds over in—I don't know—someplace really far away. The downfall of society could be precipitated just as easily by some small, innocuous event as by a major upheaval. For example, the publication of a *seemingly* innocent book. A butterfly flaps its wings, and a hurricane is stirred up on the far side of the globe. Do you see what I'm getting at?"

"It seems to me," said May philosophically, "that someone should kill that damn butterfly. I mean, it's been causing typhoons and shipwrecks and earthquakes for far too long. If you want to solve the world's problems, you should first track down that butterfly and squash it. Forget El Niño—it's that damn butterfly we need to stop."

"I'm serious, May. How do we know what kind of destructive forces, what far-reaching chain of events, might be unwittingly unleashed by the smallest, most insignificant incident."

"And why is it always a butterfly?" asked May. "Don't you think it's time we came up with a new metaphor? Does it always have to be a butterfly? Why not a dung beetle in Aberdeen causing a sudden increase in arthritis among New Zealand sheep farmers? I think this whole 'butterfly flapping its wings' scenario is getting a bit stale. How about a housefly in Arkansas tipping over an oil tanker in the Sea of Madrid? Or how about—"

"I don't know why I even try," he said, and he was clearly pissed off at this point. "Seriously, May. I'm not kidding. I have a bad feeling about this. We didn't spend any money on promoting *What I Learned on the Mountain*. Not a penny. We didn't send out a single review copy, and in turn we didn't get a single book review. And yet, within weeks, it just took off. How do you explain that, May?"

"Edwin, you know as well as I do that the greatest sales tool we have is word of mouth. It sells more books that anything else. You can have the biggest, slickest marketing plan available, but poor word of mouth will still kill the best-laid plans of mice and publishers. That's what happened here, only the other way around. It's like *The Celestine Prophecy*. Remember that? The author couldn't find a publisher for love nor money, so he ended up publishing it himself, hawking it out of the trunk of his car, going from bookstore to bookstore—"

"And that took years, May. Years of persistence. What happened with *What I Learned on the Mountain* took only a matter of weeks. And no one was driving around with copies of it in the trunk of his car. This was purely word of mouth. And you know what? Paul down in marketing did a reader survey when sales first started to soar, trying to figure out what was going on—you know how reactive marketing is; always trying to catch up to the latest trend and then take credit for it. Well anyway, Paul tested reader satisfaction with *What I Learned on the Mountain*, and do you know what he came up with? One hundred per cent satisfaction. That's right, 100 per cent, May."

"Come on, Edwin. You're going to take anything marketing says seriously?"

"I asked Paul. I said, 'One hundred per cent satisfaction? That's statistically impossible. How many people did you test? a dozen?' He said, 'No, we surveyed hundreds. Thousands. We inserted a questionnaire in the last print run.' Now, normally we'd be happy to get a mail-in reply rate of 10 per cent. Do you know how many of the questionnaires came back? All of them. Every single one. And then Paul says, 'Well, it wasn't really 100 per cent, of course. I mean, we round up. It was 99.7 per cent satisfaction.' And you know something, May? I find 99.7 per cent more scary than 100 per cent. I don't know why, but I do."

"So what, Edwin? So people are happy with the book. I don't know why that bothers you so much. What is the worst that could possibly happen? People feel good about themselves. They feel happy. Where's the harm?"

"That, I don't know," said Edwin. "But I tell you, it just isn't right. It isn't normal."

"Being happy isn't normal?"

"No, it isn't. I edit self-help books. Trust me, I know. Everyone is looking for something, but the whole point is that they never find it. Everyone needs help. Or at least, they *think* they need help. I know I do."

"Well," she said, her hands reaching under the table, her voice dropping, "maybe I could help you with that erection of yours instead?"

And she squeezed it, under the table, surprising them both.

They ended up back in May's apartment in a swirl of hormones. Like May, the room was a study of eccentric disarray. There were books and cat toys and beaded door-hangings everywhere. There was even an old manual typewriter tucked away in one corner.

Edwin and May fell into each other, a frantic tangle of limbs and lips, as the cat looked on disapprovingly. Things were so confused and hurried that everything got jumbled and out of order. They had barely started kissing when May's breasts, soft and full, made a sudden, unexpected appearance. May was already tugging at Edwin, her fist moving up and down, before he even had time to take off both his shoes. So there he was, with one shoe on and one shoe off, trying to gain traction on a throw rug that kept slipping every time he reared up in less than stallionesque glory. His overcoat became caught up over his head, the band in his wristwatch got snagged in her hair, and her pantyhose became knotted around her ankles. It was all very poorly choreographed. Certainly not the most graceful or cinematic coupling ever seen. They rolled off her futon, consecrated their passion on a stack of magazines, rolled back up, kneeling on each other's legs, getting in each other's way, awkwardly shifting positions. At one point, Edwin licked long on exposed flesh, only to discover it was his own forearm.

It ended as much from sheer exhaustion as anything else. May came in shudders; Edwin was wet with sweat.

They lay there, half on the futon, half off, senses spinning, gulping air in ragged spasms. May's cat had fled the scene, assuming it was a strange human wrestling ritual, and at some point someone had kicked over a fern.

As always, moments like these tended towards religiosity.

"Oh, God. Oh, my God."

"God. Oh, God."

"I need water," said May. She staggered to her feet, wrapping herself in a sheet, and padded barefoot to the kitchen. Edwin kicked off his second shoe. Stretched back. Thought about Jenni and was surprised at the lack of guilt he felt. And then, just as quickly, he felt guilty about not feeling guilty.

Edwin looked down, grinned, and shouted out, "May! My erection! It's gone!"

"I should hope so," she said, coming back in with a glass of ice water. "Here, take this. You look dehydrated."

"You don't understand. It's gone. I'm exhausted. I'm absolutely exhausted. This is how sex is supposed to be! I'm sitting here, feeling unsettled, a bit awkward, vaguely guilty. This—*this* is what sex is all about. It's not meant to make you feel at one with the universe. Nothing that intimate ever should. With my wife, sex is just too, you know, too *perfect*."

"Perfect," said May, and her voice had grown cold, but Edwin went on unaware.

"That's right: perfect. Everything is arranged just so. Clean, crisp, precise. Sex with my wife is just too good, you know? Sex isn't supposed to be clean and healthy. It's supposed to feel kind of dirty, kind of wrong. Ambivalent. That's the word I'm looking for—ambivalent. It's supposed to be ambivalent." He took a long, deep drink of water. "I feel great!" he said.

There was an icy pause.

"Edwin, I think you should leave."

He was genuinely surprised. "Why? Was it something I said?"

"Just go. Now."

"But, May—"

"Do you remember the Sheraton Timberland Lodge? Do you?" Her face was flush with anger and sadness. "Do you?"

"Of course, May. I think about it all the time. Every day at work, every time we pass in the hall."

With this, her resolve faltered slightly. "You do? I didn't realize . . . I mean, I never imagined it meant that much to you. I didn't know it was so meaningful."

"No, no," said Edwin. "I felt awful. I regretted it so much. You know, 'Oh, why did I do such a stupid thing?' My feelings were all mixed up. There was this ambivalence."

"Ambivalence." She said the word flatly.

Edwin was shoved out the door, jacket and shoes in hand, pants only half on, necktie lassoed loosely around his neck, stunned-bunny look on his face. "What did I do?" he said, even as she slammed the door in his face. He could hear the locks go up inside, could hear her closing herself in, raising the drawbridge, turning the deadbolts.

"May?" he said, softer this time. "May?" He waited in silence for a reply that never came.

And behind the walls of her fortress, curled up on her loveseat with her cat, Charley, in her lap, May sat rocking back and forth, back and forth, letting her eyes fill up and then spill over. Again and again. It wasn't because of what he said; it was what he didn't say.

She was crying because she knew she would never feel close to him again, would never *let* herself feel close to him again. Edwin de Valu: a high-strung, blithely insensitive book editor with a Stepford wife and a tendency to fly off the handle. What was May thinking? How could she ever have let herself fall in love with someone like that? What was she possibly thinking?

Ah, but she wasn't thinking. That was the problem. (It always is.)

Chapter
Twenty-three

"Lipstick," said Jenni, and Edwin stopped dead in his tracks.

"Pardon?"

"On your collar," said Jenni. "See? Here, here and here. That's almost a cliché, the husband coming home with lipstick on his collar." She stepped closer, looked more carefully. "A new shade, but still the same line. I'd recognize it anywhere. It's what's-her-name. The chubby one."

"Steve?"

"No, not Steve. *May*. That was her name, right? So what happened?" Edwin swallowed hard. He had no alibi. He had no plan of evasion. He was, in fact, choking on silence. He thought of the other lipstick: the lipstick on his chest, streaked across his back, between his toes. He was a walking road map of infidelity. "Well," he said. "You see, it's, um—"

But Jenni plunged on without giving Edwin a chance to stammer out his non-answer. "So what happened?" she said. "Were you two horsing around at work and May tripped into you? Or maybe she got some bad news and you felt sorry for her, so you gave her a hug, you know, to comfort her?"

Edwin cleared his throat. "What you said. The first one."

"Horsing around?"

"Yes. Horsing around. We were horsing around. At work. I mean, it was definitely at work. That's where we were. When we were horsing around—Hey, why don't we order out tonight? Maybe Thai? I don't know about you, but I'm starving."

"Sure," said Jenni, a familiar sly smile resurfacing. "But save some of your energy."

Edwin knew what *that* meant, and his heart sank in a pool of despair. "Energy?" he said.

"You know, for Li Bok." She trailed a finger down his chest. "Now, why don't we go into the bedroom and work up a proper appetite first."

Like a prisoner being led to the gallows, Edwin followed, head hanging down—and then, with a start, he remembered the lipstick patterns May had left across his body, those temporary tattoos in places private and personal. They would be a little more difficult to explain away.

"Just give me a moment first," he said. "I've had a long day. I really need a shower."

"Okay," said Jenni. "But make it quick. 'Cause I'll be waiting." She singsonged that last line, sending a shiver of dread down Edwin's spine.

Chapter
Twenty-four

"May, listen. About yesterday."

"No. There is no yesterday. There is nothing we need to discuss. Nothing."

"Listen, I feel terrible. The truth is—"

"The truth, Edwin? The truth is, I was using you. I was feeling a little frisky, a little sexy, and you just happened to be the nearest halfway decent male around." She shrugged. "It didn't mean anything." Her delivery was excellent: offhand, dismissive, breezy. And so it should be. She had been rehearsing this moment all night as she lay awake, unable to sleep. "It didn't mean anything. You weren't using me, I was using you." This was her mantra; this was her prepared statement to the press, to the mirror. She had repeated it so often she had even started to believe it.

"Really?" said Edwin.

"Yes. I'm sorry, but that's the way it is."

"I see." Edwin didn't know what to say. "Well, um, here's your coffee. I was—"

"Over there," she said, with a wave of her hand. "Leave it over there. Now, if you'll excuse me, I have work to do." And she turned her attention to a pile of papers, feigning a deep and unnatural interest in their contents.

Edwin did as he was instructed. He put the coffee on her side table and was about to leave when he turned in the doorway. "May, I just want you to know that no matter what happens, I will always—"

"Stop it," she said. "There's no need for any of this. Just go." And then, softly, she spoke a single word, a word that hung like a question mark between them: "*Razbliuto.*" Only that: *razbliuto.*

Instead of going back to his cubicle, Edwin strode down to Panderic's backlist stack, found *The Untranslatables* on the bottom left row and looked up the word May had spoken. Edwin flipped through the pages, followed the headings down to the entry. *Razbliuto*: a Russian word meaning "the feelings you have for someone you once loved, but now do not."

Edwin stared at the definition, stared at the word and all the cascade of subtext it contained, and he felt the wind go out of his chest. *Razbliuto. Once loved, but now do not . . .*

He might have gone back right then and there. He might have gone to May, might have said, "I am so sorry," might have said, "I never realized. I never knew." He might yet have swept her into his arms, might have kissed her lips, her full, deep lips. He might have held her warm softness in his stick-figure embrace. He might have done that and more, but the details of life got in the way.

"Mr. Mead wants you in his office! ASAP!" It was Nigel, standing, hands on hips, in the doorway. "We've been looking for you. You weren't in your cubicle where you belong."

Edwin reshelved *The Untranslatables*; he couldn't even work up the rancour to give Nigel a gratuitous zing. "Tell Mr. Mead I'll be there soon."

"Soon isn't good enough, Edwin. He's been waiting five minutes already."

"He can wait another five. I need a moment alone."

"If it wasn't for *What I Learned on the Mountain*, you wouldn't get away with any of this," muttered Nigel.

Edwin stood there a long time, staring at the vast wall of books, all Panderic, many of them his, and he thought about May. He thought about May. And about words. And the meaning of both.

Chapter
Twenty-five

"This Tupak Soiree fellow . . . I don't like it. He's too reclusive." Mr. Mead had indeed waited another five minutes, without complaint, and he was now standing by the window, looking out across the city. He turned, determination in his posture, jaw firm, eyes set. "Dammit, Edwin. We have to do something. We can't afford a hermit. That kind of gimmick may have worked for Salinger, but it carries no cachet with the self-help crowd. We have to get Soiree out there, pimping his book. Sales have almost hit two hundred thousand. And you know what that means: it's starting to peak. We have got to get started on a full-scale promotional tour."

It was a typical backwards theory, the type with which publishing is ripe—namely, the more successful the book, the more money you spend promoting it. After all, if a book isn't a blockbuster, why waste money pushing it? The result? The books that need it the least get the most money.

Edwin sighed. "I've faxed Mr. Soiree on several occasions. He's still in Paradise Flats, still out on the edge of the desert. He says if we send even one reporter out to interview him, if we give his address to even one journalist, he will—and I quote—'Tear us a new asshole.'"

"Oh," said Mr. Mead. "Well, that's not very holistic of him."

"Mr. Soiree spends eighteen hours of every day meditating under a very hot sun without food or water. I think it affects his judgment. Tends to make him cranky."

Mr. Mead nodded. "Desert will do that. Why, I remember once in an ashram in India, or perhaps it was Sri Lanka, I fasted for forty-eight hours and consumed only hallucinogenic mushrooms proffered by sutra-chanting monks. As you might imagine, I found the entire experience—"

"Sir? We were discussing the author?"

"Oh, yes, of course. Tupak Soiree. I don't know why you even brought up the topic of mushrooms. That was completely off-track. Sometimes, Edwin, I worry about you. Now then, as for our so-called reclusive, so-called author. We somehow have to entice him out of hiding."

"He's a spiritual man. Perhaps we could play on his sense of altruism. Underline how he would reach more people, make a bigger impact."

"And you think that would work, do you?"

"To tell you the truth," said Edwin, "I don't have a good feeling about Mr. Soiree. I find the entire chain of events unsettling. There's something about this book, something . . . well, something evil."

"Evil? Ha. There you go, being melodramatic. I really should transfer you over to our Romance and Gothic House." (This was considered a fate worse than death among editors, worse even than self-help—if such a thing were possible.) "I need ideas, Edwin. Ideas. Not vague premonitions."

"Well, I could fax Mr. Soiree a heartfelt plea from a young girl stricken with leukemia. That worked before, remember?"

Mr. Mead smiled warmly at the memory. "Ah, yes. *The Girl Who Loved Wayne Gretzky.* That was certainly a coup. But I'm afraid our lawyers warned us against performing such a stunt again. Still, it was inspired. Absolutely inspired."

"Thank you," said Edwin, taking credit for something in which he had played no part.

"Was that whole leukemia thing your idea?" said Mr. Mead. "I had completely forgotten."

"Panderic's success is the only reward I need, Mr. Mead."

"Good, because if you think you're going to get any extra money out of me, you're sadly mistaken. As for Soiree, forget about playing the altruism angle. Altruism is so passé. Instead, we'll appeal to Mr. Soiree's baser instincts. Money, Edwin. Cold, hard cash. Filthy lucre. We'll offer him a kickback for every interview to which he submits. We'll pay the bugger."

Edwin was taken aback by this. One of the unwritten rules of publishing was that no one ever got paid to do an interview. "Sir, I really don't think the magazines and television stations would stand for it. If we start charging them for author interviews, we could trigger a backlash against us which, in the small, incestuous world of publishing, could have grave—"

"Not the media, Edwin. Us. What if *we* paid Mr. Soiree, say, five grand per interview? Under the table, of course. Do you think he'd go for it?"

Tupak Soiree's reply came back with remarkable speed. The reclusive author was still using the Paradise Flats Municipal Library fax machine, which tended to slow down communications. But not this time. No, sir.

> Dear Mr. Edwin: May the divine light of understanding shine ever forth upon your upturned buttocks as you kiss Mother Earth in deep gratitude. (An old Nepalese blessing.) I hope everything is well on Grand Avenue. The answer to your question is *yes*. Yes. I would love to do interviews. I would thrive upon them. It behooves us all to seek more direct means of spreading my worldly wisdom and cosmic awareness. (Note: my bank-account information is given below. Make the payments direct, transit #32114.) Indeed, feel free to book as many interviews as you wish. I will be paid *per appearance*, correct? Just give me a few days to get ready, to properly attune myself with the Great Lyre String of the Universe.

And so, three days later, unexpectedly and for the first time ever, Edwin de Valu found himself speaking one on one with the great and mysterious Tupak Soiree.

"Hello, Mr. de Valu! It is I, Tupak Soiree, telephoning you today." The voice, steeped in some sort of generic East Indian accent, came lilting over the phone lines.

"Wow. This is unexpected." Edwin scrambled to maintain his composure. In spite of himself, he felt a tinge of awe seeping in. "Thank you—thank you so much for calling, Mr. Soiree. I'm glad you could find time. Your landlord said you were out in the desert."

"My landlord? Ah, yes, McGreary. A most disagreeable man, no? My lessons of love have fallen on deaf ears with him. But still, we must love every creature, great and small. Even bugs. Well, maybe not the really gross ones. You know, the ones that live in dung and whatnot. But pretty much every other creature. They need love, each and every one. Love, love, love. All we need is love. Love is all we need. This is what I learned whilst meditating this morning: every one of us must be loved. For love is like water. We need it to grow. And also when we get thirsty. Oh, yes, oh, my. I was indeed out in the desert for three days, and I was thinking about water an awful lot. My goodness, it was so very hot. Hot and dry. But when news came that you were wishing to speak with me, I came quickly back."

"Thank you," said Edwin. "It's about Oprah. She'd like to have you on her show. She's thinking she may include *What I Learned on the Mountain* in the new re-launch of her book club, and you know what a Lord Almighty cash cow that is. Spiritually speaking, of course. Now, I realize you don't like doing interviews—"

"Oh, no. Goodness, no. I *love* to do interviews. Especially Oprah. Such a special woman. And so famous, too. Oh, yes, I watch her every day. Did you see her program last week, when Will Smith was her special guest? Oh my, that was so—"

"But . . . but I thought you spent your days out in the desert?"

There was a pause. "Of course. What I meant is, I watch Oprah when I get back from the desert. You know, once the meditating and whatnot is taken care of. I tape her show and then watch it when I get back. From the desert. When did you say my first royalty cheque is due?"

The next day, Tupak Soiree couriered an 8 x 10 glossy to Panderic's publicity department, and the photo was quickly slapped into promotional pamphlets and sent out in mass mailings across the country.

Soiree was a striking figure. Not handsome, or even attractive, really. But very soothing; almost bovine in his appearance. Calm and oh so very guru-like. Within days of the mass mailings, the phone was ringing off the hook.

Oprah was to be Tupak Soiree's grand coming-out party; it would be his first public appearance, but by no means would it be his last.

"Yes, indeedy," said Mr. Mead. "I do believe we have a winner." And he personally wrote out the first cheque for $5,000 under the misleading heading of "Promotional Costs." It was no such thing, of course. It was a bribe, bald and unapologetic. And it was made to a man who claimed to have discovered the underlying patterns of time and space itself. Money, it would seem, still fit into the cosmic picture—and probably always would.

Chapter
Twenty-six

The response was unprecedented. Forget Beatlemania; that was limited to impressionable young adolescents, a notoriously easy group to whip into a frenzy. No. Tupak Soiree madness was less contrived and more widespread, and it cut across demographic lines. When Tupak appeared on *Oprah*, entire cities came to a standstill. The hype that had preceded the reclusive author's public debut sent the Windy City into media overdrive. It was the only thing the papers and radio call-in shows wanted to talk about. You'd have thought the Dalai Lama had appeared alongside Christ Himself.

Jenni recorded the *Oprah* interview for Edwin, and they watched it together when he got home.

"He is *so* sweet," said Jenni. "He's perfect."

Mr. Soiree was dressed in a simple white cotton robe, the type favoured by charlatans and gurus alike since time immemorial, and he beamed magnificence—*beamed* it—at the audience, at Oprah, at the millions of fans watching in their living rooms. Tupak looked surprisingly young for someone who had unlocked the secrets of the universe.

He had wild, curly hair and soft, puffy features, as though his face had been slightly overinflated. His eyes sparkled, and he smiled easily and with deep, endearing charm.

As Tupak flirted innocently with Oprah, squeezing laughter and "*Awwws*" from the audience, and as America fell in love with him, fell headfirst into giddy worship, Edwin sat looking on in horror. He was reminded of what May had said about the banality of evil and the banality of talent. Here, thought Edwin, was a combination of both. Tupak Soiree was evil. Pure evil. Of this, Edwin was now convinced. He didn't have any empirical evidence, but he didn't need any. He could feel it in his bones.

"Oh, Edwin," said Jenni breathlessly, her face shining in a distinctly Tupak Soiree manner. "He is absolutely perfect!"

"Yes," said Edwin. "He is perfect." Perfectly evil.

Chapter
Twenty-seven

Oprah invited Tupak back the following week, and the week after that as well. He soon became a semi-regular, and his appearances always sent the ratings soaring. Fan clubs and chat lines dedicated to "the Soiree message" multiplied on the Net, as book sales went through the roof. Panderic had to contract the printing out to half a dozen different companies just to keep up. More televison appearances followed, more gushing love-ins, more beaming magnificence. Edwin stopped watching after a while. It was always the same: Soiree would repeat his standard pseudo-mystical nonsense by rote, and the audience would wallow in it. Soiree was simply quoting random passages from *What I Learned on the Mountain*, stuff that people had heard over and over again, and still they couldn't get enough.

Panderic Inc., meanwhile, made a quick windfall licensing Tupak's image (with a hefty kickback to Tupak himself, natch), which was then plastered on coffee mugs, inspirational T-shirts and dorm-room posters across the country. *People* ran a cover-story profile; *Time* followed suit, and so did *Newsweek*. And still they kept referring to him as "the reclusive Mr. Soiree." It was starting to drive Edwin up the wall. "Reclusive?" he would shout at the magazine stands and the televison screens that daily bombarded him with Tupak's image. "Reclusive? The man is a media slut!"

And then, one day, the unimaginable happened. One day, the slush pile simply . . . *disappeared.*

It had been pouring rain all morning, and Edwin came in from lunch like a grumpy stray dog, his newspaper damp, his jacket soaked, his umbrella turned inside out. He stomped water from his feet and walked, foul cloud over his head, towards his cubicle sanctuary.

But he stopped in mid-stride.

"Irwin?" he said.

Irwin the Intern had a desk just across the corridor, and usually Irwin was not visible. All you ever saw of Irwin was a tuft of hair sticking up behind a mountain of manuscripts. He had been shovelling slush for so long, in fact, that no one really remembered what he looked like. Today, however, Irwin was completely visible. The stacks of unsolicited manuscripts were gone, and Irwin's desk was clean and polished. His notepads were arranged by size, and his pens and paper clips were lined up neatly in a row.

"Where's the slush pile, Irwin? Didn't the mailboy come through?"

"He did. But there wasn't anything for us today."

"No manuscripts? No proposals? Nothing?"

"Nope."

"No," said Edwin, a clammy feeling running across his already clammy skin. "No. This isn't good. This isn't good at all."

"Actually, I thought it was a nice break," said Irwin. "It's been slowing down all week. Yesterday it was just a trickle, and today—nothing."

"You don't understand," said Edwin. "The slush pile is society's early-warning line. *Think,* man! Would-be writers are the forerunners of every motivational fad there is. They are the bellwethers, the litmus test, the canaries in the coal mine. Slush-pile writers are our vanguard, Irwin. We need them. We need our unknowns. We need our masses of unfulfilled souls, struggling to rise above the limits of their own abilities. We need our fictional novels and our three-part trilogies. We need our jet blond hair and our bear hands. Society needs its slush pile, don't you see? Once the slush pile goes, the rest will follow. This is not good. This is not good at all."

Edwin didn't bother drying off. Still dripping rain, he stormed across to May's office, found the door open and entered without knocking. "Tupak Soiree is a fraud!" he shouted.

May looked up, her face absolutely devoid of interest. "Edwin, go away. I'm busy."

"The slush pile is gone, May. It's gone! Don't you see? That's the beginning of the end. Today the slush pile, tomorrow it's life as we know it." His voice sounded wild, even to him.

"Edwin, leave my office. I don't have time for this."

"Monkeys didn't write that book, May. A computer did. Tupak Soiree is a fraud. He isn't a writer, he's a computer programmer. He just punched in the numbers. He entered every goddamn self-help book ever written, and then let the computer do the rest."

In spite of herself, May found her interest piqued. "A computer?"

"Listen, I was in a deli over on Lancaster, having a bite, when I hear our esteemed author being interviewed on some noontime radio call-in show. It was the usual lovey-dovey, aren't-you-the-insightful-one crap. But then, in an unguarded moment, Tupak makes a slip. A small slip, but a revealing one. They were talking about how you can find beauty in everything—and I tell you, I was tempted to call in and say, 'How about ugliness? Can we find beauty in ugliness as well?' But anyway, this guy calls in, says, 'I think *numbers* are the most beautiful thing in nature.' In nature, mind you. And Tupak replies, 'Ah, yes. Numbers do have their own inner charm. I know I find the binary code to be a cosmic dance of beauty. When I was programming Unix code, I often felt—' And the host says, 'But I thought you were born and raised in a village in northern Bangladesh, where there was no electricity or running water?' And Tupak says, 'Yes, but I studied computer programing after I came to America.' And the host says, 'But didn't you arrive in America just last year? You were living on a mountain in Tibet before that, remember?' And then Tupak says—and you can hear the panic starting to build, you can tell he's getting flustered—'That is true. I was on a mountain. I have been many, many places. For life is a journey. We are all but travellers. Everybody hurts. Everybody heals. We must love every living creature.' And off they go, back on script, spouting platitudes. No one else caught the slip, but I did."

There was a long pause. "Don't you see, May? Don't you see what I'm getting at? Tupak Soiree is a computer hack. He developed some sort of master system. A program. One that allowed him to create the ultimate self-help book. He didn't need a million years; he only needed a million bytes. Or whatever the hell the correct term is. Don't you see? That's why he didn't want me to change one word. That's why it was so important not to alter the content whatsoever. It was a program, May. That's what produced the book. It wasn't cosmic enlightenment, it was a computer program."

"Edwin, the manuscript was hand-typed."

"Exactly! That's the genius of it. He probably *programmed* a computer to hand-type it! And the daisies? What a cornball touch. But perfect in retrospect. I mean, who would suspect a computer of putting little stickers of daisies on a title page? It's brilliant!"

"Edwin, I don't want you coming into my office any more. You take up far too much of my time and energy. You rant and rave about nothing. And worst of all, you don't bring me coffee."

"What?"

"You heard what I said. You don't bring me coffee anymore."

"You're quoting Neil Diamond now? This is bigger than coffee, May. Tupak Soiree claims to have unleashed paradise on earth. But I know better."

"And what if you're wrong, Edwin?" May rose to her feet, looked at him with a cold, hard stare. "What if Tupak *has* released heaven on earth? What then? What if we are living in hell right now? This city, this building, this office. Maybe hell is right here. Maybe the American Dream is simply Hell on Earth, an endless, ceaseless, pointless chase. Maybe we're trapped on a Merry-Go-Round from Hell, Edwin. Have you ever thought of that? Maybe Tupak Soiree is simply offering us a way to stop the ride and get off. Listen to me, Edwin. Tupak Soiree is *not* the Anti-Christ. Nor is he a demonic software developer. Nor is he an evil computer programmer. And neither is he a saint. He's just the latest flavour of the month. His message will soon start to fizzle, just like all the others before him. It's only a book, Edwin. And happiness can't be found in books. Trust me, I know. Now, maybe I'm wrong. Maybe Tupak Soiree has indeed achieved the impossible. Maybe he has 'unleashed paradise.' Well, I for one will not mourn the loss of sadness."

"Oh, yeah? Listen to this!" Edwin fumbled about. He unfolded a creased photocopied page and began to read from it: "'This is a panacea for all human woes. It is the secret of happiness, about which philosophers have disputed for so many ages, discovered at last.' The secret of happiness. Do you hear that, May? *The secret of happiness.*"

May was baffled. "So someone liked the book? So what? How is that a bad thing? What's wrong with producing a 'panacea for all human woes' or 'the secret of human happiness'?"

"Do you know where that quote was taken from? Do you know who wrote that? It was an Englishman named Thomas de Quincey. And he wasn't talking about *What I Learned on the Mountain*—he was talking about opium. It's from an 1821 book, *Confessions of an English Opium Eater*. The author ended up having his life destroyed by this 'heavenly panacea,' emotionally, physically, intellectually. Self-help is the opium of our age, May. And we have cornered the market. This isn't a publishing house. We aren't dealing in books, we're dealing in opium."

"Oh, for Chrissake, Edwin. Stop being so damn—"

"An opium den, May! That's what this world of ours is fast becoming. One big, vast opium den. An opium den of the mind, one that leaves you listless, lethargic—and full of bliss."

"Is it?" said May, and her voice now had an edge. "Or is it something better? Something bigger. Maybe what we are witnessing isn't a fad. Maybe it's the dawn of a new collective unity. The Javanese have a word, *tjotjog*, 'a unique and harmonious convergence of human affairs.' It describes those moments, ever so fleeting, when people fall in step with each other, when everything clicks, when society moves *together* instead of at cross-purposes. Collective harmony, when divergent goals and desires come together as one: *tjotjog*. Maybe that's what we are witnessing. Maybe that's what Tupak Soiree has achieved. An alignment of our collective compass points. Collective harmony."

"Oh, come on, May! That's ridiculous."

"And a 'vast opium den of the mind,' that's rational, is it?"

"May, listen to me—"

"I think I have had just about enough of this. I want you to leave."

"May, listen—"

"Now."

Chapter
Twenty-eight

"I don't know. I think he's dead."

"Dead?" Edwin was once again on the phone with Jack McGreary, Tupak Soiree's surly and relentlessly uncouth landlord. "*Dead?*"

"Haven't seen him in days. After his last appearance there on *Oprah*, he walked out into the desert, alone. No food. No water. I seen buzzards circling the sky yesterday; I figure Soiree must have kicked the bucket. And about friggin' time, too. I was getting sick of the guy."

"But—but I need to talk to him. I have some questions about the book. Are you sure? Dead?"

"Maybe. Maybe not. Who cares? I told you, the guy's a crackpot."

"You don't understand," said Edwin. "This is urgent. I have a bad feeling about what's happening. I'm afraid . . . I'm afraid this book of his might very well have set in motion a chain of events so horrible, so devastating, that—"

"Listen to you. You sound like you're talking about the end of the world or something."

"I am," said Edwin. I am. "Listen, if you run into Mr. Soiree, can you give him a message?"

Jack grumbled a sigh and said, "I suppose so. What do you want me to tell him?"

"Tell Mr. Soiree that I'm on to him."

The tobacco industry was the first to fall. It toppled like a huge redwood: impressive and magnificent, but dead on the inside. It was suffering from terminal dry rot, and it crashed to the forest floor as a harbinger of things to come. Cigarette consumption plummeted more than 70 per cent. Entire fortunes were ruined. The "one-time, self-correcting anomaly" reported in the *Times-Herald* became a headline and the headline became a panic and the panic became a stock-market stampede. Sell! Sell! Sell! Those tobacco executives who hadn't thrown themselves in front of trains, leaving oily, nicotine-scented stains on the tracks, simply . . . walked away. Across America, more and more high-powered business executives were wandering away from their posts, as though stricken with a form of contagious Alzheimer's. "Gone fishin'," the signs read. *Gone fishin'.*

Newsmagazines scrambled to get on top of the trend. Self-important neo-con columnists (not to name names, but one of them was George Will) began churning out pontificating essays on how, just as they had always predicted, America had become a tobacco-free nation virtually overnight, not because of government taxes or regulations, but because of pure, undiluted human willpower. The right wing insisted that these events supported its views on the sanctity of individual choice. The left wing (or rather, the middle wing, there being no real left wing in America) was just as adamant that years of government intervention had finally paid off—and in a most spectacular way. Everyone was taking credit for it.

Extra cleaning crews were employed to scrape up the nicotine splats left by plummeting tobacco executives, and the companies that made NO SMOKING signs went quickly bankrupt, but for the most part, the effects were not as widespread as many analysts had predicted. Or feared.

Then the alcohol and illicit-drug industries collapsed. Cocaine. Hashish. Acid. The demand dried up, as it did with less respectable consumer items. And the panic started anew. The newspapers now spoke of a "massive paradigm shift in spending habits," but even then media commentators did not connect the upheaval directly to Tupak Soiree's book. Instead, they spoke of *What I Learned on the Mountain* as "part" of the trend, not the cause. Some went so far as to say that the book had helped "spark" the sudden shift, had served as "a catalyst for change," but they were adamant that the conditions had been in place long before. (They were even now hastily scouring the archives, looking for evidence of past conditions.) Commentators began to speak of a New America, of a New World Order, of a New Consumerism.

And yet, even as the country was plunged into economic uncertainty—"a time of great adjustment lies ahead," said a solemn, frowny-faced President on the demise of the tobacco and alcohol industries—street crime began to fall. You could still buy booze, of course, and you could still kill the odd bystander with a handgun, but the trend was certainly downward—and steep. Junkies were given copies of Tupak Soiree's book. Alcoholics Anonymous went belly up. Drug-detox centres began to close.

"This is a sad, sad day," said a spokesman for one of the nation's largest chain of substance-abuse rehab centres. "We have been forced to shut down almost our entire operation due to a lack of clients. A dark day indeed."

It was only a matter of time before certain groups began to think: *revenge*.

Chapter
Twenty-nine

Edwin Vincent de Valu was propelling his wife's car along mainly through the power of profanity. He swore at and cursed the gutless little two-door hatchback even as he popped the clutch in and out, even as he jerked and stalled his way through the residential lanes of South Central Boulevard. Edwin had soon expanded his web of rancour and had taken to arbitrarily cursing pedestrians, pets, and even the occasional shrubbery. Edwin hated Jenni's car, just as surely as he hated Jenni's smug sense of satisfaction, just as surely as he hated her cat. It was too damn perky (the car, not the cat; the cat was a great, overfed, overgroomed lather of feline laziness). Jenni's little yellow car had no get-up-and-go. It just toddled along; it didn't *roar*. Edwin wanted a car that would roar. Everything about Jenni's car was silly, even the horn. Especially the horn. When punched upon by one's fist, the horn would emit a chirpy little "toot-toot" that didn't really capture the feelings you had when someone cut you off and you had to lay it on. "You son of a bitch! *Toot-toot*." It ruined the entire mood.

Not that there was a lot of traffic to tangle with. Quite the contrary. Usually a trip to the supermarket involved approximately six death threats, four near-fatal collisions and at least one threatened fist to the face. Today, the streets were calm. Road rage was nowhere in evidence. The birds were singing. The sun was shining. More and more people seemed to be walking, which was a shame, because when your wife sends you out to get fenugreek at 4:00 p.m. on a Sunday afternoon right when you are watching a perfectly good rerun of *Who's the Boss?*, well, hell, you *wanted* to fight your way through traffic, if only to justify your own petulant mood. But today the streets were as tranquil as a TV commercial. The sun was filtering through leaves; couples were strolling arm in arm along the sidewalks. Edwin pulled up in front of the Holistic Sunshine Happy Health Food Emporium (formerly: "Safeway"). There were no cars in the parking lot, but the store itself was packed. Everyone seemed to be taking their time, languidly shopping, slowly accepting their change, calmly leaving the store. It was absolutely annoying.

"Live! Love! Learn!" said the wispy-bearded clerk as Edwin stormed out with his bag of all-natural hand-picked fenugreek.

Outside, a car had pulled up alongside Edwin's and it sat with the motor running. "That's odd," said Edwin. "With the entire lot empty, why would they want to park right beside me?" Three men in silk suits got out and stood, arms crossed, as Edwin approached.

"Hey!" said Edwin. "You're leaning on my car."

Another man appeared, a smiling, sun-freckled yup dressed in tennis pastels with a sweater twisted in carefree perfection around his shoulders. "Well, hello there!" he said, stepping forward, his face full of grin. "Edwin de Valu, am I right? How the heck are you? Wonderful day, dontcha think? Makes you glad to be alive."

Edwin's Spidey sense was tingling. "Have we met?"

"The name's Jay, as in blue or O." A hand extended. Even the grip was cheery. "I'm what you would call a freelance problem-solver."

"Meaning?"

The man's smile hardened. "Meaning, I'm what you would call a freelance problem-solver." There was an uncomfortable pause as the man stared into Edwin's eyes. "But, hey, enough about me," said the freckled man. "Let's talk about *you*, shall we? Edwin de Valu. Married. No children. Works for Panderic Inc.—which is very hot right now. Lives at 668 South Central."

"What is this about? How do you know who I am?"

The smiling man with the freckled face and the sniper's eyes looked past Edwin to the parking lot behind him. "Listen, Ed—can I call you Ed? Why don't we go somewhere less public. Say, an abandoned warehouse down by the docks where no one can hear your plaintive cries for help." He gave Edwin a slap on the shoulder. "Don't worry, Edwin, I'm probably kidding." His voice dropped. "Now get in the fucking car."

They held the door open.

Edwin stepped back, but one of the hire-a-thugs had slipped behind him, and Edwin found himself backing into a giant slab of humanity, a refrigerator stuffed into a silk suit. The man put a hand on Edwin's shoulder, a heavy hand ripe with menace. "You're not going anywhere, my friend."

Edwin bolted. He ducked down, slipped under the pending embrace and ran, blindly, straight down a dead-end. *Damn!* The alleyway beside the health-food store ended in a chain-link fence. It was like the punchline of a particularly bad joke.

The men started down the alleyway towards him, silently, without hurry, as though the outcome were inevitable and they were simply playing out the scene.

"I warn you," said Edwin as they closed in, "I bruise very easily."

Chapter
Thirty

Edwin came to in darkness.

His face was hot and sweaty with his own breath; a heavy cloth bag had been pulled over his head, and he turned, this way and that, trying to shake it off. He couldn't, and the feeling was both claustrophobic and terror-inducing.

Footsteps. Murmured voices. A sudden tug at his neck, and the cloth sack was yanked away. Edwin blinked, squinting in confusion. Across from him, he could see a row of stark lights, and beyond that, figures in the shadows. He could smell and hear the sea. Packing crates were stacked high around him and—he struggled—his arms were tied behind his back. He tried to speak, but his throat was dry and raspy.

"Where am I?" he said.

There was a rumble of laughter on the other side. "See? I told you. That's always the first question. 'Where am I?' Remember when we whacked Coloné? Even as we were tying the cinder blocks to his chest and even as we were putting the plastic bag over his head, he kept saying, 'Where am I? Where am I?' Like it mattered." More laughter.

Out from the shadows, the freckle-faced man stepped forward. He had a look of abject and utterly insincere pity on his face. "Mr. de Valu, I must apologize for my somewhat stereotypical use of heavies. Person-ally, I prefer a more subtle approach, but these are desperate times. And it is getting so very hard to find good help. Especially with this whole 'niceness fad' going on. Cigarette?"

"I'm . . . I'm trying to quit."

"Good thinking. These things will kill you." The freckled man lit a cigarette, took one long, almost transcendental draw and then dropped it to the floor. He exhaled a calming cloud of blue death. And then, with the casualness of someone reaching for a pen, he slid a hand inside his jacket and retrieved the inevitable prop. He pressed the barrel against Edwin's temple.

"Tell me, Edwin. Are you a betting man?"

Edwin spoke and his voice was small. "No, not really. I play the Scratch-and-Win on occasion, but . . ." His voice trailed into nothingness.

The freckled man nodded. "Just as well. Because I would say the odds of you getting out of here alive and with all your limbs still attached are just about nil." He withdrew the gun, reholstered it and said, "You want that cigarette now?"

Edwin nodded, mute with despair.

The man placed the cigarette between Edwin's lips, almost tenderly, and struck a match with his thumbnail.

"You want I should loosen his ropes?" said a voice to one side.

"Edwin, I would like you to meet one of my junior associates: Sam 'the Snake' Serpent. He's young, he's hungry and he's the worst kind of lad there is: one with something to prove. So whatever you do, try not to piss him off."

Sam stepped up, a twitchy kid full of tics and false bravado. "You want I should kill him slow or fast, regular or extra crispy?"

The freckled man sighed. "Just undo the ropes for now, okay, Sam? We'll get to the logistics of killing him later. One thing at a time." He shook his head and gave Edwin a smile, as if to say, "Kids, eh?"

Once Sam had untied the ropes, Edwin rubbed his wrists and looked around, trying to get orientated. He could see other figures in the background, half-lit and cloaked in smoke. In front of them, in a semi-circle of chairs, sat four men, silent, faces backlit and lost in shadows.

The freckled man leaned down and spoke into Edwin's ear. He was so close that Edwin could smell the scent of tobacco and Brut. "Mr. de Valu, are you or are you not the shining star behind a book entitled *What I Learned on the Mountain*. Don't lie, because we already know the answer."

"I was the editor, yes. But that's all. Really, you should be accosting the author directly. I would be more than happy to give you directions to his house, maybe even draw a map. He lives in Paradise Flats, just outside of—no wait, he moved. He's building a compound near Boulder, somewhere up in the mountains. I'm sure he's the one you want to whack, not me."

"Unfortunately, Mr. Soiree has a fleet of trained bodyguards protecting him twenty-four hours a day. You"—and here the man laughed in spite of himself—"you drive a yellow Chevette."

"My wife's, actually."

"Mr. de Valu, that book of yours has caused certain people a great deal of financial harm. Cigarette sales have fallen. Alcohol consumption is down. Drug use has been shockingly reduced. Each one of these gentlemen before you has been personally hurt by your actions. Allow me to introduce them. From left to right: Mr. Davies from the Tobacco Institute, Mr. Brothman from the Liquor Commission, and Mr. Ortega from the Colombian Drug Cartel and Cultural Exchange Program."

"And the—the last gentleman?"

"Oh, that's Mr. Wentworth. He runs a chain of drug and alcohol rehabilitation centres. As you can imagine, he is as dependent upon the continued consumption of vice as anyone. Mr. de Valu, you have cost these gentlemen millions and millions of dollars in lost revenue."

"Is it too late to say, 'I'm really very terribly sorry?'"

Sam cut in. "*Hey!* Don't get smart with us. You have any idea who you're dealing with here? I'm Sam 'the Snake' Serpent. I'll eat your fuckin' heart."

There was a long and excruciating pause. Edwin squirmed; he knew he shouldn't say anything, but he couldn't help it. "Um, I know this isn't important, but it's just, it's the editor in me. If your last name is already

Serpent, why would you need the nickname Snake? I mean, it is kind of redundant, don't you think?"

When Edwin regained consciousness, he was lying on a tabletop, strapped down and looking up into a bright white bulb. "Where am I?" he asked.

"Mr. de Valu," said the freckled man. "If you do not start giving me some straight answers, Sam here will begin biting off your fingers one by one. And when that's done, Lewis will start in on your toes."

"Man," you could hear Lewis' voice off to one side. "How come I always get stuck with the toes?"

"Listen," said Edwin. "You've got to believe me. I don't have any influence at work. I'm absolutely insignificant. I'm just a meaningless cog in a much bigger machine. I can't stop the press runs, and I can't pull the book. The guy you want is Léon Mead. That's whose fingers you should be chewing off, not mine. Mr. Mead, he's the one in charge; he's the one making the decisions. And while you're at it, you might want to kidnap and terrorize a guy named Nigel as well. He's an editor like me, but he's got more seniority."

Sigh. "I find your attempts to incriminate your friends sad and appalling."

"So do I," said Edwin. "But you have to admit, it was worth a shot. Not literally, of course. Please. I'm sure we can come up with some sort of—"

"Time to say goodnight, Mr. de Valu."

"No, no, no, no, no, God, no." (Except that when Edwin said this, it was without commas, in one hysterical burst: *nonononoGodno!*) "Killing me won't solve anything! But if you let me live, I can turn things around. I know I can. I'll convince Mr. Mead to pull the book. We'll do a full recall, we'll pulp current shipments and stop future runs. I can turn this trend around, I swear I can. Listen, I'm not worth anything to you dead. But alive, and with a death threat hanging over my head, I can help you. I *will* help you. Please let me help you."

The freckled man interrupted the interrogation for a quick huddle with the tobacco and alcohol people. Edwin could hear murmured agreements, some assorted hemming and hawing, and then: "Mr. de

Valu, we are prepared to give you one week. That's it. You have one week to convince your Mr. Mead to stop future printings of that . . . that book. One week to rectify the situation. And be advised: we know where you live. We know your wife's name. We even know your cat's name."

"Oh, no. Not the cat. Not Mr. Muggins. Please, whatever you do, don't kill the cat—not even, you know, as a warning or just to scare me. No, please, don't kill the cat, although that certainly would send me a message and make me take you much more seriously. Not the cat, anything but the cat."

"Heh, heh, heh," said Sam. (Or words to that effect.)

Chapter
Thirty-one

"Edwin, what took you so long? You've been gone two whole days. Did you at least remember to get the fenugreek?"

Edwin staggered in, shell-shocked and still shaking. They had thrown him from a car somewhere just across the state line, and he had spent the last two days hitching rides and camping out in culverts.

Jenni looked him over. "What happened to you?"

"I was kidnapped, beaten, and then thrown from a moving vehicle."

"Oooh, sounds tough. Now, before I forget, Alice and Dave from next door are coming over for dinner. So scoot along and make yourself presentable before they get here."

Edwin stood there, marvelling at her lack of perception, marvelling at her ironclad resolve not to let anything ruffle the surface of her life. Marvelling at this person, this person he had married.

"Hun, did I mention that the mafia has a contract out on my life," he said. "Well, not the mafia *per se*. It's more of a cartel of tobacco, alcohol and drug-rehab directors. I have only one week left to live. They put me in the trunk of a car and they hit me on the head repeatedly with very hard objects and they took me across state lines."

"Ho-o-o-oney?" She was speaking in the tone one would take with an unusually slow child. "You told me that part already, remember? Now, then"—she turned a small pirouette, frowned at her bum in the hall mirror—"Do I look fat?"

Chapter
Thirty-two

If, on a certain stretch of a certain highway in a certain area of Bayou County, in the early hours of a moody Monday morning, you stopped and listened—really listened—you would have heard, beneath the sound of the bullfrogs and the sweep of the wind through the Shilo trees, a scratching. A faint, faint scratching. You might have missed it, so low was the sound. But if you walked in among the hanging vines and Spanish moss forests, if you pressed your ear to the wet peat, if you closed your eyes and listened, you would have heard, deep in the earth, the sound of scratching. Scraping.

No one knows who sent Dr. Alastar a copy of *What I Learned on the Mountain*; no one knows whether it was meant to be a mocking gesture or one that was genuinely sincere. But either way, it didn't work. Dr. Alastar (you may know him better as "Mr. Ethics") went into a wild rage. First, he threw the book against the wall of his prison cell. Then he picked up the book and threw it again. The next thing he did was kick it. Then he urinated upon it. And then he set it on fire. (Truth is, after he had peed on it, the book didn't light very well. He did manage to scorch the cover slightly, though.) And finally, in a grand and symbolic finale, the good doctor broke the spine and flushed the massive book down the toilet. Or rather, he attempted to. The book got wedged in halfway, and when the doctor tried to flush it through, the entire system backed up. This was not good, because it meant a guard had to come down with a mop and clean up the cell, and a plumber had to be called in to pull the piping out of the wall and then reinstall and reseal it.

This did not make the guard particularly happy, and the guard, being a somewhat inarticulate man, chose to express his displeasure with actions rather than words. He ground his sour soggy mop into Mr. Ethics' face. "Ha' you lack that?" asked the guard. "Ha' you lack it? Not so good, huh?"

That night, the poor doctor lay on his bunk, seething amid fantasies of vengeance and retribution, as the moon rose pale and blue across Bayou County. Tomorrow was Monday, which meant ten hours in a chain gang, followed by a program of macramé and assorted arts and crafts. Mr. Ethics hated jail. Hated the chain gangs. Hated the firehose showers. Hated the endless awareness sessions and the group-hug therapies. And as he lay there, deep in his own bile, raging at the way his life had turned out, he heard a small *plonk*—like the sound a banjo makes when you pluck it. Rolling over on his side, Mr. Ethics stared at the darkness until the details emerged. Under the pipes of his toilet, a drop of water was building—and then falling. *Plonk.*

Mr. Ethics crawled over, crouched down, and found the source of the leak. When he ran a finger around the seal where the pipe entered the wall, he found the putty still soft to the touch. He then checked the base of the toilet. Same thing. The sealant hadn't hardened, nor had the mortar around the replacement blocks. The plaster was as pliant as Camembert cheese. And Mr. Ethics began to laugh, softly, to himself. (As a later judicial investigation would reveal, the plumber brought in to fix the burst pipes and toilet had used the wrong type of sealing mix: it wasn't the quick-drying variety, but rather an older cheap plaster mixed with a rubber-based bond.)

Mr. Ethics is a small man, almost petite, but he is in no way a weak man. He put his back into it, and the entire toilet shifted. The water hose twisted but held. (Had it snapped, the ensuing flood might have alerted the guards when they sloshed through the puddle on their rounds. But no, for the first time in a long time, in a very long time, Mr. Ethics' luck held.) He scrambled back, stuffed his bed with lumps of clothes in case someone shone a light into his cell, and without further ado, he slipped in, under the skin of the building, and escaped.

He hugged himself to the piping, shimmying down and then across, through the intestinal network of the prison's sewer lines. Water flows downhill, Mr. Ethics reasoned, and eventually the prison's waste had to be pumped out into the swamp or perhaps a treatment facility. Sure enough, the pipeline he was following grew larger as it descended, as more and more lines branched into it. The only light came from the orange glow of control panels and the tiny reading lamp Mr. Ethics now held between his teeth. The warden had allowed him that: a single small lamp. The bulb was hard plastic and the light it emitted was meagre, but deep in the wet, dank tunnels below Filoxum Prison 901, it was a godsend, an angel's finger pointing the way.

And so it was that Dr. Robert Alastar (a.k.a. Mr. Ethics, a.k.a. three-time convicted felon) slithered and crawled and made his way to freedom. He had to dig out the last part by hand. (The pipes had disappeared into a sickly green brackish pool, and Mr. Ethics decided to go through the side instead.) The earth pulled away easily in great wet clods as he squirmed through and then pushed himself free, out into the pre-dawn darkness, like a calf being born in moonlight.

Sputtering and coughing, the doctor wiped the black dirt from his eyes and face. In the distance, he could hear the lapping of water, and he followed the sound down and waded in. In a primal baptism, as the sun washed peach across the sky, Mr. Ethics splashed the water up and over, up and over, washing the mud, washing the earth, washing the very prison from his skin.

"Well, well, well. If it ain't the good doctor himself."

Mr. Ethics stopped dead in the water. He spun around and saw, for the first time, that he wasn't alone. Someone was sitting on the bank, watching him. A fishing pole was wedged upright, the line lying languid across the bayou water.

"Bubba?" said Mr. Ethics.

It was one of the meanest guards the prison had ever produced, and he was looking at Mr. Ethics with a rock-steady gaze. "Now isn't this an interesting sight," said Bubba.

For a moment, for an awful gut-wrenching moment, Mr. Ethics stood, knee-deep in water, facing Bubba on the shore as he tried frantically to decide what to do. Obviously, he needed to kill Bubba, but how? The man was a trained prison guard twice his size. The tax auditors had been easy. Mr. Ethics had slapped them to death with their own attaché cases. And even then, his neighbours had chipped in to help him hide the bodies. "A tax auditor, you say? No problem. Let me get my spade."

With Bubba, it would be more difficult. Perhaps the doctor could wrestle the fishing pole away from the guard, use it as a javelin to impale him . . .

"So," said Mr. Ethics, buying time. "Any luck?"

"Naw. I'm just watchin' the fireflies jig and the catfish jump."

"Haven't seen you back at the prison for quite some time."

Bubba nodded. "True enough. Don't rightly work there any more. One day, I just up and decided to go fishin'."

"Yes, I can see that."

"No, not *fishing*. But fishin'. Inside here." He tapped his chest. "Fishin' in my heart."

"I see. Well, it was very nice talking with you. I think I'll be on my way now. I was paroled, you see, just recently."

"Is that a fact?" said Bubba. "Because I saw you come out of that hole in the riverbank over there. It sure didn't look like early parole to me. If I didn't know better, I'd say you were trying to escape."

"No, no. Not escaping, Bubba. I was just—you know, taking a break. Gone fishin'."

Bubba nodded thoughtfully. Toyed with the line awhile. "Doc, will you promise me something?"

"Anything."

"Will you promise me that once you've had your time out, once you've realigned the ball bearings of your life, you'll go back to prison? You'll turn yourself in. Will you promise me that? Will you give me your word?"

"Sure. No problem."

"That the truth?"

"Hey, would I lie to you? Come on, I'm Mr. Ethics."

A big grin from Bubba. "Trust is what we give, not what we earn. Page 47. And that's the truth, it surely is. Truth with a capital 'T'. Say there, you need some cash? Or a ride someplace?"

Mr. Ethics hesitated, wondering how far to push his luck. "I could use some money and a ride into town. And maybe a change of clothing."

"Sure thing," said Bubba. "I'll go an' get my truck. And you know, I am sorry about all the full-cavity body searches and random brutality. Hope there's no hard feelings."

"Hey," said Mr. Ethics, quoting Spinoza or perhaps Aquinas, "it's water under the bridge."

"So where you headin', anyway?" asked Bubba as they walked up the riverbank.

"Oh, let's just say I have a rendezvous," said Mr. Ethics. A rendezvous on Grand Avenue—with a certain publisher at a certain office at a certain company that had left Mr. Ethics out to dry. Vengeance was at hand.

Chapter
Thirty-three

It turns out Edwin was a gambling man after all. He just wasn't a very astute gambling man. Evidence of this lay in the way he had pinned his every hope on what the people in marketing were saying. Indeed, he was betting his very life on the wisdom emanating from marketing, which only underlines just how desperate he had become. (In terms of reliability, marketing is only slightly above the study of chicken entrails.) Edwin had one week to live, unless he could convince Mr. Mead to pull the book. Which he couldn't. It was too late for that. Panderic had already licensed more than a dozen spinoff titles and copycat projects. (Mr. Soiree, oddly enough, showed a distinct, and to Edwin's mind suspicious, lack of interest in writing any more of the books himself. "Oh, goodness no. Let the radiant words of other journey-questers fill the great vision. Let other authors carry the crusade forward. I'll still be getting 15 per cent on sales, right? And that's list price gross revenue, correct?")

What I Learned on the Mountain had spawned an entire self-perpetuating industry. It was like some sort of mythical beast, a thousand-headed monster impossible to slay. But if Edwin could go to Mr. Serpent and the others armed with impressive charts and complex sales figures, if he could convince them that *What I Learned on the Mountain* had peaked and was in fact already on its way down, he might yet walk away with his life and most of his limbs intact. Edwin would have to sell his would-be killers on this view. "The trend is already waning, gentlemen. The fad has passed. Happy days are here again!" It would be the sales pitch of Edwin's life. And it would all come down to what the people in marketing were telling him.

It began with an offhand comment made in the cafeteria ("This Tupak Soiree book has got to peak sometime!"), and soon became a working assumption ("Word is, the Soiree book is going to peak any day now"), before finally hardening into the presumptive authoritative ("The sales for *What I Learned on the Mountain* have peaked. Definitely").

The only thing that was needed was a formal report with lots of pie graphs and a heart-monitor chart showing sales poised to plummet. Marketing was working on that right now, and Edwin took a moment, cleared his mind, and said to himself, "I might just pull this off." He was already rehearsing the pitch he would give to Mr. Serpent and the others when they next abducted him: "Gentlemen, if you will turn your attention to the chart on the overhead screen . . ." (He made a mental note: "Make sure an overhead screen is on hand for the presentation.")

But then everything started to unravel.

The problem began, as so many things do, with a single small tweak: a twist in your consciousness, an apparently minor, apparently inconsequential detail that almost goes unnoticed, but once focused upon, suddenly looms up in all its horrible ramifications. With Edwin, it began when he happened to come home exhausted (again), and had kicked the cat (again, Mr. Muggins having somehow eluded entire platoons of Cosa Nostra hitmen), and had downed a beer (again), and had stumbled into the living room to be met (again) by his wife's usual welcome-home greeting—namely, "Do I look fat?"

"No," he sighed. "You look fine."

Then, just as he was about to trudge off to the shower, the full, terrifying consequences of her statement hit him. He turned. "Why would you ask me that? Why would you possibly ask me that?" His voice was rife with panic.

Jenni blinked at him. "What are you talking about, grumpy face?" She tried her usual crinkle-nose, melt-your-heart pout, but this time it didn't work.

"Jenni, why would you keep asking me if you look fat? Why? You've read Tupak Soiree's book. You've read the section about self-actualizing and accepting one's appearance as an affirmation of self. Of living *within* your body, not against it. You've read about how you should find the weight that is healthy and comfortable for you, not one that society dictates. Now for Chrissake, Jenni, why would you ask me that question?! Why would you possibly care if you look fat? *Answer me!*" Edwin was screaming at this point. He knew full well what the answer was, and could see how awful and far-reaching the impact.

"Edwin," she said, "calm down. I just haven't got to that part of the book yet. I've been meaning to, but I haven't. I read the section on Li Bok first, and the part about organizing your daytimer. And I tried those turnip-stew recipes, but I haven't got to the part about dieting or weight loss or anything. I've been meaning to, I just haven't had any spare time."

"Spare time? *Spare time?* You're a telecommuter, for God's sake. All you have is spare time! You get paid for doing nothing!"

"I was going to take tomorrow off. I was going to finish the book then. I don't see why you're getting so upset."

Edwin stumbled into the hallway, could feel a cold sweat break out. "Procrastinators," he said. "I never factored in procrastinators. I'm dead. I'm a dead man. They will kill me and chop me up and feed me to the fishies, or whatever it is they do now. It's over. It's all over. I'm a dead man."

He repeated that phrase again and again, part mantra, part lament: "I'm a dead man. A dead man."

"Will you quit saying that?" Jenni was leaning in the hall entrance, watching her crestfallen husband. "You're ruining my mood."

"May," he said. "I have to talk to May."

Edwin ran from the house like a man fleeing a burning building. He ran seven blocks, all the way to the Devonian Hotel, where a line of taxis lay in wait. Edwin leapt into the first cab, shouted out May's address and said, "Make it quick!"

"Ah." The driver turned, smiling like a saint. "The flow of time is nei-ther helped nor hindered by our own desires. It exists independently, yet envelops us in its warmth."

Edwin's eyes shot up, wild and filled with hate. "You've been reading Tupak Soiree."

"That I have." And the taxi driver held up the book, with its nauseat-ingly familiar cover, with its cheesy two-tone colour and unimaginative Verdana font caps, and he beamed rays of banality at Edwin. "I am almost halfway through. Such an eye-opener."

"You listen to me," said Edwin. "If you don't want me to shove that book down your throat, you'll stop spouting quotations and put your goddamn foot on the goddamn pedal."

"Out of my cab."

"What? You can't do that."

"Out of my cab. Anyone who insults the words of Tupak Soiree has no place in my cab. Now out, *out!*"

Edwin eventually found a cab driver who hadn't read the book ("I've been meaning to, but I just haven't found the time"), and he arrived at the door of May's apartment building after dusk. He buzzed and buzzed, holding the button down with a force far stronger than necessary.

May had been making tea, and the kettle was just starting to whistle when Edwin barged in, arms waving, gestures flying every which way. "It's worse than we ever imagined! Much worse."

"Edwin, you can't just show up like this," said May, cradling her cat in her arms, a warm purring hot water bottle covered in fur. "I might have been with someone."

"But you're not."

"Yes, but I could have been."

There was an awkward pause. He had just assumed she would be alone. And she was. *Sola et casta.* Alone and chaste.

"Edwin," she said, "I have a lot of work to catch up on." She gestured to an unfinished crossword and an open TV guide on the table. "So I think you should go."

"May, listen to me. We are on the brink of destruction. The very brink. It's like a roller coaster poised at the top of a suicide drop. If we don't derail this, we're going to be in a lot of trouble. Do you hear me? A lot of trouble!"

The kettle was shrieking at this point, and so, basically, was Edwin. May plunked a tea bag in her cup, filled it with hot, sputtering water and turned a harsh expression on her unwanted guest. "Did you need a cup of tea as well?"

"What? Sure. If you're making some anyway."

"Good. There's a coffee shop on the corner. Why don't you go have a cup there and talk to yourself like the crazy street person you're becoming—and leave me out of this."

"Procrastinators, May. I forgot about procrastinators. Don't you see? All those people out there who have purchased the book or were given it as a gift and still haven't got around to reading it. Think of the millions of people who have that book sitting on their shelves. It's a time bomb, May! A ticking time bomb set to go off at any moment. The upheaval we've seen so far—the tobacco industry, the collapse of the liquor companies—that's nothing, May. That's just the first wave. We have almost ten million copies in print, and that's only the first wave. The worst is yet to come."

"Edwin, what part of 'fuck off' don't you understand?"

"May, everything is about to collapse around us. Everything. I'm talking society, country, economy. It's the end of life as we know it. And why? Because of Tupak Soiree and his computer-generated formula for human happiness. You said, 'So people become happy. What's the harm in that?' May, our entire economy is built on human weaknesses, on bad habits and insecurities. Fashion. Fast food. Sports cars. Techno-gadgets. Sex toys. Diet centres. Hair clubs for men. Personal ads. Fringe religious sects. Professional sports teams—there's vicarious living for you! Hair salons. Male mid-life crises. Shopping binges. Our entire way of life is built on self-doubt and dissatisfaction. Think what would happen if people were ever really, truly happy. Truly *satisfied* with their lives. It would be cataclysmic. The entire country would grind to a halt—and if America goes, you don't think the rest of the Western World will follow? We're talking about a global domino effect. The end of history."

"So Fukuyama was right," said May. "So? I have other things to worry about."

"Like what?" sputtered Edwin. "What could possibly be more important than this?"

"Well, getting a crazed former lover out of my apartment for one."

This stopped Edwin even as he was building up steam for another rant. "Former?" he said.

"Do I have to call the police? Do I have to get a restraining order? Do I have to—"

And he kissed her, hard on the lips, like you would in a movie, like you would when the music swells in the background and the waves break along a pristine shore in a pristine world. He kissed her, hard and long, and then stepped back like Errol Flynn to smoulder awhile in her eyes.

"Get out," said May. "*Right now!* And if you ever try that again, I'll have you arrested."

"But, but—"

"You heard me!"

So much for the movies.

"We spend our lives constructing elaborate mansions made of cards—and then spend the rest of our lives waiting for someone to bump the table. *Hoping* for someone to bump the table. We dress for yesterday's weather. We hold our breath. We confuse our memories with who we are . . ."

May Weatherhill was sitting alone by lamplight, reading from the book in a stage whisper to an empty room.

"A poet once wrote, 'If equal affection cannot be, let the more loving one be me.' Ah, but I say to you, that poet was a fool. There is no 'more,' no 'less,' when it comes to items of the heart. There is only need, desire, and heartache. Why do we choose the wrong person, again and again and again? Why do we *choose* to choose the wrong heart to hold? Is it because we are secretly in love with our own sadness, secretly in love with our own mistakes? I give you *bliss*. Not passion, which sparkles and sears, but bliss. Pure bliss. The bliss of eternity."

May peered into her mirror, saw herself for the first time, the first time ever, and she felt the layers of illusion slowly separate and drift apart.

Something shifted. Something just beneath the surface, like a vein under skin.

Chapter
Thirty-four

The diet centres and bodybuilding gyms were the next to go, followed closely by the home-exercise market and miracle baldness cures. Overnight, commercials for "ab crunchers" and "thigh busters" and "butt masters" vanished from the television screens of the nation, unmourned and unmarked. Bald men, having taken Tupak Soiree's advice to heart ("It is not enough to accept one's baldness, one must *embrace* one's baldness"), stopped rubbing placebo potions into their scalps, stopped combing long mutant strands of hair over their bald pates, stopped fluffing and moussing and fretting and trying to deny their male pattern baldness. And they stopped more or less en masse. Sales for *What I Learned on the Mountain* topped 45 million, with no end in sight. It went beyond fad, or even phenomenon. It was a firestorm, an earthquake, a typhoon that levelled entire industries overnight. And very few were spared.

The fast-food industry took a body hit. Once people had learned to separate their childhood need for love from the instant oral gratification of processed cheese and all-"beef" patties (heavy editorial quotations on the word "beef"), sales plunged. Across America, McDonalds and KFC outlets began to close. Some franchises, those quick on their feet, switched to all-natural salad bars and vegetarian soy-and-tofu pitas and managed to stay afloat. Most did not.

Oddly enough, Americans did not suddenly lose vast amounts of weight. Far from it. Instead, the very *notion* of what was attractive and what was not became—in the words of Tupak Soiree—"realigned." Because Soiree's book sought to shift one's fundamental identity, it managed to change the value structures that underpinned people's personalities. *What I Learned on the Mountain* focused on the habits, insecurities, shortcomings and frailties of people not as problems in their own right, but rather as symptoms of something deeper: a self-image and self-esteem that was out of tune with its surroundings. It was, again in Tupak Soiree's words, "a bottom-up approach." Once you had learned, through creative imaging and other pseudo-hypnotic techniques, to "reset" the foundation of your personality, everything else fell into place.

The obese lost weight, true. But most people simply adapted their thought processes and underlying assumptions to fit their bodies— rather than the other way around. Tupak Soiree had turned the entire process upside down. People no longer felt estranged from their bodies. They felt connected. For the first time, possibly ever, Americans began to feel comfortable with who they were. Cosmetics went unsold; department stores stood half-deserted. Expensive perfumes were marked down and sat gathering dust. *GQ* magazine switched its emphasis from men's fashion to articles on "fostering happiness." Dour Calvin Klein models stood on street corners, holding up signs: "Will pout for food."

By now, the momentum was clearly on Tupak Soiree's side. The upwardly mobile urban class was the first to be swept under (theirs was an entire lifestyle built on fads, and once those fads were stripped away, there was no anchor left holding them in place). Ironically, because of the slowness of book distribution, the outlying rural areas held out the longest. Hundreds of small towns continued on, only vaguely aware of the huge upheaval that was consuming the cities. The more trendy and cutting-edge the city, the quicker it fell. Seattle went down almost immediately. Toledo chugged along with only minor disruptions—at first.

Fashion died without a fight. People started letting themselves go. Or, more accurately, they started letting go of themselves. The newspapers—those that were still operating—called it the "whatever style," but in truth it wasn't a style at all. It was the opposite of style. People simply wore whatever they happened to have in their closets, whatever they happened to grab. Any colour, any fabric, any time, anywhere. It was casual day every day of the week. It was a sloppy, sitting-around-the-house-on-a-Sunday-afternoon approach to clothing.

The centre of fashion now shifted from the cities to the smaller outlying regions. Towns like Upper Rubber Boot, North Dakota, and Hog River, Idaho, were now the fashion meccas of America. If you wanted to see men in matching socks or women with makeup and hairspray, that was where you had to go. These small backwater towns were now the last proud bastions of the American self-preening instinct.

The book-buying public is a very small segment of any society. But it is a highly influential segment, and that was the key to the disaster. This class of people, what author Robertson Davies called the *clerisy*, comprised those who read books for pleasure. Not the professional critics or the scholars or the students who read because they have to, but rather, the people who read books as an end in itself. The true readers. The clerisy is the crucial element in any societal shift, and this is something every successful despot knows. The notion of the rabble-rousing mob of peasants overturning the social order is a myth; real revolutions begin with the clerisy. It is only after the old order has started to crumble that the mobs show up, pitchforks in hand, ready to take credit. The "angry mob" is a reactive entity, in every sense of the word. No, it is the people who read books who instigate the changes in society—for better or for worse. And by hitting first among that very class, by taking the clerisy by storm, *What I Learned on the Mountain* had struck at the very heart of society. Or, more accurately, the head.

But that was only the beginning.

Panderic had unleashed an entire flood of Tupak Soiree–related items: comic books, motivational one-quote-a-day notepads, inspirational calenders, audiobooks. The message was now reaching an entirely new, non-literate audience. There were radio broadcasts, public readings, "share groups," learning circles, television specials, cyberspace multimedia editions.

"Dear God," said Edwin, as the full scope of the disaster became clear. "It's gone airborne."

At this point, there was no way to stop it, even if you wanted to. There was no way to get the genie back in the bottle, the toothpaste back in the tube. There was no way to kill the beast, no way to weed the Triffids from the garden. *What I Learned on the Mountain*—and its innumerable, insidious offshoots—had wormed its tendrils into every aspect of America. The nation now reminded Edwin of a grand mansion, a once proud exemplar of human vanity and conspicuous consumption, now overrun with vines that were slowly choking it to death.

America had become—or was in the process of becoming—a Very Happy Land. The Valium of Nations. And no corner of the country was safe. Not even Panderic Press itself . . .

Chapter
Thirty-five

"Nigel, where the hell is your leash—I mean, your necktie? You know full well that we have a dress code." It was Mr. Mead, and he looked very annoyed.

They were having their usual Monday morning meeting—the last such meeting of Edwin's life, as it turned out—and Nigel Simms had shown up dressed in a sun-faded grey tank top and a pair of lime green sweatpants.

The meeting room was eerie and nearly empty. May had taken the day off, had said she wanted to be alone, and most of the other staff had long since deserted. Paul in marketing was the first to hang up a "Gone fishin'" sign, but he wasn't the last. Panderic was now operating with a skeleton crew; so thin had the staff grown that Irwin the Intern had been hastily promoted to the head of the sci-fi department, where he quickly approved a futuristic novel entitled *I Am Adam, You Are Eve* (which sort of gave away the ending, you know?).

Not that it mattered. Sales were in free fall right across the board. Entire genres had died, suddenly and without so much as a single death-rattle gasp. Romance ended along with diet centres and makeover clinics.

(Like diets, fashion trends and liposuction, romance—the very concept of romance—relied on unrequited yearning. It was just such a yearning that was now melting away.) Business empowerment books went unsold. Adventure travel was barely hanging on. Cookbooks were sporadic.

And sports books? The fantasy life of fans (mainly male) no longer needed to be fulfilled by overpaid professional athletes playing children's games on astroturf. Sports books were remaindered by the truckload. Pro teams across the country were struggling to stay alive, and the drop in attendance was reflected in the dismal sales of such weighty tomes as *Football Greats* and *Golf Heroes* and *Lawn Bowling Legends*. Mind you, sports activities themselves were up across the country, but not pro sports and not organized leagues. It was local neighbourhood toss-the-ball-around Norman Rockwell–type pleasures that were now being played. Games without rules. Games without structure. Pointless. Non-confrontational. The mouth-frothing sports fanatic, obsessed with statistics and overcompensating for his own shortcomings, was now all but extinct. Faltering teams were forced to slash budgets, and one after another they collapsed into bankruptcy. Like the pro leagues themselves, the once-lucrative genre of sports-writing was now on the brink of death. Euthanasia was just a matter of time.

Gardening books, however, were up. As were celebrity biographies, but only those of the "Tupak Soiree variety," wherein former adulation junkies recounted in mindless joy how their careers as self-important movie stars had been hollow and empty—until they "discovered" the Soiree prescription for happiness. These books weren't so much biographies as they were testimonials, and as such, they were just a small part of the wider Tupak Soiree juggernaut. Panderic Inc. was raking in the profits, but virtually every cent of income was related, either directly or indirectly, to *What I Learned on the Mountain*.

Even Mr. Mead's overhyped fried-pork cookbook had been cleverly retitled *Eat Pork and Be Happy! The Tupak Soiree Way*. Panderic had been transformed into a Tupak Soiree conveyor belt, repackaging various "insights" and "cosmic principles" into handy consumer-sized bites. More than one disgruntled competitor had muttered that they should change the name of the company to Tupak Books. And there was both truth and a sting to that claim.

The merchandising rights for *What I Learned on the Mountain* alone brought in more money than had Panderic's entire textbook line. British rights to Tupak Soiree's book had been purchased, and sales were already climbing across the UK. The Canadians (French and English alike) were flocking to the Tupak Soiree message, and translated versions were rolling off the presses in German, French, Italian and Spanish, with the Japanese, Mandarin and Korean versions already in the works. Even the Australians were on board.

The process wasn't without its problems, however; some of the translators tended to wander off halfway, leaving behind cryptic multilingual messages that basically amounted to "Gone fishin'" and "Capture your bliss." Panderic went through four different Parisian translators in a row before the French-language version was finally completed. Still, the sale of foreign rights for *What I Learned on the Mountain* had been a huge bonanza, a financial windfall of unprecedented scope. The money was flooding in from every side. Panderic's bean-counters could barely keep up.

In light of this, one would have supposed that Mr. Mead was now a very, very happy man. But he wasn't. If anything, he seemed more surly and more sour than ever, even as fresh, new, glowing sales reports came pouring in.

And what are we to make of Edwin, sitting there at the conference table, a certain half smile on his face, a certain wry, sardonic look in his eye? Why does he seem so self-contained? Shouldn't he be perspiring profusely and squirming in his seat? Shouldn't he at least be fidgeting on this, the last day of his life?

The freckle-faced sociopath had given Edwin until tomorrow to turn things around, and not only had Edwin not succeeded (or even made a token effort), but sales for *What I Learned on the Mountain* had in fact continued to shoot upward at an ever-increasing, ever-alarming exponential rate. Marketing (here's a surprise) had been completely wrong in its predictions. *What I Learned on the Mountain* hadn't even begun to peak. The books were now rolling directly off conveyor belts and into booksellers' waiting vans. This was only the tip of the iceberg. And a very large iceberg it was, one lying in wait as the USS *Economy* plowed straight ahead, full throttle, band blithely playing even as disaster loomed.

So again, why is Edwin de Valu smiling? Why is he watching this meeting—the last such meeting he will ever attend—with such benign bemusement? Is it perhaps because, like the condemned man that he is, Edwin has finally made peace with his fate? Has he, like a character in a Camus novel, learned to accept "the benign indifference of the universe"? Has he prepared himself to face death bravely? No. Not our Edwin. Quite the contrary. Edwin is more determined than ever to be the master of his own destiny. Why is he smiling? He is smiling because he knows something. He knows something that no one, not Mr. Mead or Snake or Nigel or anyone else, is aware of. This morning, on his desk when he dragged himself despondently into work, there was an envelope waiting. And inside this envelope was a notice. A simple, succinct notice informing Edwin that the United States Treasury was about to release past funds with full interest. In spite of several judiciary hearings, the Treasury had been unable to detect any crime. The money was rightfully his. And in the wake of a recommendation by a non-partisan panel of three judges, Edwin de Valu's lost fortune was about to be returned to him.

As of 8:00 a.m., Tuesday morning, Edwin would be a millionaire. True, the recent surge in inflation as the market fluctuated sharply on "shifting consumer purchasing patterns" had reduced the real amount by almost 30 per cent in just under a month, but it was still more than enough. More than enough to escape. More than enough to set himself up somewhere far away with a new name and a new identity. More than enough to send for May (once he had moved his money out of the country, had carefully erased his tracks, had shredded the paper trail, burnt the bridges, wiped the slate clean).

That is why Edwin de Valu is smiling. That is why he doesn't fidget, doesn't squirm. His thoughts are elsewhere; his mind is floating free as he conjures up images of a reunion with May on a long white beach beneath a polished blue sky. Freedom beckoned.

Mr. Mead, however, was not quite as befogged with daydreams as Edwin. For a man who was now at the head of the single most successful publishing venture in American history, he looked downright cranky. And lacking any real target or valid reason, he had now focused his ogre-like wrath on Nigel. Nigel, with his ratty grey tank top and his lime green sweats. To Mr. Mead, this was an affront: a senior editor in the country's number-one publishing firm dressed in such a dishevelled, haphazard manner—and lacking even the courtesy of a necktie.

"I'm waiting," said Mr. Mead. "Are you going to explain yourself?"

Nigel smiled, a gentle, airy smile. "Clothes are only a thin veil, Mr. Mead. In life, we must learn to see past the veils."

"Veil or no veil, I don't give a damn. Company policy requires a necktie. So unless you've got one tied around your dick—"

Edwin came out of his puff-pastry fantasy world just about then and looked across at his old nemesis. It was unnerving. Nigel's eyes, they were . . . *devoid*. That was the only word Edwin could come up with. Devoid of anger, devoid of rancour, devoid of cunning. Devoid of personality. It was the same bland happiness he had seen reflected in Rory the Janitor's eyes. The same blank, benevolent stare he had seen out on the street, again and again. It made him think of *Anna Karenina*, and it put a revealing twist on Tolstoy's original insight. Unhappy people are unhappy in their own way, thought Edwin. Happy people are happy in the same way.

Nigel was one of the Happy People. And it wasn't a mere transitory moment of joy in an otherwise unpredictably chaotic world. No. Nigel's was a deep, existential happiness. It was a calming of the storm at the very centre of one's soul.

Nigel Simms was gone. He had vanished like the Cheshire cat, leaving only a trace behind. Nigel was gone. And a gentle, generic shell had been left in his wake. Normally, Nigel's downfall would have elicited from Edwin delicious feelings of *Schadenfreude*, but Nigel, now lifeless and brimming with bliss, didn't evoke in Edwin any such response. If anything, Edwin felt a certain anti-*Schadenfreude*: "a feeling of sadness one experiences over another's happiness."

"Nigel? I asked you a question." It was Mr. Mead, and his patience was wearing thin. "As long as you work for me, and as long as you work at Panderic, there are certain specific codes of conduct to which we ascribe. Now, if you think—"

"Oh," said Nigel, with that same disarming, placid smile, "I don't work here any more, Mr. Mead. I'm going away. Far away."

And in that moment, Edwin saw in Nigel the very downfall of Western Civilization. When one thought about the many varied products and cultural influences that Nigel both reflected and epitomized: the hair gel, the teeth whitener, the electric nose-hair clips, the alchemist's approach to cologne, the tailor-made suits, the eyebrow pluckings, the shaving lather, the skin moisturizers, the manicures, the fashion magazines—the complex, cross-referenced multi-layered lifestyle. Entire industries depended upon Nigel for their survival. To see him go from *GQ* to this, to see him transformed into a smile and a vacant stare, to see his once sleek presence reduced to a tank top and a pair of old sweatpants . . . well, it was nothing short of tragic. Because if you went past the standard complaints about modern consumerism and amoral advertising and the packaging of identity, etc., etc., if you took that away, you would have seen in Nigel Simms an eternal human desire. A striving. A futile (but vital) quest for self-actualization; a yearning to be something more, something bigger, richer, faster, better-looking. It was the Great Chimera of Self-Perfection, which, while never attained, had nonetheless fuelled mankind for thousands of years.

Far from being a Gen-X prat with a weakness for trends and grooming, Nigel represented a fallen hero, a figure from Greek mythology. Prometheus of the present day.

Even Edwin was sorry to see him go. "Nigel, listen. About the incident with the necktie and the pencil sharpener—"

Nigel held up his palm in a small fluid motion, like a Buddhist monk preparing to stop traffic, and said with a soothing voice: "Yesterday's weather, Edwin. Do not worry about the necktie. There is no need to apologize."

"Apologize?" said Edwin. "You still owe me 140 bucks. Isn't that right, Mr. Mead?"

"Yes," said Mr. Mead. "You're right. Nigel still owes you for that. Not to worry, Edwin, I'll make sure that amount is deducted from Nigel's paycheque—from Nigel's *final* paycheque."

"Thank you," said Edwin. "I appreciate that." And he smirked at Nigel, hoping to provoke some sort of reaction, or at least some sort of inkling that the old Nigel lay lurking just beneath the surface. But there was no inkling, and there was no reaction. It wasn't Nigel; it was an automaton standing before them. A happy automaton, to be sure, but an automaton, nonetheless.

Nigel slowly gathered up his papers with that same Bodhisattva energy, looked around the near-empty conference room at the scattering of people in attendance, touched his heart, wafted his feelings outwards, and then looked at Edwin and said: "How about I give you a hug?"

"How about I throw you down an elevator shaft?" said Edwin, but the fun was gone. It was like trying to spar with a puppy—an especially warm and fuzzy puppy.

Nigel turned and quietly left the room. There was a long, sad silence in his wake.

"To hell with him," said Mr. Mead. "We're better off without him." And the meeting resumed in a shuffle of papers and subdued round-table discussions.

Edwin never saw Nigel again.

Chapter
Thirty-six

After the morning meeting had finally petered out, amid long awkward silences and continued complaints from Mr. Mead about the poor turnout and lack of fresh ideas, Edwin went back to his desk to clear out the last of his belongings. He hadn't told Mr. Mead that he was quitting—he didn't want to telegraph his intentions to anyone—and as he looked around the small cell-like cubicle in which he had worked and schemed and seethed for more than four years, he felt a twinge, ever so faint, of melancholy. There was very little worth keeping: Edwin had posted no pictures, had hung no potted plants, had gathered no personal mementoes about him. He found the Workers' Appreciation Day silver Zippo lighter that Mr. Mead had given to everyone the year before. (When Edwin had taken it to a dealer to be appraised, he had discovered that the lighters were Hong Kong fakes, and not even good fakes at that. But, hey, they still worked.) Edwin pocketed the faux Zippo, looked once more across his cubicle and sighed. He grabbed a stapler and a couple of ballpoint pens—on principle more than anything, departing theft being something of a corporate tradition—and he left. The halls echoed with his footsteps. And his footsteps echoed into silence.

Edwin left 813 Grand Avenue and started towards the nearest Loop station, but he stopped short. He cocked his head, and he listened. It was something he had never heard on Grand Avenue before: silence. Traffic still flowed, taxis still moved in yellow-line processions, and fleets of pedestrians, their numbers vastly diminished, still crossed intersections on stoplight command. But there were fewer cars than before, less raw kinetic energy, less frantic motion. No one was swearing, no car horns were blaring, and the once-permanent white noise was gone. It had echoed itself away, had dissolved into mist and floated upwards into the ether. Grand Avenue was now subdued, and the silence was warm and cocooning, like a flannel embrace. Like a silk-lined coffin.

Edwin felt nauseous. If nothing else, he was grateful—grateful that he was about to escape, grateful to be leaving. Edwin used to loathe the ordeal of Grand Avenue, but now he mourned its passing. Even the graffiti had changed. Instead of gang tags and incoherent rage, there were quotes from Tupak Soiree spray-painted on storefronts: *Live! Love! Learn! . . . Capture your bliss.*

"I don't belong in this world," said Edwin.

It was time to take flight. Time to cash in his money, set up an offshore account and change his identity. Time to flee. Edwin was no cad; he would leave enough money behind so that Jenni would be able to live comfortably. He would even write a heartfelt note explaining why he had to go. (Anything but "Gone fishin'.") Edwin would then set up a new life in a new land, far away. And he would send a message to May. He would find someplace where Tupak Soiree had not yet penetrated, someplace where people still cursed, still complained, still worried and still laughed—laughed not from the heart, but from the belly. Someplace where people still tried, still failed, still tried again. Someplace, over the rainbow, where people fought, fucked, drank and smoked with a reckless human abandon. It would be like one of Irwin's bad sci-fi books. He would turn, say, "My name is Edwin." She would say, "My name is May, and if you try to kiss me again I'll have you arrested."

Edwin walked down the now serene sidewalks of Grand Avenue, feeling like Charlton Heston in *The Omega Man*: alone, awake, alive.

Louie's Hot Dog and Pickle Stand no longer offered hot dogs or pickles—or caffe latte mochaccinos either. Louie (a.k.a. Thad) now ran a hug-therapy stand. For twenty-five cents and a smile, Louie would step out and give you a big ol' hug. And Louie's hugs were in high demand. People were lined up down the street, quarters in hand. "There's another hug-and-hot-dog stand a couple of blocks down," Edwin heard someone say. "But I prefer Louie's. He gives the best hugs ever!"

In the end, Edwin eschewed the subway entirely and decided to wander up to O'Callaghan's for a drink instead. But the pub was closed. Of course. A handmade sign hung on the front door, and on it—Ah, but you already know what was written, don't you?

"Shit," said Edwin to no one in particular.

O'Malley's was closed as well. O'Shannon's was being converted into a volunteer drop-in centre. And O'Toole's had a notice out front advertising "healing clinics and happiness therapy—the Tupak Soiree way!" So up past the statue of Gerald P. Gerald, the father of the Great Potash Boom of 1928, and down along the edge of Park Royale, Edwin wandered aimlessly: a man overtaken by events, a man no longer in step with the world around him. He tried one bar after another, but no salvation was to be had.

"A bar?" said one girl when he pounded on the door. "Gosh, no. We sell macrobiotic organic health fibres now."

Edwin looked at this pert, pleasant girl, and he recognized instantly the glassy stare and ingratiating smile. "So what the hell are you doing here?" he asked. "Shouldn't you be out tending an alfalfa field somewhere?"

A big, beaming smile. "How did you know? My boyfriend and I leave tomorrow. Not alfalfa, but maize. We're starting our own micromanaged non-profit farmers' collective co-op aimed at empowering young people to—"

But by this point in her spiel, Edwin had already left. A stranger in a strange land. No matter. This time tomorrow, he would be on a plane. A plane to somewhere else.

"*Psssst,* kid. Looking for booze, are you?" It was an old man, half-hidden in the shadows of the alleyway. (And yes, he really did say "pssssst.")

"What the hell do you want?" said Edwin, unnecessarily rude at this point. "Spare change? A hug? Well, forget it. I gave at the office."

"Oh, I don't need a hug. Not from some young snot like you."

This perked Edwin up considerably. Bad manners? Did such a thing exist any more?

"You look like you could use a drink, kid."

Now *that* got Edwin's attention. He heard the tell-tale rattle and clink of bottles, and when he walked into the hidden alleyway entrance to investigate, he found an entire mini-bar stocked with bottles of Johnnie Walker, Southern Comfort, Albino Rhino, Kokanee Gold. There was even a case of Lonesome Charley.

"I thought most people had stopped drinking," said Edwin.

"Most people did. But 'most people' ain't *all*, kid. There's huge stocks of this stuff sitting at the dock, piled high in warehouses, gathering cobwebs in boarded-up wholesale outlets. Our national supply of vice will take years to consume. Years, I tell you. I got cigars as well. And reg'lar smokes. And some crack cocaine and a couple of back issues of *GQ* and *Maxim*."

"Hot damn!" Edwin began rummaging around in his wallet. He stocked up on cigarettes, bought some liquor and even purchased a couple of out-of-print men's fashion magazines, and as he walked away, decidedly uplifted, he had a Vision. A Vision so clear and so inspiring it almost brought him to tears. He could see it now, spreading outwards across the country: a network of rebels, an entire subculture of non-happy people—the new minority, driven underground and forced into a shadowland of black-market deals and secret handshakes. He could see it: a subterranean world of people who refused to give up their bad habits, who steadfastly (and nobly) refused to "capture their bliss." It cheered his soul, the prospect of this fringe counterculture group keeping the flame bravely alive during the dark years that lay ahead. It warmed Edwin's heart, it made his senses soar and then—and then Edwin was abducted. Again.

"What the hell? You said one week!"

Sam "the Snake" Serpent gave Edwin a smile. Edwin returned it, unopened. They were crammed into the back of the Snake's car, tinted windows hiding the drama inside from the rest of the world. Two henchman sat on either side of Edwin, and one of them held a snub-nosed barrel tight against Edwin's rib cage.

"My, my. What do we have here?" said the Snake as he confiscated Edwin's contraband cigarettes and black-market bootleg. "Funny, don't you think? You stocking up on booze and cigs."

"A week, goddammit. You said I had a week!" Edwin was genuinely upset. The mafia had welshed on a deal. What were the odds of that?

"You had a week," said Snake. "We picked you up on a Sunday. Held you for two days—"

"Exactly! You let me go on a Tuesday."

"That's right. And today's Monday, so it's been one week."

Edwin was beyond indignant at this point. "One week from Tuesday is not Monday! It's the following Tuesday. I have one more day."

"No," said Snake thinking aloud, "that would be eight days. Count it out: Tuesday, Wednesday, Thursday . . ." He began ticking them off on his fingers, which was difficult because he was missing one or two digits to begin with.

"The first Tuesday doesn't count!"

"Sure it does. Why wouldn't it?"

"Look," said Edwin. "If you see someone on, say, a Friday, and you tell them, 'Okay, see you again next week,' do they show up on the following Thursday? Of course not! To the average person, 'one week from now' means 'same day, next week.' I have until tomorrow."

The Snake frowned, looked to his henchmen for help, but they hadn't exactly been hired for their canny intellects, and no consensus was reached.

"One more day!" yelled Edwin. "I get one more day!"

"Fine," said the Snake, conceding Edwin's point. "I can understand your confusion. So tell you what—I'll let you go and give you another twenty-four hours. But I'm still going to have to break your thumb or something."

"Why?" said Edwin. "Because you don't want to admit you made a mistake? You don't want to admit that, yes, you are human after all? Listen, Snake, there's no shame in saying, 'Hey, I goofed. I made a mistake.' Nobody's perfect. So let's start anew tomorrow, shall we? New day, fresh start. What do you say, big guy?"

* * *

The emergency ward at San Sebastian Hospital set Edwin's thumb with a plaster splint and gave him a bottle of extra-strength painkillers to dull the pain (even as the doctor on call urged Edwin to consider Tupak Soiree mental pain-blocking first, to which Edwin had explained: "Just give me some friggin' painkillers before I kill you!").

And so, doped up and with a swollen, purple-and-black, throbbing broken thumb—which had indeed become *completely* opposable once Snake had got through with it—Edwin came staggering back to . . . an empty house.

Not empty in the "no one at home" sense, but empty in the "nothing inside" sense. Edwin stood perfectly still for a long while, agog at the sight. It was gone. Everything. The furniture. The drapes. The wall hangings. Even—he checked the kitchen—the goddamn fridge and the goddamn stove. Jenni had cleaned him out.

Mr. Muggins appeared, mewing in confusion and rubbing up against Edwin's legs. Edwin didn't even have the energy to step back and give the cat a decent punt, so drained of life force had he become.

"She took everything," he said, as though repeating the obvious would somehow diminish the impact. "Everything."

A note, written on flowery scented stationery, was in the middle of the living-room floor. Edwin didn't have to read it. He already knew. "Dear Edwin: I have decided to leave you—" Edwin looked around at the empty room. "Thanks, but I figured that part out on my own."

> I am about to depart on a voyage of happiness and discovery. I sold all our so-called belongings to help fund my journey. (But really, Edwin, they are only things. Remember: we do not own our possessions, our possessions own us.) Yes, Edwin, the time has come for me to realign my identity in accordance with a higher principle. I'm not really sure what that means, but I'm going to do it anyway. I have decided to become Tupak Soiree's concubine. I phoned Him late last night (His home number was in your e-mail archives.), and I offered Him my heart and soul. He, in turn, said we all must shed our bodies and become one with the textures

of our life. He then asked me for my measurements, you know, so that He could properly banish my shallow outer shell and seek my true inner beauty. He was quite impressed. He then asked me to fax Him a photograph. (I sent the one of me in my red swimsuit, from our trip to Acapulco. I think it really shows the "inner me.") I was so worried that He would think I was spiritually unsuitable, but no, to my joy and relief, He graciously consented to allow me to join His "holy band of God-desses," as He so poetically put it. I hope you'll under-stand, Edwin. I must be with the Great Teacher now. Sorry. I never really loved you, anyway. Don't take that personally, but it's true. Oh, and I sold all your suits to a wandering minstrel band of journey-seekers. (I got $5 a suit, which will come in awful handy in the days ahead. Thanks.) Alas, I can't take Mr. Muggins with me on my Great Journey of Life because, darn it anyway, it turns out the Supreme Enlightened One has an allergy to cat dander. But I know you'll take good care of Mr. Mug-gins, Edwin. You two were always so close.

Sincerely, Jennifer

P.S.: I know about May. I always knew about May. I just didn't care.

Edwin slumped to the floor, note in hand, thumb throbbing. Although he was poised to collect more than a million dollars the following morning, Edwin knew that his life was adrift, knew that the centre was not holding. His wife had joined Tupak Soiree's inner circle, the mob was stalking him, his thumb had been broken, his belongings had been sold to a band of travelling freaks, and he was about to flee the country. Alone.

In spite of the fantasies he had concocted, Edwin knew full well that he might never see May again. He would send her a clandestine mes-sage, asking her to join him, but there was no way of knowing if she ever would. He might very well have lost her—forever. Indeed, that was the overriding sense Edwin now had: one of loss. He could have checked off an entire shopping list of losses, had he wanted to—and if the Snake hadn't broken his right thumb, the one he needed to write. ("Not the right thumb! Not the right!" followed by a wet snap, a shriek and an insincere apology. "Sorry, Mr. de Valu, but them's the rules.") Edwin had lost almost everything. He had lost his wife. His home. His best friend (one is tempted to say his "only" friend).

"I guess it's just you and me now," said Edwin sorrowfully as he stroked Mr. Muggins' fur. "Just you and me." And he wondered what else could possibly go wrong.

That night, as Edwin lay sprawled out on the living-room floor in a drugged and drunken stupor, as he gasped and tossed in fits of delirium, as the city slept and the moon rose, Mr. Muggins peed in Edwin's shoes.

Dulce domum. "Home, sweet home."

Chapter
Thirty-seven

At the border between Beecher and Bower counties, on a half-deserted highway deep in the swamplands, where the air rolls pungent and mosquito-ridden from the waters of the bayou, and where the Nazarene vines hang limp and green, a single hand-painted sign points the way: "The Beecher/Bower Ammo Shop and Family Fun Centre."

A quirk of county zoning has made this largely inaccessible corner of the bayou a haven for gunrunners and amateur enthusiasts alike. In light of a recent preschool incident involving armour-piercing bullets and titanium-enforced assault rifles, Beecher County had banned the sale and distribution of said shells, reasoning: no bullets, no bad guys. ("Impressionable young children don't kill people; armour-piercing bullets kill people" had been the legislature's cry.) Now, over in Bower County, they took a slightly different tack. They banned the guns but didn't bother targeting specific ammunition, reasoning: no assault weapons, no assaults.

The logic appeared impeccable on both sides, but gun dealers quickly spotted the loophole and learned to exploit it. And so, out here in the dark wet wilds where the two counties met, a gun shop was quickly erected, straddling the border. On one side of the store you could buy armour-piercing bullets (for "recreational use only"), and on the other side you could buy the corresponding rapid-fire, high-impact assault rifles ("perfect for squirrel hunting").

Now, they don't read a lot of books in this neck of the woods. True, the local schoolmarm and the parson's wife had been prattling on lately about some fellow named Tupak, but for the most part illiteracy and a high degree of inbred DNA had conspired to keep Beecher and Bower counties relatively thought-free. Which is why, when the small man with the darting eyes showed up at the gun shop, he went unrecognized. No one said, "Hey, I know you from the photo on your book jacket. You're Mr. Ethics!" No. He managed to slip in without being noticed.

"What can I do you for?" asked the large man in the too-tight T-shirt. (A T-shirt the colour of dead flesh, appropriately enough. It had been bright orange when the large man bought it at the County Fair and Gun Show eight years earlier, but the dye had faded over time, even as the shirt itself shrunk and the belly beneath grew.)

"I need a weapon," said Mr. Ethics. "One that can kill a man."

"Now, wait one darn minute, mister," said the clerk (in strict accordance with the state gun laws). "It is illegal for me to sell any recreational firearm if I suspect it may be used to commit a felony."

"Fine then. I need a sniper rifle with which to hunt squirrels."

"Good. Now what size squirrel are we talking 'bout?"

"Oh, about the size of a man."

The clerk took down his pride and glory: a combination crossbow and grenade launcher. "Now this here is very popular with our more avid sportsmen."

The small man frowned. "Looks expensive."

"Not necessarily. Our distributor down in Galveston went bankrupt—the CEO just up and went fishin' one day—so we're practically giving these babies away at the discount fire-sale price of $7,400. Of course, you need to purchase the exploding grenade canisters on the other side of the store—across that big red line you see painted on the floor."

"I'm afraid that's a bit out of my price range. Do you have anything less sophisticated, but still lethal?"

"How much money are we talking?"

The small man emptied his pockets onto the counter. There were a few coins and a couple of wadded-up bills courtesy of Bubba the Reborn Prison Guard and a handful of quarters he had stolen from a small child who had been out collecting for UNICEF. Mr. Ethics silently cursed the cheapskates of the county; it was shameful how little they had donated.

The man behind the counter picked through the offerings, and said, "Well, you got $42.81. It's not a lot. But don't you fret. I think I have something you can afford."

And with that, he leaned under the counter and slid out a large metal army case, drab olive green and covered with dust.

"Here you go," he said. "I'll give it to you for forty bucks."

Stencilled across the case were the distinctive letters of the Cyrillic alphabet. Backward R's and lowercase capitals. It was Soviet.

Chapter
Thirty-eight

Edwin left the front door open and a full bag of cat food out for Mr. Muggins.

This was the morning that Edwin de Valu would cease to exist. This was the morning he would disappear. Edwin walked briskly through the sun-washed streets of an early dawn, down to the neighbourhood bank, where he waited for the doors to open. He had worked out his plan in careful detail and was now about to set everything in motion. First, he would transfer his million-odd dollars into several separate accounts as a sly diversionary tactic. He would then immediately take a taxi to the airport and catch the very next plane out of the country. It didn't matter where. It would be better to make it an entirely random decision. Were he to make a premeditated choice, someone might later be able to second-guess him. No, it had to be a matter of pure chance. He would be on the next international flight, regardless of whether it was going to Istanbul or Singapore. He would then repeat this process as soon as he arrived, taking the next plane out to wherever it was heading. It didn't matter where—just that it was away.

He would leave a trail of assumed names and misdirections in his path, and then, once he was convinced he had escaped cleanly, cash in tow, would he pick a final destination. Only then would he contact May. (He was already working out the details of the cryptic but romantic message he would send her.)

By the time the bank doors opened, a small line had formed behind Edwin, and Edwin, feeling generous and having slept off his late-night narcotic blues, stepped aside and held the door for an elderly lady. "Please," he said. "After you."

"Why thank you," said the lady. "You're such a dear."

And with that single, gracious gesture, Edwin lost everything . . .

There was only one teller (staff levels at the bank had been dropping lately), and the elderly woman he let in had presented a complex, convoluted chain of transactions that needed to be burrowed through before the teller could get to Edwin and the others. It dragged on forever. Edwin waited and waited.

By the time the dear old lady had fastened up her purse and shuffled to one side, Edwin's previously generous demeanour had soured considerably.

"Stupid old bag," he muttered as he approached the teller. "I want to set up four floating accounts," he said, "connected electronically, with the same password but under a separate transit route. And make it quick."

The teller, already frazzled and exhausted, sighed wearily and punched in the numbers. Edwin's account information appeared on her screen. "And how exactly would you like me to divide the $1.47 that you have in your account, sir?"

If Edwin hadn't been so stunned by this, he might have noted her use of sarcasm, might have commended her for being sardonic, might have seen in her a kindred spirit. Instead, he stammered, "But—but, that's impossible. I have more than a million dollars in that account. It went in first thing this morning."

"A million, huh?" She clearly didn't believe him, but she reviewed the day's transactions nonetheless. "You're right. The account was empty as of this morning, but $1,800,611.47 was deposited at exactly 8:07 a.m."

Edwin felt a wave of euphoria and relief wash over him. "Thank God," he said. "Now then, I'd like to divide that amount into four separate—"

"And it was then withdrawn at exactly 8:22 a.m."

"Withdrawn?"

"Cashier's cheque, for the full amount—rounded down to the nearest ten dollars."

"What are you saying?" Edwin knew exactly what she was saying.

"It's gone. Someone must have had access to your account. They cleaned it out, sucked it dry. Do you have any idea who might have done this?"

"Yes. I know—I know exactly who. It was my wife. My ex-wife."

The teller gave him a sympathetic, tight-lipped smile. "They'll do it every time."

Edwin stumbled from the queue, felt his inner ear spin like a gyroscope. He thought he might faint, he thought he might start to dry heave uncontrollably. He had no backup plan, no secret avenue of escape. The only thing of value Edwin had were his credit cards, and they were pretty well maxed out. And anyway, there was no way he could fund a continent-hopping escape on Diner's Cards and Uncle Visa. (It was even worse than he realized. That very morning the Visa Corporation, citing "a fundamental shift in consumer lending patterns," had filed for bankruptcy.)

Edwin sat down in a customer courtesy chair and put his head between his knees. "You can do this," he said. "You can pull this off." But he wasn't convincing anyone, least of all himself. Maybe he could join a co-op, change his name to Moonbeam, spend his time in hiding, hoeing turnips and gathering flax. "Think, man. *Think*." And then, just when he thought it couldn't get any worse, it did. Edwin looked up and saw, through the front window, a familiar black car lying in wait.

"Shit!" With his face averted, Edwin sidled up to the teller, cutting in on mid-transaction. "Excuse me," he whispered, "but does this bank have a back door?"

Of course it didn't. Not for customers. So Edwin stepped back and took a running leap. He sprang across the counter, vaulting over in one fell swoop as papers flew and chairs toppled over. The aged security guard on duty fumbled ineffectively with his holster, to no avail. Edwin was already sprinting towards the employees' exit. He kicked the door open in a flying leap that was more Don Knotts than Van Damme, and ran out, into the rear parking lot. He was searching for an escape route when he heard, behind him, the sudden squeal of tires on asphalt. The car came rushing up from the rear and veered sharply across Edwin's path. He was cut off, all but pinned against the wall.

A tinted window rolled slowly down. It was the head sociopath himself, the freckled man with the cold eyes and the fake smiles.

"Twenty-four hours!" yelled Edwin, full of fear. "Snake said twenty-four hours! I have until this evening."

"Come here, Edwin."

"No way! Snake said twenty-four hours! It's not fair!"

"Edwin, I have something to give you."

"Sure. A bullet to the back of the head. No thanks, think I'll pass. Twenty-four hours! That's what he said."

But still the hand beckoned, still the voice called, soft and treacly. The last time this happened, Edwin had been given a missing manuscript. This time, who knew what awaited him? He stepped forward hesitatingly, the way a schoolboy steps forward to face a caning.

"Edwin, hold out your hand."

No, not another finger. "Please, no. For the love of God, I'm an editor; I need all the fingers I can get. Can't you just sprain one of my toes instead, or maybe pull my hair really hard?"

But the freckled man did not want to snap another one of Edwin's bones. Instead, he held out his own hand and, gently, placed something in Edwin's palm. He then closed Edwin's fingers around it and said, "Goodbye, Edwin. I have enjoyed tormenting you so, but I am now about to debark upon a journey-quest. Farewell, Edwin. Live, love, and learn. Sorry about your thumb."

And off he drove, leaving Edwin alone, chest still pounding and legs still trembling, in a bank parking lot on a beautiful blue morning in South Central Boulevard.

Edwin opened his hand, looked down. Inside was a single small daisy.

Chapter
Thirty-nine

The entire building felt empty and barren. As Edwin strode through the once hectic clutch of cubicles and lab-rat corridors of Panderic Inc., it was as though he was walking through an abandoned movie set. One would be hard pressed to realize that Panderic was now the largest and most successful publisher in the world, with revenues higher than those of many mid-sized countries. Panderic's cash reserves alone could have easily toppled several Third World Latin American regimes. The entire place was afloat on money.

Yet none of that showed. Edwin had heard of ghost towns; this was a ghost office. Cubicle after cubicle was empty. The hallways were silent. The hum of fluorescent lights now seemed improbably loud. The petty office politics, the gossip, the envy, the anger, the laughter—it was all gone.

Mr. Mead, the King of Panderic, was slouched in his office, his back to the door. He was looking out across the rooftops below, a drink in hand, his posture slack. When Edwin came in, Mr. Mead didn't even bother to turn around.

"What is it now?" he growled.

"It's me, Edwin. I've come to hand in my resignation."

Mr. Mead waved vaguely to one side. "Just put it on the pile with the others."

Edwin turned to go, stopped, and said, "One more thing, sir. Fuck you."

At this, Mr. Mead spun around. "What did you say?" he roared. "What did you just say?"

Edwin's resolve began to give way. This wasn't quite the scenario he had expected.

"I said, um, fuck you, sir. I quit."

"Ha, ha! That's wonderful. That's the best thing I've heard in days. Come on, Edwin. Pull up a chair. Have a drink with me."

"You did hear what I said?"

"Of course, of course. So what are you drinking? I've got— What do I have? Boodles Gin. Santiago Red. Some kind of brandy. I've got a little bit of Kaluha left. And some sort of horrid Chinese wine. It was a present from our Taipei distributors. I've had it for years. It tastes like cough syrup, but what the hell, it does the trick."

"Gin is fine."

"What happened to your thumb? It's all bandaged up."

"Long story, sir."

"No matter. This will cure what ails you." And he handed Edwin a glass. Mr. Mead wasn't drunk, or even all that tipsy. But then, the day was still young. "Edwin," he said, "be careful what you wish for, because you just may get it. Cheers! *Skoal!* Down the hatch."

They swigged back their drinks, and Mr. Mead immediately sloshed more into Edwin's glass. "These are dark days, Edwin. These are dark, dark days."

"But you've won, sir. You have turned Panderic into the most powerful publishing company on the face of the earth."

"No. Tupak Soiree turned Panderic into the most powerful publishing company on the face of the earth. I just oversaw it. I was like the hat-check girl at a whorehouse. I smiled and collected the ticket stubs."

"But, sir, you have vanquished your enemies. Doubleday, Harper-Collins, Random House: they've all gone under. Panderic stands alone, unchallenged, at the top of the compost heap. You've won, sir."

Mr. Mead tossed a copy of Panderic's spring catalogue onto the desk in front of Edwin. It landed like a slap. "Have you seen our catalogue?" said Mr. Mead. "Have you seen it?"

Edwin flipped through. It was all Tupak Soiree–related: cookbooks, calendars, testimonials. *Right Living: the Tupak Soiree Way. Home Repairs and Solar Energy: the Tupak Soiree Way. Tupak Soiree for Christians. For Jews. For Sceptics. For Heathens.* The underlying themes contained in Soiree's original book had proven to be completely protean, meaning radically different things to radically different people, yet still gently herding everyone towards the same vanishing point, one of bliss and banality. Trying to pin down Tupak Soiree was like trying to nail Jell-O to a wall; no matter how hard you hammered, something essential always managed to slither free and elude you.

Tupak's message had even become vertically integrated, reaching both down and up the generational ladder: *Tupak Soiree for Seniors; Tupak Soiree for Teens; Tupak Soiree for Single Pregnant High-School Students Still Living at Home* (subtitled: *It's Not Your Fault—Nothing You Do Ever Is!*). There was even a parental guide titled *Tupak Soiree for Toddlers.* The once innocuous children's section had become infected as well: *Harry the Humph and the Tupak Soiree Surprise.* There were colouring books based on the principles behind *What I Learned on the Mountain;* there were even "spiritual mysteries," in which the hard-boiled detective tried to figure out which "great cosmic principle of life" had been violated, and in which everyone learned an important self-validating life lesson at the end.

"The bookstores have become vast Tupak Soiree clearing houses," said Mr. Mead. "They have become the purveyors of happiness."

"I'm missing something. All this talk of happiness, doesn't that play in your favour? Didn't you recently trademark the term?"

Mr. Mead nodded. "That's right. From now on, the word 'happiness' has to be followed by ™, and Panderic collects a royalty every time it's used. Of course, we can't do anything about people using the word 'happiness' in common conversation, but yes, when it's used in the Tupak Soiree sense, happiness is now a Panderic trademark. We have cornered the market on happiness™. Haven't you noticed? There are very few actual bookstores left, Edwin. They call themselves Happiness™ Centres instead, and they're stocked almost exclusively with Tupak Soiree and his spinoffs. It's funny; we used to joke about the difference between 'books' and 'book-shaped objects.' Well, there are almost no actual books being produced any more. Certainly, here at Panderic we're producing only book-shaped objects. They're all related to happiness™, they're all instant bestsellers and they all rake in great mounds of cash. The company's coffers are full."

"So why are you so glum?"

Mr. Mead swallowed a mix of Kaluha and Chinese cough syrup, winced, and said, "Have you read that book? *What I Learned on the Mountain*? Have you read it?"

"I edited it, sir. Remember?"

"I know that, but did you read it? Did you *honestly* read it?" (It was quite possible, and indeed probably quite common, to edit an entire book without ever actually reading it or thinking about what it had to say.)

"Yes, I read it. I read it backwards and forwards, sir. I know it inside and out, and upside down."

"So why aren't you walking around serene and peaceful and at one with the universe?"

Edwin hadn't really thought about it. "To tell you the truth, I'm not sure. Maybe I'm immune. Maybe it's because I *was* the editor. You know what it's like, sir. An editor doesn't see a book the way normal people do. An editor sees the structure, the syntax, the transitional devices; everything is laid bare. It's like looking at a building but seeing a blueprint instead. It's like looking at an X-ray. I see the skeleton. I see the flaws. I see the way a book is put together. I see the seams and the support beams. I see the tricks and the tics and the quirks. It's like a professional magician watching some bogus psychic fooling people with a cold reading. I'm not fooled by *What I Learned on the Mountain* because I know better. In the land of the blind, I'm the one-eyed king. Maybe that's why I never quite fell under the spell." He took a long, hard drink. "And how about you, sir? Have you read the book?"

"Sure. Several times. Frankly, I don't see what the big fuss is about. It's just a lot of New Age hooey and warmed-over platitudes arranged in a very shoddy, slapdash sort of way. You did a terrible job of editing it, by the way. Christ, it reads like a first draft. But you know what pissed me off most? Do you know what really irked me? The part about male pattern baldness. The part about how 'we must not merely accept baldness—we must embrace it, we must celebrate it.' When I read that passage, I knew then that this Tupak Soiree fellow was full of crap. Let me tell you something, Edwin. Going bald shouldn't be something we 'embrace.' Going bald is a sign of aging. Just like wrinkles, just like liver spots, just like grey hairs. You want to know something, Edwin? I have arthritis. I'm fifty-four years old and already my hands are turning into claws. My fingers are stiff, my knuckles are knotted like cheap pine. I can barely hold a pen. I have arthritis, I'm going bald, and I don't like it one damn bit. Why? Because it's a constant, nagging reminder of my own mortality. And that, my friend, is not something we should ever gloss over. Mortality is not something we should 'embrace.' And it sure as hell isn't something we should 'celebrate.'"

"Do not go gentle into that good night," said Edwin. "Rage, rage against the dying of the light."

"Dylan Thomas. Well cited, Edwin. I should have put you in our poetry department." (Okay, so there was something worse than romance and self-help.) *"Do not go gentle into that good night* . . . It's funny," said Mr. Mead. "Everyone always made snide comments about the comb-over artists. You know the guys; the baldies who grow their hair long on one side and then plaster it over in oily strands across their heads. It looks ridiculous, so we ridiculed it. But the reasons behind the comb-over are *not* ridiculous. Not in any way. The men who combed over their hair were denying their own impending mortality. The result may have been silly, but the gesture itself and the underlying motivation was not. In its way, it was sad and somewhat poetic. Almost heroic, really. Haven't you noticed? You don't see the comb-over any more."

It was the one thing Edwin never expected he would be sorry to see go, but now, with a few drinks in him and Mr. Mead's eulogy still hanging in the air, Edwin couldn't help but feel sad; sad to see all those balding men with the combed-over hair giving up the fight.

Mr. Mead sat back, shook his head in slow mystification. "I just don't get it. I read that damn book, and I thought it was a piece of poorly written pap. What is it I'm missing?"

"Nothing, sir. You're just part of the 0.3 per cent. When marketing did a survey, they found a 99.7 per cent satisfaction rate. In any epidemic, there is never a 100 per cent transmission rate. You must be one of the ones who isn't susceptible. And even if *What I Learned on the Mountain* invades every single home in America, there will still be that stubborn 0.3 per cent that aren't caught up in it. That doesn't sound like much, but in the U.S. alone, that works out to be something like 90,000 people. Even the most lethal virus doesn't have a 100 per cent kill rate."

"A virus?" said Mr. Mead. "Is that how you see it?"

"Sometimes."

"You're wrong, Edwin. That book isn't a virus. It's exactly what it claims to be: a panacea. No one was forced to read *What I Learned on the Mountain*. They all chose to. That's how the market works. It was a combination of free will, the herd instinct, and the eternal allure of the quick fix. Virus? No. It isn't a virus. It's much worse than that, Edwin. It's a cure. A cure for all our modern woes; the cure for all our problems—real or otherwise. The funny thing is, people like you and me, maybe we were secretly a little bit in love with the malaise. It isn't a virus, Edwin. It's a prescription. Only problem is, the cure is worse than the disease. Oh, yes, beware of what you wish for, Edwin . . ." He went to take a drink and found the glass already empty. "Beware of what you wish for."

"It's time for me to go, sir."

"Yes, I suppose it is. I hate to see you leave, Edwin, but I understand. It isn't much fun working here any more. May Weatherhill quit this morning as well. She's in her office, packing up. Make sure you stop in and see her on the way out. She was asking for you."

Edwin hesitated. "Before I go, sir. I have a favour to ask."

"May's gone. You're gone. Nigel—who the hell knows where he is now. There's just me and Ned down in accounting. Everyone else is gone, long gone. The rest of the work is being done by volunteers. Can you believe it?" Mr. Mead laughed out loud, a single ironic bark. "People dedicated to the Tupak Soiree message, they've been volunteering their services right down the line. Artists, layout, distribution: they're working for free, just to get the word out. So not only are we reaping the biggest profits in our sixty-year history, but we don't have to pay anyone either. Is that hilarious, or what? You remember Irwin? The intern? I bumped him up to the head of our sci-fi department, but he quit within a week. Put up that stupid fishing sign—God I hate that. Why can't they just go already? Why the cute little farewell? Anyway, Irwin quits, puts up a 'Gone fishin'' sign, and then two days later, he shows up as a volunteer. He's doing the same work as before, but now he's doing it for free! Can you believe it? What a moron."

"So why Ned? Why is he still here?"

"Ned? In accounting? Oh, it turns out he honestly enjoys adding up numbers. He says accounting is his 'bliss.' So what the hell, I keep him on the payroll." Mr. Mead got up, made another haphazard raid on the liquor cabinet. "More gin?"

"No, I can't. I have to catch May before she leaves. But I would like to ask a favour of you."

"Anything. Shoot."

"You know how you mentioned Panderic's huge profits, vast cash reserves and low overhead? Seeing as how I was largely responsible for Panderic's current financial surplus, I was wondering if—well, if I might be granted a special one-time severance bonus. Just to help me get started somewhere else."

"A bonus?"

"Yes, a kind of farewell package. You know, in light of everything I've done for Panderic."

"What?! Are you crazy? I'm not made of money, you know. Didn't I give you a Zippo lighter just last year? Didn't I? You bloody ingrate. Get the hell out of here, you make me sick."

Edwin sighed. "Yes, sir."

I really should have gone with "puke face" and a ponytail pull, thought Edwin as he left the room.

Chapter
Forty

May was indeed packing up her belongings. Cardboard boxes were everywhere—on her desk, atop her filing cabinet—the pictures of her cat had been taken down and her ferns were boxed up and on the floor.

"Edwin," she said, looking up. "I'm glad you came over. I wanted to say goodbye."

But Edwin hadn't come for farewells; he had come to sweep her up in his arms and carry her away. He had come as Conan of the Cubicles.

"No," he said. "No goodbyes." And then, with a deep breath and a fluttering sense of vertigo, he took the high-flying plunge from the top of the cliffs. "Come away with me, May. I want us to be together. I have nothing to offer. I have no job, no money. My future is bleak, my thumb is in a splint, and I haven't had a bath in two days. The mafia has been trying to kill me, and Jenni left and took all my stuff. I don't know where I'm going or what I'll do—but I want to be with you. Only you. Come away with me, May."

She turned and looked at Edwin, really looked at him, as though seeing him for the first time. "It's too late," she said, ever so softly.

Edwin nodded. "I see." There was a long pause. "Are you sure?" he said.

"Yes, Edwin. It's too late."

He turned sadly, without any Bogart epigrams with which to sign off, no nimble, wry goodbyes with which to end the scene.

"Goodbye, Edwin."

"Wait a sec!" He turned back suddenly. "Wait one goddamn second!"

"Edwin?"

"Your lips!" he shouted. "Where the hell are your lips?"

"My lips?"

"Those big, red wax lips of yours. Where are they? And—your eyes! Where is the sadness? Where is the wistful intelligence? Where is the mascara? Where is the eyeshadow? *And where, goddammit, are your lips?*" And then, quieter and with a sense of creeping horror, he asked, "Who are you, and what have you done with May?"

"Edwin," she said, and her voice was calm and soothing, and her eyes strangely serene. "Makeup is just a veil, and I have outgrown the need for veils. I am finally giving myself permission to be me."

Edwin staggered back, his finger stabbing the air, his mouth contorted like someone in *The Invasion of the Body Snatchers.* "You—you've been reading that book!"

"Edwin, I'm happy now. At long last, I have learned to make peace with myself. It was like my entire life was off-kilter, and now I have found equilibrium. I have captured my bliss."

"No," he said, and the way he said it you could tell it was a vow made to the heavens themselves. "I refuse to let this happen. Not to you."

"Live, love, learn," she said.

"*Never!!*"

He grabbed her by her shoulders and hustled her out of the office and into an elevator.

"Where are we going?" she asked, her voice tranquil and untroubled even as she was being kidnapped.

"You owe me this, May; you owe me one last moment. One last chance."

The elevator descended to street level, and Edwin hurried May through the lobby and out onto the street, where he waved frantically for a taxicab.

"Edwin, there is nothing left to say. Your words can have no effect on me, because I have moved to a place beyond words."

But Edwin pulled her into a cab nonetheless, told the driver to leave the city—"escape" is how he phrased it—and they spun away, down along the harbourfront and then up above it on the elevated Callaghan Overpass. It was a long drive, one lost in silence and the oppressive sense of end-game.

"Edwin," she said, softly. "Look. The sea. It has captured the sky and made it a brighter blue."

"Condoms and used needles wash up along this shore all the time," said Edwin.

"And the Ferris wheel. Do you see the Ferris wheel? In Candle Island Park? Do you see it silhouetted, just over there? Do you see how beautiful it is?"

"It's rusted and worn out, May. And Candle Island is garish and shoddy and filled with cheap trinkets and small-time hustlers. The world isn't shimmering with magic, May. It's shimmering with sadness."

She watched from the window as the amusement park drifted by on her right. "I used to go there as a girl," she said. "My father would take me. He'd buy cotton candy, pink and silk-spun. It melted in your mouth even as you tried to taste it." Then, turning to Edwin, she said, "I miss him, my father. Sometimes I wonder where he is. And I think about the cotton candy, impossible to hold."

The gates of Candle Island floated past, and May saw a terrible sight. So terrible, it made her stare in disbelief. The gates were padlocked and chained shut. A sign out front said "playground closed." It shook May almost free of her bliss. "When . . . ?" she said.

"Last week," said Edwin. "They shut it down without a word of farewell. Turns out, happy people don't need cheap thrills or gaudy distractions. Happy people don't need to be dazzled by lights or Tilt-a-Whirls. They don't need to flirt with death or throw darts to win sawdust-filled toys."

May said nothing. She just closed her eyes, closed them so hard that tears began to form, and she thought about the cotton candy and that insubstantial taste of spun sugar, soft on the tongue, dissolving into memory. "I'm happy," she said. "I'm happy. I'm so very happy."

Edwin had the driver stop at the first motel they could find, which took some time; most of the seedier establishments were now boarded up and sinking into neglect and tangled weeds. The Bluebird Motel was still open, however: a long, low line of doorways in a gravel driveway with a faded sign that said COLOUR TV and another, just below it, that advertised AIR CONDITIONING in blue letters with icicles hanging off them. Twenty-five years ago that sign had been a bright beacon of modernity, now it was as antiquated as a paleolithic cave drawing. *Colour TV?* Was there ever a time when television wasn't colour?

As the taxi pulled in, scrunching gravel and rolling to a stop outside the motel office, there was an embarrassing moment.

"That'll be $71.50. Eighty with the tip," said the driver, a dark squat man who clearly hadn't read Tupak Soiree's chapter on the spiritual poverty of demanding money from others.

Edwin cleared his throat. "You wouldn't happen to take Diner's Card, would you? No?" Edwin turned to May, feeling sheepish and a tad bit less than Conanesque.

In spite of her new-found bliss, May laughed at Edwin's request, admired the absurdity of the situation. "Let me get this straight," she said. "You want me to pay for my own abduction?"

"It's just that I'm a little short."

May fished out the cash and handed it to the driver. "Live, love, learn," she said sweetly.

"Yeah, right. Whatever, lady." (The taxi driver had lost a spouse and four family members to Tupak Soiree happiness™ already, and was not in a charitable frame of mind when it came to gratuitous epigrams.)

The deprogramming of May Weatherhill began with a handful of chocolates and a heartfelt plea. Edwin kept May locked up alone in the room for more than an hour, and when he returned he found her sitting cross-legged on the floor, breathing in tandem with the pulse of the universe. The room itself was a press-wood furniture, threadbare sheets and mildewy carpet sort of place. May's meditations couldn't have seemed more incongruous had they occurred atop a Ferris wheel.

"May!" shouted Edwin as he barged in. "The money you lent me has not gone to waste. Do you see what I have? Chocolates, May. Not for your soul, but for your hips. Empty calories, May! Delicious, guilt-inducing, and completely unnecessary. That's what America lives on! Empty calories. We are a nation sustained by empty calories." He dumped an armful of old Mars bars on the bed and then scattered Smarties across the sheets like a Balinese wedding offering. "But wait, there's more!" With a flourish, he fanned out a selection of glossy magazines. "*Cosmo! Swirl! Women's Monthly Weekly!* Look at these back issues, May. Look at all the things that are wrong with you. Fashion tips, makeup, relationships. On this page they have an article on how to lose weight and—*ha, ha!*—on the very next page they have a recipe for double-fudge chocolate cheesecake. You can't win, May! Isn't that great? It's one step forward and two steps back. And look, I've got sports magazines for me, so I can read about richer, faster, stronger men than I who are living out my childhood fantasies. That's right, I can pretend I'm some sort of Iron John archetypal figure, when in reality I'm an office worker in a grey suit. I make no difference! I'm insignificant, May! Do you see the kind of emptiness that lies right here, right here—" he hit a fist against his chest. "Do you see all the mechanisms and makeshift solutions we have created? Do you see how we staunch the symptoms, how we try to fix punctured hearts with cheap band-aids? This is who we are, May. This is the sadness at the core of all things. *Mono-no-aware*, May. This is what makes us human: not happiness, but the sadness underneath."

"No," said May. "I will not accept that. I will not accept that this is how the world must be."

"Tough!" shouted Edwin. "Because the world doesn't care. We can't wish reality away. We can't simply agree to close our eyes and hug ourselves into believing that old age, death, and disillusionment don't exist. They do, May. Whether we like it or not. Life is just one damn thing after another, but it's still the only game in town. We can't afford to sleepwalk through it, because we've only got the one go round. *Dum vivimus, vivamus!* 'While we live, let us live to the fullest.' *Dum vivimus, vivamus.*"

But May was one of the few people who could meet Edwin blow for blow, word for word, arcane term for arcane term, and she countered his Latin with an untranslatable of her own. "*Kekau*," she said. "An Indonesian word. It means 'to awaken from a nightmare.' But what's happening here is something else entirely, Edwin. We are waking up not *from* a nightmare, but *into* a dream. The world is finally waking up. Waking up into a dream. A wonderful, wonderful dream. A dream as ethereal and as sweet as—" she caught herself.

"As cotton candy," said Edwin. "As saccharine and insubstantial as cotton candy. A spun-sugar world. Is that what we've been reduced to?"

"Not reduced," she said. "Released."

Edwin flopped more magazines onto the bed, one after another. "Look. I found a bunch of old celebrity-gossip magazines. Remember the concept of gossip? Well, these magazines are chockablock with scandals and heart-wrenching tragedies. Now we can feel both pity *and* resentment towards complete strangers!"

Edwin swung a battered valise up onto the magazines. The valise clinked, glass on glass. "I've got whisky. I've got gin. A bit of hashish. A carton of Luckies. Even"—he produced a single metal tube with a conjurer's sleight of hand—"lipstick."

But at this point, he was looking less and less like a magician and more and more like a condo salesman who was running out of tricks. He instinctively grabbed the small sign sitting on top of the television. "Ha, ha!" he said, and by this point his *ha ha's* were becoming noticeably strained. "What do we have here? Porno! Channel 13. In-house videos, May. Now we can live vicariously at even the most private level. We can pay to watch strangers have more fun in ten minutes than we will have our entire lives!" He cranked the dial to mid-band, flicked over to the pay-per-view channel. It came up in sickly green skin tones and wavering reception. "Porno, May! People using people. This is what life is all about."

On the screen a radiant young woman and a curly-haired man dressed in white bathrobes smiled beamingly at the camera. "Watch this," Edwin crowed. "Any moment now, they are going to have acrobatic, completely unmotivated sex."

The announcer's voice came on: "Coming up next, former adult-video stars discuss their innermost feelings."

"What?" Edwin almost choked on his disbelief. "Former porn stars? *Former*?"

The girl on the TV screen swished back her long blonde hair—rendered a swampy green by poor reception—and said, "I first read Tupak's book on the set of my last movie, a sequel to *Shaving Ryan's Privates*, and I thought to myself, 'Hey, this guy is really on to something'—"

"No!" Edwin screamed. "No talking. Get naked!"

The young man, smiling blissfully, chimed in, "The last film I starred in was titled *I'm Not Feeling Myself Tonight*, and though I thought it had definite artistic merit, I couldn't help feeling—"

"Feel!?" screamed Edwin. "Don't feel. Don't think. *Do*. Just do!" Edwin's arm gestures were getting more wild by the moment. "You're a disgrace to base human horniness, both of you! You ought to be ashamed to show your faces in public."

May, her meditation and bliss now totally disrupted, rose to her feet, straightened her simple blue skirt—the "whatever" skirt she had happened to pick when she reached into her closet that morning—and she said: "I am going to go now, Edwin. I gave you your final moment, and it was a mistake. You have nothing to offer me, just old magazines and stale cigarette smoke. This"—she gestured to the contents of the room, the flickering televison, the bedside offerings—"this is just yesterday's weather. I have moved beyond that. I've changed, Edwin. The world has changed. A new dawn is breaking."

"A new dawn? And what kind of world will it be? A world without a soul. A world without laughter. Without *real* laughter. The kind that makes your heart ache and your eyes go blurry. No one laughs in heaven, May. And no one laughs in paradise. Is that where we are heading? A world that has forgotten just how *sad* real laughter is. Tears and laughter, May. Two sides of the same coin. You can't separate them. *Nemo saltat sobrius!* 'Sober men don't dance.' James Boswell wrote that, and it was true in the eighteenth century, and it's just as true today. We need our vices. We need our cotton-candy fluff, because life *is* sad and short and over far too soon. Why do we spend so much time tinkering with our identities? Why are we so captivated with trivialities? Because these small, petty things are so important."

May was no longer listening, and Edwin might as well have been arguing with his own shadow. (Which, in a way, he was.)

"May, I don't know what the meaning of life is, but I do know this: the two most important phrases in the human language are 'If only' and 'Maybe someday.' Our past mistakes and our unrequited longings. The things we regret and the things we yearn for. That's what makes us who we are."

He waited for a response. He waited for a glimmer of hope. But none came.

"I feel sorry for you, Edwin." She unchained the door, stepped outside and walked away, into sunlight and bliss.

Edwin sunk back onto his vice-strewn bed, despondent and beaten. Had he only thought to run out after her, had he only thought to spin her around one last time and kiss her, just one more time. She was waiting for this. She was waiting and she would not have pushed him away, not now. Not ever. She would, in all likelihood, have kissed back, hard and desperate, the way a drowning person gulps for air. But we'll never know.

We'll never know because Edwin let her go. He let her leave, he let her call a taxi, and he let her stand alone by the side of the road in the warm autumn sunlight with her eyes closed, waiting. Waiting for something—waiting for someone.

Chapter
Forty-one

Inside the Bluebird Motel, a familiar face had appeared on the television screen. It was a face from Edwin's past, and Edwin sat watching in stunned disbelief. Rory the Janitor (a.k.a. Rory the Financial Wizard) was appearing via satellite on this, "The Tupak Soiree Channel: All Happiness™, All the Time!" (formerly: "The Hot Wet Sex Network: All Sex, All the Time!") The host of the show was an amiable man with happy soul-dead eyes and a slack, almost apathetic smile.

"Now, Mr. Wilhacker—or Rory, if I may?"

The host's deferential attitude turned Edwin's stomach. "Fraud!" he yelled at the screen. "Fraud!"

Rory was expounding upon the nation's current economic woes, which he described not as a catastrophe, but rather "a readjustment."

"Every crisis contains within it the seeds of opportunity," said Rory serenely. "We are in the midst of a great upheaval. We are witnessing a momentous turning point in the history of the world, one surpassing even the Industrial Revolution itself. From this great upheaval, from this great disruption, a new economic order will blossom like flowers after a heavy rain."

"Or mushrooms," yelled Edwin. "Poisonous fungal mushrooms growing in rank bullshit!"

"Now, now," tut-tutted the host. "Unemployment *has* soared, the federal reserves *are* depleted, the economic landscape *is* littered with the corpses of once-great industries—"

"Ahh." Rory held up a finger. "I object to the word 'great.' The industries that have recently died deserved to die. After all, *money is never neutral.*" (Edwin recognized this immediately as an aphorism lifted directly from the book.) "Money is anchored in morality. It can be moral or immoral, but it can never be simply neutral. The slave trade was once a vibrant, boisterous industry. Are we to have mourned its passing as well? In sheer economic terms, wasn't the slave trade one of the 'greats'? Immoral industries deserve to die, whether it is tobacco, alcohol, or fashion. A new reality is taking root, one based not on greed and temptation, but on love. Our aim must now be to generate wealth *through* human happiness, and not the other way around. That was always the fatal flaw: we tried to capture happiness by using money, when we should have been doing the exact opposite. We thought that accumulating more and more things, more and more material wealth, would somehow give meaning to our lives. This has always been the central mistake of our existence."

"You talk about the end of temptation. Are you speaking in the biblical sense? Are we, perhaps, undoing the lessons of the Garden of Eden? Are we, perhaps, returning to an oceanic state, a state of grace that existed prior to that of original sin?" (The interviewer was a former Catholic bishop who had "followed his bliss" into public-service broadcasting.)

"Sin?" said Rory. "What is this thing you call sin? For me, sin is only a symptom of a life out of balance. That is all. The consequences of sin may be terrible, but the sin itself exists only from a lack of understanding. If we know good, if we truly understand good, then we must make the right choice. The *moral* choice. In this sense, temptation—whether it is economic or personal—is a very real challenge. For example, I was once a custodial engineer for a large office tower, and at a certain fateful moment, I found myself in the position to crush a certain person—a person I had long despised."

"When you say crush, are you speaking figuratively?"

"Oh, no. I mean, I could have physically crushed him. He was in my garbage compactor, you see, which was against safety regulations, I should note, and I had only to press one button, and that would have been the end of him."

This brought Edwin up cold.

The host laughed. "Were you tempted?"

Rory smiled, that same bland smile he had given when he told Edwin, "I always hated you." He said, "Oh, I was very tempted. In fact, I tossed a coin and it came up heads. So I let him live."

Edwin swallowed hard, felt a cold sweat form on the back of his neck. *A coin toss?* That's what it had come down to? Surely Rory was kidding. He had to be kidding.

"I'm not kidding," said Rory. "But I learned an important lesson. Moral decisions—and the economic policies that follow—must not be left to chance. No more coin tosses of the soul, that is my motto now. *No more coin tosses of the soul.*"

The host nodded at this trite observation as though Rory had uncovered the secret of relativity itself. "Brilliant," he said. "Absolutely brilliant. Now, I understand that the White House is in quite a tizzy over our current economic realignment. Have they contacted you, perhaps requested your aid or advice?" (The way the host asked the question, signalling his intent, made it clear that he already knew the answer.)

"Yes. The President's personal secretary phoned me just this morning. He said, 'Mr. Wilhacker, we need your help.'"

Edwin was watching with the morbid fascination one gives an impending car crash. Was this for real? Was Rory P. Wilhacker (a.k.a. Jimbo, a.k.a. the Janitor from Hell) really poised to become a personal adviser to the President of the United States? Was Rory P. Wilhacker about to start dictating economic policy to the White House?

They began taking calls.

"We have Miss Starlight on the line from Boise, Idaho. Go ahead."

It was one sickly love-gush after another. Caller after caller wished Rory a calm heart and a steady hand. Or maybe it was the other way around. Not that it mattered; the message had become the medium, and the medium had become one long, stupefying blur. Edwin felt his mind going numb . . .

But then, like a blast of cold air, one caller suddenly began shouting abuse and logic at the guest. The Great Rory had just proclaimed the death of free enterprise and was elucidating on the micro–co-op neighbourhood-based economy of the future.

"This is worse than absurd," shouted the caller, gruff of voice, strong of mind. "It's self-defeating! Mr. Wilhacker would have us believe that we can become a nation whose wealth is built on taking in each other's laundry and staying at each other's bed-and-breakfasts. Is this entire country under sedation? Do you realize that science has now ground to a halt? Do you even care? Medical advances. Research. Exploration. It's being replaced by spiritual New Age bunk. Our colleges and universities sit empty and so do our minds. Education has been abandoned, so has art, so has literature. There is no longer any debate in this country because there is no longer any disagreement. We inhabit the muddy middle ground, and you call this progress? This isn't a step forward, it's a step back! And that quack guru of yours, Tupak Soiree, he's the biggest scam artist to ever peddle his feel-good placebo wares in the marketplace of public stupidity, and the sooner we—"

But that was quite enough. The host cut the man off. "Thank you for calling, Mr. Randi. Peace, love, and inner calm always." He smiled warmly. "And don't ever call here again, you vile sceptic, you."

"*Credo quia absurdum*," said Edwin. "'I believe because it is absurd.'" It was the motto of every major religion, the rallying cry of the New Age, the anthem of the entire self-help movement. And it was now fast becoming the motto of the United States of America as well. *Credo quia absurdum*. A medieval theological creed had been given a new lease on life. Randi was right: this was a step back. A leap back. The last 500 years of human development, progress, and thought; the Renaissance; the Enlightenment; the hard lessons learned from the ideological wars of the twentieth century; the triumph over dogma: the great strides in health and medicine: it was all about to be erased. Human nature, at its best, had always been based on a deep heroic restlessness, on wanting something—something else, something *more*, whether it be true love or a glimpse just beyond the horizon. It was the promise of happiness, not the attainment of it, that had driven the entire engine, the folly and the glory of who we are. *The folly and the glory*: the two were not mutually exclusive. Far from it.

And now this: Rory P. Wilhacker, in wavering shades of green and blue, about to enlighten the nation. Rory had settled back into his easy chair and, with a self-satisfied smile, had launched into a long-winded spiel about the future of money. Much of it was quoted verbatim from Tupak Soiree. ("You have to understand that all monetary theory is fundamentally flawed from the start because it attempts to capture the fluidity of motion with the geometry of numbers. Money is constantly in flux, neither energy nor matter, but something in between. Attempting to assign formulas to it is like taking a freeze-frame of a cheetah in flight. The motion itself is lost in the process.") Other gems were from some of Panderic's follow-up books by other authors, in particular *The New Economics: Money and Finance—the Tupak Soiree Way!* ("I have seen the future, and it is small. Small and powerful. We are seeing a profound move away from old, outdated concepts of the Corporation vs. the Consumer. Instead, we have entered an age of micro-economics and self-supporting co-operatives, a perfect blend of capitalism and altruism.")

On and on it went. A narcotic web of words that lulled the listener first into a state of acceptance and then into capitulation. Perhaps the paradigm shift was real. Maybe this was the end of the old order. Maybe Tupak Soiree was right. Maybe—Edwin shook his head clear. *No, goddammit.* He stumbled to the washroom, threw water onto his face, looked at himself in the mirror—cracked and yellowed (both the mirror and his face)—and repeated with stubborn conviction the only thing he knew with certainty to be true: "Tupak Soiree is a fraud. I plucked his rambling overwritten manuscript from the slush pile, and I made him who he is today. Without me, Tupak Soiree would not exist." Edwin looked at the face in the mirror and the significance of that last sentence imploded within him, collapsing inward with a sense of guilt and despair. "Without me, Tupak Soiree would not exist."

And then, from the other room, he heard someone laughing. It was a familiar lilting laugh, and Edwin's mind snapped awake.

"A saint? Oh, no, no," said the voice. "Surely not a saint. My accomplishments are most modest. I am a humble man of humble means."

It was Tupak Soiree himself, full of coy modesty and flirtatious giggles. It was Tupak. The Devil Incarnate. Edwin hurried back, sat on the bed and watched in queasy silence as the architect of ruin smiled and laughed and flirted shamelessly with the audience—that vast televison-viewing audience, which was even now held in thrall by the force of Tupak Soiree's pat answers and cuddly little comments.

Tupak had won. And now he was gloating.

Even worse, at that very moment, Edwin's wife was winging her way towards Tupak Soiree's spiritual retreat somewhere high in the snowy mountains of the American heartland. Edwin's money was even now on its way into Soiree's fat, bloated bank account. Tupak Soiree had taken everything Edwin had: his wife, his wealth, his career and his future. Edwin could have lived with that. But Tupak Soiree—a monster unleashed by Edwin himself—had also destroyed May Weatherhill, had sucked the life and sadness out of her, had made her an empty and singularly unremarkable person. For that, Tupak Soiree would have to pay.

And so it was that as his Royal Portliness chuckled his way through yet another interview, and as millions of televison viewers watched with unadorned love, a thought formed in Edwin de Valu's mind. It formed so smoothly and so quickly it seemed almost to have congealed from substances already present, as though the thought had always been there, waiting for Edwin to recognize it. It was a single thought, so beautiful, so pure, so heroic, that Edwin almost threw his hands heavenwards with joy.

"Tupak Soiree must die." That was it. That was the perfect Platonic Ideal, the single forceful idea that formed in the mind of a distraught ex-editor in a seedy motel this side of the Candle Island Amusement Park: *May must be avenged. Tupak Soiree must die.*

Chapter
Forty-two

Early evening, at the dockside. Edwin and the Serpent.

"You want him dead, he's dead. Simple as that."

"And how much would this . . . what is your price for doing this? For killing him."

"Fifty. Thirty now and twenty on completion."

It had long been an open secret at Panderic Inc. that Léon Mead kept an undisclosed amount of ready cash on hand in case he was ever forced to flee the country. Everyone knew Mr. Mead had been skimming money off of Panderic's pension fund for years and salting foreign bank accounts in several inconsequential countries with the undisclosed "income."

Edwin de Valu had now come to reclaim some of that lost money, a good deal of which was from Edwin's own pension fund. Edwin arrived at dusk, as the night watchman was meditating and the security guards were sharing marshmallows, and with a bluff of purpose, he walked briskly towards the elevators. In spite of his outwardly confident manner, Edwin's heart was pounding as he made his way to the four-teenth/thirteenth floor and entered the darkened halls of Panderic Inc.

The door to Mr. Mead's office was locked, but Edwin had come pre-pared, and the crowbar he had hidden up his sleeve slid easily into his hand. Edwin first attempted to pry the door open, but he eventually gave up and began pounding the handle into submission, the loud reverberating bangs echoing across the cubicles. Face sweating and hands shaking, Edwin managed to splinter the wood around the metal housings and was able to squirm in a few fingers and pop the lock. The door to Mr. Mead's office swung open.

Edwin moved like a greased ocelot, over to the mahogany desk, flick-ing on the lamp, searching through the drawers for anything that looked like a key. There was none, but then Edwin hadn't expected it to be that easy. No. He would have to use his brain. He would have to out-smart the absent Mr. Mead.

Everyone knew where the secret safe was located: it was hidden behind a large Warhol print of a can of soup that hung directly beside Mr. Mead's wet bar. (The print wasn't a real Warhol but a clever forgery—the fact that "Campbell's" had been misspelled was the first clue—but this, ironically enough, had only increased its value. Turns out, original Warhols are a dime a dozen, but authentic fakes are much rarer.) Edwin hated that stupid can of soup, and he considered punch-ing a fist through it as an act of vengeance, but who would have guessed canvas would be so tough? He punched and punched, but managed to make only a few fist-sized indents, barely visible. Which sort of sums up the relationship between Edwin's generation and Mr. Mead's. But enough of that. Enough of Warhol and Campbell's soup. Edwin had more momentous things to deal with.

The safe had a touchpad key-control time-release lock. Meaning that without either a blowtorch or a password, one's chances of getting inside were very slim. Edwin wiped the sweat from his forehead, took a deep stabilizing breath and began to talk it out. "Think it through. You can do this. You can pull this off." Mr. Mead was a man with a very small brain. How hard could it be to break his code? "Woodstock?" Edwin punched the code into the touchpad, turned the dial and pulled. Nothing. "Peace." "Love." "Watergate." "LSD." "Kent State." Nothing. And Edwin was fast running out of Baby Boomer references. "Self-important." "Overblown." "Overrated." Nothing worked. Damn it anyway. Could Edwin's life be going any worse than it was? When the mail had finally been delivered that afternoon (owing to staff shortages, postal service had been cut back to twice a week), Edwin had discovered a writ of sale for the brownstone. Jenni had sold it for a pittance and was going to have it converted into a Rainbow Drop-In Centre, whatever the hell that meant. And then, taking salt into the wound, Edwin had opened a second daisy-festooned envelope and found a stack of legal paperwork filled in with a pink ballpoint pen with smiley faces over the i's, along with a booklet entitled *Divorce with Love: Learning to Let Go, Learning to Let Grow* (gotta love those clever wordplays) *the Tupak Soiree Way.* And Edwin thought, "Great. I'm being dumped by a spinoff."

It was with these lovey-dovey divorce proceedings and legal theft of property weighing on his mind that Edwin summoned the anger to attack the wall safe. He hammered the dial with the crowbar, splitting the outer casing but achieving little else save a vibrating elbow and sharp pains in his wrist. "Damn you!" he yelled. "'Jesus Christ Superstar!' 'Eleanor Rigby!' 'Tet Offensive.' What?" He punched in code after code and pulled and pulled. Nothing.

"Try 'postmodern sensibilities,'" said Mr. Mead.

Edwin turned in shock as his former boss entered the room. "Shit," said Edwin.

"Is that all you have to say for yourself? Just 'shit'?" Mr. Mead stopped to right a picture frame that had toppled when Edwin had rifled through the desk, and then, with slow, caustic deliberation, said, "So when I wouldn't give you a bonus, you decided to steal it from me anyway."

Edwin picked up the crowbar, stood firm. "I need the money, Mr. Mead, and I'm not leaving without it. I'll take you down if I have to."

"A threat? Is that a threat? You break into my office like some second-rate burglar from a pulp detective novel, and you think *you* can threaten *me*?"

Edwin had always assumed that Léon Mead, beneath the bully-boy bravado, was a cowardly lion. But Mr. Mead was advancing towards Edwin with grim resolve, and his pace never faltered. Edwin raised the crowbar like a batter in a practice range. Head? Shoulders? Knee-cap?

"Mr. Mead, I swear. I'll do it. There's just the two of us here. No witnesses."

"Exactly," said Mr. Mead, a tight smile playing across his lips. "No witnesses."

Edwin gulped, felt the crowbar start to slip in his wet palms.

And then, in an abrupt eye-aching flash, the entire room was flooded with light. A small man with wild eyes stood by the doorway, his hand on the light switch, and he cried out: "Vengeance is mine!"

Mr. Mead turned to face the intruder. "Bob?" he said.

The small man took a dramatic step forward, raised a rifle to his shoulder and took aim at Mr. Mead.

"Actually," said Edwin, "I think it's pronounced 'Bubba.'"

The man with the rifle balked at this. He looked down at the name tag on the front of his shirt and said, "What? This? This isn't mine. These clothes were given to me by a"—he was going to say "friend," but that didn't sound right—"by a former colleague. From my prison days. That's right, it is I! Dr. Robert Alastar. Better known as Mr. Ethics!"

"I thought I recognized you!" said Edwin. "You look bigger in your author photo."

"Yes, well. I've lost a lot of weight recently. The dietary standards at your average maximum-security prison are absolutely appalling. Now then, where was I? Ah, yes. Revenge! *Revenge!* You betrayed me, Léon; you left me for dead. And I have come back to exact a terrible justice." He stepped closer, took a near-pointblank bead on Mr. Mead's head.

To Edwin's amazement, Mr. Mead did not flinch or duck or drop to his knees and beg for mercy. Instead, he took a cigarillo from his desk-top stand and, cool as all get out, flicked the top of a Zippo lighter, lit up and took a deep satisfying inhalation. "Shklovsky, V.B. MK-47," he said. "Standard issue on the Vladivostok Front. Soviet Red Army sen-try duty and armoured personnel. It fires advance-gauge shells in rapid sequence. The last plant to make the MK-47 closed down in 1982 on the Afghanistan frontier. The rifles were decommissioned soon after as unreliable. That's an antique, Bob. Even worse, it's a Soviet antique, meaning the odds are 10 to 1 that if you try to shoot me, it will either misfire or blow up in your face. You *have* test-fired it, haven't you, Bob?"

Mr. Ethics' eyes narrowed. "You're bluffing."

"Am I?"

"Vengeance is mine!" screamed Mr. Ethics, and he pulled hard on the trigger.

The gun exploded. The chamber burst, deafening Mr. Ethics and showering shrapnel across the room. The blast punctured the air, and left Edwin stunned and Mr. Ethics reeling.

"Six years of Tom Clancy, asshole!" roared Mr. Mead as the would-be gunman, dazed and ears ringing, stumbled and fell.

Then, calmly and without a word, Mr. Mead reached over and took the crowbar from Edwin's hands. He sat back on his desktop and, shaking his head, surveyed the sorry scene before him: a bungled burglary by a traitorous former employee; an escaped convict and ex-author rolling on the floor holding his ears and sobbing; and at least $5,000 in damages to the wall panelling and door frame of his office.

"We'll start with you, Edwin. You came here to rob me. Why?"

At this point, exhausted and defeated, Edwin could see no reason for lying. "I wanted to hire a hitman to kill Tupak Soiree."

"Really? Let me see if I understand this correctly. You wanted to use *my* money to hire someone to kill *my* top-selling author."

"That's right."

"I see." Mr. Mead placed the crowbar across his lap like a college lecturer with a pointer. "Well, don't hire Bob here. He's about as good an assassin as he is a tax-dodger."

Mr. Ethics lurched onto his knees. His hands were still over his ears, but the sobbing had, for the most part, subsided. His face was wet with tears of pain and useless rage. "God damn you all to hell, Léon!"

"You managed to escape from a maximum-security prison? I'm impressed, Bob. Or can you hear me? Should I talk louder?"

"Yes, yes." He sounded utterly broken. "I can hear you. It's just . . . it's just not fair. It's not."

"Another brilliant insight from Mr. Ethics," said Mr. Mead. "*The world isn't fair*. Bravo. I eagerly await further updates. Perhaps you have noted that the colour of the sky, incredible as it may seem, is blue. Or that when released, objects tend to fall downwards. Or that rich people can do whatever they want. Or that politicians tend to lie. Or that—"

"Enough," said Edwin, softly. "You've won, so spare us the patronizing tone. It's obvious you're enjoying this."

"Oh, I am," said Mr. Mead. "Absolutely. But not in the way you assume. No, I'm enjoying this because it proves that all is not well in Happy Land. It proves that the world is still a nasty, messy place. *This* is the way it's supposed to be: editors trying to kill authors, authors trying to kill publishers. I find it"—he searched for the word, the right word—"*inspiring*."

Mr. Ethics rose slowly to his feet. "So you're not going to turn me in?"

"Turn you in? God, no. I would sooner read another stupid Tupak Soiree book. Now then, do you still favour blond cognac over walnut brandy? You do? Philistine. Let's see now," he put the crowbar to one side and began looking through his cabinet. "Ah, yes. Olson's Own. The finest Norwegian cognac from the catacombs of Oslo. What say?"

Edwin and Mr. Ethics exchanged glances, each trying to second-guess the situation, neither wanting to make the first move.

"None for me, thanks," said Edwin just a little too casually. "Think I'll mosey along. You two will want to catch up on old times, swap some stories. Maybe get falling-down drunk and maudlin. I'll catch up with you later." And he headed towards the door, all but whistling with his hands in his pockets.

"Not so fast," said Mr. Mead, and Edwin froze in mid-saunter. "Aren't you going to tell me how much?"

"Sorry?"

"How much do they want? What are they asking?"

"To kill Tupak Soiree? The price I was quoted was $50,000. Unfortunately, I'm a tad short."

Mr. Mead nodded. "And you think this is moral, what you're doing? You think it's appropriate behaviour, having a beloved author snuffed out on your command?"

"Well, I don't know about moral. But I think it's the right thing to do." Edwin wasn't sure where this conversation was headed.

"Why don't we ask the expert. Bob?"

By now, Mr. Ethics was hunched over, drinking his cognac with both hands huddled around the cup, and he didn't catch the question. "What did you say? My ears are still ringing."

"Is it ethical to have Tupak Soiree killed?"

"That depends," said Mr. Ethics, slowly at first but soon warming to the topic. "It depends on whether you take a Kantian or a Utilitarian approach. A 'let justice be done though the heavens fall' view versus 'the greatest good for the greatest number.' And Mr. Soiree certainly has provided a great many people with a good deal of happiness™."

There was a brief pause as they mulled this over.

"I'm with Kant on this one," said Edwin.

"Me too," said Mr. Ethics. "Let's kill the fucker. I'll chip in for your hire-a-hitman fund. I've got"—he rummaged through his pockets, came up with a handful of loose change, mainly pennies and dimes—"eighty-nine cents. Now that may seem a meagre amount, but one's moral contribution must be put in a proper, proportional context. That eighty-nine cents is everything I have."

"Let me see," said Edwin, working it out in his head. "That leaves us about, what, $49,999 and ten cents short. I think I've got ten cents here somewhere. As for the rest . . . Mr. Mead?"

Mr. Mead said nothing for a long, long time. And when he finally spoke, it was with what seemed to be a typical Mead non sequitur.

"Robert Lewis," he said, and there was a long pause. "Robert Lewis. That was the name of the pilot who flew the *Enola Gay*. Captain Robert A. Lewis. That was the name of the man who dropped the bomb on Hiroshima. August 6, 1945. And do you know what his immediate reaction was? Do you know what he said when he saw the blinding light and the cloud uncurling? He said, 'My God, what have we done?' That's how I feel right about now. I published Tupak Soiree's book, I promoted it once it started to take off, I repackaged and resold it in a hundred different forms. And now, the only thing I can think is, 'My God, what have we done? What have we unleashed upon this world?' And now you're asking me to join your vengeful little crusade. You're asking me to help you have Tupak Soiree killed." Léon took one last long draw on his cigarillo and then stubbed it out in the tortoise green ashtray with the gold-leaf trim. "Let's do it," he said. "Let's kill him."

Edwin was just about to pump the air with his fist and say "Yes!" but his decorum got the better of him and he opted instead to nod solemnly.

Their attention now turned to the wall safe behind the mini-bar. "Is the code really 'postmodern sensibilities'?"

"No," said Mr. Mead. "It's Wordstock. *Word*, get it?"

"Ahh," said Edwin, pretending to laugh. That zany Baby Boomer humour—you just can't beat it.

"But I'm not opening the safe," said Mr. Mead. "Fifty grand? Forget it. What do you think, I'm made of money?"

Edwin was taken aback. "I thought—"

"You want something done, you do it yourself. Now go fetch me another drink, Edwin. I have something to show you. Something better than money." Mr. Mead slid his hand along a side panel, found the hidden G-spot and pressed. A cabinet opened up and Mr. Mead said, "You remember *Balkan Eagle*? Mad Dog Mulligan?"

"Ah, yes. The General. What ever happened to him?"

"He runs a Tupak Soiree anger-management course somewhere out in Iowa. Changed his name to Mildly Peeved Dog Mulligan. It doesn't really have the same ring to it, but what can you do? Anyway, before he got blissfully at one with the universe, the General gave me a little present, a token of his appreciation." Mr. Mead reached inside the cabinet with both hands and withdrew the future itself: cold and shiny and lethal. "Atku-17. The next generation in home defence. It's got all the bells and whistles. Exploding magnesium-tipped shells. Nightscope. Laser lock. You just point and shoot. It's the instamatic camera of high-tech weaponry. And let me tell you, Clancy would be green with envy if he knew I had one of these babies. This gun"—Mr. Mead cast a disparaging look in Mr. Ethics' direction—"is idiot-proof. A complete fool could use one of these. I mean, you'd have to be a moron, an absolute—"

"All right already! I get the drift," said Mr. Ethics.

"So who does the deed?" asked Edwin.

"We draw straws," said Mr. Mead. "The loser kills Tupak—or the winner, depending on your point of view. Personally, I would love to do it, but I can't. Arthritis, you see." He held up his gnarled fingers.

"Broken thumb!" said Edwin quickly, displaying his own bent digit.

"Oh, come on," said Mr. Ethics. "You don't pull the trigger with your thumb. Besides, you're the young and spry one. I nominate Edwin."

"Yeah?" said Edwin. "Well, you managed to escape from prison, so you must be pretty spry yourself."

"That's true," said Mr. Mead. "He's got you there, Bob."

"But," said Mr. Ethics, "I failed in my attempt to kill you, Léon, remember? Which only proves that I am indeed a poor candidate for the task. I say, 'to each according to their abilities.' Léon provides the weapon, I provide the ethical overview, and Edwin here provides the youthful vigour. It's an *a priori* assumption that wars are to be fought by the young."

"This is generational discrimination," said Edwin bitterly. "Why can't I provide the ethical overview'?"

"Because you don't have the necessary life experience," said Mr. Ethics. "Wisdom takes time, Edwin. It requires a certain sense of perspective, something woefully lacking in today's youth."

Mr. Mead had had enough. "Let's just draw the damn straws, shall we?"

Edwin and Mr. Ethics exchanged sullen glances and then nodded in agreement. Straws it was.

"Fine," said Mr. Mead. "Straws it is. But before we do, perhaps Edwin would like to explain what happened to my authentic Warhol forgery?"

Chapter
Forty-three

High in the alpine heights of his mountain retreat, as snow filtered softly down onto spruce boughs and the crisp cool air broke across distant peaks . . . Tupak Soiree was picking his nose. He had his index finger wedged up good and tight, trying to dislodge what felt like a piece of wet putty.

Tupak Soiree was not the Anti-Christ. Nor was he an evil mastermind. He was, in fact, a fairly affable chap once you got to know him, even if he was, you know, responsible for the downfall of Western civilization as we know it. He lived in a spacious, luxurious cabin overlooking a panoramic mountain valley. (Though the word "cabin" should probably have editorial quotation marks around it as well; it was a sprawling complex of interconnected pseudo-rustic mansions, and not simply a "cabin.") Tupak owned half of the town below and most of the mountains in the vicinity. He hadn't wanted to be a messiah, and he hadn't revelled in the cult of personality that had formed so quickly around his book—not at first. But hey, he was still human, was still a man, and as such was as susceptible to flattery and temptation as the next guy. (Provided the next guy in line was a randy lech with a leather fetish.) When women started writing to him, offering him their "cosmic sensuality," who was he to deny them such happiness™?

Tupak Soiree, like most self-proclaimed gurus, was surprisingly unimaginative when it came to fulfilling his every desire and whim. Lots of sex and the constant fawning of underlings, that was about it. He had racked his brains, and that was the best he could come up with.

And truth be told, Tupak had already become bored with the bevy of beauties who paraded through his life, had grown tired of his "happy holy harem" and their constant niggling demands. Especially the newest member, the one who called herself Sunshine Happy, the one who was always pestering him. "Do I look enlightened? Do I?" "Yes," he would say wearily, for the 400th time that day. "You look enlightened." "Really? You're not just saying that?" "No, no, you look fine. You look completely enlightened." "Because I just don't *feel* very enlightened today." True, she had brought some spare change with her when she arrived—not much, less than two million—but still, it was a nice gesture. (Tupak spent more than that on refreshments in a month. When Sunshine Happy turned over the money, which she had apparently stolen from her husband, Tupak had simply tossed it on the pile. Hardly a day went by without someone showing up proffering Rolex watches or bags filled with rubies. It was starting to get downright stale.)

"Do I look enlightened? Do I? Really?"

After about a week of this, Tupak had suggested that she go off on a "vision quest" down by Danger Ridge. "It's deep in the forest," he said. "Just keep walking—and maybe keep your eyes shut for better concentration. That's how I first attained enlightenment."

"But I thought that happened in Tibet."

"Tibet. Colorado. What's the diff?"

But alas, she hadn't wanted to stray from his resplendent side, not even for a moment. Not even for a single goddamn moment. "Do you mind? I'm trying to pee."

It wasn't easy being the Supreme Enlightened Spirit of the Universe. It wasn't easy being the Most Revered Thinker of Our Age. You always had to be "on," always had to think of something clever to say when the conversation lagged; you could never say "I dunno" or "beats me."

Tupak often wondered if Sir Isaac Newton or Albert Einstein had experienced similar difficulties. He often wondered if they had felt the same "pressure to perform."

The fringe benefits of being a guru were nice enough: money, fame, lavish ostentation and endless media appearances. Tupak loved giving interviews, loved meeting celebrities. He had been giddy with fanstruck awe when he first met Oprah, and once, backstage, he had shared a green room with—ah, but no never mind. Now the celebrities were coming to him. There were times, late at night when everyone was asleep, when Tupak Soiree would pace the halls of his sprawling mansion and wonder: Why do I feel so sad? Why do I feel so melancholy? What is it I'm missing? *If only . . . Maybe someday . . .*

He missed his childhood (which was not in Bangladesh; Tupak could barely spell Bangladesh), and he especially missed his carefree college days. Maybe he should have majored in computers instead. He had taken a single course in Unix code, back in second year, and had marvelled at the stark beauty of the binary system, had been absolutely enchanted and fascinated with the clean procession of 1s and 0s, that endless either/or from which unlimited, intricate patterns could be shaped. It was the closest thing to enlightenment Tupak had ever experienced.

And as he stood, bathed in moonlight, picking his nose, he sighed, "Maybe I should have stuck with computers instead."

When he first built his mountain retreat and then purchased the town below, he had toyed with the idea of creating a vast computer learning network with the latest state-of-the-art equipment and only one pupil: himself. He had outfitted a lecture hall with the most sophisticated computers money could buy. Except that they were free. A gift from what's-his-face, that goofy guy with the glasses and the bad breath. What was his name? The acolyte who was always offering to wash Tupak's feet. Bill? *Billy?* Yes, that was it, Billy Gates. Tupak had asked Gates to give him some pointers, maybe show him how to use the chat lines (they were almost all about Tupak Soiree anyway, so maybe he could eavesdrop, sign in under an assumed name). But Billy had protested in mid-kowtow, "No, no, no. I couldn't teach you such things. You are far too divine to soil your hands with matters as profane as surfing the Internet."

So Tupak had him flogged.

This was a grave mistake on Tupak's part. Flogging Billy Gates, along with keeping a harem and his habit of appearing on one too many talk shows, had provoked a quick and stinging response from M.

It was a terse note, and it made Tupak quake in fear:

> Mr. Soiree: You seem to be enjoying yourself a little too much lately. I'd advise you to curtail some of your more distasteful excesses. Remember, I know your secret. I know the truth about you. I made you, and I can tear you down just as easily. So lay off the bullshit, or I will personally go up there and kick your flabby ass down the mountainside. This isn't a threat. It's a promise. Yours truly, M.

Panicked, Tupak had cancelled future television appearances and had convened an assembly to tell everyone to stop calling him the Enlightened One. "It's just a book," he said. "It's just a self-help book."

"Yes, O Enlightened One," they chanted.

And now this: he had something wedged right up deep in his nose, and no matter how much he dug around, he couldn't get at it. "Damn these daily manicures; they make picking one's nose absolutely impossible." Even worse, in a fit of pique over having been scolded by M., he had cleared the entire east wing of lackeys, so there wasn't even anyone on hand to pick his nose *for* him. He would have to manage it himself. Life just wasn't fair.

High above the mountain retreat, Edwin de Valu was crouched in the underbrush.

Hands trembling, heart racing, he screwed in the Atku nightscope and adjusted the lens. He was having a hard time controlling his breathing, a hard time trying not to hyperventilate. How did Edwin de Valu, a lowly editor, come to be bushwhacked in a forest, poised to fire upon the very slush-pile writer he had once rescued from anonymity? Simple. Edwin had picked the short straw. "Well then," said Mr. Mead. "It's settled." "Hear! Hear!" said Mr. Ethics. Edwin had demanded that they make it best two out of three, but he lost again.

So they tried rock-paper-scissors, but Edwin was the odd man out each time. They then tried three-card monte and one-potato-two-potato, and Edwin lost every round. "Fine," he said angrily. "I'll do it. But you two have to provide backup."

It had taken three days to get to Colorado and two more to reach the base of Tupak's secluded mountain compound. With Ethics and Mead holding down the fort at one of the few local motels still open, Edwin swung the gun over his shoulder and prepared to make the long trek alone. "Don't worry," said Mr. Mead. "We'll be right here, poised to act should anything go awry. Isn't that right, Bob?"

"Sure," said Bob as he pillaged the room's mini-bar. "We'll be right behind you. Hey, look! Cashews!"

They walked Edwin out to where the trail began and wished him "godspeed" and "good luck" and other talismanic protective farewells.

As Edwin de Valu trudged up the mountain, Mead and Ethics retired to their motel room. "I ever tell you about my younger days?" asked Mr. Mead as they walked back. "In college, when I was working the carnival circuit?"

"You were a carny?" said Mr. Ethics.

"Oh, yes. Sleight of hand, three-card monte, ring toss, the works."

Edwin, legs aching, shoulder straining, fought his way through the snow and pine branches behind Tupak's compound. Fortunately for Edwin, Tupak's crack team of bodyguards had long since been infiltrated by "the message," and they now spent most of their waking hours in the avid pursuit of bliss. Edwin crept noisily by one guard as he sat in his shelter, legs in a pretzel, echoing the *aum soiree* chant.

If you could go back in time, would you kill Stalin if the opportunity arose? This is the question Edwin was asking himself. And the answer, inevitably, was yes. Edwin de Valu would have killed Stalin, would have killed him in an instant. And Tupak Soiree was the Stalin of the New Age. He had released a neutron bomb of love upon the world, and he had to be stopped. Edwin knew in his heart that he was right, but he still felt sickened and racked by doubts. It was one thing to muse philosophically about an issue; it was quite another to pull the trigger.

Edwin peered through the lens.

"You can't miss," Mr. Mead had assured him. "It's idiot-proof." In the liquid green world of night vision, the walls and windows of Soiree's alpine compound swam in and out of focus. Edwin was tracking along the inner wall, probing the interior, when in sudden sharp relief, Tupak Soiree's face came starkly into view. It was so unexpected that Edwin gasped out loud. Then, forcing himself to stay calm, he ran the laser sight up the side of Tupak's face and slowly slid his finger onto the trigger.

Tupak was walking back and forth, finger up his nose, but Edwin managed to keep a lock on him, the way a cougar will keep its prey in sight. "This is it." Edwin took a deep breath. He thought of May. And in the pause between heartbeats, he squeezed the trigger.

The side window shattered in a hail of glass. A spray of blood and gristle exploded from Tupak Soiree's head, and the guru reeled to one side and fell.

A grip of silence followed the explosion. Edwin peered through the nightscope, watching and waiting. Nothing. Tupak Soiree had landed behind an end table, and Edwin could see the hole punched by the bullet in the wall behind. He knew that if the shot had gone clean through Tupak's head, there would be no chance of survival. (Mr. Mead had explained that the shells they were using exploded on exit, and that the vacuum wake this created sucked out pulp from behind.) It was over. Tupak Soiree was dead, and Edwin was just about to click on the safety, sling the rifle over his shoulder and slip away into the night when he caught a glimpse of—*something*. Movement. Was it an assistant rushing to Tupak's side? No. It was worse than that. Far worse.

Tupak Soiree reeled back onto his feet, bellowing like a stuck bull. He held up his hand and looked in horror at the spurt of blood where his digit had once been. In his fear and pain, Tupak had inhaled sharply and his missing index finger was now lodged firmly up his nasal passage. "Oh, my Dod! Hap me! Tumbuddy hap me."

Edwin panicked and squeezed off three more rounds without taking a proper sighting, the bullets hitting brass mirrors and Ming vases, showering rose petals and water into the air, as Tupak fled, screaming in a muffled, stuffy-nosed wail.

"*Shit!*"

Edwin went scrambling down the hillside, not bothering to skulk, and kicked open the back patio doors. *Why couldn't the son of a bitch just die?* He found Tupak cowering in a corner, paralyzed with fear. "Whad do you wand? Whad do you wand?"

Edwin was out of breath. His heart was pounding and his face was wet with sweat. "I'm sorry," he said. "But I have to kill you." Edwin fumbled with the rifle. This wasn't the way he had imagined his first face-to-face meeting with Tupak Soiree would go. "I'm sorry," said Edwin. "But I have to."

Edwin was just about to scatter the heavenly brain matter of Tupak Soiree, Messenger of Love, Apostle of Bliss, when he noticed the finger, still twitching, that was embedded in Tupak's nose. That was no way for a man to die . . . Without thinking, Edwin reached over and twisted the finger out of the guru's nose, and then, using a tatter of curtain, he tied a rough tourniquet around the stump. "Put pressure here," he said. "It isn't bleeding that bad. Maybe the heat from the blast cauterized the wound. I don't think there are any arteries in your fingers, so it's probably not as bad as it looks."

"Thank you," said Tupak, voice quavering.

"There, you see?" The bleeding had pretty much stopped. "Keep the pressure on and your hand elevated, and you'll be fine, okay?"

Tupak smiled bravely through the pain and tears. "Okay," he snuffled.

"That's better," said Edwin. "And now I have to kill you."

"No, no, no, no, please, God, no. At least—at least tell me who you are."

"I'm, um, your editor."

"I have an editor?"

"At Panderic? Remember? The book? We talked on the phone several times."

Tupak's fear softened. "Edward?" he said.

"*Win*. Edwin. Now, I hope this doesn't sour you on the editor-author relationship, which should be one based on mutual trust, but—" he stepped back and raised the barrel. "Goodbye, Tupak."

"But I didn't do anything! I didn't even write that book."

"*I knew it!* A computer, am I right? You're some kind of evil wizard. You programmed a computer to manually type a thousand-page manuscript."

"No, no," sobbed the guru. "I'm not a genius. I'm not a mastermind. I'm just an actor."

"An actor?"

"My name is Harold T. Lopez. The 'T' stands for Thomas. Please don't kill me. I'm a graduate of the Tri-State Community College Drama Program. I've never even been to Bangladesh. Please don't kill me."

Edwin lowered his sights. "Harry? Your name is Harry?"

The guru snuffled back a sob and nodded.

"But if you didn't write that book—who did?"

Harry Lopez (a.k.a. Tupak Soiree, a.k.a. Master of the Universe) searched frantically through his desk drawer as Edwin sat to one side, Atku-17 at the ready. Harry's hand was throbbing with pain and was bundled up in a messy homemade bandage, which made it difficult to handle papers, but Harry did his best. The threat of impending death tends to concentrate one's mind.

"Here," said Harry. "Here, do you see? This is my resumé and this is my 8 x 10. It's not the best picture; I mean, the camera puts on ten pounds at least. See? Those are my film credits. This list is live theatre, and that's my drama instructor. You can call her if you like, she'll vouch for me."

Edwin looked it over in quiet disbelief. It was indeed the resumé of Tupak Soiree. "You're listed as 'ideally suited for swarthy Latin outlaws and/or lovers.'" He raised an eyebrow.

"My agent's idea," said Harry, somewhat sheepishly.

"Can you really tap dance and play the sax?"

"No. I mean, not really. But everybody embellishes their resumé, right?"

Edwin put the bio to one side, and he asked the question, the only question that mattered: "Who is Tupak Soiree? The *real* Tupak Soiree."

The answer he got was not what he expected. "There is no Tupak Soiree," said Harry. "There never was. It's a scam. You've been set up, Edwin. I was just hired to act as a stand-in, and that was only because your boss started offering money for interviews. I was hired to handle the media, to do the interviews, to help flog the book, to help give the readers a focus for their adulation. Tupak Soiree doesn't exist. He's just a role, a role I was hired to play."

"*Who*, Harry? Who hired you?"

Harry took a deep breath. "Some guy down in Paradise Flats. Some guy named McGreary. Jack McGreary."

Edwin sat back. "McGreary. Why is that name so familiar? Wasn't he your landlord?"

"No," said Harry. "He was never my landlord. I didn't even meet him until he showed up at the casting agency in Silver City. I was doing Little Theatre, one-man mime introspectives, some experimental works—I did one deconstructionist play that consisted entirely of a single sound: 'Moo.' It was very well received, especially among the alternative press. The local arts community hailed it as a—"

"Harry? I have a gun, remember?"

"Sorry. Where was I?"

Edwin made a sound halfway between a sigh and a growl. "You were doing community theatre in Silver City."

"That's right, and Mr. McGreary comes in, asks me if I'd like to make a lot of money and live in a big mansion. I said yes, for obvious artistic reasons. I mean, it was the role of a lifetime. He asked me if I thought I could play an East Indian mystic. Well, my mom was Italian and my father was from Mexico, so I didn't think I could really pull it off. What do I know about India? But Mr. McGreary says, 'Don't worry about it. Remember Archibald Belaney? A blue-eyed Englishman who convinced the world he was a Native elder named Grey Owl? He had 'em fooled for years. People see what they want to see.' So what the heck, I took the part. No audition, no callback. Just a straight hand-shake and a cut of the box office, so to speak. I was hired just before the first *Oprah* interview." Harry came closer, sat down, looked imploringly at Edwin. "You have to believe me, I never dreamed it would end up like this. It got way out of hand. At first, I spent most of my money paying off former friends. You know, bribing past class-mates, dishing out hush money to old college instructors. But then they started to read the book and they began returning my money. Said I was a genius, even when I told them I never wrote one word of it. I only memorized a few key passages."

"I know," said Edwin. "I've seen you spouting insights by rote."

"I'm sorry," said Harry. And he was. He shifted in his seat, keeping his bandaged hand elevated, and he said, "It's not that I'm a bad person—I'm just a bad guru. You have to understand. It was a gig. I mean, I was *acting*, that's all. I kept waiting for someone to catch on, but no one ever did. It was like they wanted to be fooled. It was like they preferred the illusion to the reality. I mean, I couldn't even get the accent right. I only ever took an introductory course in dialects, and even then I didn't study East Indian variations. I took a dozen different brands of Cockney and every British accent there is, but we didn't learn Pakistani or Hindu dialects until second year—and I took computers for non-majors instead. That's why Mr. McGreary chose some obscure village in northern Bangladesh as my hometown; he figured the odds were better no one would know it. I had real trouble with the accent. Which is too bad, because my Irish one is excellent. It really is. I got a B+. Want to hear it? 'Faith and begorra, me lassie child. 'Tis a wee fair sight for Irish eyes.'"

"Spare me the leprechaun shtick," said Edwin.

"But I do an excellent Limerick," said Harry, ever so earnest.

"Gun, Harry. Remember?"

"Oh," said Harry, his chest deflating.

"I don't care what grade you got in Dialects 101, okay?"

Harry looked down, discouraged. "That's what Mr. McGreary said too, only he wasn't as polite. He said, 'You stupid twit. Who the hell is going to believe an Italian-Mexican–American with an Irish accent and a name like Tupak Soiree?' He kept hitting me on the head. He wasn't a very nice person. I really think he needs to get in touch with his inner child."

"Where is he now? This Mr. McGreary, how do I find him?"

"Far as I know, he's still in Paradise Flats."

Edwin stood up to leave. "Thank you, Harry. It's been a pleasure. Sorry about your finger."

"Listen," said Harry. "If you go to Paradise Flats, be careful. He's mean."

Chapter
Forty-four

May Weatherhill changed her name to Cotton Candy, and she floated like gauze on a warm autumn wind from one open community to the next, before eventually settling into an upstate Happiness™ Convent (Oneida Community, Branch 107), where she was surrounded by like loving people.

In the convent, the days bled one into another and time seemed to dissolve. There were no calenders, no clocks, no way to divide the world into hours, minutes or days. There were no dismal Monday mornings, no joyous Friday nights, no lonely Sunday afternoons.

May wandered the herb gardens, met and made love with a procession of similar white-garbed strangers, and smiled until her face and heart grew numb. She could feel her world swing slowly into balance. Into stasis. She kept having the same conversations. The people changed, one radiant, glowing face replaced with another, but the talk itself was interchangeable. No one made caustic remarks. No one gossiped. No one ever cried—and nor did anyone ever laugh until their chests ached and their eyes went blurry. No laughter. No tears. It was, in the truest sense of the phrase, Heaven on Earth. Everyone was always agreeing, always flitting from one circle to another. No one knew anything about May, and yet they loved her very deeply. The sun was warm and the people were beautiful: holistic loving vegetarians dressed in simple homespun clothes. There were flowers scattered along the thresholds and spinning wheels turning endlessly in the evenings, and the evenings were long and twilight gold. *All that's solid melts into air* . . .

And May was happy. She was so very, very happy. The surface of her life was placid and calm, and when she looked in a mirror she no longer saw an incomplete person, no longer saw an arrangement of flaws and shortcomings. She hardly even saw herself. Not that it mattered. On the seventh day, the Sisters of Happiness™ removed the mirrors from the convent, banishing pride, insecurity and vanity with one simple act.

Perhaps it was the proximity to the Sheraton Timberland Lodge that first began to undermine May's calm demeanour. Every day, on the long barefoot walk to the local farmers' market, May passed the now deserted hotel, overgrown with vines, and as she passed she would whisper a name—the one name that continued to confuse her, enrage her, beguile her, annoy her: "Edwin de Valu." Edwin, conspicuous in his absence, cast dark ripples just beneath the surface of her calm, creating dangerous eddies and unpredictable currents that threatened to capsize everything.

The days continued to bleed, one into another. The herbs grew, and the hotel crumbled. May's life was caught in a Möbius strip—the days endlessly repeating, the smiles never faltering.

And then one day, a letter arrived. It came like a stone through a stained-glass window, smuggled in under the guise of bliss and happiness™, with the message "Glory to Tupak Soiree!" written large upon the envelope in a shaky but determined hand (Edwin was still getting used to his crooked thumb, was still having trouble keeping his words lined up).

Inside the envelope, the writing was just as shaky, but the sentiments were not. It was a message writ bold and clear, and across the top of the page, in large capital letters, Edwin had scrawled: *A MANIFESTO FOR MAY.* And below it:

> I know now what is wrong. This isn't about smoking too
> many cigarettes or using too much makeup or eating too

much junk food. It goes much deeper than that. The central flaw in the entire Tupak Soiree philosophy is this: he doesn't understand the true nature of joy.

Joy is not a state of being, May. It's an activity. Joy is a verb; it's not a noun. It doesn't exist independently of our actions. Joy is *supposed* to be fleeting and transitory, because it was never meant to be permanent. *Mono-no-aware*, May. "The sadness of all things." The sadness that informs everything, even joy itself. Without that, joy cannot exist.

Joy is what we *do*. Joy is a naked dance in the rain. Joy is pagan and absurd and tinged with lust and sadness. Bliss is not. Bliss is where we go when we die.

I am leaving. I am on my way south, towards the desert, towards a final confrontation. I am going to rescue us all from happiness. I am going to restore joy and pain and the guilty pleasures of life to their rightful place.

I am going to save the world, May . . . And then I'm coming back for you.

Across the bottom of the page, underlined forcibly and littered with exclamation marks, Edwin had written: *mbuki-mvuki!!*

And for the first time in a long, in a very long time, May began to laugh. Out loud. A belly laugh. A deep, soul-purging laugh. *Mbuki-mvuki*, indeed. May knew the word very well; it was one of her untranslatables, a Bantu word meaning "to shed one's clothing spontaneously and dance naked in joy." It was a word of *doing*, a word of letting go, of raising hell.

May had the image of Edwin dancing naked in the rain, a scarecrow figure, stick arms waving, in a comic ode to vice. She laughed and she laughed. Edwin. Her Conan. Her man of the grand, meaningless gestures, naked in the rain. *Mbuki-mvuki!*

"Excuse me? Cotton Candy?"

May turned, startled. It was one of her fellow Sisters of Eternal Happiness™, an older lady with large doe-like eyes. She looked concerned. Very concerned. "I heard you laughing—we all heard you laughing—and I must say, it didn't sound like *proper* laughter. It didn't sound like the calm, peaceful laughter of someone who is at one with the universe. Indeed, if I didn't know better, I would even say it sounded a little bit malicious."

But this only made May laugh harder. "Oh, it was malicious. It was very malicious." And with that, she slid the Banner of Bliss from her shoulders, folded it carefully, and handed it over to the sister. "I think I've had just about enough happiness™."

"Oh, dear. Are you sure? Is there something wrong? Aren't you happy here?"

"Yes," said May. "I *am* happy. That's the problem."

And so, even as Edwin prepared for the final showdown between the forces of bliss and the forces of vice, May Weatherhill gathered up her belongings and, with a renewed vigour in her step, walked out of the garden and through the Gates of Happiness™.

She never looked back.

Part III

Ragnarök

?→

Isn't Ragnarök a little obscure?
— ed.

Of course it's obscure!
It's an "untranslatable"
STET, damnit!!
STET   W.F.

Chapter
Forty-five

After Tupak Soiree appeared in public *sans* finger, his devoted followers across the country began getting their own index fingers amputated as well. It was considered "a sign of commitment," a "symbol of one's dedication." Hadn't Tupak Himself written that the same finger that points to the moon also picks our nose? And now he, the Great Teacher, had removed his finger from the equation entirely. This was taken as a sign, a sign that from now on there would be no "I" and "thou," no intermediary, no "finger" with which to point. There would be only pure and direct experience of the truth, an instant leap of enlightenment. It was like a Zen koan made manifest.

None of this was Tupak's interpretation. A parasitic but thriving community of scholars and commentators had formed around him, intent on interpreting and explaining his every move. In fact, Tupak (as he was still known) never mentioned his missing finger. He didn't like to be reminded of what had happened, and when—in a gush of devotion—some of his senior management acolytes had suggested he preserve his severed digit as "an icon of self-actualization," Tupak had chased them away with a stick. Disgusted with the hoopla surrounding it, Tupak eventually flushed his finger down the loo.

He was weary of playing the guru, and he was, even now, plotting his escape. The first step would be to publicly renounce his divinity—always assumed but never explicitly stated. It was just a damn book, for God's sake. It talked about how to lose weight and stop worrying, how to improve your sex life and feel good about yourself. That was it. It was a self-help book, nothing more. Why did everything have to end up becoming a religion in America? Why did everything have to harden into dogma?

The next morning, Tupak Soiree began packing his bags. He didn't have a lot of belongings, at least none that wouldn't fit into a standard airline-approved overhead bin: his unbleached all-natural white cotton robes were giving him a rash, and the solid gold fixtures in his bathroom were impossible to remove. Instead, he placed a few mementoes, several large wads of unmarked bills and a map of Hollywood homes ("Where the Stars Come Out to Shine!") into his carry-on bag. It was a lonely farewell—he had many devotees, but no real friends—and Harry (as he would now be known) took one last forlorn walk through the compound. "I never even made it into town," he said. "And I own the damn place."

Chapter
Forty-six

Edwin de Valu hit the ground running.

The top was down, the motor was humming and the highway's dotted line came clipping in like a Morse code message writ in gold paint, like a line of bricks drawing him in. Beside Edwin was the owner of the convertible. "Call me Léon," he had said magnanimously. Edwin had nodded. "Whatever you say, Mr. Mead."

Unfortunately, even with the top folded down and the wind billowing through, the car still reeked of eucalyptus oil and canola seed. Mr. Mead, you see, had been experimenting with yet another dubious cure for hair loss, and his mangy mane was now slick with the stuff. *Rub into scalp vigorously three times a day during meals.* True, no one made "miracle breakthrough cures" any more, not since men everywhere began embracing (and celebrating) their baldness, but Mr. Mead had found a half-forgotten carton of tonic in the storage room of an old pharmacy. "Take what you like, as much as you want," the clerk had said. "The only price is a hug." To which Mr. Mead had punched the man in the head and said, "When I need a hug, I'll ask for one." And so, still locked in oily combat with his own ineluctable hair loss, Mr. Mead had been dousing himself with the stuff regularly ever since they left. "This isn't some bogus snake-oil claim," he insisted. "It actually resuscitates the hair follicles *below* the surface."

"Whatever you say, Mr. Mead."

Under the back seat hid a distraught Mr. Muggins, who, having survived years of Edwin's disdain and several mob attempts on his life, was now yowling plaintively. Stretched out on the back seat itself was none other than Mr. Ethics, along for the ride and hoping for a chance to "beat to death the person responsible for Tupak Soiree." ("It would not be entirely unethical to dismember this McGreary chap—slowly," Mr. Ethics had noted earlier. To which Edwin had answered, "We're not dismembering anybody. At least, not if he co-operates.")

All three crusaders—the balding Baby Boomer, the straw-thin Gen-Xer and the heartless doctor of philosophy—all three of them wore matching shades, wraparound and ultra-hip. The sky was heavy with clouds and the glare from the highway was minimal, but what was a road trip without shades? "Damn, we do look good," said Mr. Mead, examining himself in the rear-view mirror. (He was, of course, using the royal "we.") One other person was present, in spirit if not in fact: pinned to the dashboard, the way Ecuadorian bus drivers will pin portraits of Mercy or the Virgin Mary, was an old, slightly blurred Polaroid of May Weatherhill, caught in passing, laughing in a haze of wine, eyes shut, ruby lips waiting for a kiss that never came.

The cityscape had long since fallen away. Cornfields and sway-backed barns lined the crests of rolling hills. Small, anonymous towns came and went, and the desert grew closer, ever closer.

In the car, the conversation meandered about with a singular lack of purpose. At one point Mr. Mead, predictably, began to ruminate on the lost idealism of the Sixties.

"Woodstock," he said, "was a seminal event in modern history."

From the back seat, Mr. Ethics laughed out loud. "Yeah, right. Teenage hedonism parading as social conscience. Big honkin' deal. The revolution was co-opted before it ever got started."

Mr. Mead turned to Edwin and said, by way of explanation, "Bob here used to be a Marxist."

"Used to be?" said Mr. Ethics, leaning up from the back. "Still am. Let me tell you something, Marxism was more than an ideology. It was a religion. Sure, it may seem antiquated now, but back in its day, it set the world on fire. It was Capitalism vs. Dialectal Materialism. Those were the days, my friend."

"You're a Commie?" said Edwin in wide-eyed disbelief. "A real live Commie?" For someone of Edwin's generation, it was like meeting Cro-Magnon Man in the flesh.

"The funny thing is," said Mr. Ethics, "both systems shared the same underlying assumptions. Capitalism. Communism. They both started with the belief that life is primarily about conflict, about competition. Both were based on notions of unrest and inequality. One system revelled in it, the other reviled it, but both took it as a given. They were more similar than we realized. And now . . . I'm haunted by a certain, unsettling doubt."

"Which is?" said Mr. Mead.

"What if this happiness™ stuff is right? What if this is the way the world ends? Not a socialist paradise, not a capitalist cult of self-interest, but simply this: the end of conflict. The end of unrest. What if this is where the journey was leading us all along? America Generica. Watered-down and homogenous. Happy. Sincere. Bland. Bloodless."

"Is that what we were fighting for?" asked Mr. Mead. "All these years? All those centuries?"

"Maybe," said Mr. Ethics. "Maybe this is how the story ends."

Ethics and Mead were now lost in a mist of nostalgia that was both depressing and comforting, as nostalgia always is. "I miss the old religions," said Mr. Ethics. "I miss the self-important smugness, the unyielding, closed-loop ideologies. I miss the self-righteousness. I miss the sense of mission. I miss the purges and the cruelty and the consciousness-raising sessions." He sighed wistfully as he looked out the window at the landscape rolling past.

There was a pause, an awkward pause, while they waited for Edwin to chime in with his own contribution to their pool of nostalgia. But what could Edwin possibly counter with? What could he possibly offer? After Karl Marx and Woodstock, what was the next logical step?

"*Gilligan's Island*," said Edwin. "In re-runs. *Gilligan's Island* as social history. *Gilligan's Island* as artifact. Jordache jeans. Pat Benatar and big hair. Losing your virginity and worrying about AIDS at the same time. Oh, I miss those golden halcyon days of the late Eighties and early Nineties."

Edwin half-expected them to mock him, to spout the usual "Is that it? In our day, we made history, sonny boy," but the mood was one of validation, not disdain, and they gave Edwin his due. "Happiness™ has made us all dinosaurs," said Mr. Ethics.

Onwards they drove: an ex-Commie, an ex-Hippie and an ex-X. Three generations, lost and adrift, traversing a vast empty landscape littered with fallen heroes: Steinbeck, Kerouac, Knight Rider.

"How can you be an ex-Xer?" Mr. Ethics wanted to know.

"I used to be a member of that fraternity," said Edwin. "But then they got all sensitive and globally aware on me, and I found myself out of step. I was cut from the herd, so to speak. Once the Xer's lost their sense of humour, they lost everything. They lost the very things that made them better than the Boomers: their ideology-free cynicism, their sense of irony, their brutal honesty."

"Join the club," said Mr. Mead. "That's the way it always goes. At some point, you outgrow your generation. Or it outgrows you."

Chapter
Forty-seven

The pride of Paradise Flats was its library. Built during the town's glory days, before the salt mines went bust, the library—with its haughty dome and green copper roof—was the centrepiece of the county. It was also how the town got its nickname: the Emerald City. Though, in fact, it wasn't much of a city, and the rooftops themselves were copper, not emerald. The library had become something of a civic trademark, and when the City Hall and the seminary went up, it was decided to top each one with green copper as well, just in time for the summer celebrations of 1897. Only problem was, the coppered rooftops of the newer buildings were a bright penny brown, and not the stately, aged green of the older buildings. This caused a wave of consternation among members of the town council; they had been promoting Paradise Flats for months as a town known far and wide for its "majestic green-topped buildings."

When it was learned that acidity would speed up the aging process, and that human urine had just the right acidic balance, a heroic effort was launched on the very eve of the parade. Stalwart men, labourers and businessmen alike, joined forces and—amply reinforced with copious supplies of the tavern's lager (beechwood aged)—held a marathon round of urination. Sure enough, the copper turned a proper and dignified shade of green, and the Fourth of July bash went off without a hitch. Joyous crowds gathered along Main Street to admire the piss-soaked rooftops of Paradise Flats, and the future lay out before them like a shimmering mirage, alluring and seemingly near at hand.

Alas, that glorious summer of 1897 would never again be matched. With the salt mines depleted, the real-estate bubble burst and the Berton Line was shut down. The railway shifted its main route farther east, to the coast, and those who were left behind settled into interminable rounds of wistful "what ifs" and "maybe somedays." The Fourth of July celebrations shrank every year, until finally there were more people in the parade than there were watching it.

And that more or less summed up the latter years of Paradise Flats: more people in the parade than watching it. The world passed the town by, like a procession glimpsed from afar, on televison screens and in distant radio reports. Life was elsewhere, and for the past five years, Paradise Flats hadn't even bothered to stage a Fourth of July parade. Just a bake sale and an Independence Day marshmallow roast. (It used to be an Independence Day wiener roast, but the budget was cut back once the municipality filed for bankruptcy.)

The Paradise Flats town council dissipated without anyone really noticing, the way a mud puddle will dry up when you aren't looking. The county took over the town's finances, the regular churches all but disappeared, and a fringe group of snake handlers and tongue-talking Baptists moved in, following the spoor of dismal lives lived in dismal locales and finding in Paradise Flats a people yearning for spirituality. Or failing that, some homespun gospel entertainment.

Today, the main street of Paradise Flats runs wide and lonely, past boarded-up shops and vacant lots. Weeds grow in the cracks along the sidewalks, and hound dogs lie in sun-induced stupor in the middle of the road. That's the kind of place it is. The kind of place where, if a dog lies down to sleep in the middle of Main Street, he is in no immediate danger. The traffic was slow and sparse, and anyway, the drivers would probably just pull over and let the ol' dog sleep. (Chances were, they'd know whose dog it was, too, know it by name.) The streets of Paradise

Flats were all but deserted. Only tumbleweeds were needed to make the image complete. Mind you, the modern equivalent of tumbleweeds were there a'plenty: plastic bags billowing on the wind, rolling down the alleyways, gathering up dust, clotted on fences.

"Good Lord," said Mr. Ethics as Edwin slowed the car. "It's a ghost town."

Not quite. One or two shops were still open, among them a dusty, sun-bleached gas station with its rusted, lazy, wind-creaking sign.

The gas station belonged to another era. Bottles of Fresca were on sale inside an old, belly-tubbed refrigerator. "Fresca?" said Mr. Mead. "Do they even make Fresca any more?" And the bottles didn't even have twist-off caps; you had to pound them off on the edge of the counter.

"Welcome to Paradise Flats," said the proprietor, a man apparently put together from spare parts. His ears were bat-like, his eyes furtive, his chin non-existent and his neck turkey. His eyes didn't match. Hell, they weren't even lined up properly. (Which wasn't surprising. This was, after all, the heartland of inbreeding, where a man would say, "I'd like you to meet my wife and my sister," and there'd just be the one woman beside him.)

"If the theme song from *Deliverance* starts up, I'm outta here," whispered Mr. Ethics.

"Agreed," said Mr. Mead. "The first sign of banjo music and sodomy, and we're gone."

Stereotypes aside, the gas station owner was, in fact, a remarkable man of many talents. He read old algebra textbooks when he wanted to relax, he spoke Spanish and two different dialects of Hungarian, and had once built an amphibious vehicle solely out of odds and ends. (Which would have been a more impressive feat if there had been a body of water anywhere in the vicinity where he could have tried his vehicle out. Maybe he was inbred after all.)

The people in Paradise Flats liked to say they lived on the edge of the desert, but in fact there was no clear dividing line, no border between, say, scrubland and arid wastes. Certainly, the citizens of Silver City always referred to the town as being "out in the desert." Paradise Flats shimmered in the heat, waves of dry air rolled up and off the rooftops, and the baked red sands peeled and cracked like sunburnt skin.

"Haven't had a decent rain in six months," said the man in the gas station. "Last time the rain fell, the ground was so dry, you could practically hear it go '*ahhhh*.' Course, it turned the sidestreets to mud, and more than one shoe was lost in crossing, but the flowerbeds bloomed, if only for a few days, so I suppose it was for the best."

"I suppose it was," said Edwin, holding a cold bottle of Fresca against his flushed face. If there wasn't a sticky residue to contend with, he would have poured the entire drink over his head and shaken himself like a wet dog.

Mr. Mead approached the counter, flashed his best insincere city smile and said, "Say there, friend. We're looking for an old college pal o' mine. A fellow by the name of McGreary. You wouldn't happen to know where we could locate him?"

The man's eyes narrowed in instant suspicion. "College, you say?"

"That's right. The two of us go way back."

"Really? And how old would you be, exactly? You see, ol' Jack's at least eighty. Grew up in the Great Depression, served overseas in the war. Landed on the beaches of Normandy—landed in the first wave. Was hit three times, but they patched him up and sent him back in. Helped liberate Europe, he did. Now, you wouldn't have been there with Jack when he stormed the beaches at Normandy, would you?"

"Oh, did I say *my* college pal?" Mr. Mead laughed away the mistake. "I meant to say he was my *father's* college pal. They fought together in the war. Heroes, both of them."

"You don't say?" By now, the man's eyes were little more than sun-creased squints, so narrow had his gaze become. "'Cause the story around here is that Jack was dishonourably discharged, given the boot for smuggling supplies from the officers' canteen. Spent seven months in the brig for his black-market tricks, left the service in disgrace. Now that wouldn't be the same Jack McGreary you'd be lookin' for, would it?"

Mr. Mead leaned in, his voice husky and Clintonesque. "He may have made his mistakes, but Jack will always be a hero to me."

"Is that a fact?" said the owner.

During Mr. Mead's increasingly ham-handed attempt at finessing the locals, Edwin had wandered the aisles of the gas station's sad little convenience store, amazed at the faded containers and dusty inventory.

There were old kewpie dolls for sale, and postcards from the 1940s on racks that no longer turned. There were carburetors still on shelves alongside eight-tracks by Boxcar Willie, still in the original shrink wrap. And then, as he looked through a random box of odd-sized nails and old spark plugs, something caught Edwin's eye. He looked up and found himself facing a bleached, colour-drained advertisement for Red Seven Chewing Gum. It took a moment for Edwin to understand the significance, or to realize what it was about this poster, curled at the corners and reduced to pastels by sun and age, that held his attention. Edwin remembered Red Seven from his youth. They stopped making it back when Edwin was still in elementary school (something about Red Dye No. 7 causing birth defects in lab rats), though they continued to sell it in the Third World right up until the company was absorbed, gum-wad style, by Wrigley's.

What was it about Red Seven chewing gum? What was it about this poster? And then—and then he saw it. In faded letters along the bottom of the poster: the tag line. Red Seven, you see, used to be sold in a two-for-one pack, and the slogan read: "It's a Two-Pack Soiree of Good, Good Bubble Gum Flavour!" and it caught Edwin cold. He felt his skin shiver, the way it does when you walk over a grave just as a breeze rustles in tall grass. *A two-pack soiree.* They were getting closer. The hour of reckoning was drawing near.

Edwin returned to the counter, whispered to Mr. Mead, "Let's get out of here."

But by now Mr. Mead had spun his web of lies so widely that he was having trouble disentangling himself.

"So," said the owner, "your father's cousin's army drill master is trying to locate Jack McGreary to resolve the last will and testament of an anonymous donor, and he has asked you to act as the executor?"

"Yes, yes, dammit," said Mr. Mead. "Now where is he?"

Edwin, ignored by both men, sighed and looked to the displays of candy and cheap knick-knacks that were stacked alongside the cash register (one of those old cash registers, where the numbers sprang up on separate slots). And there, in front of Edwin, in a small cardboard box beside the jawbreakers and the plastic pinwheels, was a handful of stickers for sale. Daisy stickers. Ten cents each.

"I don't see Jack much. He never comes in here."

Edwin looked up from the box of daisies. "Jack McGreary comes in here all the time," said Edwin. "He wanders around, he looks through the aisles, and he bought a handful of these stickers a while back."

The man behind the counter stopped talking. He turned and looked at Edwin. "How do you know about that? How do you know about them flowers?"

"Where is he?" said Edwin.

"You know," said the man, "I don't especially like Jack. No one does. But we put up with him, always have, always will, and he deserves better than to have some fast-talking debt collectors come slinkin' around. I have a double-barrelled, well-oiled twenty-gauge shotgun under the counter. If you boys don't leave my store right now, I will shoot you for trespassing." With emphasis on the "will."

Mr. Mead snorted at this. "You can't shoot someone for trespassing in a public place during regular business hours."

"You can in Dacob County. By-law 7701. Now get, before I lose my patience in its entirety." He reached below the counter.

"Fine, fine," said Mr. Mead, and they stomped out, the screen door slamming shut behind them.

"Where to now?" asked Mr. Mead.

"The library," said Edwin.

The library, in proud late-Victorian sandstone, was still the most impressive building in the county, even though its once grand square had been reduced to a scraggy patch of brown grass around a fountain that hadn't seen water in years. The park benches, high in dry-stick weeds, were peeling paint to the point of terminal eczema. The garden path was rutted with crumbled concrete, and the front steps of the library itself were pockmarked. But the building was still magnificent, even now, even after all these years.

Inside, there was dust and darkness, and in contrast to the blistering sun outside, there was if not a coolness, at least a certain lack of heat. The librarian, a tall thin-lipped woman with a fire-and-brimstone air about her, was hiding behind a stack of old books and had to be prodded out.

"Hello? Anybody here?"

Nothing. They could see her, huddled down, pretending not to notice, hoping they would go away.

"Sorry to bother you, but we were wondering—"

"Library's closed," she said.

"The sign out front said open."

"It always says that," she snapped. "It don't matter, because it's closed. Only open in the mornings; everybody knows that."

I've seen her somewhere before, thought Edwin. *American Gothic.* She was standing beside the old guy with the pitchfork.

"We're looking for Jack McGreary," said Mr. Mead.

Her expression shifted at this, from sternly disapproving to slyly curious. "Mr. McGreary? Why, is he in trouble?"

"Possibly," said Edwin.

Her face lit up, and she all but clapped her hands in glee. "I knew it! I knew it would catch up with him."

"It?" said Edwin quickly. "What do you mean 'it'?"

"His past. His bad language. His awful lack of manners. He can't be trusted, everybody knows that. Why, Agnes over at the Lo-Food said she caught him eating sardines right out of the can. Can you imagine such a thing! She said he brought his own can opener into the store with him."

"We're not here about the sardines," said Edwin.

"You're not?" She sounded genuinely disappointed.

"No, we're trying to find him and we thought you might be able to help. I'm assuming he comes into the library fairly often."

"Oh, he does," she said, her voice thick with disapproval. "Almost every single day. Pulling out this book and that, messing up my system, carting off every volume under the sun, pushing them home in that beat-up shopping cart of his—which he stole from the Lo-Food as well, I might add. Mr. McGreary was in just this morning. He dropped off a stack of books, all overdue, with those horrid little scribblings of his in the margins. I've warned him more than once not to mark up my books, but he just says, 'Why? No one else in this darn town reads them.' Except, of course, he didn't use the word 'darn.' I took it upon myself to clean that part up. His language is absolutely foul."

Mr. Ethics looked at the stacks of books, the shelves lined up on three floors, the old rolling ladders lying rusted in their tracks. The smell of must and mildew permeated the air. The entire place was heavy with words and deep with ideas. It was less a library than a depository of lost works.

"We haven't had any new additions since the 1920s," the librarian noted with a certain amount of misplaced pride. "Most of these books are from the original boom-town endowment of 1894. We've had scholars from the university in Phoenix come down to catalogue our collection. If only Mr. McGreary would stop reading them. They are far too valuable to be read, you see. Many are first editions. Some are worth thousands of dollars. Thousands, mind you."

"Really?" said Mr. Ethics, a little too eagerly. "And which ones would those be?"

Something was bothering Edwin. "You only have old books? Nothing recent? Nothing new? These are the only books Mr. McGreary reads?"

"Oh, no. He reads everything. He abuses our inter-library loan system, I assure you. Always ordering books in from the main branch and then complaining when they don't arrive. The man is just impossible to deal with. He got so fed up he drove that awful pickup of his to the city one weekend and visited every second-hand store there was. He came back with boxes of books in the back. Boxes and boxes, mind you. And you will never guess what type of books they were. Never."

"Self-help," said Edwin. "He came back with boxes filled with self-help books. I could probably write a list of titles for you: *The Power of Positive Thinking, Simple Living in a Complex World, Building a Business the Buddhist Way, The Road Less Traveled* . . ."

The librarian was taken aback by this. "I don't know what the specifics were, but yes, they were self-help. Every one of them. Stacks and stacks of self-help. How on earth did you know?"

"Oh, I know Mr. McGreary better than you think," said Edwin, and the more he heard, the more it felt as though he was listening to a self-generated echo. And he wondered if maybe Jack wasn't in fact his own splintered reflection, wondered if maybe he hadn't been chasing himself all along.

"Well, I know this much," said the librarian. "Jack McGreary is a horrid, horrid man. He goes up to Silver City almost every week. He says it's for medical tests, but everyone knows what he's really doing." And here her voice dropped to a dramatic stage whisper. "Whoring and drinking. That's right, whoring and drinking. He is a man of very dark urges. I fear for my safety when he comes into this library, I truly do. I fear for my safety—and my virtue as well. Often he spends the entire morning in here, hunched over some obscure book he found way in the back. When we're in here, alone together, I feel trapped. I surely do. It makes a woman nervous. He has . . . he has a certain animalistic air about him. And now, if you will excuse me, I'm starting to get all flustered. It's this heat. I'm melting in it, and I must go home and lie down."

Mr. Mead stepped forward, smile blazing, with that same condescending big-city style that he had tried earlier, and failed with. This time, however, it worked. The librarian mistook his patronizing sincerity as flattery.

"Miss, I hate to be a bother," said Mr. Mead. "But do you think you might be able to help us out? We need to find Mr. McGreary. It's for his own good. The only address we have is a post-office box, and when we tried calling him on my cellphone, his number was no longer in service."

"I know," she said. "The phone company had him disconnected. Cut his phone line just last week."

"For nonpayment?"

"No, not this time. It was over crank calls. He was constantly calling up members of the Chamber of Commerce and haranguing them with his ideas. And the bank manager as well. We have only the one branch, you see, yet Mr. McGreary is always threatening to take his account elsewhere. There are rumours."

"Rumours?"

"About his money. They say he has money stuffed in his mattress. They say he is secretly a millionaire. They say he sold his soul to the devil. What do you think of that?" (In Paradise Flats, the devil was the ultimate trump card. Once played, no one could beat it. And if Jack McGreary was in league with the devil, what more could one possibly add?)

"His address?" said Mr. Mead.

"Oh, yes. He lives out in the trailer park, across the tracks from the old Compascor building. You can't miss it. You absolutely can't miss it. His is the only mobile home there. Everyone else moved out long ago."

"Tell me," said Edwin as they turned to leave. "Have you ever heard of a book called *What I Learned on the Mountain*?"

"I don't read," she said firmly. "Book-reading is for idle minds."

Edwin smiled. "I couldn't agree more," he said.

Chapter
Forty-eight

"He lives out in the trailer park, across the tracks from the old Compascor building. You can't miss it."

They *could* miss it. And they did. The "old Compascor building" turned out to be a boarded-up, cinder-block-and-tin-roof affair with no discernible features other than its utter lack of distinction. Some landmark. (The tracks themselves had long since been pulled up, but the invisible path they cut remained: a long, straight scar of omission running through the centre of town.)

"The ol' Compascor building?" The elderly man hobbling down Main Street on crutches was amazed that anyone would *not* know it. "You must be pullin' my leg. That company was huge. Everybody knows where the ol' Compascor building is. Mind you, they don't sell no insurance. Not no more. It's closed down, coming on seven years. Where would you find it? The ol' Compascor building, you mean? It's down by the ol' drugstore. Everybody knows that."

Edwin sighed/snarled and said, his patience sorely tried, "And where would the old drugstore be?"

"Oh, that's just beside the ol' Compascor building."

Of course. At which point, Edwin got out of the car, crossed over and beat the man senseless with one of his own crutches.

"We're trying to find the trailer park," said Edwin.

At this the old man balked. "The trailer park? But they shut that down years ago. There's no one out there now but crazy Jack McGreary. He's a hermit, you know. Never socializes with the rest of us. Aloof, that's what he is. He's a horse of a different colour, all right. Thinks he's better than the rest of us. A real snob. Well, I'll tell you somethin', if Jack McGreary thinks he's so damn high and mighty, he can darn well—"

Edwin sighed. "Just point us in the right direction, okay?"

"—and so Jack says to the school trustees that we can't allow no prayers in school, because schools are 'by nature meant to be spectacular.' Now, what the hell is that suppose to mean?"

"Secular," said Edwin with yet another sigh. (He had been sighing an awful lot since he got to Paradise Flats. The town has that effect on you.) "I'm sure he said 'secular.'"

"Well, he's a goddamn atheist, if you ask me. You want to see Jack, fine with me. Take Elm Street at the next corner" (there were absolutely no elm trees anywhere on Elm Street), "down to Oak Drive" (ditto), "and follow it all the way to Seabreeze Ocean Crescent" (ditto, ditto, ditto; it wasn't even a crescent, it was just a gravel lane). "You'll see a flat empty lot and a single, lonesome mobile home. That's Jack's place. But you be careful, McGreary's a dangerous man. He's a hellraiser. A regular hellraiser—and a snob. Once, at a town-planning meeting, he gets up on his hind legs, cocky as all get out, and demands to know what Ellen has been doin' with the interest from the town workers' pension fund. Well, I says to him, 'Sit down, Jack, no one cares what you have to say.' And you know what that bugger says? Do you? He says to me—"

Edwin couldn't get away fast enough. The tires spun a dry cumulus cloud of dust as Edwin stood on the gas pedal.

"Justifiable homicide," said Mr. Ethics from the back seat. "If you killed a garrulous old fart like that, no jury of your peers would ever convict you."

Edwin looked in the rear-view mirror, saw the old coot still hectoring away to the dust, and he said, "You may be right, Bob. You may be right."

Chapter
Forty-nine

The silver trailer was basting in the heat, the metal reflecting a stark glare beneath the oppressive UV rays of the desert sun. A sign, the lettering having faded to little more than memory, announced the Fairview Trailer Park Community, but other than the sole "lonesome" mobile home, there was no indication of any community, past or present, semi-nomadic or otherwise. A rusted pickup, the shocks gone, was parked in a junk-scattered front yard, and an extension cord was strung in a listing line to a distant power pole. The horizon lay flat and kiln-baked in all directions.

"Can you imagine living out here?" whispered Mr. Mead. His face was wet with perspiration, his voice was weak and dry. "A metal trailer on the edge of the desert without any shade? It must be like living in an oven."

Edwin cut the engine and the car rolled the last few feet to a stop. Silence. Nothing moved from within the trailer, no blinds were peered through, no door creaked open.

"Aren't you going to take us closer?" asked Mr. Ethics, eyeing the expanse of land that separated their car from the front door.

Edwin got out and, shielding his eyes from the sun, peered at the mobile home. Ethics and Mead joined him, and the theme song from *The Good, the Bad and the Ugly* started up, softly, in the background.

"Ever see *The Wild Bunch*?" said Edwin. "Sam Peckinpah. It ends with a gang of cowboys walking down the middle of the street to their final showdown. Well, this is it. This is our chance to make a true Peckinpah approach."

"Didn't they all get killed in the end?" asked Mr. Ethics.

"*Wait!*" It was Mr. Mead. "Did you see that? The side window, over there. The curtains moved. Just now . . . *there!* Again, did you see that?" His voice dropped. "Somebody's watching."

Mr. Mead straightened his shoulders and stepped forward with a copy of *What I Learned on the Mountain* held high above his head like a beacon. It was the same sweat-damp copy he had been carrying with him ever since they left the city, and he held it in much the same way Eastern Europeans will display amulets and garlic cloves to ward off danger. Or evil.

"Mr. McGreary!" he yelled, book up high, voice booming across the emptiness. In the stark desert plains outside Paradise Flats, it was like yelling into a vacuum; with nothing to reflect them back, sounds tended to dissolve into silence. It was a landscape without mountains, a landscape without echoes. "Mr. McGreary! Can we talk to you for a moment? We're fans of yours. And we loved your book!"

The reply was immediate and unexpected: a gunshot, a loud *whoomp* and the book exploded in Mr. Mead's hand, showering debris and shredded paper into the air.

"Jesus Christ!" Mr. Mead fell to his knees and Mr. Ethics leapt head-first into the back seat. Edwin had ducked reflexively, but he held his ground. He didn't run and he didn't hide.

"The crazy bastard's going to kill us!" yelled Mr. Mead as he scurried, head down, into the front passenger seat. It was one thing to stare down the rusted barrel of a Soviet rifle, but it was quite another to confront an evil genius in his own front yard. "Let's go!" hollered Mead. "Let's go, go, go!"

Edwin turned, disgusted, and looked down at the two men cowering in the car. "Mr. Mead, if he had wanted to kill you, you'd be dead already. He was aiming for the book."

"I don't care! It's over. Get in and drive, for Chrissake."

"I always knew you were a coward," said Edwin. (And at this point, the disgust was flying like spittle.)

"We're going," said Mr. Mead. "Right now. End of debate."

"Oh, yeah? News flash, Einstein: I've got the car keys," Edwin jangled them in the air. "And we're not going anywhere. We are going to do this; we are going to finish what we started." Then, turning his attention back to the trailer with the shimmering silver skin, Edwin took a deep breath and steadied himself. His shirt was now plastered to his back and his hair was dripping with beads of sweat, but he forced a cool calmness into his posture. "Mr. McGreary!" he yelled. "My name is Edwin de Valu. I was your editor at Panderic. We spoke on the phone, remember?"

Nothing. The silence was unnerving, and the heat made Edwin light-headed, almost hallucinatory. He took a step forward . . . and a spray of dirt kicked up in a gunshot aimed just a few inches from his feet.

"Spare keys!" screamed Mr. Mead. "Under the back mat, Bob. Hurry!"

Mr. Ethics belly-slid from the back seat into the driver's, scrunched under the dash, turned the ignition and threw the car into reverse. "Edwin," he yelled. "We're going for help! Hang tight, we'll be back."

"Stop!" yelled Edwin, running in vain as Mr. Ethics accelerated the car backwards into its own dust. "Come back here!" yelled Edwin. "Come back here, you heartless bastard!"

They were gone. Edwin now stood alone, with no place to hide. He turned, hands in the air, and waited for the next shot. None came. Instead, from deep within the trailer, he heard a low rumbling sound. It began as a chuckle, it grew into a laugh, and it then rolled out as a loud booming guffaw. Is this the last sound I will ever hear? thought Edwin. Mad Mephistophelean laughter? Is this the last sound I hear?

The sweat was now running in rivulets down Edwin's body, soaking his belt line, creasing his face, stinging his eyes with a haze of salt. He took a step forward, then another. Slowly, slowly. And then, with the angle of fire cut down, he ran—loped, really—in a fluid crouch, zigging and zagging as best he could, until he reached the trailer's front door.

"Don't shoot," he yelled. "I'm coming in, and I'm unarmed. So don't shoot!"

Ah, but that wasn't entirely true. Edwin was indeed armed. A small handgun, chamber loaded and ready to fire, was strapped with Velcro bands to the inside of his right calf. "I mean you no harm!" said Edwin. And he was lying.

The screen door swung open into a muggy darkness thick with the pungent smell of sweat and stale tobacco. "Jack?" said Edwin as he stepped inside.

He had expected to come face-to-face with a gun barrel levelled behind demonic stoke-embered eyes. Instead, he found a room stacked with—books. Boxes and boxes of books. They were piled high everywhere. About the only open space visible was a sofa bed with the sheets unmade and the cushions threadbare and faded. That and a sagging plaid recliner with the seams splitting and sandwich crusts and coffee cups circling it like fallout from an explosion. Boxes and books. Books and boxes. And there in the middle, standing in the half-light, was Jack McGreary.

The gun, a hunting rifle of some kind, was laid across a kitchen counter stacked with pots and pans and strewn with dirty dishes—and still more books. Jack was standing in his undershirt, a bottle of Southern Comfort and a cracked glass in front of him. His face was lit from the side by a spear of light through the window. It was the face of a bear. The face of a boxer. Large-jawed, jowly, broken-nosed, unshaven. The eyes were focused on Edwin through half-lens reading glasses, which added an oddly quaint touch to the man. The hair was bone white and poorly cut, and was messed every which way, as though he had just woken up from a Van Winkle slumber. The hands that reached out to pour a slosh of whisky into the glass were huge. They looked like a stonemason's hands: the knuckles clumsy and cracked, the fingers heavy, the skin leathery. They weren't the hands of a guru, or those of an author.

In later years, when the memory of this encounter had long since transubstantiated into myth, it was not the eyes—stone grey cold—or the immense girth and size of the man—six-foot-five, at least, and 290 pounds or more—that Edwin would recall. No. It was those hands, those massive, oversized hands. That was what Edwin would remember best.

The voice, when it came, was a raspy, deep baritone: a third presence in itself. "Well, well, well. Edwin de Valu. Editor and professional jackass. You finally tracked me down."

"Hello, Jack."

"A drink?"

Edwin nodded. "Pour yourself one, too." *A drink before dying.*

But Jack didn't move. He just stood there, squinting at Edwin, as though trying to focus him out of existence through an act of pure will. "Why did you come here?" said Jack.

"I'm here because I know. I know everything. I know about Harry Lopez. I know about the entire charade. Heck, I even tried to have Harry killed." The threat was implicit, but Jack was unfazed.

"So is he dead?"

"Unfortunately, no," said Edwin, and he mentally calculated the distance from Jack's whisky hand to the rifle trigger, compared it to the time it would take for Edwin to drop down, pull the handgun free, squeeze off a round, shoulder-roll dramatically to the right and maybe spout a few pithy farewell comments as he pumped shot after shot into the large man's chest. "Anyway," said Edwin. "You may have heard: Harry has given up the whole 'enlightened master' gig and renounced his divinity. Which is just as well, as he didn't play the role very well to begin with. I mean, he wasn't the greatest thespian ever to grace a stage."

"That's a fact," said Jack with a low, chuckled laugh. "He weren't no Barrymore, I can tell you that. You ever heard him do a Scottish accent?"

"No, but he regaled me with—or rather, inflicted upon me—his version of Irish."

"Same thing. He just says 'och, laddie' instead of 'faith and begorra.' A good kid. A nice kid. But not the brightest."

"Your book, Jack. It topped sixty-five million copies last week. That's not counting spinoffs or excerpts or audiotapes. Sixty-five million, Jack. And counting. We've never seen anything like it. It's unprecedented. Back when your book first started to take off, I thought to myself, Hey, we just might have the next *Celestine Prophecy* on our hands. But it went way beyond that."

Jack laughed, a laugh as coarse as canvas—as coarse as canvas torn ragged in two. "Ah, yes. *The Celestine Prophecy*. A stupid person's idea of a clever book."

"Listen, Jack." Edwin took another step closer. It felt as though he was trapped in a deadly game of Mother-May-I. *May I take one baby step forward? You forgot to say, "Mother may I."*

"Stop right there," said Jack, and his left hand slid over to the rifle. At the same time, he kicked back the Southern Comfort in one fluid motion with his right. "Ambidextrous," he said. "Comes in handy at times."

"Hey now, Jack. You can trust me, I'm your editor. Any author-editor relationship has to be built on trust."

"You're the stupid son-of-a-bitch who wanted to repackage my book as *Chocolates for your Soul*, or some such shite."

"Um, yes. That would be me. But I recognized my mistake, Jack. I saw the error of my ways. And we published your manuscript exactly as it was. We didn't change a single word or a single comma, just as you requested. I honoured your wishes, Jack, and why? Because I am an honourable man."

"Bullshit. You did it because you had to, you did it because—in your infinite stupidity—you deleted the lines in the contract that would have given the publisher any clout whatsoever. I laughed out loud when I saw that. Could you have been more dim-witted than you were? Could you have been more of a jackass?"

Edwin grimaced in a way that might very well have been mistaken for a smile. "You certainly got the better of me. Yessir. I'm a jackass, all right. But there's just one thing I have to ask . . ." ("Before I kill you," Edwin almost said). "How did you do it? How did you come up with the perfect formula? Everything worked, Jack. Everything. The self-esteem awareness exercises. The weight-loss plan. The stop-smoking techniques. Even Li Bok. How, Jack? I have to know."

"Li Bok?" Jack choked back on his cigarette, coughed a chestful of phlegm up from his throat. "Well, you see," he wheezed. "Li Bok, that's short for Lila Bauchenmier. She was a hooker I knew back when I was stationed in Louisiana. That was after the war. She had all kinds of tricks, Lila did, but the one in the book—that was her best. It was kind of her signature piece. Best twelve bucks I ever spent, kid. Jeez, that must have been, what, fifty, sixty years ago, maybe more. Last I heard, Lila was in a nursing home in Florida. She got married, you know, had kids, grandkids. Lived in the suburbs for years. I still get cards from her now and then, but her mind is slipping. Alzheimer's. Or maybe just old age. Anyway, when I wrote my book, I figured I'd better throw in some 'breakthrough sexual techniques,' and Lila's moves were always the best. I just called it Li Bok to make it sound exotic. You know, give it a mystic oriental Tantric sort of quality."

"And the section on homosexual Li Bok?"

Jack shrugged. "Everyone likes to believe that they're part of some subculture or another, but when it comes to our bodies—and our minds—we're all pretty much wired the same. The similarities out-weigh the differences, kid. I simply extrapolated."

Jack dropped his cigarette butt in a pan in the sink; Edwin could hear a faint hiss when it hit the water. And as his eyes adjusted to the dark and gloom, Edwin saw Jack's features emerge in finer detail. As he edged his way ever closer, one surreptitious step at a time, Edwin could see the spider web of broken veins that lined the old man's nose, testa-ments to a lifetime of hard drinking and even harder living.

Jack McGreary looked around him, at the boxes and clutter of his life, and said, with a gravelly sigh, "Who would have thought a mobile home this small could hold so much junk?"

There were squares of clean space along the wall where pictures had once hung, though they were all now gone, packed away in boxes. Jack lifted a stack of loose papers, what looked to be magazine clippings (they were actually pages cut out of rare books with an exacto knife), and flopped them into a cardboard carton. "Forty some years," he said. "When I first moved into this trailer park, every lot was full. Mobile homes were lined up with Prussian precision, gleam-ing in a pre-ozone-hole sun. They were the height of modernity, just like TV dinners and the Sputnik space race. Sure, Paradise Flats had already become a backwater, sleepy—narcoleptic, really—but I never thought it would fade away like it has. Every year, I think, Well, this fuckin' town can't get any smaller, but every year it does. It's like watching a corpse wither."

"You were born here?"

Jack nodded. "That I was. Born to a Finnish midwife under a half moon on a night full of stars. Or at least that was how my mother remembered it. I lived in Silver City for a couple of years. Was in the Navy and later the Merchant Marines. I went to the university up in

Phoenix for a while on the GI Bill—until they ran a background check and kicked my ass out of there. Had to do with a little mix-up I had back in Belgium."

"Black market," said Edwin.

"You've heard?"

Edwin nodded.

"It sure as hell ended my academic career, I'll tell you that much. Which was kind of a shame, because I liked college. I liked books. I liked ideas. I liked to turn them over in my head, see them from as many angles as I could. I was studying physics, accounting, literature, philosophy, whatever. I took any damn course that appealed to me."

"And you ended up back here," said Edwin. "In this wretched little dog-patch. Why? How?"

"Don't let this modest hermitage of mine fool you. I've done more in my lifetime than you would in a dozen of yours. I've been to Bangkok and Guayaquil. Been beaten up and left for dead Down Under. I've gotten drunk with kings and clowns, con men and beauty queens. I've been laid in every time zone and damn near every continent. I have scars on my body that I don't even remember how I got. I've passed out in slums and on warm tropical beaches. I've hitched rides and borrowed other men's wives, and I've circled the globe more times than Magellan. But Paradise Flats has always been home, and I always came back." He looked around at his dark, suffocating cell and said, "I always came back. Kind'a like a prisoner on day parole, I suppose."

By now, Edwin had managed to sidle right up to the kitchen counter, had even managed, casually, to shift the barrel of Jack's rifle to one side. As Edwin took a seat by the counter, he dropped a hand casually to his leg, pulled back on the Velcro, just a touch. Just to check. He could feel the gun's handle, smooth and inviting.

"You haven't answered my question," said Edwin. "How did you do it? How did you come up with the perfect formula for human happiness? It wasn't on any Tibetan mountaintop, I'm guessing."

Jack laughed at this. "Is that what I said? Tibet? I thought I said Nepal. Not that it matters."

Edwin shifted forward, dropped his voice to conspiratorial tones. "I used to think that perhaps you had created a complex computer program.

Or maybe that you were some kind of evil genius who had performed a feat of mass hypnosis, a Rasputin of the self-help set. Which is it?"

"Your drink," said Jack. "I almost forgot."

He fished a not-as-dirty-as-the-rest tumbler from the sink, wiped the rim with a corner of his undershirt and poured Edwin a shot. Edwin didn't hesitate. He grabbed the glass and tossed it back, swallowed hard, and suppressed an emasculating shiver. "Good stuff," he squeaked, in a manly sort of way.

"My old man was a crofter," said Jack. "A crofter out of St. Kilda in the Outer Hebrides. Ghost islands of granite, on the far side of nowhere. There were only five surnames in the history of those islands, and mine was one of them. There's no one left on St. Kilda, not since the 1920s. Just a few stone homes, a cemetery and endless unmarked graves. My old man came to the New World looking for something better. Came over with a bunch of others, a whole shipload of McGrearys, and they were put to work in the coal mines of Cape Breton. My old man went down the coast looking for work, following the coal seams through the Appalachians, traded his labour for shelter, and eventually he ended up here, working in the salt mines—now there's a lateral move for you. From black coal to white salt: my old man. My poor old man. Coal gets under your fingernails, but salt gets under your skin. 'We sweat salt,' he would always say. 'Never forget that.' It was, he said, 'elemental.' He fell in love with my mother, and they settled here. They worked hard and whiled away the rest of their small and uneventful lives. They're buried, the both of them, in the cemetery east of town. Side by side. Their graves used to be under some shade, but a few years back Dutch elm disease killed the entire stand of trees and now my parents' headstones are directly under the sun, without protection. Which is a shame, seeing as how they both came from colder climes. My mother was Scandinavian, you see. She used to tell me about snow, about how it felt, how it tasted, how it turned to water in your hand. It was white and pure. Elemental. 'Like salt?' I would ask. And she would say, sharply, 'No. Not like salt. Not like salt at all.'"

Jack took out another cigarette, twisted off the filter and searched for a match. He was about to crank the gas range when Edwin leaned in with a flick of his pseudo-Zippo. Jack accepted the light without comment or a nod of thanks. The interior of Jack's trailer was thick with the residue of cigarette smoke, laid down in lacquer layers, a patina of smells and oily film.

"Paradise Flats," said Jack. "Broken-backed and broken-down. My old man got hired on with the railyards, worked his way up to warehouse foreman and immediately started building his dream house. It was magnificent. A towering mansion with shutters and a sweeping staircase and a library in every room. But then the Great Potash Boom hit up north, the entire economy shifted, and right in its heyday, they closed down the Berton Line. Moved the railway east, past the hills, out to the coast, and my old man—he lost everything. His job. His home. Everything. He only ever laid the foundation. That's all his dreams ever amounted to: a hole in the ground filled with weeds and wildflowers. He would take me down there, after my mother died, and show me where it would go: the staircase, the veranda. He would point to mid-air and talk about intangible things as though they existed, as though they were really there. He was a fool, my father . . . And now you come in here, and you ask me where that book of mine came from. It came from Paradise Flats. It came from here." Jack placed both hands across his wide belly. "It came from the gut. Every book I've ever read, every drink I've ever spilled, every fight I've ever lost, every punch I've ever thrown. We're each of us a collection of cross-references, kid. Every woman I've ever seduced. Every lie I've ever told. Every sin. Every triumph. Every small victory and every great failure. It simmers inside, and when we die, we take with us multitudes. That's Walt Whitman, by the way. 'We contain multitudes.'"

"I know," said Edwin, almost in a whisper. "Whitman. 'Do I contradict myself? Very well then, I contradict myself. I am large, I contain multitudes.'"

"You want to know my secret? There was no secret. I just sat down and typed. I wrote the whole damn thing in one go, without stopping to rewrite or even to check what I had written. I figured self-help was where the money was. You want to know why I wrote that book? For the money, pure and simple."

"But why didn't you just invest in T-bills and then roll it over on the time zones?"

"Did that actually work?" said Jack.

"Millions, Jack. People made millions off that."

"Well, I'll be damned. Hell, I was just standing in line at the bank, waiting to cash my social security cheque, and I started flippin' through a pamphlet on government banking regulations. The loopholes were obvious. Any fool could see it."

"But—but the research that was needed for *What I Learned on the Mountain*. Sure, a good deal of it was simply recycled self-help, but not the core of it, and not the way it fit together. That book required vast expertise, Jack. It required years of research and profound insights into the human psyche. I thought it might even have been written under a pseudonym, by a committee or something."

"Maybe Francis Bacon wrote it," said Jack. "Or maybe it was UFOs. Or angels. Panderic publishes enough of that shite; maybe it was angels what wrote that book. A committee of angels. On a UFO. With dowsing rods stuck up their ass."

"I don't edit UFO books," said Edwin, testily. "I edit self-help."

"Same fuckin' thing. No. It weren't no committee, kid. It was just me, alone in my trailer. What I did was, I went up to Silver City and stocked up on paperbacks. I bought 'em by the boxload, and spent the next couple of weeks wading through empowerment and closure and affirmations and validations and emotional masturbations. 'It's not your fault.' 'Learn to love yourself.' 'You are special and unique—just like everyone else.' I gritted my teeth and rolled my eyes so often you would have sworn I was epileptic. Those were some of the worst books I ever read. I tell you, it's a miracle the entire self-help field doesn't collapse into self-parody. Anyway, I went through as many of those books as I could stomach, and then I sat down and knocked off my own version. What I didn't know, I made up. It took me a couple of days. Maybe a week, tops. Like I said, I didn't bother rewriting it. I knew it would sell; that was the whole point. I was just giving people what they wanted to hear, what they had been waiting to hear, wrapped up in a single-volume helping. I still have a stack of paper left over. I bought it in bulk, two thousand pages for half price up in Phoenix."

There was a pause. A long, long pause.

"That's it?" said Edwin incredulously. "You just sat down and typed?"

"That's right. I didn't have an outline or anything. I just kept typing until my wrists started to hurt and my head started to ache, and then I quit."

"And then you quit . . ." Edwin was having trouble processing this revelation. (If, indeed, revelations can ever be fully "processed.") This was *not* what he had expected. Instead of Lex Luthor tucked away in a secret villain hideout, Edwin was confronted by a dishevelled writer, heavy on the Southern Comfort, pounding out a manuscript "for the money."

"It gets even better," said Jack with an unexpected grin. "I never even sent it to anyone else. It wasn't a multiple submission, it was a one-shot affair. Hell, I couldn't afford to send it to anyone else. I barely had enough for postage after I bought those damn paperbacks."

"Why us? Why Panderic?"

"Because you people published Mr. Ethics, and I figured if you published that crap, you'd publish anything. I figured your standards were lower than most."

"Actually, that was Mr. Ethics outside just now. I drove down here with him. He was supposed to be my backup."

"Really?" said Jack. "Mr. Ethics? The one waving my book?"

"No, the other one. The one who drove away and left me to die."

Jack's face lit up. "No kidding? That is bloody well wonderful. Damn. I had him in my sights, too. I should have popped him off right then and there, as a service to literature. The English language would have thanked me for it. That man's prose is abominable, and the content? It's just warmed-over Intro Ethics 101 set to pop psychology and feel-good narcissism. Ethics? Ha. The man has debauched the very word. Aristotle must be spinning in his grave. You know, kid, ethics isn't about choosing between right and wrong; it's about choosing between grey and grey. It's about choosing between two equally desirable but mutually exclusive courses of action. Freedom or security? Courage or comfort? Self-examination or blissful happiness? Column A or Column B? Mr. Ethics, my ass. I should'a shot him when I had the chance."

Jack racked up another round of Southern Comfort and insisted that they clink glasses.

"To the written word!" said Jack, his glass raised. "To characters who exist only on the printed page. To characters who exist only in books and aren't even aware of it—who exist only on the printed page, yet live and breathe and are sorry to go nonetheless."

"To us," said Edwin, feeling disoriented and vaguely distressed.

"To us," said Jack. "Now then, Eddie. You've got to tell me: it was the daisies that did it, right?"

"The daisies?"

"That's what hooked you on the manuscript. That's why you rescued me from the slush pile. The daisies, am I right?"

"God, no. It wasn't the daisies. I thought they were dreadful. Insufferably cute. I had actually discarded your manuscript, Jack. I threw it away without looking at it. It was only later that—"

"Sure you did," said Jack, clearly not believing him. "It was the daisies. I knew it. Best seventy cents I ever spent."

"But—but dammit, Jack. You deconstructed Keynesian economic theory in eight and a half pages. You can't have done that in a single sitting. I've had professors and government policymakers call me up in an absolute panic, saying you undermined everything they believed in."

"Oh, that. Come on, Keynes' theory of market intervention is self-cancelling. Anyone can see that. The market works in spite of Keynesian policies, not because of them. I thought that was obvious."

"You studied economic theory?"

"Who needs to study economic theory? That's like studying Tarot cards. Economics isn't a science—it's just voodoo and wishful thinking dressed up as policy. The emperor has no clothes, kid. He doesn't even have a body. It's a mirage. Deconstructing modern Keynesian theory is about as difficult as deconstructing a fairy tale. It's about as difficult as pointing out that 'generally, pigs don't actually live in houses, not of straw, sticks, or brick.' I wasn't planning a treatise on economic theory—I mean, it was supposed to be self-help—but I was in the middle of writing the manuscript when a documentary came on PBS. I sort of watched it as I typed. It had something to do with John Maynard Keynes. That old frooty-toot, what the hell did he know? You never heard such stupidity. So I knocked off a section about Keynes as well, on the fly, pointing out the flaws and contradictions in his theories."

"You deconstructed John Maynard Keynes after watching a documentary on PBS?" Edwin's disbelief was rapidly giving way to dismay.

"Not quite. The signal started to go and I missed the last part. We don't have cable out here; I have to rely on that coat hanger on top of the TV, and the reception tends to come and go. I only pick up PBS and some of the local programming out of Silver City."

"You deconstructed John Maynard Keynes after watching *part* of a documentary on PBS?"

"That's right. You want another shot of Comfort?"

Edwin nodded, numbly. "Yes," he said. "I think I do. I think I do need another drink." He swilled this one back just as quickly, felt his limbs tingle with a preview of drunkenness and asked—pleaded, "But *The Seven Laws of Money*, Jack. I studied that in college. I read it and I re-read it, made notes, went over its main points, compared and contrasted it to other theories. Surely, you didn't simply—"

"*The Seven Laws of Money?* Oh, yeah. I read that one on the shitter. Skim-read it, really. The silly mystical conclusions are invalid, but the basic premise was sound. So I incorporated that as well, threw it on like another lump of mud. Why?"

"I think," said Edwin, swallowing his whisky and wiping his mouth with the back of his hand, "I think—" and at this point, he was having trouble not slurring his ideas. Indeed, at this point, he was practically sweating Southern Comfort, the whisky dripping from his pores, his senses swimming in it. "I think I have heard just about enough. Mr. McGreary, you are a fraud and a cheat. You are no better than Stalin. Your book has caused unspeakable damage to the people I love—to the person I love. You took the sadness out of my best friend's eyes. And for that, you must pay the price!" He lurched down, reaching blindly for the gun strapped to his calf, but the sudden motion sent him reeling and he toppled, headfirst, into the edge of the counter and then onto the floor. Damn his bent thumb, he couldn't do anything nimbly any more! Edwin was struggling in vain with the strap—and who would have guessed Velcro would hold so firmly—when he felt something cold and smooth touch him, lightly, on the side of the head. It was (of course) the barrel of Jack's rifle.

"Here's a handy tip," said Jack. "And you may want to jot this down: when ambushing someone, shoot first and drink later. Reverse the order and you stand a good chance of screwing up."

"I bet this never happened to Starsky and Hutch," said Edwin bitterly.

"Stick to editing books," said Jack. "Leave the heroics to others."

Once Jack had relieved Edwin of his handgun and frisked him for any more surprises, he forced the young man to sit right back down and share another drink. "No hard feelings," said Jack. "I've lost count of the number of people over the years who have tried to kill me."

Edwin, feeling morose and with his testicles suitably shrunken in shame, said nothing. He just stared down in sullen silence at the countertop.

"Why would you want to shoot a helpless old guy like me?" said Jack. "Seventy-eight years old, living alone in a mobile home in the middle of nowhere. Why would you bother?"

"Because," Edwin rasped. "You're a murderer. What you've done, what that book of yours has done, is murder. Mass murder."

"Really? How do you figure that?"

Edwin looked up, right into Jack's eyes without flinching. "What are we, Jack? Who are we? We're not our bodies. We're not our possessions or our money or our social status. *We are* our personalities. Our foibles, our quirks, our eccentricities, our frustrations and our phobias; remove those and what do you have? Nothing. Just happy, mindless human shells. Blank eyes and bland expressions, Jack. That's all I see now. It hasn't hit Paradise Flats—yet. But rest assured, it will. And what then? When Paradise Flats goes, where will you find refuge from happiness™? Soon everyone will talk the same, smile the same, think the same. Individual personalities are becoming less and less distinct. People are vanishing. And it's because of you, Jack. You're a murderer."

There was a long, icy pause before Jack replied. "I am *not* a murderer. I merely succeeded where Thomas More and Plato, St. Augustine and Charles Fourier, Karl Marx and what's-his-face, Huxley, tried and failed. I created not a utopia—not some concocted fantasy world, non-existent by its very definition—but a *eu*topia. That's *eu*, as in 'euphoria,' from the Greek, meaning 'good.' Eutopia: here and now. And there's no denying that the world is a far nicer place for what I've done."

"Nicer, but not better. And here's the funny part, Jack. Now that I've met you, now that I've seen you for what you are, it doesn't really matter whether I kill you or not. Your days are numbered. You with your nicotine-stained fingers and your whisky-soaked halitosis and your abysmally bad manners. You're an anachronism, Jack. The New World Order that's dawning doesn't have any place for you. In the shiny new universal Religion of Happiness™, you're a heretic. You don't belong, Jack."

"Ha. That's the best you can do? That's the biggest insult you can hurl my way? I'm *already* an anachronism, kid. And as for what happens to the rest of you—I don't care. I don't give a good goddamn. After I'm gone, nothing matters. When I go, the world goes with me. Who cares whether the future is bleak, bitter, or filled with honey and sunshine? When I die, everything dies with me. What happens after that is of no consequence."

"Don't give me that solipsist bullshit!"

"Aha," said Jack, suitably impressed. "Solipsism. Well spotted. You know your stuff."

"Of course I do!" roared Edwin, now on his feet, arms outspread. "I'm an editor! *I know everything!* My head is so crammed full of useless information it's all I can do to get to sleep at night. My thoughts are buzzing, constantly buzzing. *Nemo saltat sobrius*, Jack! *Nemo saltat sobrius.*"

"James Boswell," said Jack. "'Sober men don't dance.'"

"Exactly! The world is losing its drunken dancers. Oh, we have circle hugs and campfire sing-a-longs, but the wild, drunken dance of life is coming to an end. And it's all your fault."

"No," said Jack, and for the first time he sounded angry. "It is *not* my fault. I gave the people what they wanted: not freedom, with its heavy, burdensome responsibilities, but security. Security from having to think. Security from themselves. I know what people want: they don't want to be free, they want to be happy. And the two are often mutually exclusive. Look, I want to show you something." He pulled over a half-packed box, rummaged through it and came up with a framed photograph that had been packed away. It was a picture of a young man (circa 1973) with comical sideburns and a polyester shirt. He was staring into the camera with undisguised hostility.

"This is my son," said Jack. "Allan, from my first wife. She left me when he was twelve and raised him in Silver City, and then later in Phoenix. He came of age in the late 1960s and early 1970s. You want to know why I was so confident my book would sell? Because of Allan. Allan went through psychedelic drugs and transcendental meditation and transactional analysis. Every pop-culture trend, every stupid self-indulgent bandwagon, and he was on it. And for what? He ended up in Cleveland, working for a life-insurance company—feeding on people's fear of death and the hereafter—and going from one therapist to another. Allan isn't an anomaly, he's a bellwether. Hell, he even took past-lives regression. Turns out he used to be a king—there's a surprise. No one ever discovers they were an illiterate peasant who died of scabies and was buried in a bog. No, sir. We are all special, if not in this life, then in someone else's. Allan here has had every modern affliction known to man. He was diagnosed with Chronic Fatigue Syndrome by one therapist and with Adult Attention Deficit Disorder by another. Kind of contradictory, don't you think? He had hypnosis and discovered that I had abused him when he was a child, which was bullshit. Allan might have had me arrested and thrown behind bars if his therapist hadn't been debunked soon after. His phony repressed memories are still with him, however, and he said, 'They may not be real, but you are still responsible for them.' He then wrote me this self-serving Declaration of Independence—at the age of forty-five, mind you—telling me what an inept father I had been and how he was finally giving himself permission to be real, blah, blah, blah. I wrote back and told him to go fuck himself, and I haven't heard from him since."

"But what does any of this have to do with—"

"Let me finish," said Jack. "You want to know where that book came from? It came from Allan. It came from my son. His wife had a baby a couple of years ago, I went up to see the little guy, and Allan left the room. 'I don't want to share the same space as you,' he said. Then he marched right back in and started going on about how I had never been there for him growing up and how I was the reason he got a divorce and how—well, basically how everything that ever went wrong with his life, big or small, was not his fault. And like I said, Allan is no anomaly. He is the mainstream. So when I decided to write a book and make a lot of money, I just thought, What kind of crap would my son buy? What kind of self-satisfying message would appeal to him? What would have the broadest net? What would bring in the most cash? The result was Tupak Soiree and *What I Learned on the Mountain*."

Edwin felt sick to his stomach. How much of that was due to the Southern Comfort, how much due to the heat and how much to what he was hearing was unclear. Perhaps it was a combination of the three, but the cumulative effect was oppressive nonetheless. His ulcer was burning, his skin felt hot and itchy.

"Is this it?" said Edwin. "Is this how the world ends: not with a bang, but a warm fuzzy hug?"

"Face facts, Edwin. The days of the hellraiser are over. The Age of Nice is at hand, and there's nothing we can do about it. I didn't cause this, I just helped it along. *What I Learned on the Mountain* was simply the right book at the right time. It wasn't a book ahead of its time, it was a book *of* its time."

"*Zeitgeist*," said Edwin. "A German word; it means—"

"I know what it means. And you're right. What I captured was the spirit of our times. Our *Zeitgeist*. Our post-Reed apocalypse. Our return to the Garden. Our final white flag of surrender."

"Reed," said Edwin. "You wrote a note across the back of one page. Something about Oliver Reed. The writing was sloppy; it looked like you were drunk when you wrote it."

"I probably was."

Jack offered Edwin another drink, but this time Edwin declined.

"A cigarette then?"

"Trying to quit." Edwin turned the Zippo lighter over in his hand, looked up and said, "That was the one thing I never understood. Oliver Reed, how does he fit into this?"

"He doesn't," said Jack. "That's the point."

Edwin looked on, puzzled.

"Someday," said Jack, "when future anthropologists exhume the spirit of our age, when they reconstruct what went wrong, where we went adrift, they will no doubt trace our downfall back to May 2, 1999. The day Oliver Reed died."

"A B-movie actor. Why?"

"Oh, Oliver Reed was more than just an actor; he was the Last of the Hellraisers. And it's been downhill ever since. To Ollie!" Jack raised a glass, not to Edwin, but to the air, to the emptiness. Then, turning to Edwin, he said, "You know *when* he died, but do you know how? Do you know where?"

Edwin shook his head. What difference did it make?

"Oliver Reed died on the island of Malta after out-drinking the British Navy. He had downed more than ten pints of beer and more than a dozen shots of rum, and he was arm-wrestling sailors from the Royal Navy frigate HMS *Cumberland*. He bought them round after round, but they couldn't keep up. The sailors surrendered and staggered away, defeated. And Oliver Reed died in victory. He died on a barroom floor in Malta, and his final farewell, his last departing gift, was the tab he stuck the sailors with: more than seven hundred dollars' worth of debauchery. In this, he had the last laugh."

"Did you know him? Oliver Reed?"

"No, not really. I met him once. In Manila. He was being thrown out of a brothel by a pair of bouncers, and I dragged him away from a pummelling. We wandered the streets until dawn, he and I, and we sang and laughed and drank the darkness away. I knew him only that one night—he stiffed me with the final tab as well, more than forty bucks. We drank to death that night. We drank to the grey stalker. The grim reaper. 'To death,' said Ollie. 'For keeping things interesting.' I asked him that night. I asked him if he was afraid of dying, and he said 'Yes.' Just like that. '*Yes.*' Years later, I read some bullshit biography where he's quoted as saying, 'I don't believe we ever die, if only because we will live on through others, in their memories and in the lives of our children and our children's children.' He was a family man, he had several wives, children that he loved dearly. But he was just too big—you know? Bigger than life, and afraid of dying. 'Still, it's better to burn out than rot away,' he'd say. 'I'd rather die in a barroom brawl than in a terminal cancer ward.' You see, Ollie *seized* life. Seized it by the throat. Shook it till it bled. One woman, a writer named Gilham, I think, said 'Oliver Reed had deep blue eyes and a deep blue soul.' And I think maybe she was right. He was just too big, too big for this world."

Edwin said nothing. He wasn't entirely sure who they were discussing at this point, Oliver Reed or Jack, and the memory of a long-dead actor from another era filled the room as surely and as imperceptibly as smoke.

"Oliver Reed is dead," said Jack. "And I don't feel so good myself. That night in Manila, that night I out-drank and out-pissed and out-laughed Oliver Reed, if I could have one night of my life to live over . . ." Jack's glass was empty.

Edwin had nothing to say. Nothing to counter with. He was a spectator after the parade had passed. A parade, or maybe a funeral procession.

"Nostalgia," said Jack. "The last refuge of has-beens. That night in Manila, we shut the city down. Ollie was like a bull elephant on a rampage, with holes in his jacket and a strange wild joy in his eyes. He roared off on incoherent tangents. He challenged his own shadow to a fist fight. He splashed rum across his face and asked barrio girls to marry him. And when I dragged him away from yet another brouhaha, I said, 'Ollie, you're a goddamn troublemaker.' And he said, '*No!* You're wrong. I'm not a troublemaker. I'm a hellraiser. And there is a very large difference between the two. Troublemakers grow up to become priests and politicians and social reformers. They are always meddling in other people's lives. Hellraisers don't meddle. They rage and roar, and they celebrate life and they mourn its shortness. Hellraisers destroy only themselves, and they do it because they love life too much to fall asleep.'" There was a long, lingering silence. Jack topped up another glass, but didn't raise it. "They love life too much to fall asleep."

"Jack, about the book."

"Did you know he had a picture of a cockerel tattooed on his dick? He did. That's a fact. Or that he once got laid on centre court at Wimbledon? After the tournament was over, of course. Did you know he was the first person ever to say 'fuck' in a movie? Did you know that?"

"Yes," said Edwin, his voice suddenly small. "I knew that."

"And did you know that Oliver Reed also discovered the secret of life?"

Edwin shook his head.

"He did," said Jack. "It's true. The secret of life itself. You want to hear it?" When Edwin didn't reply, Jack went on anyway, reciting from memory. "The secret of life, by Oliver Reed: *Don't drink. Don't smoke. Don't eat meat. Die anyway.* Now then," said Jack, "do you honestly think some pasty-faced milk-fed pup such as yourself has anything to add? That's just about as brutally honest as you can get, don't you think?"

There was nothing Edwin could say, and Jack knew it. Outside, a car could be heard approaching, the sound growing louder and louder. The heat inside the trailer had grown unbearable; Edwin thought he might faint or pass out.

"Your friends," said Jack, as he looked out the window. "They're back."

Edwin nodded. He rose, started to say something, changed his mind. Words had failed him.

"Wait," said Jack. "Before you go . . ."

Edwin turned, "Yes?"

"Here," Jack slid Edwin's handgun back across the kitchen counter. "Take it. It's yours. Do what you want, I don't care anymore." He then turned his back to Edwin, deliberately it seemed, and began to fill another box with papers.

Edwin felt the weight of the gun in his hand. He looked at the wide, inviting back of Jack McGreary, and he thought, "It would be easy. No one would ever miss him. It would be weeks before anyone even noticed he was gone. He would roast in here like a mummy, like a piece of beef jerky, like an anachronism." Edwin raised the gun, pointed it dead centre, and whispered, "Bang, bang. You're dead."

Edwin then lowered the gun and walked to the door.

Jack never turned around. He just muttered, under his breath, "Coward."

Chapter
Fifty

Outside, under a punishing sky . . .

Mr. Ethics had parked the car to the rear of Jack's trailer, away from the window and the threat of sniper fire.

"Edwin!" shouted Mr. Mead. "Over here! Thank God, you're alive."

"Oh, yes," said Mr. Ethics as Edwin walked towards them. "We were worried for your safety, weren't we, Léon?"

"Worried. Very worried."

Edwin noted the bottles of thirst-quenching Fresca in either man's hand and asked, "Did you at least get me something cold to drink?"

"Oh, sorry. Slipped our mind."

"We were so worried, we weren't thinking straight. Isn't that right, Bob?"

"Yes, Léon. Slipped our minds entirely."

Edwin opened the car door. "It doesn't matter. Let's just go, okay?"

"Did you shoot him? Did you make him kneel? What did he look like? What did he say?" The questions came in a flurry.

"He was seven feet tall and made of steel," said Edwin.

"Did you kill him?"

"No," said Edwin, softly. "He was already dead when I got there. I want to leave now."

"We're with you on that," said Mr. Ethics. "Jump in the back and we'll be on our way." He leaned forward with the seat.

"I can't wait to get out of this dump," said Mr. Mead. "There is nothing to do in this town. Nothing. Can you imagine living here?"

Edwin stopped halfway in. "You're right," he said. "You are absolutely right." He slid back out from the car, looked towards Jack's trailer. "You're right."

"What are you doing?" said Mr. Mead. "Get back in the car before that lunatic comes out and starts shooting."

It all came together. It all made sense. "You are right. You are absolutely right," said Edwin, half-smiling. "There *is* nothing to do in Paradise Flats." And with that, Edwin strode towards Jack's trailer.

"What the hell are you doing?" yelled Mr. Mead.

"I'm going back in," said Edwin. "And I am going to win."

Round Two was about to begin.

Chapter
Fifty-one

Jack McGreary had moved some boxes and was slumped over in his easy chair, drinking straight from the bottle and fanning himself with a book on metaphysics. An off-kilter fan was stirring the humidity, and Jack's grey undershirt was stained with maps of sweat. When Edwin entered, Jack looked up.

"Forget something?" he said. "Like maybe your balls?"

"How long?" said Edwin.

"How long what?"

"How long did they give you?"

And the expression on Jack's face shifted ever so slightly. "Whisky's gone to your head, kid. I don't know what the hell you're talking about."

"The doctors," said Edwin. "How long did they give you?"

Jack looked at him with an expression of profound annoyance. Edwin had sandbagged him, and he knew it.

"Well?" said Edwin.

"Fuck off and leave me alone."

"A year? Six months? A week?"

"Didn't you hear me? I said, 'Fuck off and leave me alone.'"

But Edwin refused to move. "How long, Jack?"

Jack shifted his girth, looked at Edwin with a hatred that bordered on respect and said, finally, "Who knows? The doctors are a bunch of fools. They don't know shite. Could be a week. Could be a year. Once it goes systemic, it'll be a matter of days. You are looking at Job himself, kid. I have suffered ever boil and every plague and every test of faith that God in his infinite cruelty could dish out. And I'm still standing. Why? Pure friggin' spite."

"It was, let me see, one and a half years ago, wasn't it, Jack? When you first found out. And it was just after you found out that you decided to write a book, make some money. Some long-term money. The librarian was wrong. You weren't out whoring and drinking in Silver City, you were doing exactly what you said you were: you were going in for tests."

"Whoring and drinking? Is that what Rebecca told you? Ha! At my age, I'll take that as a compliment." He rolled up from the chair and onto his feet, like a walrus, like a king, and he said, slowly, "What exactly do you want from me? An apology? A penance?"

"The money," said Edwin. "What did you do with the money?" But Edwin already knew the answer.

"I blew it!" shouted Jack. "I spent it with reckless abandon. Pissed it away. It's gone. Ha!"

Edwin smiled. "No. It isn't. Your royalties must have topped $150 million by now. There is no way you could have spent it all—not here, not in Paradise Flats, not in this dead-end town of yours. You didn't even buy yourself a new pickup truck. No, Jack. You didn't blow the money. Far from it. You knew you were dying and you salted it away. But why?" Edwin stepped around a stack of boxes, shook his head. "It's funny. We sat in here for over an hour, arguing with each other like a pair of Talmudic scholars, and it never registered with me that you were leaving. You're packing up. Going where, Jack? Silver City, am I right? You're going away to die, aren't you, Jack?"

"Well, well, well. Aren't you the clever one? But if you think you're going to get your grubby little rodent hands on my money, forget it." He made a grab for his rifle, but Edwin was there first; he pulled it back and away, and then, carefully, laid it to one side.

"Oh, I know exactly where your money is, Jack."

Edwin found the box with the photographs, flipped past the photo of Allan in his bell-bottoms and retrieved instead a snapshot of a little boy, a toddler, all smiles. He had fly-away hair, a big grin, and Jack's eyes.

"Your grandson?" said Edwin.

Jack was watching Edwin with growing suspicion. "You leave my grandson out of this."

"Oh," said Edwin with a smile, "I'm afraid I can't do that. He's already involved, isn't he?"

"If you've come here planning to rob an old man, you're off base," said Jack. "You can turn this place upside down. There's no money here. Not a goddamn cent. Don't believe me? Go ahead. Look."

"I believe you, Jack. Like I said, I know exactly where your money is. And it's not here. No, there is a bank account, probably in Silver City, with $150 million in it, registered in the name of—what did you say your grandson's name was?"

Jack's bluster had gone out of him. His voice had lost its thunder. "Benjamin," he said. "His name is Benjamin. Benjamin Matthew McGreary. He's six now, that's an old photograph."

"Bright kid?"

Jack nodded. "Sharp as a fuckin' tack. And it's not $150 million, its closer to three hundred."

Edwin shrugged. "What's a million here or there?" He sat down on the counter stool. "I believe I'll have another drink, Jack."

"Go to hell."

"With ice, if you have it. It's hot as Hades out there."

Jack growled, went to his aging Frigidaire, chipped away some of the frosted buildup around the freezer (he never bothered to make ice cubes) and dropped a chunk into each glass. He topped this up with the last of the Southern Comfort.

"Well, now," said Edwin, impressed. "We managed to kill the bottle. *Salut!*"

But Jack wasn't going to raise his glass, not in a toast, not to anyone.

"You wanted to leave your grandson a legacy," said Edwin. "You wanted to surprise him, long after you were dead. You wanted to surprise him on his eighteenth birthday—"

"Twenty-first," said Jack. "I'd no sooner give $300 million to a teenager than I would lend him the keys to my truck."

"Good thinking, Jack. Still, you wanted to leave him *something*. You wanted him to say, 'The old guy wasn't that bad after all.' You wanted him to remember you long after you were gone. You wanted him to think about you. You wanted to make a final posthumous gesture. That's a far cry from the 'when I die, the world ends' line you were feeding me earlier."

"Three hundred million dollars. He'll never have to slave for anyone. He can go anywhere, do anything. The kid'll be a world conqueror."

"No," said Edwin. "No, he won't. Because there won't be any world left to conquer. Little Benjamin is going to inherit a whole lot of money and not much else. There won't be anywhere to spend it and—even worse—no way to enjoy it. You know what it was that made us who we are? You know what made us the biggest, meanest, Big Mac eating, calorie-counting, world-dominating kick-ass powerhouse country in the history of the human race? The pursuit of happiness. Not happiness. The *pursuit*."

"Listen," said Jack, but Edwin was in no mood to listen.

"The first recorded documents, Jack? The first words written down, the first things thought worthy of being written down? Shopping lists. Shopping lists and accounts of war. That's what we first pressed into clay tablets, first scratched onto papyrus. When the Sumerians began committing life to words, when they first began the written record of mankind, they made lists. Lists of *things*, of ownership. That and great deeds. This is where history begins: conspicuous consumption and braggarts' rights. The first scribes, the first men of letters, they weren't asked to write about self-esteem and getting in touch with their inner selves. They weren't writing 'We are all special in our own way.' No. It was the death of kings and the accumulation of wealth. Property, pride, and epic dreams. That's what makes us human. And this entire vast self-help, self-love epidemic we unleashed with your book—it has undermined everything. *What I Learned on the Mountain* is a crime against humanity."

"Why?" said Jack. "Because it worked? Because it actually delivered the goods? It promised to give people happiness and it did. People are happy now. That's it, end of story."

"No," said Edwin. "It's worse than that. Much worse. They're not just happy—they're *satisfied*. You know what we're witnessing, Jack? We're witnessing the end of adventure. Is that the legacy you want to leave behind: the end of adventure?"

"When Benjamin gets that money, he'll be able to—"

"Forget the money! This has nothing to do with money. Long after you are dead and gone, do you want your grandson growing up in a world without adventure? Is that what you want to leave behind? *Finis coronat opus*, Jack! 'The end crowns the work.' A man's final acts reveal the purpose of his life. *Finis coronat opus!*" He spat those last three words out as though he was punching the air with his voice. As though words alone could change everything.

Jack said nothing. Edwin raised a glass, let the ice slip into his mouth, felt the whisky-soaked coldness numb his tongue. He thought of May with her now lifeless lips and vast vacant eyes, and he waited for Jack's response, knowing full well that everything would turn on this moment.

The answer was a long time coming. Jack swilled the last of the Southern Comfort around and around the bottom of his glass, stared into the middle distance, said nothing. The Frigidaire kicked in, the compressor rattling the silence.

"What do you want me to do?" said Jack finally. "How do we undo this mess?"

"Write," said Edwin. "Write another book. Write a book not for the money, but from the heart. Set the record straight. Don't concoct fantasies, and don't spin sugar. No more lullabies, Jack. No more bliss. Clobber them over the head. Tell the readers what you *really* learned in a life of pointless adventure. Tell them about human folly. Tell them about chaos and wild girls and butterfly wings and invisible mansions overgrown with weeds. Tell them about salt mines and coal dust and the death knell of the hellraiser. Tell them about screwing and drinking and running around and not enjoying any of it. Tell them how pissed off you are that you have to die. Tell them about Oliver Reed. Tell them about Benjamin. Tell them everything."

Jack hesitated—and then said, "You type. I'll talk. The paper's over there. The typewriter is somewhere under that pile of laundry."

Except, of course, that when Jack said "laundry," what he actually meant was "dirty, smelly clothes." Edwin gingerly removed the under-shorts and tangled socks, the way someone might remove toxic waste, and then—flicking a couple of steak-bone relics to one side—sat himself down at the keyboard. He ran his fingers first along one side of the typewriter and then along the other. Puzzled, he turned it at an angle to have a closer look.

"Jack?" he said.

"There is no 'on' button, you jackass. It's manual. You just put in the paper and type. It's hi-tech, kid. I can use her anytime, anywhere. I can use her in a power failure. I can type by candlelight. No batteries required."

"Really?" said Edwin, honestly impressed by this.

After a short, impatient lesson in how to roll the paper into the drum—"Words directly onto paper," said Edwin. "That's so quaint."—and how to push the tab back at the end of each line, Jack stood, arms crossed, and in a loud, booming voice, he began to speak.

"*How to Be Miserable* by Tupak Soiree."

Edwin clattered the title down.

"Line one, page one," said Jack. "Plato wrote that human happiness was the ultimate goal of life. But Plato was a dipshit and human happiness is vastly overrated . . ."

And so, onward they went, with Jack dictating and Edwin typing. Onward into the night. Outside, the shadows lengthened, the sun went down and the desert began to cool off. Bob and Léon fell asleep in the car, neither of them craven enough to completely abandon Edwin, but neither of them brave enough to storm in and rescue him either. (They were supposed to take turns keeping watch, but Mr. Ethics—after some fine *post hoc* reasoning on the reciprocity of moral duty—decided to catch some shut-eye instead.)

As a salt-eaten moon cast its pale light across the land, and Paradise Flats slumbered and plastic bags tumbled gently across Main Street, Jack spoke and Edwin typed. Edwin's knuckles began to ache and his wrists started to cramp, and eventually Jack's voice started to go, but the two of them filled up on rotgut and pushed on in spite of the pain. They wrote away the night, filling the darkness with words until the first pink wash of dawn gathered strength on the far horizon. And still they continued. Page after page. Word after word after word.

Chapter
Fifty-two

How to Be Miserable was an immediate bestseller, and though the numbers never matched those of *What I Learned on the Mountain*, its impact was just as dramatic. (Panderic now held the trademark to both happiness™ and miserable™, so the money continued to pour in.) The eagerly awaited sequel from Tupak Soiree caused a huge uproar. Many people condemned the once-loved author for having betrayed the very movement he helped launch. A *fatwa* was issued against him, a price was put on his head and the bounty brought hundreds of hopeful assassins out from the shadows.

Poor Harry Lopez, now the target of innumerable death threats, continued to protest his innocence. "I'm just an actor!" he would plead. "Tupak Soiree doesn't exist!" But the crowds were unswayed, and they continued to chant "Heretic!" and "To the gallows!" Harry was eventually forced into hiding, where he spent his vast fortune on round-the-clock surveillance and armed (but illiterate) bodyguards. Across the country, Happiness™ Convents broke into warring factions. Schisms appeared, holistic communes fell to bickering, and many an alfalfa field was trampled underfoot. Fist fights were not uncommon. The Happiness™ Brigade squared off against the Miserable™ Alliance, and in upstate Vermont, the turmoil came to a head when one white-robed devotee stabbed another during a communal hug. "He touched my freakin' book," was how the disciple explained himself as they wrestled him to the ground.

T-shirts and bumper stickers appeared declaring PLATO WAS A DIPSHIT, and just as quickly, opposing T-shirts appeared: PLATO RULES! Competing gang tags fed an epidemic of graffiti as the two sides battled it out.

"At least they're discussing philosophy," said one professor, somewhat weakly. "It's a start."

College enrolment soared. So did alcohol and drug abuse. Having been abandoned by Tupak Soiree, many former happiness™ junkies now began to seek their bliss and fulfilment in fashion magazines, discotheques and random one-night stands.

With the FBI hot on his trail, Mr. Ethics fled to the Dominican Republic, where he wrote *On the Run: The Dummies Guide to Ethics for Wanted Fugitives Who Are Fleeing for Their Lives*. Edwin de Valu was given the thankless task of editing this notably thin book: barely 30,000 words, with margins the size of an airport runway and the sort of typeface usually reserved for VE Day headlines. Mr. Ethics went into a rage over Edwin's editorial meddling ("But don't you think 'wanted fugitive' is a redundancy?"), and was arrested at the airport when he flew back to the U.S. intent on killing Edwin. They found a loaded handgun in his luggage.

Panderic Inc., meanwhile, released a satirical book the following spring entitled *Die, Baby Boomers, Die!* by a young, anonymous author. Critics, mainly fifty-year-old men with receding hairlines, denounced the book as "impudent," "lightweight," and "jejune." They then went home and cried into their pillows. Not that it mattered. The book bombed. It was remaindered within months and ended up in the discount bin, thus killing Edwin de Valu's covert literary aspirations.

Mr. Mead got hair plugs, which didn't take, and was left with a scalp that was now both bald *and* scarred. No matter. By then, he had started to comb his prodigious side-hair up and over his forehead. He was last seen at a "major" publishing conference in Waikiki, sunning himself on the beach.

And what of May? And what of Edwin? And more important, what of May *and* Edwin?

Sad to say, things didn't work out for them. Why? Cabbage. Cooked cabbage. The Italians, you see, have a word for it: *cavoli riscaldati,* "trying to reheat cabbage." It refers to any attempt to revive an old love affair, as doomed a pursuit as trying to serve warmed-up cabbage as leftovers. Reheating cabbage is inevitably messy, distasteful, and unappetizing. It simply doesn't work, and so it was with May and Edwin. May Weatherhill left Panderic and is currently the editor-in-chief at Key West Books. She flies first class now, and has even managed to steal several of Mr. Mead's prize authors. At this very moment, Panderic was petulantly forwarding its slush to Key West. "She wants war? We'll give her war!" Mr. Mead had bellowed.

And Edwin?

Well, Edwin is still at Panderic Inc., still scratching at paper, still seething, still scheming, still dreaming of escape. He gets the odd postcard from May, filled with ironic asides and small shared secrets, but even then the friendship has faded more into nostalgia than anything else. They run into each other now and then, at book launches or trade shows, and there is always an awkward wall between them. A sad silence. *Mokita.* They have drowned in a sea of *mokita.* Edwin had saved the world and lost his best friend.

There is no happily-ever-after to this story. And that, I suppose, is the whole point.

On the Mountain

Edwin Vincent de Valu, necktie rumpled, briefcase in hand, emerged from the underground at Faust and Broadview like a gopher into a high canyon.

The day was still young, but already it was lost in a mire of weary stress and urban ennui. It was a hot, flaccid day, the kind of day when even the taxi drivers seemed listless. Sure, they swore at you, but you could tell they didn't mean it. You could tell their hearts were elsewhere—up above, on the fringe of the city skyline, where the sunlight caught the rooftops in a glowing mock of fool's gold, forever tantalizing, forever out of reach.

Edwin crossed Grand Avenue on the ebb and flow of stoplight commands, and he thought, as he did every day at precisely this time and precisely this spot: *I love this fuckin' city*.

A stack of slush-pile manuscripts was waiting for him when he entered his office (May's old office, and still warm with her memory). Edwin sat down to the endless Sisyphean grind that was his life. The latest intern had lasted only six days, and the slush pile was bigger than ever.

"Dear Mr. Jones: What would happen if a self-help book actually worked? This is the zany premise of my whacky, fun-filled fictional novel. It is a story about the end of the world and I am sure it will . . ."

Dear Sir/Madam: After careful consideration and great editorial debate . . .

Edwin had just managed to shovel his way through the first stack of manuscripts when his pager went off. It was a doctor calling from the Silver City Medical Centre.

"May I speak with Mr. de Valu?" she asked.

He could feel his chest tighten. "This is about Jack, isn't it?" He had been waiting for this phone call, and now that it had finally come, he was surprised to find his sense of dread was much worse than he had expected. "Did he . . . ?"

"No, but he has been moved to a facility in Phoenix. He listed you as his next of kin. Well, his exact words were 'heir apparent, but not entitled to one thin dime of my money.' That's what he wrote down on his admission forms. Mr. de Valu, I'm afraid it has gone systemic. It's spread to both his liver and his throat, and it has caused the collapse of the capillaries that support his—"

"Spare me the techno-babble. Please, spare me that."

"He's lost sight in his right eye and has very restricted vision in his left."

Oh, shit. "Does that mean . . . Can he still read?"

"No, I'm afraid he's almost entirely blind."

"Then he's dead."

The doctor wasn't sure if she had heard correctly. "No, he isn't dead. But I'm afraid it won't be much longer now. He told us not to bother you, but we thought we should let you know anyway. Your father may not make it through the night."

"He's not my father," Edwin started to say, but he never finished the thought. Instead, he said, "The hospital in Phoenix. Do you have a street address?"

The plane touched down just as the sun was setting. Passengers milled through the terminal, dragging suitcases, stumbling onto escalators and snapping at each other in a most un-holistic way. Edwin arrived with no baggage, and he cut cleanly through the crowds and out the ARRIVALS EXIT—and in passing he thought, "What a wonderful phrase, 'arrivals exit.'"

The taxi ride cost him fifty bucks; the hospital was clear across the city, on the far side of Phoenix from the airport, and Edwin hurried through the front doors and into the antiseptic calm of the south wing. The "dying wing," staff members called it.

"Jack McGreary?" said the nurse on duty. "Is he your father?"

"Yes. I suppose he is. Where can I find him?"

"First floor. Room 102. Down the hall, second door on your left. But, sir!" she called out as Edwin ran down the corridor, "visiting hours end in ten minutes."

"That's fine," said Edwin. "It won't take long. I've just come to say goodbye." And good riddance. And thank you. And give my regards to Oliver Reed. And I'll miss you. And I won't forget you. And oh so many more banal, trite, important things.

But Jack wasn't there.

He had escaped. The room was empty, chest-monitor tapes had been pulled away and were left hanging, the hospital sheets had been tossed aside—and the window was open. The televison was flickering blue echoes across the bed, the volume on mute.

"He's gone," said Edwin in quiet amazement. "He's escaped."

Edwin walked slowly back to the nurses' station. "Mr. McGreary, he's gone."

"Again?" said the nurse. "I'm so sorry. He does that now and then. We have to keep an eye on Jack, he's always trying to slip away. I'll send someone out to find him. We know where he is. He's on the mountain."

"The mountain?"

"That's just what Jack calls it. When your father first came in for tests, must have been two years ago at least, he used to walk up the mountain every day and just, well, sit and think, I guess. It was after he had first been diagnosed, you see."

"The mountain?"

"Yes, out behind the hospital. It's not very high, but it's a tough climb and we explained to Mr. McGreary that with his health deteriorating, he shouldn't be exerting himself. We must have told him a hundred times not to go up there, but he never listened."

"The mountain. There really is a mountain?"

She smiled. "Just a hill, really. A small rise of rock out behind the parking lot, you probably passed it on the way in. There's a bench and some shade up there, and a picnic table or two. It's not a real mountain, but still, with the countryside so flat and all, you do get a terrific view from the top. You can see almost the entire plains, and the city lights and the stars and a range of hills in the far distance. It's a beautiful spot. Even now, we call it Jack's Mountain," she laughed, and then, realizing they were discussing a terminal patient, said, overly solemn, "We didn't mean any disrespect."

"Of course not. And even if you did," Edwin smiled, "that would be appropriate too. You don't need to send anyone. I'll go and find Jack myself."

It was a steep climb: a narrow, winding footpath made its way through prickly plants and cactus fields, and by the time Edwin had made his way to the clearing at the top, he was out of breath.

A quiet night. The air coming in off the plains was scented with the memory of distant fields. Below Edwin, and spread out like the exposed interior of a transistor radio, lay the shimmering gridwork lights of the city. The sun was down and the moon had yet to rise, and on the far side of the sky a soft, surreal afterglow lingered still.

Jack McGreary was on a bench, walking stick beside him, shoulders slouched, face turned towards the wind. As he came near, Edwin could hear the old man's ragged, laboured breathing. It was the heavy, hard breathing a man makes when he is carrying a great burden.

Jack didn't turn around as Edwin approached; he just sat, face into the wind, without a word.

"Jack? It's me, Edwin."

"What do you want?" said Jack, but the tumours cut from his throat had left his once glorious baritone scratchy and weak.

"I just came to say goodbye."

Jack nodded, squinting out at the vanishing panorama before him. A long silence passed between them. And then, and almost as an afterthought, Jack said, "She's not a bad old world, is she?"

"No, sir," said Edwin. "It's not a bad old world at all."

Jack nodded and said, "Good. Now fuck off and leave me alone."

Edwin, taken aback, started to speak, but the old man raised his hand for silence.

"But, Jack—" said Edwin.

"Didn't you hear me?" said the old man as he peered out into the diminishing light. "I said, 'Fuck off and leave me alone.'"

"Fair enough," said Edwin.

And with that, Edwin de Valu turned and walked back down the pathway, laughing. He laughed: a loud, rolling belly laugh of the soul. He laughed until his face hurt and his heart went numb. He laughed until his eyes went all blurry on him.